Annie Thomas

On Guard

A novel

Annie Thomas

On Guard
A novel

ISBN/EAN: 9783337028435

Printed in Europe, USA, Canada, Australia, Japan

Cover: Foto ©Andreas Hilbeck / pixelio.de

More available books at **www.hansebooks.com**

ON GUARD.

A Novel.

BY ANNIE THOMAS,

AUTHOR OF

"DENIS DONNE" AND "THEO LEIGH."

NEW YORK:

HARPER & BROTHERS, PUBLISHERS,

FRANKLIN SQUARE.

1865.

Novels by Miss Annie Thomas.

DENIS DONNE. A Novel. By Annie Thomas. 8vo, Paper, 50 cents.

THEO LEIGH. A Novel. By Annie Thomas, Author of "Denis Donne." 8vo, Paper, 50 cents.

ON GUARD. A Novel. By Annie Thomas, Author of "Theo Leigh" and "Denis Donne." 8vo, Paper, 50 cents.

Extracts from English Notices.

Miss Thomas's writing is fresh and vigorous. Her sketches of character are full of cleverness, and *Theo Leigh* confirms the impression made by *Denis Donne*, that the writer may take a foremost place in modern fiction.—*Saturday Review.*

Miss Thomas displays an even vigor of diction which few of her sex possess. Strong power of language and clear definition are Miss Thomas's principal resources.—*Athenæum.*

Its characters ("Denis Donne"), men and women whom every body has met, are drawn with wonderful vigor, freedom, and freshness.—*The Press.*

Miss Thomas need not have either doubt or fear as to the place which will be awarded her among our modern novelists.—*Morning Post.*

Miss Thomas will, we think, rank high among that class of novelists of whom Miss Evans (George Eliot) is the first.—*Reader.*

ON GUARD.

CHAPTER I.

LADY VILLARS' KETTLEDRUM.

THE first scene opens as the last one will close probably, quietly enough; for this is to be no story of guilt and horror, of murder, mystery, or machinations. The actors in it will be of the order amongst whom we live and move and have our being. Upon these I, their historian, will rely for creating an interest to the full as deep and true as can be obtained by the powerful pourtrayal of any or all of the cardinal vices.

The season was June. Time, four in the afternoon. Place, the drawing-room of a house in a certain fashionable street in the May Fair district: a street which shall be nameless, because not a house in it stands empty at present, and the occupants of any given number might feel annoyed, might experience just indignation, at having their residence so plainly indicated.

Here I will pause for a paragraph or two in my story, to ask whether any teller of tales in print, past, present, or to come, may hope to avoid this cruelest wrong of all, of being accused of maligning places and persons, and distorting in recital occurrences which some wiseacre or other in perusal is sure to discover is "meant for so-and-so, and such-and-such." It is a bitter drop in the cup of fame, popularity, or whatever one may be fortunate enough to attain, to hear from a third and candid acquaintance that the friend of your heart is cut to that organ by your obvious allusion to him or her at p. 44! Or that the feelings of some one whom you deemed too sensible, too quick of comprehension, to be affected by it for a moment, are wrung because your promptitude of pen, and pride of power in producing copy, has led you into the unwitting error of dubbing lodgings in the locality in which said supposed sensible one once dwelt, "fly-blown." Ah me! since all have faults and follies either on or under the surface, to the one to whom is given the delicate tact to avoid mention or allusion to all or any of said faults and follies be all praise and glory! But not mine the latter, since not mine the gift.

I have made my plea. I have indicated that I intend to indicate nobody in particular, nor to allude disparagingly to any special place. Should I be so extremely unfortunate as to do other than I intend, I here crave the pardon of the offended, but nevertheless proceed with my story.

The season was June, and the time four in the afternoon. After this, need it be added that the guests at Lady Villars' kettledrum were rather warm and very sleepy. "Tea and a little music" on a Midsummer afternoon are strangely conducive to the "brother of death" (vide Shelley) obtaining at the least a partial sway.

There was a lull in the entertainment. A pretty girl had just ceased singing; or, rather, had just ceased listening blushingly to the gentle "bravas" which some amiable, well-meaning men had bestowed upon her. Silence had fallen over everything, and Lady Villars began to think herself an unwise woman in having thus collected a throng without sufficient cause.

For the brightest luminaries in her circle had refused to grace this afternoon re-union of hers. She had beguiled the many here to-day with the promise of some special shining on the part of some bright particular stars. The bright particular stars having disappointed her, the many were cross, and showed that they were so; albeit, they belonged to the upper ten thousand, and were Lady Villars' dear and devoted friends.

It was not an unpleasant place in which to be warm and sleepy, this room of Lady Villars'. A double drawing-room, with a conservatory at one end and a bay window draped with rose-coloured silk at the other. A drawing-room, the corners of which, through the skilful adjustment of furniture, were many. A room that was replete with quiet nooks, though it was at the same time an eminently comfortable and sociable-looking apartment. A room in which it was impossible for any one to hear all that was said to everybody by everybody else. A room that looked as though natural taste and careful cultivation had presided over its adornment. Yet, withal, a room that was much like many another one in the neighbourhood.

As for the people who filled it, they were as void of singularity as the place they filled. Picture to yourselves, you who may read these pages, a group of English gentlemen and ladies of all ages standing about in a state of idle irresolution, until the carriages which were ordered at five should be announced for their redemption from this sleepy slavery.

The pretty girl who had just received mild plaudits from the listless throng was the second daughter of the house, Florence Villars. She is to be one of the heroines of this book: therefore her charms shall be sung in full.

Hers was a moulded, not a chiseled face, yet it was an exceedingly delicate, or, rather, perhaps, I should say an exceedingly refined one. Her face was fresh and glowing in hue. Had her hair been black or brown her complexion would have appeared fair. As it was, the bright golden locks that were folded smoothly back over her ears, and arranged in a large loop behind her head, caused the skin that knew more of the rose than the lily to appear almost dark.

For all this violation of the usual laws of Nature's colouring, Florry Villars was a very lovely girl. The shape of her head—the yielding lines of her full rounded figure—the manner of her movements—all these were perfect. Her aquiline nose was as utterly devoid of strong-mindedness and severity as the veriest snub could have been. Her hazel eyes were as tender as the deepest blue that ever adorned another woman's face. While as for the gentle retreat her rounded chin made, it was women and women alone who had the heart to suggest that it betrayed "weakness of character." Artists, and, indeed, men generally, held that it was all that a woman's chin should be.

She had a very sweet smile, this lovely Miss Florry Villars: a charming smile—warm and pure as a sunbeam. All that portion of the world which came in contact with her knew her smile; for it was rarely absent from the soft ruddy lips and the kind hazel eyes. But at this moment when I introduce her there was more softness on the lips, and more kindness in the eyes, and more sweetness in the smile, than any one present had ever remarked before.

"I am glad you liked the song," she murmured, glancing up towards a man who leant against the wall at the end of the piano.

"I liked it so well that I want you to sit down and sing it again, Florry."

"Oh, Claude, don't ask me! What would mamma say?"

"I don't care what mamma would say; I want the song," he replied authoritatively. "I want to hear it again, Florry. I did not come here to listen to the squalls of that fat woman in green silk; and as for the little Grey girl, she opens her mouth square, and tacks on a 'ra' to the end of every word that she breathes upon. I came to hear you, and I want to hear you again at once."

Claude Walsingham infused a strong flavour of flattery into the words he used; so strong a flavour, in fact, that it robbed the words of all their arbitrariness and selfish unpoliteness to her ears. She moved a little nearer to him, and whispered—

"Don't make me sing again, Claude, just yet. I want to speak to you: I have great news to tell you."

The man she addressed stood erect in an instant.

"I will get Miss Grey to bewail something being 'So near and yet so far,' as loud as she can—she will do anything I ask her—then I will hear what you have to tell me, Florry."

The girl's eyes followed him as he walked away to the other side of the room, where sat Miss Grey, expectant.

"I hope he won't say that Stanley is foolish, or make hard-hearted speeches, and seem to look down upon the affair altogether." Then she watched him wistfully while he bent over and solicited Miss Grey for her song—watched him wistfully, to her mamma's intense chagrin.

Not that the man was a "detrimental," according to the usual acceptation of the term, or that Lady Villars was a heartless, manœuvring parent; on the contrary, Claude Walsingham, major in a light cavalry regiment, and eldest son of a good old west country house, was a prize that had been deemed worth striving after, in all honour, by the many, for some three or four seasons.

Still, a mother—a widowed mother—with two fair daughters on hand, was justified in watching keenly and feeling anxious—as Lady Villars did watch and feel whenever Major Walsingham and Florry held confidential converse. For Claudo had been in severe action with the other sex before now, and had invariably come out scatheless. Lady Villars knew that when the action is severe one of the contending parties must of necessity be wounded. Therefore she now watched Florence's fixed regard of Claude's movements with an anxious eye and a perturbed spirit. But for all that her mien was calm and her smile unwavering; for she was a woman of the world, with her daughter's future dependent on her in a great measure.

He was a worthy subject of the fixed regard Florence bestowed upon him, from the artistic point of view, for he was one of Nature's finest works—a handsome young Englishman, with all the best points of breeding and birth clearly distinguishable about him.

Stern physiognomists might have objected to a scanty development of temple and fulness of under-lip. Neither mouth nor forehead were deficient in beauty, however; so but few women thought for an instant of the possibly absent intellect, or probably present sensuousness—sensuality would be too strong a word to use about a man whose gay, glancing career had been unmarked by anything positively staining yet.

At any rate, Florence Villars had never given a thought to the possible existence of anything that could be considered dimming to the brightness of a character which she had elected for some time to firmly believe corresponded in all things to the man's glittering exterior. She had fixed her young faith upon him—adorned him with all the good traits and noble qualities a man such as he seemed should have. In short, she had given her heart to the young, good-looking light cavalry officer, and so her imagination had enriched him with all the attributes of a hero.

Despite that before-mentioned narrowness of brow and fulness of under-lip which might possibly betoken attributes the reverse of heroic, ho was precisely the style of man whom girls delight in placing upon a pedestal. The stumpy, stout man may have the better heart and the broader mind; but the stumpy stoutness blinds the eyes of very young womanhood to his worthy merits. The proportions of a god (as gods are proportioned in marble), and the air of a man of fashion, are things that appeal far more strongly to the taste, the heart, and eyes of the majority of girls under twenty.

Claude Walsingham was tall and lithe—lithe in a wiry, not a weakly way. There was vast strength in his slight undulating form, and his small, white, delicate hands were of iron, as more than one hard-mouthed horse could testify to its sorrow. He never struck you as being a muscular, powerful man; his appearance, his supple slightness, was as deceptive as was his cold, unemotional manner.

Add to this supple, slender frame a pale, fair, clean-cut face, the chief features of which were an aquiline nose and a pair of cold blue eyes spotted with reddish brown; hair of the latter hue, closely cropped, with whiskers and moustache of a lighter colour, but otherwise strongly resembling Lord Dundreary's, and the portrait of Claude Walsingham is before you.

"Now for your great news, Florry," he said, lounging up to Florence when he had planted Miss Grey at the piano, disappointing the latter, truth to tell, most cruelly by leaving her to turn over her own leaves. "Now for your great news, Florry; is it that you are going to be married?"

She blushed, not with confusion, but with pure annoyance—annoyance that robbed her sweet face of its smile for a minute or two, and rendered her incapable of speech. During the pause she made perforce, he watched her with an admiring gaze and a well-pleased smile; but Florry marked neither the one nor the other by reason of her head being bent down.

"My great news relates to Stanley, not to myself at all, Major Walsingham," she said, in a low tone, presently.

"Why 'Major Walsingham?' No, Florry, not another word even about dear old Stanley till you have told me what Claude has done to merit such painful promotion."

"I can't endure to have such absurd suggestions made to me, by you of all people."

"Florry, I mention such a possibility in sheer idleness, as I should speak of jumping over a precipice or cutting my own throat—one would be equally destructive to me as the other."

The girl looked shyly up at him, blushing hotly; but no longer with annoyance.

"Claude!—ah! what was I saying? Oh! about Stanley—I know now; he is going—what should you think Stanley is going to do?"

"Cut the Church, I hope."

"No, Claude, no; I won't have you speak in such a way of Stanley's profession; he is going to do a much better thing—marry Bella Vane."

"No!"

"Yes, I tell you: and why not—isn't it charming? Do you know her?"

"Never saw her."

"Why did you look aghast and say 'No' in that way when I said Stanley was going to marry Bella Vane?"

"I should have looked and said just the same if you had told me Stanley was going to marry Bella anybody else. I wish some one would make day hideous with her shrieks. I want to hear a full account of Stanley's insanity, and your mother's telegraphing you to leave me to my own miserable devices. Who is Bella Vane?"

"A sweet girl——"

"That of course all girls are. She isn't Stanley's rector's daughter, is she?"

"No; she is that Mr. Vane's niece. Surely you saw her last year? She was up for a time with the Leicesters. Mr. Leicester is another uncle. Stanley met her there, and she was here once or twice. I suppose he fell in love with her then, for the announcement of the engagement followed close upon that of her having arrived at Denham on a visit. We are all delighted."

"I am not delighted."

"Yet you pretend to be fond of Stanley, Claude."

"It was a terrible blow to my affection when Stanley went into that perpetual curacy; this further rush into perpetual poverty is really too harrowing."

"But it won't be poverty—I forgot to say that she is an heiress," Florry cried hurriedly. She was distressed at the disapproval Claude was manifesting about his friend her brother's new and important move on the board of life.

"That alters the case materially; I am beginning to be delighted too."

"How calculating you are, Claude," she said, sorrowfully.

"I think my bitterest foe would tell you that I am so solely for my friends, Florry. I own I am glad that Stanley has secured money, for I should not have liked the woman who had dragged him into obscurity."

"Why would it have been 'obscurity,' even if Bella had had no money? You can live on, oh! ever so little, quite nicely in the country, you know. Besides, Stanley is sure to rise—it isn't a perpetual curacy, and he will leave it by-and-by for a living, I hope."

"I hope so. I will drop him a line to-night, congratulating him, on your authority. Good-bye, Florry."

He pressed her hand gently as she gave it into his, and looked lazily over her head the while into the eyes of Miss Grey, who was willing, report said, to bestow herself and three thousand a-year upon the light dragoon.

"You will be there to-night. Good-bye," she replied, hastily.

"There! Where?"

"At Gerald's—Lady Villars quite expects you."

"I shall just look in and make my bow; I can do no more to-night, unhappily, for I am going with a man at eleven to sup with several Bohemians."

She looked disappointed. The Dowager Lady Villars never took her daughters to a ball till eleven, therefore the chances of seeing Claude at her sister-in-law's ball were not great.

"How have you travelled into that country, Claude? Who has been your guide? I thought you did not know and could not bear Bohemians."

"Have you a clear notion of what Bohemians are?" he asked, laughingly.

"No," she said frankly, she had not; she used the phrase as she used many another one, without any very definite idea as to what it applied.

"It is not a practicable thing to steer clear of them, Florry; they're everywhere—Church, army, physic, law, all assist in swelling the list."

"Then you simply mean that you are going to-night to a mixed party?"

He laughed, "Very mixed."

"I thought Bohemians were people who sang and acted, and wrote for all sorts of papers and journals, Claude."

"You did not think far wrong."

"Well, I thought——" She paused for a few moments, until he asked her what else she thought.

"Why, that you were rather too fine to know such men."

"The men are cads," he said thoughtfully.

"Still, you will give up Carrie's ball for the sake of going amongst them; now, Claude, I call that inconsistent."

"Don't attempt to prove anything, Florry; you're not a bit of a casuist fortunately. I am going to-night to hear a—a fellow with a wonderful voice—sweetest soprano I ever——"

"'Fellows' don't have soprano voices, Claude," she said quickly: "you must mean a tenor."

"I do—of course I do—mean a tenor," he replied, colouring slightly. Then he held his hand out a second time, and took hers in farewell; which proceeding, in conjunction with the long private conversation with Florry, and certain rumours she had heard respecting him, caused Lady Villars no small anxiety.

Florence drifted aimlessly about the room after his departure, and strove to amuse and be amused by the other guests, until such time as they, too, in mercy vanished. But there was little heart in her striving, and so it failed in its object, which failure was marked by Lady Villars, and her eldest daughter, Georgina.

"Florry dear," Miss Villars said to her sister a little later, when, ensconced in their mutual dressing-room, they were resting, previous to dressing for the ball, "mamma wishes that you wouldn't let Claude devote himself quite so exclusively to you; there are things said about him that mamma does not like."

"Who tells them to her, Georgie?"

"Mr. Manners amongst others, and he wouldn't malign any one, you know."

"Ah! he is such a different man. He may judge Claude harshly, Georgie; I can't believe anything true of Claude that is not good," Florence pleaded rather wistfully.

"True or not, they are currently reported, so you must be careful, darling," Georgina cried, blithely. She herself was engaged firmly and securely to the worthiest of men, about whom none but good words had ever been said. It seemed to her but a little thing to discountenance a handsome scapegrace of whom "mamma had heard things." She did not, in her own well-assured happiness, give a thought to the possible cause of the languid indifference with which Florry went through the business of the ball that night, after Claude had passed along in front of Lady Villars, in acknowledgment of her courtesy in inviting him.

It was all weariness and vexation of spirit to Florry from the moment Claude's close-cropped fair head was finally borne from the room.

——o——

CHAPTER II.

A GREAT BEAUTY.

The first scene opened on a somnorific, sultry summer afternoon in London. The curtain is lifted now upon a widely different one. The time is morning, the morning after that kettledrum at Lady Villars'. But the place is the shady low-roofed drawing-room of a secluded old rectory—a dear old sequestered house, with whitewashed walls, over which roses crept and jasmines wandered, and above which rooks cawed daily in a way that proved how entirely at home they were—and in which, truth to tell, dulness very often dwelt.

Dulness did not dwell there at this precise period, however; for bright Bella Vane was there on a visit to her uncle and aunt. The whole house, the whole village, was redolent of her, so to say. She was there in the full glow of her beauty and wealth—there with the earliest bloom of a happiness that was new to her.

In her character of beauty and heiress, she had always been an interesting study, a never-failing subject of inquiry and interest, to her uncle's parish and the neighbourhood around. Now the interest was deepened, for she had come amongst them but the other day free, and now she was fettered—fettered to no less a person than the clerical favourite of the locality, Mr. Stanley Villars, Mr. Vane's curate.

Bella Vane was what Florence Villars, in the enthusiasm of the moment for her pet brother's betrothed, had called her, "charming." She was thoroughly "charming," though it would be difficult to say precisely why she was so. About her beauty there could be no mistake; no difference of opinion even. She was not one of those of whom keen-eyed critics can say, "Yes, she's lovely, only rather too"—this, that, and the other. She was lovely, and there could in truth be no "only" or "but" raised as to the fact of her being so. Her figure was lovely, tall, and slight, yet, withal, well rounded. Her head, crowned with its dark masses of shining long hair, was shaped like one of Phidias' realised dreams of "fair women." Her oval face was perfect in the delicacy and exquisite proportion of its classical lines. And, in addition to this rare, this almost antique perfection of form, Bella Vane had expression too.

Such expression! Take your most glowing conception of Cleopatra, and refine it, and you may come near to having some notion of the warmth and force that dwelt in Bella's wonderful steel-blue eyes, and on her full, short, ruddy lips—lip I should say, rather, for the under one was not full. There was nothing coarse in her physique; it was the fair presentment of her mind. Nothing could exceed, few things could equal, the delicacy of her mouth and chin. The short, curled, ruddy upper lip, so quick to quiver, so prompt to thrill, showed that she could feel. The chin, the firm, cleanly-cut, delicately-rounded chin, that did not retreat, after the fashion of gentle Florry Villars', showed that she could think. But it was the square forehead, from which the hair was turned back entirely, and suffered to hang in loose curls behind, that told you in unmistakable language that the great beauty was likewise a clever girl.

It has been said that she was a great heiress. That she was such, had been impressed upon her understanding from the time she could understand anything; for she was the only child of an uncommonly unreserved mother, who was a widow. Those surrounding Bella had not omitted the information that she was a great beauty also; nor had they neglected to inculcate the desirability of her having very great claims socially and matrimonially. They taught her these things to the best of their ability, and they taught her little else.

The girl had had governesses and masters whose name was legion, but she had learnt little from them. Sho was idle and impulsive in childhood and very early girlhood, and the idleness made her neglect to learn, and the impulsiveness caused her to quarrel with her instructors when they attempted to insist upon her doing so The result was, that she grew up undisciplined and imperfectly educated—with a superficial knowledge of many things, and a profound belief in her own right to sway.

But though thus indifferently cultivated, she was a clever girl—quick to catch up the salient points of a subject—specially gifted with the dangerous art of "seeming to know all about it." She had wearied of all the things they strove to teach her whilst they had been so striving; but when she grew up, and was free to follow her own sweet will, she turned of her own accord to several of the neglected accomplishments, and mastered them.

She turned to them with understanding and love, surmounting all the inseparable difficulties in a very different way to that which she would have done had she been driven to surmount them. The regulation drawing and singing lessons had been odious to her. But she took the best she could procure, with industrious avidity, after her first tour on the Continent—her first experience of the art-galleries of Italy and Germany.

Her reasons for surmounting difficulties were not invariably so lofty as were those which induced her to strive to give herself, with her own hand, the sensations of delight colour and form, from the pencils of others, had imparted to her. For instance, it was less a desire to enjoy Schiller and Goethe in the original than to please Stanley Villars, which had made her so assiduously study German for the last six months. He had told her "what she lost by reading them in English;" and forthwith Bella, who had hitherto denounced German as a cross between "snarl and sore throat," found that language full and soft, mellow and expressive, beyond every other.

Miss Bella had not been wont to trouble the quiet people at Denham Rectory with her presence very often, before the man who had recommended Schiller and Goethe in the original, became her uncle's curate. After that event she inflicted her charming presence upon them frequently—and now she was settled there for a few weeks, at the least, for she was Stanley Villars' affianced bride.

I say "troubled them with her presence" and "inflicted it upon them" advisedly, for it is a fact that a beauty and heiress in a quiet humdrum household is a great bore almost invariably. Mr. Vane strove hard to obey her behest "not to put himself out for her." But he could not succeed in retaining the blessed calm that was his when she was not there. As for Mrs. Vane she had been duly impressed by Bella's importance in the latter's infancy, and had never been able to get rid of, or conceal, the feeling. Bella, alone, would have been all very well for a time, despite this wholesome awe which she had unwittingly inspired in their breasts. But Bella's steeds in their stables, and Bella's maid and own man in their house, were overpowering.

Miss Bella never went anywhere without a couple of saddle-horses and these two personal attendants. Ordinarily this retinue of hers was but a drop in the ocean of life in the mansions of the great with whom she sojourned. But this Denham Rectory was an exceptional place; accommodation was limited therein. There was a feeling of oppression over all the residents, and a pervading sensation of tightness during the whole time Miss Vane remained with them.

She was happily unconscious of what a great bore she was—this great beauty, who was generally so prompt to see and feel. She thought that it was their normal condition to be constrained in manner and uncomfortable in mind —to be dull, and decorously depressed, and addicted to habits of silence. That they were so in her presence afforded her no manner of uneasiness, not one pang of the gentlest regret. It pleased her to stay with them now on account of Stanley Villars. Whether it pleased them to have her was a matter of minor importance to the great beauty, who was just a little selfish.

Miss Vane's engagement was still a very young thing: so young a thing that she treated it still with the sweetest consideration, remaining here in the quiet country to enjoy it simply and thoroughly. How it had come about shall be told presently, together with Miss Vane's reasons for feeling astonished that it should have come about at all.

For three weeks she had been here at Denham, taking long rides in the morning, on her brown mare Vengeance, accompanied by her "own man" and her big setter Rock; dressing elaborately for the five o'clock dinner, and then wandering about the rectory grounds all the evening with Stanley Villars.

For a fortnight these wanderings had been enlivened by a certain doubt, uncertainty, and tremulousness of spirit. She felt persuaded that he loved her;—she was a thorough woman; she never remained oblivious of a pleasing fact a minute after it became one;—but she was by no means certain that he would tell her so. He was a cool, thoughtful, earnest man. Bella could see that he himself felt that there was a want of wisdom in his love for her, the impassioned, wilful beauty. So for a fortnight the young lady, who had never been baffled in one of her smallest desires up to the present time, doubted whether or not he would suffer love to be the lord of all.

He knew that there was a want of wisdom in this love of his, but battling against it was of no avail; the girl was with him too often for Prudence to retain her empire in his soul. The girl was with him too often, for the village was very small, society very limited therein, and Mrs. Vane was driven to lay forcible hands upon any one who could assist in entertaining her oppressive niece. She was with him frequently, listening to his words as though they were passing sweet to her; sparing no looks, no lure, no tone that might still further win him; flattering him with the terrible intensity of that flattery which only a woman who believes that her spurious enthusiasm, her sham sentiment, and her evanescent affection are real, true, and lasting, can employ.

Her belief in herself created in very undue time a corresponding one in him. He soon came to deem the girl all that she seemed—all that he could wish her to be. Beauty, heiress, spoilt child, wilful woman as she was, he yet told himself that she was just such a help as would be meet for him. She was a petted darling in the giddiest circles. He was a country clergyman, with no particular prospects of promotion in the profession that, for its own sake, was dear to his heart. What objections could be raised to a union, or a contemplated union, between these two? None; not one that could stand for a moment against that resistless charm of hers; not one that his manly faith in what was so passing fair did not attribute to mere worldly distrust and an unreliant heart.

It was but for a fortnight, but for fourteen days, that he rode Faith with a curb, and kept steady hand on Desire. At the end of that time it came to him to feel that to win in the race of life he must wait upon circumspection and self-denial no longer. Then he called upon his reliance on What is to be, is best; and the call was answered. He came in winner—he little knew how little ahead—of the hand and heart of Bella Vane.

I like the girl whom I have created, or rather I like the prototype from whom I have drawn her, so well, that I fear there will be pain in telling how little worthy she was of this battle in his heart—this victory, which may turn out a defeat, which he had gained. I like her for her deep steel-blue eyes, and her warm, loving smile, and the winsome charm that was diffused through all her being and her bearing. "What moral is in being fair?" This: that all to whom that which is truth embodied beauty itself, is dear, love it, sympathise with its failings, and screen its frailties.

She had shown neither failing in aught that might be expected of her, nor frailty of purpose, as yet, this fair young creature. She had broken no troth, blighted no being, betrayed no trust. But for all this internal integrity, she was not quite at peace with herself on this summer morning when I show her to you first.

She was sitting alone, quite alone, in the quaint old drawing-room of the quainter old house, on this sultry June morning. She was bereft of her usual morning amusements. It had been too hot to take Vengeance for a good, hard, exhilarating trot. Stanley was in the parish. She detested needlework, unless she had some one by to assort her skeins and talk to her. All these things were hard to bear, but harder still was the fact that she had no new books and no morning papers to read.

Any one who has been accustomed to a full supply of them for years can understand the sudden blank, the awful misery of falling short, or straying away out of the bounds of delivery, of those yellow-ticketed volumes which go to the making up of a considerable portion of nineteenth-century bliss. Bella was wont to have her interest kept on the *qui vive* for four heroines and as many heroes at one time in divers serials. In addition to this long-drawn-out excitement she was accustomed to "look over" all that everybody was doing in Central Africa, "the House," hebdomadal and daily literature, and fashionable life. Now at one fell blow she was cut off from daily intercourse with the library, morning papers, and the people of her own set. In default of these she had fresh air and Stanley Villars. But she had been in the country for three weeks; had been engaged to the aforesaid seven days; and was—Bella Vane.

"Ah, well, the women free from faults have beds below the willow." I am never tired of that quotation. To me it has as deep a meaning, is as fraught with pathos and plea and profound pity for the weak and wavering, as was "vanity of vanities, all is vanity," to the great preacher, and his great exponent in these our own days. Bella Vane was very far from faultless. She had not yet graduated for a "bed beneath the willow." She sat here in the June sunbeams twisting the week-old engagement-ring upon her finger, and wishing, with all the power of wishing within her, that Stanley could give up more time to her—that the beautiful country was not so dull—and that she had not promised her mamma to remain quiescent in it for still a month longer, in order to regain her roses, which a brisk early season in London had slightly faded.

She had arranged herself on a bay window, with her feet on the sill of the same, and a two-days-old *Morning Post* in her lap. Its being two days old was no drawback to the delight with which she perused it. Politics did not interest her one whit. Whether the North swamped the South—Denmark got its duchies—the duchies their independence—or the grandest armies were decimated for an idea—was of little moment to Bella. Such things had their importance and value she did not doubt, but they never came in her way. Had the men she knew been connected ever so remotely with the state, it would have been different. As it was, the sole diplomatist who had bowed at her shrine was a young unpaid *attaché* to the embassy at a minute court. He having spelt providence with a "*b*" in his solitary effusion to her, was regarded by her but lightly.

What made the *Morning Post* acceptable to her, whether it was old or young, was its full description of the Princess's last new ball-dress, and the list of names of those who saw the Princess wear the same. Miss Bella had run the gauntlet of but one London season, and if she had not striven to enchain a duke, would have won an earl—so everybody said. But she had striven to enchain a duke, and the duke has successfully wrestled against a fairer fate than may ever be offered him again. Now that he was pledged to a very different line of life, she remembered the scenes in which she had so striven; the duke's name amongst those of others in the columns of the paper recalled those scenes vividly. The remembrance made her sad—she knew not why; only a country village was dull, and she was a spoilt beauty, and very young.

I like the girl whom I have created. Are we not all apt to be led away into a perhaps not too well-founded admiration for the possessors of big, blue, earnest eyes, and finely-curved, expressive lips? Beauty has a blinding influence; we cannot see its faults yet awhile—"just a little longer," we are always pleading, to believe it as perfect as it seems.

I like this girl—yet I do not declare that her speedy wearying of love's young dream was right or amiable. She—the betrothed bride of a week—ought not to have sighed over the columns of the *Morning Post.* Nor was it good of her to debate seriously within herself the question of whether she should break her resolution, order her mamma suddenly back to town, and go to a grand *fête* at a villa on the banks of the Thames, which she saw announced, and to which, of course, she would be invited; and so break up the course of evening wanderings which she had been taking with Stanley Villars.

"I am happier here with Stanley, naturally," she said to herself, after a long perusal of the paper, and a longer cogitation over its contents. Then she took out her watch to see what time it was, and yawned wearily when she found that still another hour remained to be passed away before the luncheon bell would ring. "What on earth can Aunt Vane be about? I'm sick of it all!"

She had been alone all the morning, and she was a social creature, who loved to hear the sound of her own and others' voices. Neither the feeling nor the expression were very extraordinary under the circumstances. Still she wished that she could have retracted both, for she remembered that the man she had promised to marry had a prominent place in the scenes of which she was sick.

She was just resolving to eschew all mid-day sustenance, and go out for a couple of hours on Vengeance, when she heard a step on the gravel outside the window—a step that was familiar to her—a step that, despite this sudden accession of petulant weariness, was very dear to her. All traces of discontentment and dulness vanished from her face as she rose up quickly and stepped between the screening roses that fell over the window. She forgot the *fête* by the river, the triumphs of last year, and the possible chagrin of the duke at having lost her, as she came out into the presence of the man who had won her.

"Stanley, I am so glad you are come," she began, impetuously; "I have had nothing to do, and no one to speak to all the morning." Then she went on to tell him of the half-formed determination to go away for a few days, and he listened to it silently—never combating it by any of the loving words she had hoped he would use.

He has been called the pet brother of the girl whose beauty was of the soft and yielding order—fit robe of her mind. The pet brothers of soft and yielding sisters are almost sure to possess the opposite qualities in the extreme. Stanley Villars was not a hard man, nor an obstinate one; but he was not readily impressed, and even Florry said that he could be very firm.

Look at him as he stands now with Bella Vane clasping his arm with both her hands, as she tells him, half piteously, half humorously, how the dulness and heat of the day had all but routed her from the village. A tall, well-built young man, whose figure graced the garb he wore in a way that made full many a woman sigh that some more graceful garb did not adorn it. A man whose face was perfect in the correct cutting of each feature, and in a certain severe nobility of expression that is nicer on a bronze coin than in real life. His slate-coloured eyes were truly the windows of a soul in which nothing mean could dwell, even for an instant; and his mouth had the lofty beauty of an Apollo's, who had never said a word which could shame him in the utterance. His head was held high, as were his thoughts and aspirations, and it was crowned with dark, curling locks, that were, as his sister Georgina said, "rather thrown away on any one so superior to such things as Stanley." He wore but little whiskers, and no beard or moustache; what whiskers he had were dark and silky, and were long, after the fashion of the day, rather than broad.

Give the word its widest meaning, Stanley Villars was eminently "good"-looking. Many women had deemed him so, but few had accorded him so much as a flutter of the heart.

He had been struck with surprise himself when the truth came home to him that Bella Vane liked him well. He was conscious himself that extremes would meet should they ever come together, for Bella showed her true colours at once, and the thoughtful man marvelled that so fiery a nature should succumb to his icier sway. He watched her during those few meetings to which Florence had alluded in London, and he marked that she glowed beneath his regard as she never glowed at other times. He watched her more keenly still when she withdrew from frivolity, and came down to be quiet and good in the country, and he felt that the beautiful girl believed that not alone could she make his happiness, but that he could make hers. Very frequently did he pray that she might not be mistaken, or that he might be given power to wait for awhile till further trial was given her. But she was with him frequently, gently showing that she loved him, sweetly chiding him for fearing. So the prudent, Apollo-like clergyman, whom all women admired, and so few had dared to love, took the plunge, and asked for the promise that she would be his wife, from the great beauty who might have been a duchess.

———o———

CHAPTER III.

CIRCE.

Claude Walsingham rose late on the morning following that conversation with Florry Villars, with a confused recollection of having been betrayed into sundry promises under the influence of claret-cup champagne and strains from Verdi's last opera, on the previous night. Not that he had put an enemy into his mouth who had stolen away all his wits. He was a man of the present day; one of an order and period who can go very wrong indeed, and still steer clear of aught that borders on excess. But there are other things in this wicked world which are equally intoxicating as wine. There is a certain incense, compared to the power of which, when it mounts into the brain, the most potent of vintages are weak. This incense had been around him often, but its enervating odorous sweetness had never obtained so full a dominion over him as had been obtained last night.

Every man must have, at the least, an idea of what this incense, to which no name can be given, since none can fully describe it, was composed. It is the atmosphere that women, who have charms both of body and mind, can create around the man whom, for reasons noble, or the reverse unhappily very often, they are desirous to flatter and beguile for the purpose of enslaving.

He was well endowed by nature and fortune, as I have said. He was well placed; and he had the art to make the very most and best of his endowments, his place and position. This being the case, the legitimate arrows that had been discharged at him were numerous. Naturally, then, the ones that were not so legitimate were innumerable.

There was no thought of evil in the hearts of many whose shafts had been deemed wickedly reprehensible by his mother, and others who took a warm, not to say peppery, interest in his welfare. Portionless girls, with no particular pedigree, had been severely denounced for casting upon him eyes of what would, with culture —the smallest encouragement—have developed into affection. Old Mrs. Walsingham had had bad dreams about dozens of respectable young ladies whose fair faces had made an evanescent impression on her impressionable son. Her history of the snares and delusions that had been spread for him, and that he had escaped, thank heaven, was voluminous. But they had all been respectable snares and delusions, these that Claude had confided to his mother. The list of those that had been spread —that were still, alas! spreading—was incomplete.

Claude was very precious in the eyes of his whole family. His father almost wished himself dead at times, in order that the son of whom he was so proud might enjoy the estates and the glory of being the head of the house of Walsignham. The old gentleman was stopped short of wishing it entirely, by the reflection that when dead he could not see Claude in possession. He envied Hamlet's father, to whom it had been given to come back and mark how abjectly Horatio listened when the Prince elected to make a long string of high-minded remarks, and how readily pretty Ophelia went mad for the estimable orphan.

His brothers, though they were younger and their lines were cast in less pleasant places, and his married sisters, possessing other and dearer interests of their own, as might be supposed, believed in him as a handsome, generous elder brother, who, a "great swell" abroad, remains a boy in all but years at home, is sure to be believed in. They vaunted his excellencies to their husbands, they made him godfather to all their children, they gave him the freedom of their homes, they made much of him in every way, loving him above their other brothers in a way that, if he had not been Claude, the other brothers would have been jealous of. But he was Claude, therefore no one was jealous of aught that was bestowed upon him—even of that by the side of which all else dwindled into insignificance, the great and surpassing love which dwelt in his mother's heart for this glory of her race.

He was very precious to them all, but to her he was as God's sun—utter darkness would be over all the earth for her did a cloud obscure his brightness. She believed from the bottom of her heart that he was as good a man, as true a gentleman and Christian, as she had prayed night and morning from the hour of his birth he might grow up to be, and remain. He knew of her prayers and her fond belief, and never yet had he been clouded in his mother's eyes.

But his mother's eyes were not upon him always, or indeed often, for they seldom left their old western county mansion, and Claude's was a London life. When they did come, he was her own devotional boy the whole time. The happy woman and proud mother dreamt of no vapour more defiling than the cigar smoke she knew of coming over him. He went to the opera, and to theatres, and balls, and breakfasts at two o'clock P.M., as usual, while his mother was in town. But he never talked of supping in Bohemia, nor did he go down to Richmond in a much-talked-about opera-singer's barouche to dinner, while she remained. He returned his mother's love to the best of his ability—it was not in him to give back quite all she gave; but he respected her prejudices—amongst which was a colossal one against what she termed "the father of evils, playhouses, and the poor misguided ones who performed in them." The sun would have been darkened cruelly to her, poor woman, could she but have known that a bewitchingly pretty prima donna, who had made a great success by her lifelike exposition of a Traviata's woes, was singing Claude into a state of mad resentment against the world for its idle prejudice relative to marrying a woman of whose antecedents nothing was known.

They called her "Circe" amongst themselves —he and the friends who knew the case, and watched the progress of it. He was not in love with her—at least he felt that he could and should love some other woman better in days to come. But her thrilling voice made his heart leap. Her inexhaustible gaiety, her apparently unfailing brilliancy, bewitched and dazzled him when he was with her, and she took care that he should be with her often. Those suppers after the opera were bewildering things to Claude that year; the wines and women were alike sparkling and bright; and she, the brightest of them all, sparkled for him alone—he thought.

He had never seen Circe by daylight yet. She was young and beautiful exceedingly on the boards and at the after banquets. Very young as to the rich dark bloom on her cheek —very beautiful in the rare lace, black, full, and floating, which she had a trick of half shrouding herself in, after the fashion of a Spaniard.

She had been especially young and beautiful and sparkling on the previous night, he remembered when he rose. He also remembered that he had invited her and a good many of her friends to dine with him at the "Star and Garter" this day. Additionally, the recollection forced itself upon him that he had said words of which Circe might desire an explanation, and that he was very far from being competent to give one that should alike seem good to her and to his family.

"I wish I could keep clear of her," he muttered, "or that Florry Villars was like her—in some things. How easily some fellows satisfy themselves. Stanley, for instance, who has found what he considers his fate, I suppose, in a fortnight. I own that Adèle isn't the ideal Mrs. Claude Walsingham; but I do wish that some girl, who would meet their views in the West, had a particle of Adèle's charms. It's a shame to wish Florry altered, though, by Jove!"—he went on carefully adjusting a cream-coloured rose in its proper position upon the lappel of his coat—"I wonder whether the interest would deepen or decrease if I had her with me always. That's the devil of it: a dull wife with every womanly virtue, from whom there would be no escape, would bring me to an untimely grave. There was something emotional, though, and pleasantly exciting, in that look she gave me when I asked her if her great news was that she was going to be married."

So he soliloquised about Florry the while he was adjusting and readjusting the rose, and drawing on gloves that resembled the rose in hue, and ivory in polish. He was going to drive Circe and her friends, and several of his own, down in his drag, and he desired that Circe's first daylight view of him should be auspicious.

He had written to Stanley Villars the previous evening. Written in a congratulatory strain—but Stanley detected a half note of disapproval in it. "I always thought that you would marry a girl as much like your sister Florence as possible," he wrote, from which Stanley deduced that his old friend deemed that he would have been a wiser man had he not linked himself to the very opposite of his sister Florence.

At his club this morning Claude read that—"We understand that a marriage is arranged to take place between the Rev. Stanley Villars, second son of the late Sir Gerald Villars, Bart., and the only daughter and heiress of the late Philip Vane, Esq." He read it with a laughing light contempt in his eyes. "Fancy old Stanley going in for the pomps and vanities in the way of this announcement!" he remarked, pointing out the paragraph to a mutual friend, who forthwith read it and rejoined—

"Whew! Bella Vane going to marry Stanley! 'The devil was sick, the devil a saint would be.' What's the matter with her, I wonder?"

"Do you know her?"

"My dear fellow, know her! I should think I did. I adored her during the first part of her season; then I, in common with the rest of the small deer, was smothered in the strawberry-leaves. She played for the highest stake to be won last year. What has brought her down to this?"

"Villars is a friend of mine," Claude replied, briefly and coldly.

"So he is of mine. I think him one of the finest fellows that ever lived; but I shall never doubt that the stars are fire, or but that truth is a liar, or anything indeed after this. Why, man, she turned up her nose at Lord Lexley and his thirty thousand per annum. Shows you were out of town, your not feeling the shock of surprise that I am experiencing. I wonder, though, that the noise of her fame didn't penetrate even to Canada. She was the greatest flirt and the greatest beauty we have seen for years."

"Villars is just the fellow to manage such a woman, that is all I have to say about it, not knowing the lady," Claude replied carelessly; but for all this assumed carelessness, for all his own light regard of many things, he felt sorry that Stanley should have given his heart into such a woman's hand. "Cold as he seems, he will go to the bad should she ever crush it or throw it away," he thought. "Dear old Stanley, I'll go down and see him."

They went to Richmond. Down along the road that winds through pretty prosperous little Castlenau, and over Barnes Common, Claude drove his team of bays with black points in the drag that was Circe's triumphal car for the nonce. She was scarcely so lovely by daylight as, from having seen her under the lamps alone, a tyro might have expected. But Claude was no tyro, therefore he soon ceased to see her sallow; he looked straight ahead at his horses, in fact, and with his eyes averted, found her "devilish fascinating," even by daylight.

I said that Claude had promised to drive her down, accompanied by some of her friends and his own. Her friends were a pair of women whom she greeted as mother and sister when occasion seemed to call for the possession of such relatives. At other times they fell into position as the merely useful friends they were—dependent friends who managed her establishment and dressed her hair, and kept the reckless prima donna's affairs straight, and who were ready to come forward and take up the claims of kindred when a Claude Walsingham appeared to call for such evidence of respectability as a mother and sister in the flesh, and resident.

The elder of these two women gave that air of weight and age to the party that is desirable. Her most marked attributes were a power of holding her peace and adapting herself immediately to the rich clothes into which she had to rush whenever Adèle required the countenance and support of a maternal parent. The younger woman was an adept in the art of exclamation—of admiring, wondering, interested curiosity, excited exclamation! Now we all like to be admired and wondered at, to be shown that we are interesting, and to be made feel that our smallest remarks whet the edge of the listener's curiosity! Her mission in life was to amuse the friends of Adèle's current favourite, and she fulfilled it thoroughly. The young men who went down on Claude's drag to Richmond that day had plenty of height, but not too much heart, or head, or fancy. They were the right men in the right place, for height is one of the touches an artistic-minded man will always seek to give when filling-in the picture his drag should be when "going," and Victorine, Adèle's sister, suited them entirely.

———o———

CHAPTER IV.

AFTER DINNER.

They reached the "Star and Garter" about seven that evening, and found that in front of the hotel and in the yard an equine confusion, and in the house itself a savoury one, reigned, by reason of there being much company assembled for the purpose of enjoying viands that might be improved upon, and the views that cannot be. Claude, a distinguished member of the "four-in-hand," brought his horses up at the door with that suddenly arrested rush, and threw down the unstrapped reins with that celerity which is very beautiful to behold, and looks very easy till you have tried to do it, and failed ignominiously. Then he helped Adèle down, and Adèle, with much grace and mercy, stood at the door for a few minutes, resettling the Yak mantilla over her shoulders, and gazing at Claude's horses through the jewelled eyeglass which looked too heavy for her tiny, tightly-gloved hand. Every one has seen this little pantomime gone through by women who have come down in drags. Every one has seen them stand with apparently sublime indifference, and in reality perhaps with ridiculous interest, to be inspected by the common herd who have not come down in like fashion, and who are palpably in admiring awe of it.

Amongst the many equipages that were around and being led away from and dashing up (as he had done a minute before) to the entrance, Claude recognised young Lady Villars' landau. Before he had time to collect his forces, and induce Adèle to drop her glass and turn round, and sweep into the house, he saw Lady Villars descend from it, followed by her sister-in-law, Florry. So he went in hurriedly through the door by himself, leaving Adèle standing there gazing with her lovely, listless eyes at the new arrivals.

Went in and looked at the room he had ordered, and the preparations that were being made for their reception, with more earnestness than the waiters had ever seen him display before. Went in cursing the chance that had brought the Villarses there to-day, and the fate that kept him from joining them, and even Circe herself, for being the Circe that she was.

He almost loathed her, as he stood there in the room that was so radiant and so exquisitely adorned with flowers that he had ordered but yesterday for her. He felt a repugnance to that beauty of hers which she was now employed in bringing out in bold relief on the door step. He could not bear the idea of Florence—his friend Stanley's sister, his own sweet, smiling friend—passing close to, and being scrutinized by, the woman he had driven down. Still less could he bear the idea of Florence arriving at a knowledge of his having done so, and of her discovering that he had in consequence shrunk from a meeting with her. He almost loathed the Circe of this period of his life, as he stood there gnawing the ends of his moustache.

But this was before dinner.

They all came in presently, Adèle herself, with her bonnet off and a tempered bloom on her face, and Victorine ecstatic, and the respectable lady, their mamma, still great at holding her peace. Claude put away his thoughts of Florry, and would not harbour the reflection that she might perchance be in the next room. That is to say, he nearly put them away, but a sore feeling would obtain occasionally, after hearing that Sir Gerald Villars had followed his wife in his phaeton, accompanied by Lord Lexley. Lord Lexley was a man who was unfettered in every sense of the word. He had neither debts, nor a wife, nor bad habits, to the best of the world's belief.

It was horrible for Claude to contemplate this little party of four—before dinner.

It grew less horrible gradually under the influence of white Hermitage. He left champagne to the women, and what he left was not wasted. After, gradually diminishing during the dinner itself, it died out in a burst of song—the drinking song of a new opera—that Adèle gave, and she was all the queen of his soul again, *vice* Florence Villars absent, but not "resigned."

The night was very fair. Those terraced balconies leading down from the room in which they sat to the river below, were laden with flowers, and the air was heavy with their sweetness. They leant out of the window—he, the giver of this festival of which she was the queen, and Adèle—and she sang bright bursts of song that the flowers turned to listen to, and the stars wished they were below to hear more clearly still. What wonder that he saw her fair as the night—bright as the stars—sweet as the flowers that bloomed before them? What wonder, being what he was, that he forgot his mother's prejudices and Florry Villars' gentle love for him, and she rang out strains sparkling as the champagne she had imbibed, and he listened to them under the influence of the moon and white Hermitage.

They went out at last—out on to the balcony, and then down the steps, to look into the piece of water over which that willow weeps. Her dress, as she swept along hanging on his arm, brushed against the flowers, and more intoxicating odours arose, and she was very fair. He remembered all the warm mentions of her beauty that he had heard made at divers times, and forgot the sallow tinge that he had seen during the drive down, as he stood by her side, and she looked into the water, and suffered her voice to ripple in melody soft and golden as the moonlight; and he drew her arm more closely within his own, and the fumes of the wine he had drunk mingled with the woman's beauty, and mounted to his brain.

Her head, shrouded by some lace, from under the folds of which her beauty shone out lustrously, inclined nearer to him as she sang on in a very low tone now. Her scented hair fell in rich curls, from the classical knot into which it was gathered behind, upon his shoulder. Her beauty was very patent to him at that moment, and he suddenly desired to have it for his own.

"Adèle," he said, "could I suffice to you—could you live without public applause and the adoration of empty-headed fools——"

"Ah! Claude, for you!"

She said it in a tone that implied that she could be capable of anything for him. The tone said this distinctly, but she purposely made the words devoid of too clear a meaning. She had no intention of committing herself until she clearly understood the nature of the terms Claude proposed.

"Then leave them for me, and be mine alone," he cried; but even as he said it, even as he flung his arm round her, and drew her unresisting beauty closer to his breast, he could not help marvelling how she would look in the quiet, old home in the West; and what he should do with the presents other men had lavished upon her.

She paused for a minute, apparently in the quietude of very passion, in reality because she could not, for that space of time, decide which would be her wisest course. She was a queen of song now, fêted and paid as such, but her voice might give way, or another arise to eclipse her before long. It occurred to her that it would be well to fasten him to his suggestion without further delay, so she remembered her mamma in an instant.

"Claude, I will leave them all for you—even my mother. Ah! how shall I tell her and Victorine, who will die to leave me; but I must tell them."

"There's no immediate hurry, Adèle," Claude observed.

His faith in Adèle's mamma was not nearly so perfect a thing as Adèle imagined it to be. Moreover, the difficulty of disposing of those articles of jewellery—gifts of those who had preceded him—was more vividly before him every moment.

"But I could not leave her in doubt—a moment after my heart has been assured of that for which it has longed," Adèle said. The first part of her speech had the true, genuine (stage) daughter's ring about it, the latter portion was redolent of the sweet inconsequence of love's young dream.

He relaxed his warm clasp a little. It annoyed him to think that Adèle should be in such a hurry to go and talk about it. It had been due—this abrupt proposal of his—to the moonlight and the melody in a measure, and he wanted more moonlight and melody; he did not want to go in and read, in the faces of his tall young friends, that he had made a mistake.

"Tell me, has your heart longed for this assurance, Adèle," he whispered. He did not quite believe in her warm declaration that it had done so; but the declaration had been uttered in tones that the first soprano had known how to render most seductively soft, and he wanted to hear them again.

So she uttered them again, with but slight variation of words and no variation of meaning. She wisely, having once worded a phrase that sounded well, adhered to that phrase, and made no weak attempts to improve upon it. Too much revision is as bad as none at all.

Once more, therefore, she averred that her heart had longed for this assurance, and once more she asserted that it behoved her to go in and tell her anxious parent that it had been given. Then he, feeling that copious draughts of the wine of the South were needed by him in this hour of his acceptance by the daughter of the same, went in and saw Adèle make manifest how weak he had been out in the garden.

It was after dinner now, and the anxious parent was no longer so great at holding her peace as she had been. She was naturally rejoiced at what had transpired, and Victorine was vivaciously resigned to the loss of her sister, who would leave, "ah! such triumphs for this love of hers." It was after dinner, with his tall young friends also, and they laughed more than was seemly when they congratulated him on the great conquest he had made over many things. Yes, Claude had full need of the most care-dispelling vintage the cellars of the "Star and Garter" could supply, in order to be able to bear the brunt of that tide of feeling which swept o'er him in this first hour of his engagement to Circe.

What a glorious gipsy queen she looked, though, when late that night they were about to start from the door. There had been much wishing them happiness in cups of sparkling wine, and hers was the steadiest progress made by that party through the hall, not even excepting Claude's own. She swept along "like a queen in a play that night," and held her triumph-flushed face aloft in a way none of the others were capable of doing. Claude hung over her as she moved along, fairly enraptured afresh, for she was glorious, in the pomp of her beauty, grand in the management of that fiery thing, her natural manner. She would well adorn the proudest home he could place her in, he told himself. She had the physique of one who might be the mistress of a palace. How men would turn and look when he drove her through the park. How every glass would be turned to the box when she, the former queen of its board, should sit at the opera. How Florry Villars started, and exclaimed, "Oh! Claude—Major Walsingham," at this juncture, as they came suddenly in collision with Sir Gerald Villars' party at the door, and Adèle, in her scarlet mantle, bore down in proud, picturesque beauty upon her gentle, unconscious rival.

Then he cursed afresh that hour by the water, in the flower-scented garden, and shrank, excited as he was, from the caressing weight that woman laid upon his arm. She, in her pride of Bacchanal beauty, was no fitting mistress for that grand, honourable old home of his fathers—for that house whose women had all been pure and unknown. He could take no notice of Florence's exclamation; he dared not meet her eyes; so he hurried his companion on, and into the drag tumultuously, and suffered his horses to take the road home, in an eager burst, in which he was not wont to indulge them in that hilly Richmond street.

"So you went over the brink to-night, old fellow!" one of his companions said, when he had deposited Adèle and her relatives at their house in South Audley Street, and the rest were wending their way back rapidly to their respective quarters.

"I have been a damned fool; but I'd thank you not to mention it," Claude rejoined; and the man who had no wish to be other than thanked by Claude, resolved that he wouldn't mention it yet.

Claude Walsingham was in a hard, cruel humour that night. The excitement was over, and when he had put down the last man at that man's quarters, he drove on alone to his own at a hard, cruel pace The beauty of the woman who had stood out under the stars with him was less vividly before him than the aught but tame publicity she had attained. It seemed to him that with Adèle for a wife, life to be endurable must be all driving at a rate that would abolish thought, and drinking wine to the exclusion of reflection. As he came to this conclusion, he cursed his folly—the folly that would have been blind in a boy even—and lashed his horses afresh, and they rattled over the stones in Piccadilly at a rate he would not have driven them had he been well with himself just then.

But he was far from being well with himself; he was so ill with himself, indeed, that he indulged in a savage regret that he had not secured oblivion, at least for this night, through the medium of that syren wine which had lured him on to the commission of that of which he now repented. Whatever of intoxication there had been when that subtle crowning spell was thrown round him down in the garden by the river, was gone now. He was thoroughly sober, and his sobriety was a cause of regret, for it enabled him to think.

The road was tolerably clear, for the hour was late now, and the heavy, huge drag loomed out so largely that it gave fair warning of its approach, swift as that approach was, and so enabled the few foot passengers who were abroad to get out of the way. At the entrance to Grosvenor Place, however, he was compelled to pull up suddenly, in order to avoid a woman who rushed out of the dark shade by the purposeless arch, in order to be run over, or to give him the trouble of sparing her that fate. He saw that she escaped, that she was clear of the possibility of being mangled under his wheels, and with a curse at her carelessness, he was preparing to drive on again at the old pace. But there was a something in the tone of the answering cry she gave to his maledictory caution that made him pull up, and shout to one of his servants to "get out and see what was the matter."

"It's only her dog you've gone over, sir," his man told him, touching his hat, and preparing to get in again; but Claude ordered him to "stand at their heads," and jumped down from the box at once, and went back to where the woman stood with a small crowd about her now, looking down upon the ground, where a little, heaving, bleeding mass lay—dying.

The tall, fair young gentleman with the flower in his coat, and that aroma of good breeding about him which the masses rarely fail to recognise, cleft his way through the crowd in an instant. "What is the matter?" he asked very gently of the woman, an elderly dame with one of those broad, rosy faces on which sorrow sits so very sadly; and she answered him at once, touched by the gentleness of his tone, without an atom of reproach in her own—

"Oh! yer honour, it's my little dog! killed, sir!"

"Only a little mangy cur what's better dead than alive, sir," a policeman interposed gruffly. "Now you clear out, and don't be a begging of the gentleman 'carse your dog run under his wheels," he added to the woman.

"You clear out, and let me see if the poor dog *is* dead," Claude said haughtily. Then he stooped down, and with the slender hands that were so carefully encased in the cream-coloured ivory-polished gloves, he picked up the poor little mangled animal that had been writhing at his feet. There had been hardness and cruelty in his heart, as he had driven along recklessly; but now, as he stood looking at the result of that reckless driving, there was nothing but tenderness in it, and he felt inexpressibly shocked and softened.

"I would have given something not to have done it. My good woman, there is nothing to be done for him, or on my honour I'd do it." Then he laid down the dog again, and put some money in the woman's hand; and she "blest him for a kind gentleman," and tried to forgive him the death of her dog.

It was but a poor half-bred black and tan terrier, rough and unkempt in appearance, which had come to this evil end. He saw that it was just these things and no more—yes, thus much more he saw, that the poor little dog had been palpably that woman's friend, possibly her comfort. Its dying eyes had turned lovingly towards her, and he had marked that last appeal with a keen remorse. The man who made life appointments with dubious people under the influence of wine, and lived in an atmosphere which he deemed defiling, when he thought of Florry Villars or his mother, had a tender heart. Claude cursed his folly no more that night; indeed, he thought of little else save the ruin he had brought upon that humble union, and regretted nothing so much as the death of the little dog.

—o—

CHAPTER V.

BELLA TRIES THE PATH OF DUTY.

"And what have you finally decided upon doing? staying on here for awhile or going away?" Stanley Villars asked of his betrothed, when his betrothed had rapidly recited to him the divers emotions that had chased each other through her mind during the dull solitude of that morning.

"Oh, Stanley! now is it likely that I should come to the decision of 'going away' quite of my own free will! I shall stay here while I can—while mamma can spare me."

She believed herself to be speaking the entire truth. In his presence she forgot the uncontrollable desire to be off and away from this place, which had obtained dominion while she was alone.

"Then Claude Walsingham won't have his journey for nothing, as I have feared he would a minute ago. I have heard from him this morning, telling me that he means to come down and quarter himself upon me for a few days."

"Claude Walsingham! isn't he a——"

"A what?"

"Well, a very agreeable—no, that's not the phrase—a very fascinating man, Stanley; very gay and reckless, and all that sort of thing."

"Is 'all that sort of thing' so fascinating? I don't know that he is fascinating, but he is a very good friend of mine, and I shall be glad when you know him if you can endorse my favourable opinion."

"What made you say that, a minute ago, you half feared Claude Walsingham would have his journey for nothing?"

"I half feared that you would be gone."

"Oh, Stanley! you only suffer *half* fears on my account; you ought to be miserable at the notion of losing me." The great beauty clasped her little hands more closely round his arm—this pantomime took place in a leafy alley of a very secluded old garden, be it remembered—and looked up into his face with a glow of reproach on her own as she spoke.

"I should be miserable enough at the notion of losing you—miserable enough to satisfy even you, Bella; but your going away for a time, whether that time be long or short, is not losing you while we love each other."

His tone was deep, earnest, thoughtful; she knew that he thoroughly meant what he said. But for all that conviction, a less reasonable speech would have been more taking.

"Your views are too transcendental for me to share, Stanley. Perhaps you wouldn't call it 'losing me' if I went away for ever, provided 'we loved one another still?'"

"Unquestionably I should not, darling! While we both are, what I hope and believe we are, and shall remain, we cannot be lost to each for ever."

She dropped his arm with a little shiver—a little irrepressible revulsion of feeling possessed her for a few moments. He was right, she knew, in the abstract. But this knowledge did not make the enunciation of these right views one bit more palatable to her.

"Don't talk to me in that way just yet, Stanley!" she pleaded almost wistfully, after a short silence.

"In what way, Bella?" He was calm, reasonable, and superior, and again Bella's spirit revolted.

"About not caring for my love till we both get to heaven."

"My dear girl, how shockingly you pervert my words and meaning in your impatience."

"That's what I understood you to mean, Stanley; and it *does* sound cold-blooded, and methodistical besides. If you don't care for me in this world, or want me to care for you, it's a pity that you told me you did, and made me tell you the same; I should have been happier with a sinner who cared for me, than with a saint who does not."

The tears were in her big blue eyes, standing on her long straight lashes, rolling over the flushed cheeks. The pious young divine, with the well-regulated mind, was shocked, but he could not deem her a very miserable sinner. Perhaps this toleration was due to the fact of the unregenerate heart being unruly on his own account.

"Dearest, I am weak and erring as yourself."

"Oh! *don't!*" the girl cried passionately.

He thought that she was touched and affected by his allusion to himself as a fellow-sinner. Stanley Villars was a clever, good young man, but his talent and goodness left him powerless to fathom the utter weariness, the contemptuous weariness, that filled the spirit of the girl at his side as she heard him use phrases that sounded like the commonest cant to her. If good people only knew the mischief they do by putting their goodness before others in set sentences, how silent they would be very often.

He thought that he would take a more sprightly tone with this dispirited penitent—a tone that, to his mind, savoured of hilarity.

"You want something to change the current of your thoughts, Bella; you are rather down this morning, and you require a little healthy excitement."

"I know I do," she interrupted; "let us go for a ride, Stanley—a good long ride, that will keep us out until dinner."

She asked him quite joyously to join her in this pleasure, and all the brightness was back in the tones of her voice; but the joyousness and brightness were of short duration.

"I have no time for long rides in the middle of the day, Bella; you know that very well."

"You never have time for anything I ask you to do," she answered, impatiently; "what prevents your devoting such an *enormous* space of time, as from now till dinner would be, to me to-day?"

"I thought I had told you that the girls who are preparing for confirmation came to me from three till five."

"Had you told me?—perhaps you had," she replied, wearily. "Well, I suppose it's all proper enough; you undertook to do such things."

She dropped his arm now, and turned away to gather a flower, humming an opera air, and trying not to get flushed with annoyance.

"And you have undertaken to aid me in the fulfilment of my duty; remember that, Bella, dearest."

"I am a poor aid; I can only tell you that it's three o'clock now," Bella rejoined.

"You may be a great aid to me, my darling." He took her hand as he said this, and Bella struggled with herself, and managed to say—

"I will try to be, Stanley—really I will; but is it always to be like this?—am I never to be first with you?"

Then he made her feel sick at heart again by telling her that they each had higher duties to perform towards God than towards each other; and that it behoved them to attend to these higher duties first.

"I'll try to ascend to your more perfect air, Stanley," she said to him when he had concluded, "but I must do it by degrees, or the rarification of it will kill me. A stone saint, with her hands eternally clasped, would have been a more congenial wife to you than I shall ever be, I fear."

When she said that, he, despite his calm devotion to his parish duties, and that theory he held as to the impossibility of the loved and loving being ever lost, wished ardently that he could make her his own congenial wife, never to be torn from his side in either the spirit or the flesh, at once.

But this ardent desire could not be gratified, so he went off to his confirmation class, and Bella went in and strove to wear the time away by questioning her aunt, good, prosy Mrs. Vane, as to how she had come to like doing "parish work," and perpetually pottering, physically and spiritually, about and amongst her husband's flock. "For no human being can be born with a taste for it," argued Bella, "so it may grow upon me in time."

Later in the week Miss Vane had a letter from her mamma—a judicious letter, informing her that every one was wondering why she was going to marry Stanley Villars, who, as a younger son, had little besides his curacy. "I confess myself surprised," Mrs. Vane wrote; "had he been a bishop, it would not have been so extraordinary; as it is, you must change vastly before you will be fit for a mere clergyman's wife."

"Of course, I shall change vastly; I mean I shall change quite as much as there's any necessity for my changing," Bella said to herself, clinging more closely to Stanley the instant there was a doubt thrown upon the wisdom of her choice of him. "Of course, I shall adapt myself to his career; and no one has any right to dictate to me. I shall be very happy with a 'mere clergyman,' as mamma calls him. Who wouldn't be happy with Stanley, I should like to know?"

She had not seen Stanley for a day or two when she said this. His parochial duties had absorbed him entirely, he had informed her in a brace of brief notes. She was beginning to hunger and thirst for his society again, her heart told her, because she loved him so well. But the heart is deceitful above all things; so it might have been only because she had no one else to amuse her.

On the Saturday, Mr. Stanley Villars came up to the rectory, and gladdened the heart of the rector's niece. He recounted all he had done, all the difficulties he had encountered and surmounted (he hoped) in the unregenerate hearts of the candidates for confirmation; Bella listening, and trying, with all her sweet will, to sympathise with him, and failing, failing still!

She made a petition before he left. "I should like to help you, Stanley. Can I do anything for you?—copy sermons, or anything?"

Copying sermons was her only idea of helping a clergyman. She made the offer warmly, but Stanley rejected it in a way that made her feel she had erred again.

"I don't want to see my own poor words reproduced, Bella, thank you; I am not likely to need them a second time; but you can help me in another way."

"How?"

"Will you promise to try if I tell you?"

"Yes," she said promptly. She would try anything, no matter how horrid.

"There is nothing 'horrid' in what I propose, Bella; take one of my classes off my hands at the Sunday school."

"Oh, Stanley! go amongst those children?"

"You will not essay to do them such poor service as you may do them, Bella!" he said with some severity.

"If it is sure to be such poor service, why should I put myself out to render it?" she retorted.

"Simply because it is your duty."

"I'll try to do that, indeed I will, Stanley," she said, with a sudden humility that came partly from remembering her mother's sarcasms, and partly from her genuine desire to please him.

"And if you try earnestly, you will succeed, in a measure at least," he rejoined; which was highly satisfactory to Bella of course, and precisely the sort of thing to lighten that darkness of hers which he lamented.

The Sunday morning found her at the school, diverting the attention of the regular paid teachers, and wearying over the task the performance of which was to qualify her for a position on high with Stanley Villars. "If only they are good who do these things willingly, how bad I must be!" she thought to herself as she sat in an atmosphere that she thanked the Lord was not a familiar one to her, and endeavoured to concentrate the children's attention on something besides her bonnet and gloves. She could not help feeling that the wicked world of good ventilation and sweet essences was a far preferable place to this corner of the Lord's vineyard, over the door of which "Feed my lambs" was written in mediæval characters, the attempt to decipher which had driven many a child into a state of despondency as to its prospects of ultimately being able to "read off anything." She could but glance over the edge of the book she held at Stanley, and feel that he might as well have left such feeding to those who were capable of doing it to the full as well as him and herself, and who were not made to feel miserably ill through doing it. Then his patience over that from which his taste must have revolted would occur to her vividly as the beautiful thing it was; and she would put away her rebellious thoughts, and pray to feel as she ought to feel about this that he had told her was a "duty" for a while.

"I think strong women, with robust constitutions, and a deficiency of development in one at least of their senses, must make the best clergymen's wives," she thought, as she walked to church after an improving hour in the school. "I feel sick now, and I shall most likely have a headache when I have knelt for five minutes; bad air always serves me so; and to make things better, Stanley will think me a sinner for indulging in such weaknesses. He is so *good!*"

Yes, he was very good, and very dear to her. She kept on telling herself these things at intervals during the service. She employed the interims in turning the various beautiful phrases in which she would make him absolute lord of all she possessed, and implore him to leave these "duties," the fulfilment of which separated him so entirely from her; for again she told herself, "I cannot breathe in such a perfect air."

———o———

CHAPTER VI.

ON THE CURB.

Miss Vane had said to Stanley Villars, when he refused to go out for a ride with her on account of a certain duty intervening, that she "supposed it was all proper; he had undertaken to do such things." Now, after this one attempt in the Sunday school, she told herself that she had not undertaken to do such things when she promised to be his wife, and that therefore her doing them at all was quite stretching a point in the endeavour to do right. It had not been in the compact, and still she had done it once and would do it again, not because she thought that it was her duty, but because it would please Stanley.

She was very ardently desirous of pleasing Stanley—very sweetly anxious to render her course of conduct as perfect a thing in his eyes as she might render it at no trifling exercise of self restraint. But all the giving way, all the self-abnegation, must not be on her side. They both had their prejudices. That they had them was very patent, though the days of their engagement were yet young; and if she uprooted hers immediately and utterly, and asked nothing in return, his would flourish more strongly than before.

Mr. Villars came up to the rectory in the evening to dinner; and Bella did her best to listen with understanding and interest to the long, arduous conversation he held with her uncle relative to the approaching confirmation, and the fitness of the various candidates for it. Had she suffered herself to form a decided opinion that was antagonistic to one of Stanley's at this period, she (poor sinner) would have felt shocked to hear one human being deciding on the exact measure of grace that God had vouchsafed to another. But Stanley was always right—in these spiritual matters at least—and Stanley seemed to do it.

"I have a great mind," he said, "not to suffer Mary Jones to go up this time. She is far from having a proper appreciation of the awful solemnity of the responsibility she is about to take upon herself."

Mr. Vane, by way of answer to this, nodded, shook his head, and looked wise.

"Do you say that, or anything like that, to Mary Jones herself, Stanley?" Bella asked.

"I endeavour to make her comprehend that same thing in still plainer language," he replied.

"Then I wonder at her wanting to go up at all," Bella rejoined quickly.

"Why?—tell me why?" he said quietly; and Bella knew from his tone that she would get the worst of it, and be made to endure the miserable sinner's sensations freshly.

"Why! because, according to your teaching, her sins are her godfather's and godmother's affairs now. If you go and frighten her about the 'awful responsibility' she is incurring by taking them upon herself, I wouldn't be magnanimous were I Mary Jones, but I would just let them remain my godfather's and godmother's affairs still."

"It's a subject that has puzzled graver heads than yours, Bella," Mr. Vane remarked sententiously.

"Bella is so volatile," Mrs. Vane put in with a blithe tone, and a blithe smile. She hoped to avert the reproof that she read in Mr. Villars' face from the head of Mr. Villars' betrothed.

"I cannot suppose Bella so much puzzled by it as desirous of turning the subject into ridicule," Stanley said in a low voice that only reached Bella's ears. Then she felt very sorry for having wounded him, and horribly conscious that it was not in her to avoid wounding him very often, since he was—as he was, and since she was only Bella Vane.

The time in the drawing-room alone with her aunt, before he came in, deepened her penitence, It is depressing to sit for an hour on a Sunday evening in a room in which "good" books alone do dwell, with an old lady who is very sleepy. Bella was one whose heart always grew fonder during an absence that was not too prolonged. She softened to the follies of others, and hardened to her own, when she was left to herself. So now she had come to the conclusion that she had been wrong and flippant, and Stanley long-suffering and tenderly discreet, by the time of Stanley's advent.

She made room for him to come and take his place by her on the little couch she occupied, and as he seated himself he looked so like the Stanley Villars of last year's London drawing-rooms, that she forgot Mary Jones and the confirmation, and relapsed abruptly into her own bright, unclouded self.

"Stanley, I want your advice about a pair of ponies I'm going to buy."

"Indeed! well, Bella, I shall be very happy to give it."

"I have promised to be in town three weeks with mamma in August, you know." It was the first mention Stanley Villars had heard of this plan, and Bella blushed rather consciously as she said it.

"I thought you had done with London for this season, Bella."

"No, not quite; and why should I?"

"Why you should is not the point in question. I understood from you, when you came down here first, that you had done with it."

"Something has occurred to alter my plans—not so much mine as mamma's, Stanley. You wouldn't have me object to go back to my own mother?"

"Certainly not; but why must your own mother drag you back at the fag-end of the season?"

"It suits her to do so, I suppose," Miss Vane returned promptly.

"And it suits you to go, Bella," he said gravely. The thought was a grave one to him, that his future bride should contemplate a return to the pomps and vanities with pleasure.

"And does that seem a reprehensible thing on my part?—really, Stanley!"

Miss Vane said "Really, Stanley," in the partly aggrieved, partly indignant tone women invariably adopt when they feel a little guilty, and more than a little injured.

"Not a reprehensible thing; still it is a thing that I could wish was not going to be."

"You're not afraid to trust me, Stanley?" she asked tenderly.

"Honestly, no!" he replied. "No, no, Bella; were I afraid to trust you, as you call it, I would release you at once."

"What are you afraid of then?"

"Of nothing. I simply do not think it wise on the part of your mother to immerse you again in that vortex; your lines are to be cast in such widely different places, dear."

"You don't grudge me three weeks' pleasure, do you?" she said, with a warm flush mantling her face as she spoke.

"God knows I do not; but if this will be such a pleasure to you, what will the rest of your life be?"

"Dull enough," she cried impatiently, "if

these last few days are to be taken as a sample of it."

She paused for a few moments, and when she resumed it was in a much softer key.

"Stanley! I didn't mean that—I didn't indeed! Only why will you try to make me think you saturnine and grimly good? I will try to come right by degrees."

"Dull enough!—those were bitter words, Bella, if you did mean them—if they were the expression of your genuine sentiments, Heaven help me! for I shall need its help."

She saw that he was deeply hurt; and that he loved her, truly loved her, she read it clearly then; and an uneasy feeling took possession of her on the spot. Supposing that frequent bursts of that grim goodness from which she revolted eventually alienated her love! what of him then?—would she not have a terrible thing to answer for?

"I did *not* mean it—how could I have meant it, Stanley? But I have to defend myself against so many small charges, it seems, now; you find a little wrong in so many things that I do and want to do."

"Can you only bear praise?"

"I would never hear anything else from you, Stanley," she said, recovering her spirits with a little effort; "in fact, to tell the truth, the idea of being blamed until I was married never entered into my head. But you haven't advised me as to my ponies. I could get a charming pair—greys—dark greys, matched to a hair, fourteen hands high, for two hundred pounds, but they have only been driven in the country, and if I took them into the parks I might distinguish myself unpleasantly."

"You are determined on a pair. Have you heard of any others?"

"Yes, a pair of chestnuts, regular park ponies, with splendid action, that I could have for four hundred pounds. Cheap, isn't it, for they're perfection?"

"I should take the greys, I think, were I you. Country work is what you want to get out of them, therefore they will answer your purpose quite as well as the chestuuts that you would pay two hundred pounds more for."

"Oh, as for price, I shouldn't consider that; only I like the greys, so I am undecided; but I shall want them for town work too, Stanley."

He looked down at her, at the great beauty who had had her own way all her life, and smiled.

"I should be very sorry to see you driving a pair of high stepping ponies through the park after this year, Bella."

"We shall go to town every year, shall we not?" she cried, eagerly.

"Probably we shall."

"Then why shouldn't I drive?"

"Bella, ask yourself. Would it be consistent; remember I am a minister of God; would it be consistent?—more than that, would it be right for my wife to make herself conspicuous in such a way?"

"Stanley—I can't help saying it—I think it's accusing God of possessing very petty feeling to fancy He can care what His ministers' wives drive. There, I dare say you are shocked; so am I at your narrow-mindedness."

She did not say this crossly at all. She said it brightly, but earnestly withal; as though she thoroughly meant it in fact; and Stanley Villars was shocked.

The evening—the end of it at least—was as miserable as that morning in the stuffy schoolroom had been. She was glad of his presence, for she loved him dearly whenever he came down and was of the earth earthy. But still she had a sense of restraint in that presence; a feeling of being in the wrong place, that is very antagonistic to love.

If he would only have been interested in her proposed ponies; if he would only have seemed to think it in the order of things that she could drive and still be deserving. But he could not; he did not; and she felt that he never would. Had he been sympathetic she would have given up so much that was pleasant to her now right gladly. But she could not give up anything when the sacrifice was evidently expected of her. "With what," she asked herself, "would her driving through the park be inconsistent? Why should she not go there to see and be seen?" Oh! her engagement began to weight her horribly, spite of her love for the man to whom she was engaged. For she saw him quick to carp at such little faults, prompt to see such tiny specks on her brightness, and she wearied over the prospect of having to urge something in extenuation of something else so long as they both should live.

While he thought that she would require much correction both at God's hand and his own before she would be that perfect help mate to him which he prayed she might be eventually.

She spoke no more of her ponies that night. She only sat and listened quietly while he recommended a new style of dress for her adoption when she went to the Sunday school.

"Well, Stanley," she said once, "if my bonnet causes a weak brother to stumble, I'll go in my hat next Sunday, shall I?"

"If I believed you serious I would argue with you, and point out your bad taste," he replied.

"It would be bad taste, wouldn't it? It must matter so much above whether you say your prayers in a bonnet or a hat. Don't be frightened though, Stanley; it wouldn't only be fast, but it would be bad style to go to church in a hat."

"That is the lowest view of it."

"Indeed, I think you are mistaken, now; there is nothing low in avoiding doing a bad style of thing. Well, Stanley, there's only one weakness I will stipulate to be suffered to carry through; let me take a Rimmel's vaporiser the next time I rush into parochial tuition."

"If you enter into it in that spirit you had better abstain from it altogether, Bella."

"Then you would think me a pagan."

"God forbid that I should ever think the woman I contemplated marrying a pagan!"

"You wouldn't contemplate marrying me after you once thought it, I'm thinking," she said recklessly, for she was weary of essaying to climb to praiseworthiness, and of eternally slipping back again into what he regarded as perdition. She was sadly, sadly weary of it already, and she could not help remembering that it would last so long.

"You wouldn't think of marrying me if the possibility of my being a pagan in reality occurred to you?" she repeated; and on his not answering she went on, "would you? would you?"

"I would not. But why do you utter such idle folly, my own darling? You cannot be conscious of the grief such light speeches cause me, though I know that they are not serious."

"Then if you know they are not serious, why do you let them cause you grief? Don't be so abominably severe, Stanley. It's my habit, and the habit of my set, to say many things that won't stand being picked to pieces. I have not the slightest doubt but that my flow of spirits will decrease as much as even you can desire, in a year or two."

"Bella, I hardly understand your humour; you may be merely trying me, or you may be uncertain of yourself; which it is I do not know; but, remember, for every idle word you will have to give account."

"As you're so fond of scriptural quotations in and out of season, perhaps you'll preface your next reproof with a peculiarly apt one. Would you like to know which I mean?"

She leant forward, laughing now, but still a little flushed and angry; and he shook his head, and looked reproachfully at her.

"'I speak as a fool!'—those are the words I would recommend to every self-ordained reprover;" and when she said that, Stanley Villars felt a keen pang of conviction of the error he had made in asking this woman to be his wife.

"I must see you to-morrow, and speak seriously to you for both our sakes," he said, almost sternly. Then Bella shrugged her shoulders, and replied she "hoped not more seriously than he had been speaking to-night."

He went away shortly after this, leaving her bitterly penitent for having been stung into the utterance of sharp things, but still feeling, despite the bitter penitence, that all the fault was not on her side. She declared him to be harsh and unbending, and obstinate in a cool, sensible way, that was infinitely aggravating. It did not mend matters at all that in the commencement of the dispute she had been wrong and he had been right. He had gradually shown himself to be harsh, obstinate, and masterful; and though Bella was sorry for what she had said, she could not forget that he had deserved it.

The girl went to her bed thoroughly miserable that night for the first time in her life. She had never been thwarted in the whole course of her career, and here now this man arrogated to himself the right to condemn her pursuance of habits that were harmless in themselves, and that had become essential to her through long indulgence in them. Hitherto her most flagrant derelictions from good sense had been regarded as flashes of something like genius by admiring friends. Now, when her path was one of wisdom in comparison, she was corrected and checked, and made to feel the bit at every turn.

"I shall feel constrained and uncomfortable, and sure that I shall not be free to do as I please in the tiniest matter all my life, if he goes on like this," she said to herself, with hot tears in her eyes, and a tight cord round her throat. "I've made a mistake—and yet I love him so!" Thus she wailed herself off to sleep long before Stanley Villars thought of retiring to rest that night. He stayed up considering what he ought to do in this difficult case of Bella's, and resolving to be very "gentle and firm with her, and very patient, and very particular." All these things it behoved him to be with her, and all these things he resolved to be. He did not misjudge her as she fancied he did. He neither thought her very wicked nor very foolish. He only thought her undisciplined; and he resolved (feeling fully capable of it) to discipline her. In truth, he would have guided her well—for he dearly loved her—had she but given herself up entirely to his management; but his hand was so heavy, and she had been accustomed to "have her head."

——o——

CHAPTER VII.

ADRIFT IN THE WORLD.

THERE are many more agreeable things in life than a row and a reconciliation between a pair of people who, with the proverbially keen vision of jealous love, are quicker to see one another's faults and follies than is the rest of the world. The word "row" may scarcely be used to describe the—well, I will call it "the little explanatory scene"—that took place between the betrothed lovers on the Monday morning. But "the little explanatory scene" was as painful to them both as any row could have been, and the reconciliation that followed was one of those fraught-with-feeling affairs that render one lachrymose.

They had each been impatient—they had each been exacting—they had each, in fact, been wrong. They told each other this over and over again. Bella made her recantation of error hearty and complete, but Stanley made a reservation: he "had been impatient and exacting, yes; but wrong, no; his dear Bella must admit, no!"

His dear Bella admitted "No;" his dear Bella, indeed, was in that frame of mind when all kinds of admissions can be torn from the breast. She had been very anxious and unhappy—of that she was sure; and she wanted to have her anxiety removed, and to be forgiven, and petted, and made happy again. She was not at all particular as to terms; she was ready to admit anything, provided moral peace and sunshine were hers immediately on the admission.

So there was reconciliation full and complete between these young people who had been guilty of the grand mistake of binding themselves to each other; and then Mr. Villars remarked that "while they were on the subject, perhaps he had better mention to Bella some things of which he could not approve;" and Bella put her hands up over her ears, and pleaded "not to be told them yet, till she felt stronger." She wished the disagreeable subject to be put away into the background altogether; while it could be avoided it should be avoided, she was determined.

"We have had dreary talk enough for one day, Stanley. No one ever made my eyes so red before; and to think that *you* should have done it, when I haven't been engaged to you a month, sir! I won't hear a word more to make me sorry to-day at any rate. Tell me, when is your friend coming?"

"Claude? Coming to-day, I believe."

"He will be too tired to come up here with you this evening," Bella said, suggestively.

"He's not a girl, to be knocked up by a short railway journey; still we shall not come up to-night: you will have a respite from my society to-night, Bella."

"That's very considerate of you, upon my word!" she said, sarcastically. "When you get an amusing man' down to this place you keep him to yourself, and pretend to make a merit of it."

He got up and walked to the window, and she took up a local paper and abused it for the badness of its type and the poverty of its intelligence. Presently he said, without turning round—

"You didn't see Claude in London, did you?"

"Never saw him, and never want to see him; don't trouble yourself to bring him here."

"What a thoroughly feminine speech, Bella!"

"Well, you know that I hate being here of an evening without you, Stanley," Bella replied, somewhat irrelevantly; and when she said that he came away from the window, and relapsed from stoicism for a period.

"What I was going to say to you just now," he resumed, "was that at one time Claude was supposed to be rather sweet on Florry. I never thought it myself."

"Brothers very often are blind in such cases. I have heard that, Stanley; and also that Florence was rather sweet on Claude Walsingham. That is why I am so anxious to see him," she continued animatedly. "And when he's down here, Stanley, if he seems likely to stay, *do* let me ask your sister to come to me?"

"Oh, no!" he replied, shaking his head, "oh, no! I'll have nothing of that kind."

"You won't have me ask your sister to stay with me?" she interrupted, and her head went up quickly—she was feeling the bit again.

"Not for the purpose of throwing her in any man's way; not even in Claude's, whom I love as a brother."

"You might give a helping hand towards turning him into a brother, then, I think."

"No, Bella; you will see what Florry is by-and-by, and then you will understand that she is not to be hawked about."

"And who on earth would accuse me of being guilty of such a low idea, save you yourself, Stanley?" she asked, indignantly. She felt aggrieved in every way. She had fancied that in his refusal to bring this bosom friend of his to see her at once, there had been a tinge, the faintest tinge, of jealousy; and this she had desired to assuage by professing a warm interest in, and a desire to further, the attachment which might possibly exist between Claude and Florry. This being the case, it was hard to be found guilty on that count too. To be had up and reprehended for a venial error against good taste, that had been expressly designed to cover a suppositious error against good feeling! It would be a difficult matter to please Stanley when the time came for her "to be with him always." Bella acknowledged to herself with a sigh that it would be difficult—nay, more than that, impossible.

The explanatory scene and the complete reconciliation drifted off into mere weariness and dissatisfaction again after this trifling misunderstanding respecting Florry and Claude. Bella affected to be afraid to venture upon any topic for fear of alarming Stanley's sensitive delicacy, and Stanley was very unaffectedly annoyed with her for professing this fear. They were neither of them—these people who had been engaged for life for the space of one month—very sorry when the hour of parting came, for they felt chary of saying anything more to each other.

Bella was terribly discomposed for the remainder of that day. "Out of sorts," her aunt called it, and her aunt pitied her accordingly—"knowing well what it was," she said; but, ah! she never could have known the tenth part of "it," with her equable temperament and the Rev. Mr. Vane.

"I shall have Vengeance, and go out for a long ride, and give Rock a run," Bella said, when the dinner, not any of which she could eat, was nearly over.

"Mr. Villars does not like you to ride out with only a groom at night, Bella," her aunt protested.

"Then Mr. Villars might accompany me himself, aunt."

"I hardly think it right myself," Mrs. Vane went on, more humbly, for her niece's tone startled her.

"Oh, nonsense!" that young lady replied, with decision; "I shall have Rock—dear, honest, faithful Rock with me; and though he may not be quite so prudent as—as some people are, he's plucky, and that is more to the purpose."

It was about half-past six in the evening when Miss Vane started for her ride. The brown mare Vengeance had been idle for several days, and she consequently was full of corn and courage. She came up champing her bit, and curving her head round, and striking the ground with a quick, impatient foot, in a way that was very pleasant in her mistress's eyes. Bella liked to see her mare full of play, and scarcely able to restrain herself before she was mounted. She always went off in an inspiriting burst when that was the case, as soon as her rider was seated, that left dull care behind.

Dull care commenced retreating as soon as Miss Vane saw her horse this evening. "She'll take all my time to-night," she thought, with some of the triumphant sensations a belief in one's ability to cope with the animal is sure to engender. Rock, too, came up with the evident intention of making things as pleasant as possible by accompanying his mistress. In fact, there was no disappointment—no falling short of her hopes of them, in either her horse or dog.

"If I were you I should ride along the high-road to Burton and back," Mr. Vane suggested, when his niece was settled in her saddle, and had gathered up her reins. The suggestion awakened the spirit of contradiction which Stanley Villars had roused in her in the morning, and she replied—

"The high-road is so uninteresting. I shall try some of the by-lanes."

So she went off, Vengeance with her head well up, and with that springing quick action that speaks of restrained impatience.

Bella eschewed the road that led through the village; that road would have taken her past Stanley Villars' house, and she did not wish to exhibit herself to him and to that friend of his about whom she had been unable to say right things. She rode away in a contrary direction, and took the first by-lane that she came to, "because it looked like a good riding road," she said to herself, but in reality because she hoped she might miss her way and become involved in a labyrinth of by-lanes, and so be compelled to take Vengeance home across country.

The idea of doing this was very gratifying to her to-night. She half-fancied that Stanley would not quite approve of her doing it in this neighbourhood where his quiet clerical reputation was so well assured. He might, perhaps, think it a fast and uncalled-for proceeding on her part, that she should ride in any other than an orderly and sedate manner when only her groom was in attendance. Then, if he expressed this opinion, she could tell him that she had been driven on to this obnoxious course through having nothing to do, and nothing to look forward to for the evening, when he, of course, would be penitent both for his neglect and for the censure he had passed, and all would be well between them again.

The lane she had taken was one of those "flowery conceits" that Nature does occasionally indulge in, even in prosaic England. It rambled in zig-zags about the country, it lost itself amongst fields, it embowered itself between lofty overarching hedges, it merged imperceptibly into other lanes, it completely achieved Miss Vane's object, in fact, for, after riding for an hour, she found herself she knew not where, and on looking back, the entrances to many lanes gaped around her on every side.

She had attained her object; she had lost her way, and her groom's powers of observation proved to be of no exceptional order. He could only reiterate her assertion as to the way being lost, and regret that it should be so. He could bring no original ideas to bear upon this subject.

The other part of her scheme proved impracticable. The part of the country in which she found herself was not to be "crossed" with impunity or advantage, or at all even. The hedges rose high on all sides, for agriculture was not in the ascendant, and Vengeance and Vengeance's mistress, though they would have flown anything lightly and gaily as birds, were not equal to scrambling through apparently impenetrable masses of time-honoured thorns.

"The only thing to be done, Hill," she said, after a few minutes' conversation with her man, whom she had signalled to ride up to her side, "the only thing to be done is to turn round—we must be going away from Denham now—and ride straight away in the opposite direction; we must trust to the mare's instinct whenever we are not sure (which I shall never be), and to Rock's."

Now, both the mare's instinct and Rock's were very good things in their respective ways, but they were scarcely equal to this emergency. The mare was skittish and evinced a desire to take every turning to which they came, and on the face of it, it was utterly impossible that every turning could be right. Rock was not skittish, but he was worse, solemnly depressed, in fact, as if he felt sorry for his share in this transaction, and was disposed to regard himself and his mistress as wandering sinners who had strayed from the path of right, and who were not, under the existing aspect of affairs, at all likely to get back again.

Miss Vane had been excited—pleasurably excited, nothing more—when she first made the discovery that she was adrift in the world. But presently she began to feel less pleasurably excited, and by degrees, as she rode on and on, and found no landmarks that were familiar to her, and observed the signs of the dissolution of the day that were around and above her, she grew unconditionally uncomfortable.

After a time she came to an open space, a wild sort of common, which she had never seen in any of her rides before. It was covered with heath and gorse, and, arguing from analogy, she decided that it must be a certain Welling Heath of which she had heard frequent mention made, and which, to the best of her knowledge, was situated in a north-easterly direction from Denham.

Once more she summoned her groom up for the purpose of—not so much "consulting" him, as I was about to write, as of declaring her conviction aloud that she "knew perfectly well where she was." "If this is Welling Heath we are all right, not more than ten miles from Denham Hill, and it is Welling Heath I know."

Hill, still suffering from a paucity of original ideas on the subject, touched his hat and fell back again, and Rock relapsed into his normal spirits, and dashed wildly over the common after a rabbit.

There were two roads on the opposite side of the heath to that on which Bella had come upon it, and she, without much deliberation, took one of them and went along it at a sharp gallop, for, lovely July evening as it was, it was palpably getting late.

It was a very solitary road; still it was the turnpike road, and the hedges on either side of it were trimmed down in a way that permitted her a free view over the country on either side, and the hope was father to the thought that it "looked very much like the land about Denham." She made this asseveration to herself several times as she galloped on, and the belief in her own statement grew weak in exact proportion to the increasing determination of her tones.

A finger-post at last! She pulled up close to it as suddenly as she had come upon it—pulled up so abruptly that Vengeance nearly settled back on her haunches. The girl was getting anxious to be home, for the road was very lonely, and the day was dying in the sky.

By its last grey light she read eagerly the names that were written up on the moss-grown old finger-post. They were names of places of which she had never heard; they were names of places of which Hill had never heard; and they were all eight or ten miles off it seemed to her, as well as she could decipher the figures. It was useless, she deemed, to turn down any of the roads that led off from the one she had taken in faith when on the common. It was useless to pause in deliberation. It was useless to do anything save gallop straight ahead as hard as Vengeance could lay her legs to the ground.

It was a lonely road. I have said that about Denham agriculture was not in the ascendant, which fact was patent to the most ignorant in such matters who caught sight of the high, luxuriant hedges. But here they were cut down and kept in order, and were in all respects utterly devoid of the characteristics of the hedges around Denham.

"Surely a strange part of the country!" This thought would obtrude itself upon her mind, but she put it behind her to the best of her ability and galloped on, straight on, with her heart beating rather more quickly than even that pace warranted, and with a profound conviction that she would have done better had she followed her uncle's advice and ridden along the well-known road to Burton.

No houses yet; no semblance of a village or inn, or of the merest wayside hovel even. For all she knew, houses full of people, who could have guided her back to Denham with a word, might be lurking a field or two off from this road that was innocent of human habitation. But it would have been neither possible nor pleasant to explore unknown corn and pasture lands, and the increasing darkness prevented her seeing the smoke that might be rising up from the chimneys of the probable houses.

It was a lonely road; she thought that she had never seen so lonely a one as she pulled up and walked the mare for awhile, for fear of overheating her. The hedges ran along still unbroken save by the gates that opened into quiet fields full of ripe corn, and the moon arose, and the stars came out, and there was a deep peace over all things.

No danger could come to her, she felt sure of that, let the road be lonely as it would. With her trusty groom behind her, and resolute Rock by her side, she had no fear of midnight marauders even should she be so luckless as to be roving about till midnight. But unpleasantness might and surely would arise from this unintentional escapade of hers.

Those who have ever ridden along a road in pleasing uncertainty as to where that road may lead them, and who are accountable to anxious friends for their outgoings and incomings, and those alone, can realise the sensations which crowded through Miss Vane's mind as the night and the road went on, and she was no nearer Denham. Looked at broadly, no harm would be done even were she compelled to ride about all night; her horse and herself would both be a little fatigued probably, but fatigue is a thing to be got over. But she could not look at it broadly for more than two consecutive minutes. She could not help remembering that there were some things which could not be got over so speedily as the fatigue; and amongst these things would be the conventional wonder and reprobation she would cause, and Stanley Villars' annoyance at the same. She thought the subject over from every possible point of view as she went along at a "a ready-for-anything" trot; and when she had exhausted it she pulled up again, and still the road was lonely.

——o——

CHAPTER VIII.

FOR THE FIRST TIME.

It was not a hopeful state of affairs. The mare was flagging in a way that told Bella, to the full as much as her own fatigue, that she had been on the road for many hours. Vengeance was like a good many ladies' horses—her powers of endurance were to be exhausted. With her horse nearly spent, and her mind heavy with thoughts of "what would be said about it," Bella Vane was in rather a pitiable plight.

The entrance to a village; better still, to a town! She came upon it abruptly in the night; came out suddenly from a lonely country road upon masses of architecture looming high above her; came out at the foot of a hill, which the flagging mare had no sooner climbed, than Bella found herself between rows of houses, even in a paved street.

A quiet street, with but few signs of life in it. Darkness dwelt in its lower windows almost without an exception; but a few of the upper chambers were still illuminated in a sober respectable way that was pleasant to behold—it proved to her that all the world was not gone to bed.

Her groom was riding nearly abreast of her at this time, and now she told him to keep a sharp look-out for a respectable inn with signs of life in it. Miss Vane had no idea as to what this place might be to which she had drifted; she only saw that it was a quiet town, and a feeling came over her that it was old and extensive.

A wild hope, too, shot through her heart, that she might have been riding in circles, and that so, though she had been over much ground, she might still not be so far from Denham, but that the sheltering wall of its rectory might be gained by her that night. The thought of the uproar and dismay that was most surely reigning in that usually quiet old house smote upon her heart painfully, and when she thought about what Stanley must be feeling and thinking of her, she could hardly keep the saddle.

They came directly upon a busier part of the town, a part that was broader awake than the street through which she had passed. A few fitful and uncertain strains from a brass band, with a want of unity of purpose in it, struck upon her ears. Then she saw a well-lighted house, with a red lion swinging on a post before it, and she turned into the yard of this house with a feeling of relief.

"Go in, or ask an ostler the name of this place, and how far it is from Denham, and hear if I can hire any one to guide me back there at once," she said to Hill, as she pulled up in a quaint old yard, round three sides and a half of the fourth of which buildings ran, and in which a stagnant pool in the centre reposed beneath a weeping willow.

In answer to her inquiries, an ostler came forward, and told her that the town was the cathedral town of the county; that Denham was seven-and-twenty miles distant; and that the hour was half-past eleven. Thus she learnt that she had been riding five hours, and that it was out of the question to expect Vengeance to carry her home to-night. Additionally she heard that her arrival there was inopportune, as the house was full of rifle officers, there having been a volunteer review at an adjacent park that day.

The mistress of the house, hearing a rumour of a lady in distress in the yard, came out at this juncture, and Bella dismounted, and went in to rest for a quarter of an hour, and to hear whether she could have a carriage and be taken home.

The broad entrance, that was more than a passage and less than a hall, became alive with men in grey tunics turned up with red, as she passed through; for the gallant officers of the Blankshire Rifles had heard the rumour of her advent in distress, as well as the landlady, and forthwith the majority of them made missions across from one to another of the many rooms, in order to see her. There had been a great dinner at the "Red Lion" that night, and the strains of their own band, together with the military ardour which is apt to fire the breasts of worthy country gentlemen on such occasions, had been too much for many of them.

So Bella—beautiful Miss Vane—was compelled to run the gauntlet of what appeared to her most impertinent, presumptuous, admiring observation. She felt indignant with these men, so full of wine and insolence, who came out and gazed at her daringly, as no men had ever gazed at her before. In her well-cut habit, and the hat with the big tulle bow behind, she was an unexpected apparition at that hour of the night unquestionably. With her anger heightening her beauty, she passed through them to a quiet room, leaving them not dumb with amazement at her charms, but chattering loudly in their praise.

Fate was against her. The "Red Lion" kept neither chariots nor horses, and the two rival hotels, who were the proud possessors of post-horses, demurred about obliging a guest of the "Red Lion's." That is to say, though they made the excuse of their horses having been out all day with "parties" at the review, it "was jealousy of our having the dinner that was at the bottom of the refusal," the hostess of the "Red Lion" told Miss Vane.

"What am I to do? What am I to do?" she said, appealingly, in her despair. "My mare has been going stiff for the last hour. I shall spoil her if I take her out again, poor thing; and I *will* get home to-night."

The landlady having nothing to say herself, replied, that she would go "and hear what could be done."

Bella sat disconsolately in the dull inn parlour into which she had been brought, and gazed round at all things with a feeling of distaste and loathing. The parlours of old country inns, even though they be dubbed "hotels" to suit the modern ear, are not wont to be pleasant places. There was a certain hardness and angularity about the table, and chairs, and the couch, that was anti-pathetic to her; and there were thick glasses on stems, without any sparkle about them, on the sideboard, that were odious to behold.

She was not left to herself long. The landlady came back presently with a proposition. She had been mentioning the "young lady's little difficulty to some of the gentlemen," she said (Bella winced at the whole county hearing of it), "and one of them, a gentleman who didn't belong to our corps, but who had come from the review with a friend of his, and who had his own horses, said *he* would drive her home if she was bent upon going, and would permit him the honour."

Bella was not given to calm dispassionate thought. Still it did seem to her that there was something out of the way, and something more than slightly unconventional, in this proposed plan. It was bad enough for her to be at large in the world in the night in this way. To be at large in the night with a strange man, on whom, to say the least of it, she could not have made the impression of being rigid, would be worse still.

But she wanted to be at home. "Almost anything," she told herself, "would be better than staying here in this horrid, horrid place, that was full of men, free to roam about and look at her, with eyes that were bloodshot from much wine, when she moved from her present seclusion. It was a painful position in which to be placed, and her having placed herself in it unaided, did not make it one whit the less painful. The landlady took a motherly, patronising tone towards her, too. Altogether, she could not bear it, it was too much for her. There would be nothing 'wrong' in being driven home by this strange gentleman; and even if there were, the commission of a little further wrong in order to make things right the sooner, would surely be justifiable."

"Ask the gentleman to come here and speak to me; and you may come with him, please," she added, hastily.

He came at once, the landlady hovering behind him, her voluminous robes and portly person making a background of propriety for his figure. There was an element of romance in the affair directly he appeared; Bella could not resist recognising that there was, despite her dissatisfaction with what had gone before, and her dread of what was to follow.

"You have been kind enough to say that you will take me home, away from this place at once," she exclaimed, rising and bowing to the tall, fair young man who entered. Then he bent low before her, and declared that he regarded himself as being singularly fortunate in being there, and in being able to assist her. "You may have heard my old friend, Stanley Villars, mention my name, Miss Vane," he went on; "I am Claude Walsingham."

"Oh, dear! then I dare not go home with you," the girl cried out, candidly; but she quickly made him feel that there was nothing derogatory to him in that fear she had expressed, for she went forward to him with extended hand, and with a smile, bright as one of those sun-gleams that flash upon us in the boyhood of the year, on her face.

"What did you think, Major Walsingham, when you heard of me arriving here at this hour?"

"I thought that it was extremely unfortunate that you, and extremely fortunate that I should be here; despite that declaration of fear as to going home with me, I think so still."

He was just what she had expected him to

be—tall, and manly, and chivalrously deferential. Bella was not one bit disappointed in Claude Walsingham.

Nor he in her. She was precisely the great beauty—the thoughtless, careless girl—utterly unsuited to his friend Stanley, whom he had anticipated meeting. He was not at all disappointed in her, and he could not help remarking, as she took off her hat, and lent her head against the back of the couch, how far fresher and more brilliant and blooming she was than the woman who had looked down into the water with him the other night at Richmond.

"I hardly know what to do, Major Walsingham; you see, if I stay here there will be talk and anxiety, and if I go home with you there will be the same; I think *you* shall decide," she continued: "they will be annoyed at Denham at whatever I may elect to do, but your decision will be more respected."

She was in the habit of throwing the onus on to another's shoulders whenever she could. She did it now without scruple.

Claude Walsingham saw in an instant why she had hesitated about accompanying him when first she had heard his name. He read in that hesitation a little fear of Stanley Villars. "Can he have developed jealousy, or is she acting?" he asked himself. Then he looked at the bright beauty again, and was fain to confess that she acted very prettily.

"It seems to me that of two evils you will be well justified in choosing the lesser," he said; "I would not be the cause of your giving a moment's annoyance at Denham."

"We must come to some conclusion quickly which is the lesser evil," she said.

He paused thoughtfully for a moment, and during that pause he reflected that his first proposition was an impracticable one. Miss Vane was right; she must not be driven home by him that night.

"I will tell you what I will do," he exclaimed, "you must remain here, Miss Vane, and I will go over to Denham and tell them where you are, and assuage their anxiety. It will not be pleasant for you to remain here, but there is nothing else for it."

She looked up to him and blushed.

"Let my groom go, or send some one else. Don't you leave me here, Major Walsingham."

"But, Miss Vane——"

"But, Major Walsingham, I know as well as possible what you are going to say—that I ought to go to bed and sleep the sleep of the just while you scour the country in search of my agonised friends. Well, I shouldn't do it. I should sit here all night, and be worn out with sorrow and remorse—don't laugh; I should. If you will *send* to Denham, and let me have the knowledge that I have a friend in the house, I will go off quietly to one of their dormitories; but not else."

What could he do? She had held out her hand to him when she had asked him to let her have the knowledge that she had a friend in the house. He could but take the hand and promise to stay, and feel her to be a flirt.

"I will send off your man at once on one of my own horses," he said to her; "he will be able to tell them how it came about better than a stranger, and I will stay here myself, as you desire it, Miss Vane."

So he went off and despatched the groom, and lingered about in the stables, looking at her horses and his own, for a few minutes, half hoping that Miss Vane would retire without waiting to bit him a last good-night.

He told himself while lingering there that this Bella Vane was a strange kind of girl to be the bride elect of Stanley Villars; but at the same time he felt that she was a very sweet kind of girl—sweet, and remarkably pretty, and with animation enough about her to keep any man alive.

She sat meanwhile awaiting his return rather impatiently. There was no occasion for her to remain there till he came back, she knew that very well; but she argued that it would be more polite to do it, and Bella could not be guilty of an impoliteness. So it came to pass that his lingering was of no avail. When he came back, hoping to find the room vacant, Miss Vane sat there in unclouded brightness, without a trace of fatigue in face or manner, ready to receive him.

"What an extraordinary thing it is that we should have met here! Why are you not at Denham to-night, Major Walsingham—Stanley fully expected you?"

"The colonel of our regiment came down to review these volunteer fellows at Rollerscourt Park to-day; he induced me to see him through it and the dinner that was to follow. I had my trap and horses sent on here, and I meant to drive over to Denham to-morrow morning."

"How very odd that I should have come here of all places in the world," she said meditatively; "it looks like fate, does it not?"

She coloured as she asked it, and he grew red on the brow as he laughed and replied—

"It does. Fate has been kind to me for the first time."

"I ought not to sit up here talking, ought I?" she asked abruptly.

"You ought not, indeed," he replied.

"The thought of going away to one of their wretched rooms makes one shiver," and she shivered accordingly, imparting a rippling motion to her lithe form that was pleasing to look upon, and that was as far as anything well could be from representing either nervousness or cold.

"Nevertheless, you had better go. Really, Miss Vane, you will be quite knocked up to-morrow. As your self-constituted guardian, for this night only, I will order you off at once."

"For this night only," she repeated after him, in low soft tones. "Well, it's nice to be pleasantly controlled even for a few hours. Good night, Major Walsingham."

"Good night," he said; and then he touched her hand for the second time that night, and touched it more coldly than he had done at first. Her tones were very soft and low and sweet, and her face was very lovely; but—he had been in Canada when she flashed out free, and now she was engaged to his old friend, Stanley Villars.

For some reason that it may be as well not to analyse too closely, Bella said her prayers very devoutly that night. She felt humble and penitent as soon as she was away from the influence of Claude Walsingham's presence. She collected all her tenderest memories of Stanley, and in the innermost chamber of her heart felt guilty of having done something that might justly call forth his anger. What this thing—this possible wrong—might be, she could not decide. It was not that she had lost her way; she had been innocent of intending that great offence against decorum. She began to have a glimmering notion that it was because she had come to the "Red Lion" and found Claude Walsingham there.

"It will be very unjust of Stanley if he is annoyed with me about it," she said to herself, as she went from one end of her room to the other with an impatient step. "I have suffered quite enough; it will be horribly unjust, it will be a shame if Stanley says a *word* to me about it." Then she stopped in her walk, telling herself that he had no right to utter words to her that would give her pain, and that she was very foolish to dwell so much on what Stanley might think and say on every occasion. "A woman may so soon subside into a mere slave if she strives to trim her sails to every breath of wind; he would not cease for an hour from one of his soul-wearying pursuits the other day to please me."

This she said some little time after the devoutly-uttered prayers: their humbling influence had begun to wear off already.

Circe's indescribable charm began to wane in Claude's mind as he recalled the form, the manner, and the face of the girl his friend was going to marry. He told himself that Adèle and Miss Vane could never, under any circumstances, be friends, and that the impossibility of friendship existing between the women would cause a gulf between Stanley and himself. "I should be sorry for that, I should be devilish sorry for a coolness to come between us," he thought; and then he, too, busied himself (just as Bella was doing above) in recalling all his kindest, warmest memories of Stanley Villars. He said to himself that the latter was so true a man, so thorough a gentleman, so worthy in all respects of the best a woman or man could give him of love and regard. In addition, he reminded himself that Stanley was Florence Villars' favourite brother—his own old familiar friend. But the end of all his recollections that night was, that Bella Vane would be there with him in the morning, and that Bella Vane was engaged! His blood leapt through his veins as he thought of her; but "that will pass," he said; "she is just a woman to strike a man off his balance when he sees her for the first time."

——o——

CHAPTER IX.

WAITING.

Mr. Stanley Villars was not of the impatient order of mankind. He was not one to hear in the rustle of every leaf the footstep of the coming man, or to find the minutes hours after the time had passed when the expected one should have appeared. But for all that patience and perfection of judgment as to time, Mr. Villars did wonder more than a little why Claude Walsingham was so late.

It has been seen that Mr. Villars definitely refused the proposal of his affianced bride as to the disposition of his evening hours on this day, with the events of which my story is now dealing. He had told Miss Vane distinctly that he should not go up to the rectory that night; therefore he would not go up; though Claude's non-appearance by the last train that stopped at Denham—the nine o'clock one—removed the just cause for that abstinence from her presence against which Miss Vane was girding in her heart.

The just cause and impediment which had hitherto existed (in his own mind only, be it remarked) was removed, and still he would not go up to the Vanes, and assist in making the hours pleasant to the Vanes' niece. Still he sat in his own study in his bachelor quarters, and perused reviews with a lax interest, and smoked a cigar in a desultory manner, and waited, not for the "coming man," the time was past for his advent, but for the coming darkness which should oblige him to light his lamp and do something.

It came at last, and with it his page, who opened the windows wider, and drew the curtains over them, and placed the lighted lamp on his writing-table with a quick, deft hand. Then he departed, and Mr. Villars fell to work at once, covering slips of paper with strong, steady, regular characters, writing with a speed in which there was no hurry, and with an absence of hesitation in which there was no thoughtlessness: writing, in fact, as one who has ideas of his own on any subject, and words at command to express them in, would write.

Stanley Villars was in capital working order that night. He was not one to require adventitious aids to enable him to pour forth his sentiments on paper. They poured themselves out, unassisted, freely, but not too fast. Indeed, there was no occasion for them to come out with a rush and tumult, for all that Stanley Villars did was of his own free will, and at his own gentlemanlike leisure. He was an unpaid *attaché* to the staff of two or three journals of too elevated a character to make money a consideration with their contributors. His censure, and praise, and summary of the majority of occurrences, were not to be had for filthy lucre.

Bella had no idea that her lover dabbled even thus delicately in literature. He had been very merciful to her, and had spared her this truth; for he knew that were she once cognisant of this fact, she would imagine that it behoved her to read what he wrote—a proceeding which would surely be puzzling, and most probably be painful to her. He intended that it should dawn upon her by degrees, when custom would render her careless of his printed words of wisdom to the degree of not insisting upon distressing herself by perusing them.

There was no rush, no hurry, no false excitement about the circumstances under which Stanley Villars' papers (he always called them "papers," not articles) were written. Shall it be added that there was no rush, hurry, false excitement, or "go," about the papers themselves? They were sombre things—"massive, closely-reasoning" things, his friends said—things that their producer felt a respect for himself, they were so very weighty. He was not the kind of man we are accustomed to conjure up before our minds when we speak or are spoken to about a journalist. He prepared his copy in the midst of calmness and comfort, never winding up abruptly because a diminutive "devil," with eager eyes and a dirty face, was clamouring vicariously for that which was not ready. The bloom was on literature still to this gentleman, as far as he himself was actually concerned. He knew that bad hours and much brandy, and finally being broken down, made up the life-histories of too many press men, and of too many, alas! who are not mere press men. But these things had never come near him. He looked upon them from afar with a sorrow that was strongly dashed with contempt. He could not understand how it came to pass that men of a high order of intellect could degrade themselves to the degree of pouring out unconsidered, careless, faulty work. Nor could he feel gently towards them for seeking inspiration—more than that, even physical power at times—from ignoble sources, to enable them to get through with that which was to them existence, and would be vended to the world at a penny on the following morning.

He was in admirable working order: it came out, that which he had to say, without effort, as it is apt to come out when commercial occasion for it is lacking, and it feels itself to be the offspring of its parent's free will. Stanley Villars did not live in an atmosphere of gas and excitement, about things that appear to be vital only in the light of the same. He knew nothing of the strain, and so rather looked down upon the signs of it when he found them—which he did, not unfrequently.

In his prosperity—for all things are relative, and Stanley Villars had no tastes and no temptations to lead him to exceed that income which made him appear a prosperous man at Denham—and happiness, Mr. Villars was rather hard in his judgment on those who made literature their trade. It came under the head of fraudulent transactions in his mind that the literate few who represent public opinion should pander to the illiterate many, even in trifles. He was intolerant to long laments over that which was not remarkably lamentable, and to a column and a half of virtuous indignation, meant expressly for the perusal of the people, about the vices of the upper ten thousand. In short, he was not lenient to those who leant to the times, and strove to make the times support them. He was very hard on the hot phrases about nothing that men penned at night, because they were compelled to pen something. He was very hard on the careers they ran; and held that the course they pursued, when none other was open to them, was damning evidence of their incapacity for that position in journalistic literature which forced them to pursue it.

So he sat there till eleven o'clock, comfortably penning his exalted notions by the light of a paraffin lamp and a brace of wax candles.

At eleven he was disturbed—just as he was glancing over some of his phrases, and unconsciously despising those who, with brilliant abilities, would not give themselves "time" to do equally well—by a message from the rectory—"Would Mr. Villars go up at once, for Mrs. Vane was very anxious about Miss Bella?"

He went up, more enthusiastically than he would have liked any of them, or Bella herself, to suppose he would have gone, even on her account, and found dismay presiding. Mrs. Vane, in her first sentence, pleaded ardently for his opinion as to the cause of Bella's non-appearance, to be given at once, as she had found herself, she declared, unable to form a single one—a statement she immediately proceeded to strengthen by avowing her fixed and unalterable conviction that Bella had done divers irreconcilable things, all more or less unpleasant. "I begged her not to go out for a ride on a horse at that hour—I did, indeed, Mr. Villars." She went on as if the desirability of Bella going out on a horse for something quite the reverse of a ride, or going for a ride on something quite the reverse of a horse, were painfully before her; "but she would go, and now, of course, something dreadful has happened; and yet I feel sure that there is nothing serious. I quite believe she is only staying away to alarm us."

"Bella would not do that, Mrs. Vane; she may have lost her way, but she would never stay away purposely to distress us."

"More likely she has been thrown and hurt," Mrs. Vane replied, with the tears starting into her eyes; and when she made that enlivening suggestion Stanley Villars winced. The picture of Bella injured—Bella mangled—Bella suffering and away from him, that Mrs. Vane's words conjured up, was too much for him.

It was useless to stay up at the rectory, he felt that was useless as well as trying when he had been there about an hour. They did but aggravate his anxiety by starting innumerable theories of evil that might have befallen her, and he was powerless to assuage theirs. Besides, theirs was unpleasant to him, as being of what he deemed a spurious order. He could not quite realise that contradictory surmises and fuss could be co-existent with heartfelt suspense.

It was useless to remain at the rectory. It was useless to mount his horse and scour the country, as Mrs. Vane once urgently requested him to do. Bella had ridden out of Denham by a road that branched off at the distance of half-a-mile in five different directions, and no one could tell which of these she had taken. He was anxious, unhappy, and longing to serve and see her; but scouring the country was not the way to do either more efficaciously than was Mrs. Vane's plan of running to the gate at brief intervals and calling "Bella" in a loud, firm voice that was carried on the night air for at least ten yards.

He went back to his own house, after charging them to send for him on the first sign of her approach, and instead of finding the house wrapped in slumber, as he had hoped, he found the mistress of it, together with his own boy, up, eagerly awaiting tidings of Miss Vane. It irritated him to be compelled to answer well-meaning inquiries. It outraged him to hear the good woman declare that she should not go to bed till something was known. The sound of Vengeance's light hoofs was the sole sound he desired that night—the night of his first introduction to his nerves.

He went into the room where the lamp and candles still burnt brightly, and he turned the former lower, and put the latter out, and sat down miserably to wait and feel—to write freely and think forcibly no longer. He was miserably anxious about this beautiful love of his—this bright flower who had been so well guarded all her life—being out in the dim night unattended, save by her groom. All his love for her welled up in that hour, and he began to understand that the man who goes down under a cruel wrong may be a trifle higher in the scale originally than the beasts that perish.

The thought arose to torture him, that even at this moment she might be exposed to insult, injury, danger! and then the well-arranged room in which he had but just now penned exalted notions became a very hell to him, and the distant creak of his landlady's boots, as she vigilantly roamed about, caused him to regard her as a fiend incarnate. There was no distraction to be gained from anything, poor fellow, after that. He sat there maddened nearly by the stillness; maddened a little more by the smallest break; pitiably alive to the fact that his great anxiety was capable of aggravation from small causes.

That creak again! Who does not know what it is to sit in a room alone, and hear the first sound emanate from the sole that is going to tread one's own soul into an abyss of nervous woe from which there is no rising? It commences in an insinuating way, especially if it be overhead. You hear a pleading, plaintive squeak, that appeals to you piteously to listen to what is to come. It is prolonged, this first sound, and then just as it seems to be dying away, animation seizes it, and it changes into the creak defiant, and the producer of it appears to rock upon that foot, and to have no sense of fatigue.

Mr. Villars' landlady, in common with the majority of wearers of creaking boots, was gifted by nature with that order of head familiarly described as one that "would never save her heels." She had a habit of making the greatest number of journeys in a given space that arithmetic could calculate. Afterthoughts incessantly arose, especially on this night, which involved a fresh journey of a yard and a half, a fresh plaintive squeak, a fresh defiant creak, and, finally, a fresh continuous rocking, of uncertain duration. She was one of those who always see something that they want to "go and get," and whose hands have the extraordinary property of always holding something that they want to "go and put down." And in the stillness of this hour of agony all her evolutions grated distinctly on the ear of the man who was waiting.

By-and-by she elected to do what was even harder to endure than her habit of rocking on the foot that had the most creak in it: she became "humbly anxious," as she phrased it, and opened the door of his room to ask him "if he had heard anything yet." Which inquiry caused him to do what he had broken the little boys of the village of doing, in his presence at any rate, namely, to swear in a soul-relieving way. But there was worse to follow; he felt persuaded that she would close the door with a hand so sympathetically hesitating that he should be uncertain whether or not the latch had fastened itself into its socket. He knew that there would be no decisive reassuring "click" about a door drawn to by that woman's hand that night. As in a dream he saw that it would be gently, deprecatingly, feebly done; and what he felt, and knew, and dreamt, came to pass.

It was no use reason telling him that he could promptly remedy the evil by walking up and banging the door firmly. There was no compensation, in this course that was open to him, for those moments which had elapsed from the dawning of the dread that she would do it, to the death of the half-hope that she might not. There was no alleviation, in doing that, for the way his brain had tingled, and something had waltzed rapidly round in his head when he saw it left undone. He made wine his friend that night; and when it showed him things in a less sombre hue for an instant, even he acknowledged that men might get to regard it all too kindly without being by nature bad. Despairingly he began to make wine his friend at about the same moment that Bella, in her desolation, began to make Claude Walsingham hers.

——o——

CHAPTER X.

SUNSTROKES.

The morning light broke pleasantly through the diamond-paned window of that chamber in the old inn which had been Miss Vane's resting-place—broke in with the sweet, lazy radiance we look for when we wake in sultry June; and the sleeper on the couch aroused herself to meet it; and all thoughts of the errors and misgivings of the last night were obliterated from her mind as she sprang up with the elasticity that was the offspring of complete rest, and a feeling that the day was very young and fair, and all before her too, and that life was the same.

It was a quaint old yard, that on which her window opened. Time's hand had touched it in every part gently but perceptibly. The dark brown bricks of the building (they had been red long, long ago)—the lichen that grew in luxuriant patches about the same—the solid, heavy, iron-barred doors of the stables and coach-houses—the ivy-covered porches that jutted out from two of the entrances to the side of the house which her window commanded—the deep air of quiet, which not even the unwonted presence of the volunteers could dispel—all these made up a picture of antiquity that was pleasant as the bright day itself to look upon.

It was a quaint old scene. It made the essentially modern young lady at the window feel historically romantic as she gazed upon it. This was her first experience of an old English hostelry. It came to her like a page of James or Harrison Ainsworth, and she liked the idea of reading more of it in Major Walsingham's company.

For he was new to her too, though he was a man of her own day and her own class. Still he was new to her, new and very interesting—as Stanley's friend, as Florence's possible lover, of course. How kindly he had come to her rescue last night! How honestly he had told her what she ought to do! How pleasantly he had coerced her into retiring when it was right she should retire, though by doing so he had defrauded himself of an agreeable hour! How handsome he was, and how manly, and what a charm there was in his voice!

Her thoughts of him as he had been were interrupted in this juncture by the sight of him as he was. He had come out into the yard with two or three officers, and she heard him—for her window was open to admit the warm young morning air—order out her mare; and when that order was obeyed, from her position behind the curtain she perceived him critically inspecting Vengeance, running his hand down her legs, and treating her pasterns as if he distrusted them.

He was ready to receive her in the room in which they had met the previous night, when she went down: and he greeted her with the intelligence that her troubles would be shortly at an end. The carriage had arrived from Denham, and was at her service—at least, not unconditionally at her service, for the coachman had orders to wait a couple of hours to rest his horses before starting on the homeward journey.

"I mean to ride home," she said, in reply to this communication.

"But that is impossible, Miss Vane——"

"Not at all," she interrupted; "I am not tired, thanks to your prudence in sending me off to bed last night." She delighted in giving him credit for discretion, even to her own heart and himself alone. It was soothing to praise him.

"Your mare is tired, though; and not alone tired, but lame," he replied.

"Poor Vengeance," she cried earnestly, "she is so good; what a shame of me to have ridden her so carelessly!"

"No amount of care would have been of any avail. Vengeance is not suited for these country roads. I cannot echo your declaration that she is 'so good.' She is all very well for a park hack, but she is a terrible screw."

Bella frowned. The mare was *her* mare, and she had been wont to declare that Vengeance was the best lady's mount she had ever met with. It was humiliating to be told authoritatively by a man who seemed to know all about it, that the mare was a "terrible screw."

"It is of no consequence a lady's horse being screwed behind," she replied carelessly; "she goes the easier for it."

He laughed. "Vengeance is more than a little 'screwed behind,' Miss Vane; she has not a leg left this morning; and I think, when you see her try a little canter (she's free enough, I allow), you will be disposed to accept the carriage arrangement."

"What in the world shall I do at Denham without Vengeance?" Bella asked almost piteously. "Oh dear! something is always happening to make everything else unpleasant." Then she poured herself out a cup of tea, for the breakfast was on the table all this time; and recovering her spirits abruptly, she asked—

"I like the look out from my window so much, that I want to see more of the town. We must wait, I mean I must wait, here a couple of hours, you tell me; can't we go out and walk about?"

He made one feeble protest against a plan that was very pleasant to him.

"You won't like to walk about in your habit, will you?"

"Why not?" she asked, opening her eyes with a little stare of inquiry. They were such lovely eyes, those of hers—they were so very blue! "You don't imagine me to be one of those women who are awkward in a habit on the earth?"

"I do not imagine you to be one of those women who are awkward at anything or in anything," he replied. "Yes; let us go out, by all means. You will permit me to be your escort, won't you?" Then he added, in a lower tone, "And you will forgive me for having disparaged Vengeance to you?"

She smiled brightly, and nodded, and told him "there was her hand on it, if he liked." Then he took the hand in his, and felt that he had better not kiss it, and that the sooner they went out for their stroll through the town, the better.

They went out, with Rock at their heels, through the yard Time's hand had touched—past steady ostlers attending to respectable horses—past little groups of not yet disbanded volunteer defenders of their country—past a veritable English mastiff, who was chained, and who growled at Rock—out into the quiet streets, where the sunbeams lay in mellowed masses of golden light on the one side, and the early dews of morning nourished the ferns and mosses that were about the gratings of old houses on the other.

What a dear old town Bella Vane thought it! It looked as if it might have attained to its present position of solid, unostentatious prosperity a thousand years ago, and had remained stationary ever since. It was not bustling, thriving, fussily active in a small way about smaller things. It did not look as if it were doing anything for a living, and aspiring to be considered "go-a-head." People did not rush through its narrow streets, but walked calmly along, as if it were not of the slightest consequence whether they were "there"—wherever that might be—five minutes sooner or later. The small boys even were not addicted to chaff, but looked as if ever before them loomed this great fact—"I, too, may be a chorister, and wear a little white surplice, and elevate my little alto in the cathedral diurnally, if I look—not sharp."

The streets were very narrow through which the lady and her companion wended their way, and from many a window in those beetle-browed old houses on either side did eyes gaze, half-wonderingly, wholly admiringly, upon the fair young pair. She—Bella Vane—was adjudged to be all sorts of things that she was not by old ladies of a speculative turn of mind, and young ones too. She must be Lady Moretun, they said, the wife of the Colonel of the West ———shire

Volunteer Corps; or perhaps she was the wife of the real live soldier, the genuine man of blood and carnage, who had come down to review them. Then they told over their breakfast-tables how Lady Moretun was notoriously careless of what people thought about her, and afflicted with horsey tastes, and a habit of escaping from her husband's society whenever she was able to do so. Thus heads were shaken over her, though they knew not that she was Bella Vane.

She meanwhile was very happy walking along by his side, and talking, not of the life they both knew so well, or of Stanley Villars, but of the quiet scene before them—of the tall old houses and their moss-grown bases—of the placid age of the town, and the equally placid youth of it in the form of its boys—and of how it was altogether like a page from a book, this coming there, and meeting, and walking together thus.

She did not tell him that the carol of the song-birds above them sounded more sweetly in her ears than ever similar strains had sounded before. She was unconscious herself of how very deeply the beauty of the day, and the calm in the air, and the song of the birds, was affecting her. All she knew was, that emotions the like of which had never thrilled her before were thrilling her now. All she regretted was, that life could not be all walking through old towns in the mellow sunbeams, with one on whom the gloss of novelty still lingered, and not being compelled to analyse why the doing so was sweet.

There were broad, thick avenues of beeches and of elms in the cathedral close, and walking in the shade of one of these, with the sunbeams flickering down through the leaves upon their heads, the morning chants came floating by, and fell upon their ears. They paused there to listen to the sweetly solemn strains, and time went by, and they were very silent.

It ceased at last—the peal of the organ, and the choral strains, and the silence that those who had listened to these things had kept. With a half glance at the sky, as if he expected to see a cloud there, with a half frown on his brow, as if the shadow of the expected cloud had already fallen on it, Claude Walsingham spoke—

"By Jove! that is one of the things that are over for ever!"

The girl's lips moved nervously for a moment or two, but no sound emanated from them.

"You are tired, Miss Vane?" he interrogated, relapsing abruptly into common-place tones.

"Not of being here, or of walking," she replied, and she looked full into his eyes as she said it.

"But it is clear that you are tired of something. I shall suppose that something to be my society, if you do not tell me what it is."

Again there came that little nervous quiver over her lips that he had marked before, but it merged into a smile this time.

"Would you feel at all sorry if you knew that we should never come here again?" she asked.

"I can't say that I should have any very deep feeling on the subject, as I can only suppose that our remaining away would be the act of our own free-will."

"I shall feel that I am leaving something for ever, perhaps, that I am very sorry to leave, when I drive away this morning."

"Will that something be the town? No, no, Miss Vane; it is a bright morning and all things look well in its light, and a combination of untoward circumstances has given birth to some new ideas in both of us. Ask yourself, have you not felt the same before? and with your temperament, are you not tolerably certain to feel the same again?"

She shook her head impatiently.

"I don't want to build up a romance from the sunbeams, and the green leaves, and the flickering light. You need not fear that I did, Major Walsingham."

"They were not your sole materials. You have left out the most important ingredient in your catalogue. Let us walk back to the 'Red Lion,' Miss Vane. I think I have got a sunstroke."

"Which you will recover from as speedily as I shall from the effects of my sorrow at leaving this pretty day and town behind me," she said, in a low tone. "When I tell Stanley, how he will laugh at the idea of the strains of the organ having made me sentimental for an instant."

"*When* you tell Stanley, I have no doubt but that he will laugh as you say. What a power of mischief the sun has to answer for; it has affected my head, I believe: if I verify that belief, I shall not go on to Denham."

She would not look at him when he said this, for she knew that she had the name of a flirt—that she was so dubbed by the idle-tongued majority who knew nothing at all of the matter—and it occurred to her that he might be testing her "while yet there was time," for Stanley's sake. So, though his declaration that this morning's sun had affected his head made her tremble with a feeling that had more joy and hope than pain in it, she would not look at him to read the truth in his eyes.

She was a flirt. It was the curse of her nature to long for love. Bella was not one to care for attention and superficial admiration alone; she never sighed to be made much of—to be put upon a pedestal before people; but she had a dangerous yearning for that sort of good will, between which and love it is so extremely difficult to draw the line. Directly a man proved himself capable of interesting her, she desired his friendship; desired him to feel warmly interested in her, tender to her errors of judgement, and himself a better man for being under her influence. Miss Vane had a great notion of elevating and improving so much of mankind as came under her influence. But lately a doubt had arisen as to how far her efforts in behalf of the many might be compatible with her duties towards the one she had promised to marry. This morning the doubt assailed her more poignantly than ever, as she walked along by Claude Walsingham's side, and listened to his words, and feared to look in his face.

He, meanwhile, was thinking her very lovely and very dangerous, alike as a friend for himself, and a wife for Stanley Villars. He saw how undesigning she was, how terribly addicted to making herself pleasant, how hopelessly incapable of being entirely discreet! There was no evil, there was not the shadow of guile, he did her the justice of discovering, in that winning way, which looked so strangely what it was in fact—an earnest attempt to make him think as kindly as he could of her. There was no idle coquetry in her softened tones and looks when she addressed him, in the delicate flattery of her averted eyes, in the quiver of dread which possessed her when she spoke of departing and leaving the scene, the hour, and himself, behind. There was no bad design, no low, idle coquetry in all this, but it was very dangerous. Claude Walsingham felt the full force of the danger, and wished with all his heart, since he had met her, and she was engaged, that it had been to any other than his old friend, Stanley Villars.

Miss Vane fell a prey to remorse during the latter part of their walk home. It occurred to her that they had long outstayed the specified two hours. "I never thought of asking you to see what time it was, and I never can wear my watch when I ride," she said, as they approached the "Red Lion," and essayed to shake off some of the feelings the calm of the close and the environs of the cathedral had engendered.

"And it will be useless for me to look at mine, for I forgot to wind it up last night," he replied. He could not bring his mind to deciding precisely the exact period he had passed under this phase of feeling that was new, and dangerous, and delightful to him. He could not bear to limit it, though the doing so would not shorten its duration by one instant. He rather desired that it should remain a dreamy joy—shading off into the Nothing that must surely follow by imperceptible gradations.

Promptly upon the dread that she had outstayed the two hours that had been vouchsafed them in mercy to the horses, there dawned another. Stanley would surely be annoyed by that forgetfulness of hers which might savour of forgetfulness of him. He would probably say something calm and disagreeable to her when she returned, weary and worn out, to Denham. He would blame her—she told herself—for what she could not have helped had she been Discretion herself, and think and say that she might have done sundry things which she had not done, and have left undone several acts which she had committed. He would be hard to her, she feared—hard in an affectionate, masterful manner that might not be put aside—and he would blame her judiciously, and counsel her wisely, as she hated to be blamed and counselled.

Her eyes kindled as she pictured to herself the scene that would probably ensue, and her cheeks grew rosy. It was hard for the petted daughter, the autocrat of her own house, to feel that she might be reproved and censured, and that she had no appeal against it. In the innermost depths of her soul she acknowledged that she was a little in awe of this man, whom she had promised to marry. A little in awe of him, and a great deal in love with him, of course; but still just a little weary of being in awe of him already. It was a case of rarefied atmosphere disagreeing with her, that was all—a repetition of the old Guinevre and Arthur story, a new edition of the eternal difficulty of breathing in a "perfect air."

Miss Vane's heart went very low indeed when she entered the hotel yard, and found her uncle's carriage standing, with the horses put to, already awaiting her. But it went lower still when, from the ivy-covered porch to the right, Stanley Villars advanced to meet her. She almost felt, as he came towards her, that he was her foe, and that the man by her side was her natural protector against him, and involuntarily she exclaimed—

"Major Walsingham, what shall we say?"

"The truth, I think," he replied, in a low voice; then he cried aloud, "Villars, I have done my best to make Miss Vane feel the time she was compelled to wait here as little disagreeable as possible: she must tell you whether I have succeeded or not."

"My dear Claude, I am only happy that you were here to take care of her, whether the time has been disagreeable or not," Stanley Villars answered heartily; and Bella Vane felt, as he spoke, that she had prepared her defence against what he might feel and say for nothing, and that he had unbounded confidence in his friend. It was better that it should be so—far, far better; but still she was conscious of a little disappointment.

"I suppose there was a perfect tumult last night at Denham on my account?" she asked.

"You would not be pleased were I to tell you that Denham was indifferent to your non-appearance, Bella."

"No, of course I shouldn't; but shall I have to explain how it came to pass that I lost my way in tangled roads that I didn't know, and fondly hope I never *shall* know, because rather than do that I would flee my country. I shall hate to talk about it. I have lamed Vengeance—that ought to be held sufficient expiation for all my sins."

"We will soon replace Vengeance," Stanley Villars said, cheerily. He was so rejoiced to find Bella safe and in honourable keeping, that he would scarcely suffer himself to remark that her tones were querulous, and her manner constrained.

"Indeed, we can't soon replace Vengeance!"

"Clearly, we can't replace her here this day," Claude Walsingham said, "still I think it may be done in time. "Don't you think the sooner we all get away from this place the better Stanley?" he added, in a low tone, to his friend

"Decidedly. Are you ready to start, Bella?"

"Oh! quite ready. How did you come over—on horseback, Stanley?"

"Yes; but I shall leave my horse to be led back with Vengeance."

"I shall be but a poor companion—I'm too tired to talk; and, in fact, I hate talking when I am driving," she said, wearily. It was not a graceful thing on the part of the beauty to say this to her betrothed, but she was not in a graceful humour just then.

"Well, I was thinking that as Claude Walsingham had his horses here, and as the roads are so intricate, that I would get him to drive me over to Denham, and so do away with the possibility of his losing his way," Stanley Villars rejoined hastily. Then Bella fell penitent—oh, those agonizing interludes of penitence and said, "Oh, Stanley!" deprecatingly; and Claude watched the pair attentively to mark whether by word or sign she would strive to make Stanley alter his determination.

But she did not. She made no further appeal than those two words, "Oh, Stanley!" and Stanley took no notice that was visible to Claude of them. Somehow or other, it was almost a relief to the man who had seen her for the first time on the previous night to find that her future husband was not proposing to go back to Denham in the carriage with her, and even greater relief was it still to mark that she did not desire him to do so.

They put her into the carriage presently, offered her the last services of handing her in, and saving her habit from the wheel, and putting one window up and the other down, as seemed good to her. Then she said good-bye to them both, and in reply heard from Stanley that he "should come up to the rectory in the evening to see how she got on," and from Major Walsingham that he hoped to have the honour of seeing her again shortly. But yesterday she had pleaded so warmly for Stanley to do this very thing he was now pledging himself to do, and then he had refused. Well, she could not unlive the past few hours and feel as she had felt yesterday, that was all. She nodded assent to his proposition, and drove away with a sense of the tender grace of the day being gone, though the sunbeams still lay in mellowed masses around her, and the birds still carolled high and clear above her head.

Fervently,—as the old town and the events which had happened in it appeared to recede from her, rather than she to move away from them,—did she wish that "none of it" had happened. There was no harm done, but her routine had been broken up, and she had a vague sense of discomfort and of doubt, as to whether she should take quite so kindly as was desirable to routine again. It had been a bit of pure romance while it lasted; but it had been such a tiny bit, and had lasted such a very short time, that she could but wish she had never come upon it at all. She had been fraught with a certain ecstatic feeling as she had walked through those narrow streets, and stood under the sombre beeches. It must have been because she saw them all "for the first time," she told herself; for something whispered to her that, even could she persuade Stanley to ride over to the picturesque old town with her again, the ecstatic feeling would not return—that was over for ever.

The same indescribable sensations which had caused her on the past night to be extra devout, made her now dwell upon so much of Stanley Villars' magnanimity and general superiority to suspicion and distrust as she could recall. She reflected upon how entirely satisfied he had seemed when he found that his old friend had been guarding her the whole time; how entirely satisfied, how warmly reliant, how pleased, that Claude should have been there, since he himself was absent. The reflection made her wince, and move uneasily; it was very perfect trust that he had evinced in her and in Claude Walsingham; and from any other man to any other man, about any other woman than herself, she would have regarded it as a very natural trust too; indeed she would have scoffed at the notion of aught else being possible. But it was about herself, and she was exceptional; and about Claude Walsingham, and he was the same. The loving trust in her faith, the unquestioning reliance on Claude's honour, seemed burthensome to her, she knew not why. Perhaps it was that she was conscious that it would not have been felt and expressed, had every heart-throb of hers been heard by Stanley during that morning walk, or had Claude Walsingham's complaint of the effects of the sun sounded in the ears of his friend as it had in hers.

—o—

CHAPTER XI.

CLAUDE'S CONFIDENCES.

The two men watched the carriage drive away out of the yard without speaking. When it was no longer in sight Claude turned round, took a cigar from his case, offered one to Stanley Villars, and then elaborately lighted his own, and puffed away at it for a few seconds.

"Come and look at my horses, Stanley," he then said; and before Stanley could accede to his request, he added, "Come, and I'll introduce you to my colonel."

"Is he here? Certainly, I'll be introduced to him."

"Of course he is here. It was his coming brought me down. He came to review Lord Moretun's corps; and as it sounded like being in your neighbourhood, I thought I might as well come with him, and see him through it, and the dinner that they threatened."

"It is a very fortunate thing that you were here," Stanley rejoined. "Miss Vane would have been unpleasantly situated indeed, if she had not met with you."

"Oh! you're very good to say so," Claude replied, in a slightly embarrassed tone. "You overrate my services, old boy; however, I did my best—on my soul, I did."

"You need give no such strong assurance to me as that, Claude," Stanley Villars replied, gravely.

"Don't drop on to a fellow for forgetting for an instant that you are not as you used to be, Stanley. Come and look at Miss Vane's mare."

He seemed excited—almost agitated. Still, there being no valid cause for either excitement or agitation, Stanley Villars would not permit himself to observe it.

"Poor Vengeance! she fell lame, I understand. I must find some steady fellow to take her home quietly."

"My man's here; he shall take her home," Claude interposed, "he is to be relied upon in the first place; and in the second, he will be well out of the way, as I have several things to say to you that he would overhear if he went with us. I have got a new trap—come and look at that."

"What shall we do?" Stanley Villars asked, laughing. "You are fruitful in propositions; but you don't carry one of them out. What do you want me to do first?"

"We will order my cattle in at once; then I can send off my man with the mare," Claude replied. "You don't care about staying here any longer, do you?"

"Certainly not."

"Damned hole. I wish I had never come to it," Claude growled. He, too, was suffering from a revulsion of feeling, and it made him unconditionally ill-tempered.

"I can't say that, Claude. However, I am willing to get away as soon as you please."

They walked into the stable now, to look at Vengeance, who was standing in a loose box, with a cloth on, and with pads upon her knees.

"You will never let Miss Vane ride that beast again, I should hope, Stanley," Major Walsingham said, as he went up to the slender-limbed brown. Then he remembered that Bella had called the mare "Dear Vengeance," and an access of softer feeling set in, and he repented him of that term he had used towards Miss Vane's pet horse.

"I can supply her with a horse while I am with you," he went on; "that is to say, if you'll permit me to offer her a mount, I can lend her one of the nicest stepping horses you ever saw. Come and look at them."

"Unquestionably, I will permit it, and look at them too," Stanley said, as they walked on into another stable, where a pair of iron greys were stalled. Then the pride of ownership in good horseflesh came to Claude Walsingham's aid, and he ceased to be either ill-tempered or embarrassed.

"That's the best ride of the two," he said, pointing to one of them. "I always put him in on the off-side; I used him as a break-horse for the others, for he's as mild as he is game. There's strength there, eh? strength as well as speed?"

When Stanley had eulogised the horses to the heart's content of their owner, he was conveyed by Claude to the coach-house, where the trap stood.

"But you don't see it to advantage here," he said; "in fact, it looks nothing till the horses are in; so we'll have them in at once and go, shall we?"

He was indeed strangely undecided; Stanley Villars regretted that the rush and hurry of London life should have set its mark so unmistakably upon his friend.

They got away at last without that introduction to the colonel coming off of which Claude had at first made a point. "He's linked in for the time being with a lot of cads, from whom he can't escape," he explained; "it's all very well for him, for he will go off directly, and be out of it; but you're in the neighbourhood, and you mightn't like it if you met them again." The truth was, that he was afraid ribald jokes might be uttered relative to that damsel in distress, whom he had been so prominently squiring that morning; and Stanley Villars might take such jests amiss.

The trap afforded them food for conversation for some distance. It was a new style of thing altogether—a combination of double dog-cart and phaeton that went very well together. The one man declared it to be more useful than a mail-phaeton in the country, and the other agreed with him, without knowing why, in the most affable manner; and they both averred that it showed the horses off well—that it made less noise than any vehicle they had either of them ever chanced to occupy before, and that it ran lighter than anything the imagination of either had ever conceived They talked "trap," in fact, as long as it was possible to do so, a little perhaps because they were desirous of staving off other subjects till they had become more accustomed to each other.

At last, when they had been on the road some time, and the horses had got into their stride, and the hedges were going by them at the rate of fourteen miles an hour, Stanley Villars paved the way to return to the old confidential intercourse that had existed between them, by asking—

"Have you seen anything of my people lately?"

"I was at Lady Villars' (your mother's I mean) one afternoon of last week—no, the week before. Your sister told me then about your engagement."

"Which sister?—Florence?"

"Yes, Florence," Claude replied, driving very carefully now, and bestowing vast attention to his reins.

"Florence and Bella don't know each other yet, but for all that Florry is intensely pleased about it."

"She expressed herself delighted to me." Then he drew back a little to get his horses together before they came to the brow of a declivity, and went on—"I congratulate you, old fellow, heartily, heartily!"

"Thank you; your written congratulations sounded less warmly."

"Don't be annoyed at that, Stanley. I think you now a devilish lucky fellow, and congratulate you accordingly. When I wrote I didn't think you a lucky fellow, and so I failed in putting the warmth in, I suppose."

"My dear fellow, annoyed! I do not believe that the opinion of the whole world would weigh with me on such a question as my marriage; that is too entirely to myself for me to care even what you thought about it when once I was assured that I was acting wisely myself."

"You are assured of it?"

"Perfectly!"

"Thank God! I wish I could say the same about myself." Then he went on to tell Stanley of what the wine, and the warmth, and the witchery of that woman, and the hour, had done for him at Richmond but the other day.

"It is out of the question that I marry her, you know—that you must perceive?"

"Why?" Stanley Villars asked gravely.

"Why, if you don't know, I will refrain from telling you more than that it *is* out of the question. She is very charming, and deuced pretty by gas-light, and no man, I am assured, can 'breathe a word against her.'" Then he flicked his horses, and as they burst into a faster trot he burst into a laugh, and cried, "Just fancy my marrying a woman about whom I am *told* 'not a detracting word can be breathed!'—by Jove! just fancy it!"

"What do you purpose doing? It seems to me that you must do something, since you have asked her to marry you," Stanley said indignantly. He was inexpressibly grieved and shocked that this man, whom he had half-unconsciously designed for his pet sister, Florry, should have been wasting the firstfruits of his heart, and offering his first vows on a shady shrine. But for all that he could not bear to hear light mention made of that shrine's claims on its self-ordained devotee.

"Oh! get out of it some way or other; it is one of those things that can be done. Don't look disgusted, Stanley; don't you see, old fellow, the facts are these—my breaking that lightly-offered and accepted vow won't cause any more than half an hour's annoyance; my keeping it would make my whole family miserable, and kill my mother, I believe. I hardly know why I have named it to you at all," he said, meditatively.

He did hardly know himself that he mentioned this, that he meant to be a mere passing folly, to Stanley, only because he desired to make Stanley aware as early as possible that no secret tie of feeling still bound him to Florence. This was his motive, but he barely acknowledged it to his own heart. To plot ever so remotely about Florry seemed too foul a thing for him to deem himself capable of doing it. It was not plotting! He told himself that it was not plotting! It was precaution—precaution pure and simple—nothing more.

Claude Walsingham essayed too determinately to be as he had ever been with his old Eton friend, for the event to repay the effort. The result is almost invariably poor when so much labour is bestowed upon the working of it out. Unlimited confidence, perfect understanding, friendship flawless and unalloyed, are things that are best portrayed by a few bold strokes. Laborious fillings in, and tonings down, and shadings off are apt to destroy the resemblance to the thing to be represented. Stanley Villars felt, and felt with a sorrowful foreboding, that Claude was more utterly unlike the Claude of old, at the time when he most carefully attempted to reproduce himself by countless allusions and reminiscences, and spontaneous assertions of unaltered feeling, than at any other moment. He was changed!—changed much in many things, but in nothing so much as in that peculiar manner, half-boyish, half-brotherly, which had been his of yore to Stanley, and which he now endeavoured to render with photographic accuracy.

Indeed it was rendered with photographic accuracy, for it was like, and yet odiously dissimilar to the original, It was a hard, dry, material copy of what had been, and no one could be more conscious of its failures than the man who made it.

But he was very frank with Stanley as to his prospects and plans. Far more frank and outspoken, indeed, than he would have been had compass this natural ambition, and that if his father supplied him with it, the property would suffer in a way that it would be humiliating to the Walsinghams that their property should suffer, though the suffering came through the hope of the house. "A corner of the estate that we don't want could be sold well enough; but then it would be devilish unpleasant to have to make open confession of having overshot the mark in that way, you see," he said in conclusion. And Stanley said, "Yes, it would," and wondered silently why Claude would not avert the necessity of abolishing the unwanted corner of the estate, by taking what he might have for the asking—Florence's portion, namely, and her own sweetly willing self into the bargain.

Naturally, Stanley did not say this aloud. It was just one of the things that, though it might possibly do much good, and could possibly do no manner of harm, may not be said aloud. He commenced a brief argument with Claude on the absurdity of the latter, wishing to get out of a regiment that he found to be too expensive for his means into one that was more expensive still. But he shortly saw the folly of arguing with a man who was bent on having his own way, and who was apt to put out the mild light of sober, common sense with sparkling social reasons for doing as he pleased.

Major Walsingham brought his greys into Denham, to the admiration of the whole village, about an hour after Miss Vane had made her advent. The youth of the day was gone, but it was not anywhere near its decline though; there were a good many hours to be got over before he could see Miss Vane again, and gain a further insight into the character of the girl who would exercise, in all probability, a large influence over the career of his friend. It was a large, rambling, old farmhouse, the one in which Mr. Villars lodged, and behind it there was a large, rambling, old garden, with a streamlet running through the midst of it, and seats close to the streamlet, and fruit trees "delightfully situate" with regard to the seats. There he placed himself, with all that was latest in literature that he could find, and what with a cigar and the happy consciousness of having nothing to do, and nobody being near to see him do it, he managed to get over the afternoon. The hours did not fly precisely, but they were not leaden-winged. A brief period in such a place was all very well—renovating to mind, body, and estate in fact. But he caught himself marvelling how Bella Vane could have pledged herself to remain in it, and similar scenes to it, for the term of her natural life.

Major Walsingham had altered his mind as to the desirability of speedily recommencing his study of Miss Vane's character when evening

Mr. Villars had no special desire for the society of his friend. He wanted to hear an account, before possible collusion, of what had transpired that morning before his own arrival. Not that he was suspicious of Claude or distrustful of Bella; but still he did want to hear about it. So he went up alone, leaving Major Walsingham on the sofa, feigning sleepiness and an indifference to the duration of Stanley's visit to Miss Vane that he was very far from feeling. It was not a pleasant thought to him, lying there, that the man who had just gone out from his presence had gone up to the girl who had listened to the organ's swell, and the low, mild summer whisper of the trees, with himself that morning—gone up armed with legitimate claims on her affection that she might possibly pay.

How he cursed the fate that had brought him there—not there to Denham, so much as to that old town, whose quaint, old, quiet poetry had aided in the creation of this feeling, whatever it was, that began to oppress him. How he cursed that fate, and also that fatal facility for being touched when it was not well to be touched, which he was fully conscious of in himself, and half-fearfully recognised in another. The man grew half afraid of himself as he sat there alone. "I will be off to-morrow," he said to himself; "if a night's rest, and the knowledge that there's nothing to be done, even were I blackguard enough to wish to do it, doesn't cure me." Then he thought again of that pair up at the rectory, and chafed sorely at the thought of them, and went into a very Inferno, without the faintest hope of a Beatrice guiding him through it.

——o——

CHAPTER XII.

MRS. VANE PUTS THINGS IN A PLEASANT LIGHT.

On the whole it would have been better for them all had Claude Walsingham risked possible neglect or mortification to himself, and gone up to the rectory that night. Had he been there he might have been a distressing diversion to Stanley, and an obstacle to Miss Vane's unconditional return to that path of right from which, in the innermost recesses of her soul, she felt conscious of having strayed. Moreover, he might have been slightly oppressive to Mr. Vane, who always essayed to be hilariously hospitable to young men when first they entered his house, and who speedily relapsed into a low frame of mind on making the disheartening discovery that his hilarity was not contagious, and that they would prefer his hospitality without it. Mrs. Vane, too, would have been subinevitable, therefore he finally appeared, and was immediately seized upon by Mrs. Vane, with the healthy avidity old ladies do occasionally display in grasping hold of what is apparently the least important point. "Major Walsingham! you don't say so?" Mrs. Vane had exclaimed when Bella made her hasty mention of him. "Well, it's one of the most extraordinary things I ever heard! Here, Mr. Vane, do listen; quite a coincidence; tell it again, Bella. Is he tall?"

"My dear aunt, I really can't say. Besides, what does it signify?"

"Oh no, only his coming here makes it seem so strange. Did he seem very much pleased to meet you?"

"No."

"*Not* pleased! Well, I am sure all Mr. Villars' friends might be pleased without any very great exercise of toleration. Did he say anything about the engagement?"

"Really we did not go into the question," Bella replied, coldly, and for a few minutes Mrs. Vane was shut up.

Later in the day she started the subject again, for there was a lack of new and original matter in that retired little village, and Mrs. Vane made the most of that which she could get. It did not occur to her that her beautiful niece was suspiciously reserved about the stranger. It did not strike her that this reticence was an exceptional thing. She always found Bella wanting in the spirit of detail; always regretted that Miss Vane did not disburden herself of every word and look that others had given to her, and she to others, on her return home from the tamest excursion. Now her regrets were aggravated, for this had not been a tame excursion. She longed to hear all about it, and Bella, as usual, would not tell her without being questioned.

"Did they seem nice and respectful at the 'Red Lion,' Bella? In my young days there was no hotel like it in the town. We always stay there now when we go to the festival."

"Yes, they were very nice and respectful," Bella answered. "I should like to have seen them other, indeed, to me."

"Did they give you a good breakfast?"

"I believe it was good. It was hot, and there was an immense lot of it, as there always is at those horrid inns, I suppose; but I couldn't eat."

"Not eat! Ah! poor child! though how could you, sitting down alone."

"I didn't sit—I mean, how should I, indeed."

"You didn't sit! why not?"

"I didn't sit down alone, I mean to say," Bella said, laughing.

"Don't say that I said much about him."

"I won't. But you haven't said much about him. Of course, I should very carefully avoid saying anything that could make Mr. Villars uneasy."

"It wouldn't make him 'uneasy;' it isn't that; only men always hate to have an adventure made out of nothing, and a hero out of the same."

"Oh, I understand," Mrs. Vane replied, "and I'll be very cautious." Then Bella felt that her aunt overcautioned would be thrice as dangerous as her aunt cautioned not at all.

So it came to pass when Stanley Villars cursorily alluded to the subject in the evening, that Mrs. Vane fell to making palpable mysteries about portions of it, and Bella began to evince nervousness. Now this was not a habit of Miss Vane's, therefore it alone would have caused Mr. Villars to be on the alert; but, in addition, Bella laboriously tried to conquer her nervousness—to hide it from him, and seem as she had been before.

"I suppose Bella has told you all her adventures, Mrs. Vane?" he said; and Mrs. Vane replied that "Bella had; but, oh dear! they were not worth speaking about, she could assure him."

"There I differ from you. When a young lady loses her way in a strange country, and then falls in with a stranger who turns out to be the familiar friend of her own familiar friend, it is worth speaking about; it's a prize subject, in fact—a thing that you may not hope to have happen to you twice in your life, Bella."

He was evidently desirous of taking a semi-jocular view of it. He was clearly above suspicion. Bella felt better.

"Ah! but I'm *sure* Bella wouldn't wish it to happen again, Mr. Villars; she would *much rather* have had you there to take care of her than your friend, whatever you may think."

Mrs. Vane was painfully in earnest in her vindication of her niece, and her niece began to experience sensations of nervous dread of what might possibly follow.

"I can well believe that—still a change is pleasant sometimes; isn't it, Bella?"

"Very. Let us change the subject," Bella replied.

"I don't see why you need desire to change the subject, my dear," the amiable, well-meaning old lady struck in, with charming simplicity; "there's no reason for it. You said very little about Major Walsingham, and thought very little about him, I'm sure: it was not your fault that circumstances threw you together in a way that of course made you more intimate for the time being than mere casual acquaintances are usually—not your fault at all."

Mrs. Vane positively beamed as she spoke. It appeared to her that she was placing the thing in the most agreeable light for all parties concerned.

"Unquestionably it was not her fault," Stanley Villars replied, stiffly.

"Then why blame her for it?" Mrs. Vane asked, cheerily.

"Blame her! You are accusing me of what I should never have presumed to do, even had cause for blame existed," he said, quietly; but he gave a quick, passionately-interrogatory glance at Bella as he spoke, and Bella shuddered under it.

"Pray, Stanley, don't think a moment longer about such nonsense," she whispered.

"Don't be uncomfortable then; if you don't blame her, don't make yourself uncomfortable," the good-natured setter to rights of all things that were wrong, interposed, affably. "Bella *did* tell me not to say a word, especially about Major Walsingham, as she saw you were uneasy; and I wouldn't have said a word, if I hadn't seen that you could not quite get over the little feeling, whatever it might be."

"Oh, aunt, you make things worse!" Bella cried, indignantly.

"Uneasy! make things worse! Good God! what is it all about?" Stanley ejaculated. "What made you request your aunt not to speak of my friend before me, Bella? what reason could you have had for desiring that silence should be maintained when there was no cause for it?"

He had risen from his seat on the couch by her side, and was walking up and down the length of the room as he spoke. It seemed to Bella that there was more anger than sorrow in his tone, and her spirit rose.

"Aunt, you have blundered egregiously, in common with the rest of us," was the sole notice Miss Vane took of his questions.

"You are right; we have all blundered egregiously," Mr. Villars exclaimed. "I believed in you so implicitly——"

"Believe in me still, Stanley," she said, very gently, going up and laying her hand on his arm; then she went on in low, caressing accents—"because I am excused awkwardly before I am accused or guilty, are you going to be unjust to me and to yourself?"

"What did she mean by that nervous anxiety to clear you from the shadow of reproach before it had fallen upon you, Bella?"

"I don't know—that is, I do know, but——"

"You would rather not tell me?"

"Not that, but I hardly know how to tell you in such a way as will make you fully appreciate all the bearings of the case at once." Then she paused reflectively for a minute, and in that minute she arranged her speech, and made herself believe that she meant it.

"I know so well the dislike you have to hearing things talked up and made much of, and I felt that it couldn't be pleasant for you to feel that I had been roving about late at night with only a groom; so I asked aunt not to enlarge upon the topic when you came, and as a reason for my request I said that you would not care to hear Major Walsingham's name mentioned in conjunction with mine too often. She has been over anxious to obey me, and has done the very thing I wanted her not to do."

"Don't plot in a small way against me, Bella. Why should you imagine that I should be annoyed at hearing your name and Claude's coupled in the sole way they can be coupled—as far as I know."

"I didn't think you would care," she whispered, "I only said so."

"Why tell stories?"

"Now you are harsh and unjust: besides, I *did* think it, in a measure—I judged by myself;

it would not be pleasant for me to hear *your* name coupled with any other woman's."

"Would you care?"

"Of course I should," she replied, rather absently. She had made her peace with him, she felt; the excitement was over, and now she was beginning to wonder whether the game was worth the candle—whether the prospect of a lasting peace was pleasant enough to pay for the trouble that had been given her to make it.

One thing, certainly, was pleasant. She was proud of her tact, accustomed to receive congratulations upon it, to hear that it was perfect, and to be told that it was of a quality to extricate her from any difficulty. She liked to bring it into play on the smallest emergency, and was rather addicted to believing that she set things right that had never been wrong. But this had been a genuine occasion; for Mrs. Vane's well-intentioned speeches had clearly rendered Stanley both angry and distrustful. Then, while anger and distrust were young and lusty in his soul, she had aired and exercised her tact, and all was well again!

Outwardly, all was well again. He had appeared to accept her explanation of those small reserves which were to have been observed; and she knew him well enough to feel sure that what he appeared to do, he did. But though she had forced herself to believe in her speech while she was uttering it, she began to doubt its perfect-integrity now that it had been made and accepted. So, though all was well outwardly, all was not well inwardly; and Bella Vane had a conviction that this "would grow."

She mooted the subject, after awhile, of Florence's coming to stay with her during the remainder of her visit to Denham. "You would not listen to a proposal I made the other day, Stanley," she said, "but I shall venture to make it again. Let me ask your sister Florence down here; then, when I go to them in town, I shall not be a stranger to the whole family."

He was half conscious of a change in his own sentiments since the other day, respecting this proposed visit, and more than half conscious of the cause of such change.

"If you really wish her to come," he began, dubiously.

"I do," she interrupted, eagerly; "I am quite sincere in it. Let her come—let her, do!"

"Certainly, if she will. What has made you set your heart on it in this way?"

"I hardly know," she replied, with an increase of colour. She had one of those faces whose colour is always increasing or decreasing. "I hardly know. I am sympathetic with your sister, I suppose."

He paused in silence for a minute or two; then he said—

"Come away to the window, where what I tell you won't be overheard." So she went over to the bay-window with him, and stood there, looking out into the night, listening with beating heart and throbbing brow.

"I am not quite certain that we shall do well in getting Florence down here, Bella. You have seen her, though you don't know her yet; you must see how sensitive she is."

"Well," was all the answer she could make; she was feeling painfully that the identification of himself with her contained in that sentence, "not quite certain that *we* shall do well," was grating harshly on some newly-strung chords in her soul.

"Well! She will see more of Claude Walsingham than will be 'well' for her, perhaps, if she comes. I should like her to be with you, unquestionably, but it may turn out a dangerous experiment for her."

"Why? Let her come, Stanley," she pleaded, "let her come; let them meet and love each other if they will."

She was struggling fiercely with herself at this juncture, and it seemed to her that Florence's presence would materially aid her in her endeavour to do what was right, and honourable, and womanly.

"She may love him, but he will never care for Florry again, I fear," Stanley said, rather mournfully. He was thinking of his friend's infatuation at Richmond the other night. Bella immediately fancied that his words referred to Claude's dawning admiration for herself. Yet, if they did, how could Stanley bring himself to utter them? She was perplexed.

"At any rate, let her come; good may come from it—good to us all in every way," she murmured. "I am so much alone here, you know, Stanley, and I shall have less than ever to do now poor Vengeance has gone lame. Do let me have your sister for the few weeks I shall be here."

"Write to her to-morrow, if you will; she will be only too glad to come. As to your riding, though, I forgot to tell you that Walsingham has commissioned me to offer you a mount, as you would find some difficulty in replacing Vengeance down here."

"One of the horses he drives?"

"Yes."

"I shall not take it; I shall not like to deprive him of it. You and he will be wanting to drive about while he is with you, and I shouldn't think of using his horse after he has left."

"The offer only held good for while he was here, my dear child. I do not believe he contemplated, for one instant, leaving the horse with you," Stanley Villars said, laughing.

Even in the semi-darkness of that bay window he saw the blood surge up to her face.

"It would not be so much for him to do for me, after—after—" She stopped abruptly; she had commenced in a ringing, impetuous tone, and her sudden pause sounded strangely.

"After what?"

"Oh, nothing! After having been your friend for so many, many years, I was going to say," she replied. "There, don't let us speak about horses any longer, Stanley. Vengeance's lameness is too fresh a thing for me to be calm on the subject yet. Let us talk of Florence—is she clever?"

"Clever enough to have made all who know her love her," he replied, fondly.

"Is she bright, I mean?"

"Perhaps hardly, in your sense of the word."

"What do you take to be 'my sense of the word?'"

"She is not brilliant and flashing. There is a great deal of repose in her soul; consequently

: manner. However,
describe her; you'll

ie right sort of wife
n, Stanley; for there
her his soul or man-

very improbable she
replied impatiently.
that impression of
ways regard him as
possible."
it likely he is," she
ably he was put out
, and guard me from
ct is," she continued,
window, and burying
weary, in the corner
felt myself bound to
about him, as I had
Observations made
are apt to be rather
w."
ars took his leave, in
st be worn out, and
rest," he said. In
asked her for a rose,
ie had worn in her

g," she said, placing
"an old, worn, faded
shall not have it. I
of them, a bouquet
breakfast to-morrow

will gather? No,
ne."
led. All the leaves
reached home; and
to walk in with a
green leaves in your

t look imbecile?" he
not tell him, so he

rapidly. He took a
ctory grounds, and
joined that rambling
the streamlet ran.
r of communication
ck, of which he had
he admitted himself
saying to himself—
ude will have bored

of the garden as he
preparatory to taking
he saw Major Wal-
ench on the opposite

out: "you are like
lay beside a rivulet,

myself," Claude an-
rning to walk to the
least I was beside
stay here for a time.
back to-morrow."

es—not to be disre-

Stanley said affec-tionately; "for heavens don't go if you can possibly remain. I shall feel that there is some cause for your departure that I could ill bear to exist. Don't go if you *can* stay."

"On my honour, it is only service matters that would take me away," Claude replied confusedly. Then he suddenly added—

"I will stay, whatever comes of it. One is apt to get false notions when alone under the moon, you know."

———o———

CHAPTER XIII.

FLORENCE COMES.

The morning after these events occurred, Miss Vane sent off her note of invitation to her future sister-in-law. She made it very brief and kind. I will leave to the reader to decide whether or not it was graceful. I deem it entirely in keeping with her character myself.

"*Thursday, Denham.*

"My dear Florence" (she wrote),

"It is your brother's wish, and my great desire, that you should spend a short time with me down here at my uncle's. Will you give us this pleasure? and will you commence giving it at an early date—say by coming the day after to-morrow, if possible? That will give us Sunday—always an idle day—to learn as much as may be necessary of each other.

"Yours always affectionately,

"Bella Vane."

She glanced her eye rapidly over the last line or two when she had written it, and said to herself, "I *will* let that go about Sunday being an idle day. Perhaps she won't like it; she may be starchy; but I will let it go."

So she let it go, and Florence, who was far from being starchy, saw no guile in that simple statement of a fact, but nevertheless found that she could not get away from town before the following Monday, "when I will be at Denham by the five P. M. train," she wrote.

The intervening days passed slowly to Bella, and wearily, wearily to one other sojourner in that village. Stanley left his flock to attend to their own salvation, unaided by his supervision, and devoted himself to the entertainment of his friend. But the entertainment he provided palled upon his friend, and his friend was powerless to conceal from him that it did so. The days dragged, in fact, and, fatal comparison! the evenings were dangerously delightful.

Dangerously delightful in a fitful kind of way. The two young men were always with the Vanes in the evening, and the elders of the Vanes went for their due worth, which was but little in the estimation of the visitors. The girl was the fountain-head from whence emanated all that was pleasant, and the girl was engaged to one of the men, and it was the other one who felt that there was a danger in the delight he began to feel in her presence: that sitting with her, as he too often did, in the half-light of the warm, soft July evenings, contrasted with fearful pleasantness with the long oppressive mornings he spent fishing with Stanley; for Stanley had retained this single sporting taste, and would carry him off to distant streams that had, to Claude's sorrow, a reputation for trout. Now, Claude hated fishing with a line and fly, from the bottom of his soul. It was to him like going out to tea, or home to a birthday feast, or any other inoffensive and tedious pastime. But he concealed his feelings as well as he could from every one (even from himself!), and entirely from Stanley; for to the latter something whispered that he owed, or would owe, all of reparation that was in his power to make.

But the mornings alone, quite alone, with the friend of his youth and the companion of his riper years, were long, and dull, and void; and the evenings were fleeting, exciting, and full of a feeling that was dear to his heart as his hopes of heaven, and yet he cursed his fate when he found that it was shared.

The Sunday, the day that she had termed "an idle day," came, and Stanley was all the parish priest again, as was meet and well. While, as for Bella, she was all her own rebellious, undecided self—that was all. Only she suffered more than people to whom it is given to be wise on all occasions, and always to know what they mean, can readily imagine.

Once more she went down to the schoolroom, but there was less heart in her effort on this than on the former occasion. "I will try while I can, but I shall never succeed," she said to herself when she came to the door; "but I will try, for his sake."

She did try: she tried to do what was in the path of what Stanley had declared to be her duty, and what she told herself would be her duty all her life if she married him, and the effort made her faint and weary—with a faintness and weariness that but a short month since she had fancied she could not feel on the treadmill, provided only that Stanley was with her: with a faintness and weariness that she knew must deepen, for she could not battle with it even now that it was so young a thing, and that would, therefore, finally overcome and beat her down.

She could not battle with it; and he, sitting there piloting his own class through the intricacies of the gospel for the day, saw that she could not battle with it, and that it was mental more than physical. Then a sharp pang assailed him at the sight, and he prayed a passionate prayer that a certain bitter cup, now faintly outlined, might be suffered to pass away from him. For he loved this woman well!

That day passed "much as usual," Bella would have said had she been asked about it; but no one asked her, therefore she was spared the utterance of the story. In truth, it did not pass as ordinary Sundays had passed at Denham since her advent; for there was turmoil in the breasts of all three when they came together—turmoil that would not be toned down.

Once more—late on that Sunday night—Claude made one more attempt to do what was just.

"Don't take it amiss, old fellow," he said to Stanley, "but really I ought to go away—that is, I ought to go back to town to-morrow."

Then Stanley combated this resolution with all the power of eloquence he had in him. He partly fathomed the motive of it, and even to himself (spasmodically unhappy as he had been this day) he would not allow that there could be danger to any of them in a prolongation of Claude's visit. How should there be, indeed, if Bella were faithful, and Claude honourable, and he himself worthy of being dealt honestly by? He would not doubt or distrust even them or himself; he would rely on the woman who had vowed to love him, and on the man who had never lied to him, and all would be well.

So he urged Claude to remain—urged him heartily: told him, with apparent unconsciousness, that Florence was coming to stay with Miss Vane, and that then, as there would be two ladies, they could go for wonderful drives behind those matchless iron-greys. "You will cut off our chief hopes of happiness if you go, Claude. You will indeed. Don't think of going yet: I won't hear of it," he said; and Claude, after one brief protest, succumbed to his fate and his friend, and agreed to stay.

Florence was to come by the five P. M. train, and Bella proposed that, to obviate aught like embarrassment or ceremony, they should "all walk up to the station in procession to meet her." "It will be a delightful, refreshing, wholesome little bit of exercise after the railway journey," she said, "and will show her that her advent is a welcome thing indeed."

"I suppose Miss Vane's whim must be gratified," Claude had said to Stanley when he heard of the plan, "but it strikes me as absurd. Much better send the Vanes' carriage for your sister, Stanley. Florry won't care for this sort of triumphal entry."

"Oh, I don't know, we may as well walk up," Stanley answered. He was blindly acquiescent in all Bella's schemes at this period, and Bella marked the change in him, and knew sorrowfully well the cause of it. He would keep her at any cost to himself, she saw. Would he keep her at any cost to her?

Four of them set out to meet Florry. Solemn-faced Rock was the fourth, and he was a welcome addition, for whenever one of the party found a difficulty in either speaking or keeping silence, his or her gloves could be thrown over the hedge for Rock to fetch, and as Rock invariably packed away all articles that he retrieved in the back of his throat, these proceedings kept their hands occupied, and their minds too, in a measure.

They stood upon the little platform, the boarded back of which had no advertisements hung upon it which might amuse the expectant, and waited for the train. When it came up, and a blooming face, with a radiant smile upon it, beamed upon them from the window, Bella put her hand hurriedly on Mr. Villars' arm, and then, instead of approaching the carriage, turned to look at Claude, and mark the effect of that blooming, beaming face upon him.

He had stepped forward to open the door and give her his hand to help her out. Such at least had been his design when he stepped forward, but he checked it when Bella turned to look at him. Checked it, and suffered Florry's brother to pass him; and Florry saw that he so checked himself, and felt that "but the other day Claude would have been first."

Before Florence could speak to Claude, or indeed think of him further, Miss Vane had recollected herself, and many other things. She went up to the new arrival with a pretty gesture of greeting, in which both her hands and her head, and in fact her whole slender, graceful figure, bore a part. "We met in London without knowing each other, dear," she said; "but we shall know each other well soon, I hope." Then she kissed Florence, and saw that she was very pretty; after quite a different pattern of beauty, though, to her own.

"I had no idea that I should find Claude here," Florry said, when she had responded to Miss Vane. "When did you come, Claude?" she continued, turning to him and giving him her hand.

"I have been here several days. Did they not tell you?"

She shook her head. "No. Why didn't you mention it, Stanley?"

"Simply because I have not written to you since he came," Stanley answered.

"And I did not, simply because when I wrote I forgot it, I suppose," Bella said, lightly. "Come on, Florence, we are going to walk home if you have no objection."

"Whether she has any objection or not, it seems to me, since there is no carriage here," Claude interposed.

Then, of course, Florence protested that she should delight in being compelled to walk a mile, and that she was not a bit tired, and that it was just the very thing that was most pleasant, &c. All of which they affected to believe, as becomes well-bred hypocrites, and inwardly distrusted.

Rock was not so essential to their well-being on their homeward journey. There were four without Rock now, and four is a very pleasant number under certain conditions. So Rock, being superfluous, and feeling the same, jogged along by the side of the one who was least likely to make manifest to any living thing that it was so (superfluous), and that one was Stanley Villars.

They came out four abreast into the high-road from off the railway-station yard, and for at least a hundred yards they kept up an unbroken stream of talk and an unbroken line. Then it occurred to Bella that to cross the fields would be pleasanter than to keep along the dusty highway, "if Florry didn't mind stiles."

Florry was amenable immediately to any alteration, whether great or small, in their route. So they stopped at the entrance to a field-path, and looked at it in the dubious way people are apt to look when it is over a tall stile which has but one step, and that one very near its summit.

As may be supposed, however, they surmounted it. Naturally they would do so in the pages of this book, whatever they might do in real life; I being desirous of getting them into the field, enter it they must. They surmounted it as creditably as women may hope to do in the garb of the present day. They neither fractured their bones on the single step, nor their dresses. But when they walked on again, it was to be perceived that something was fractured, and that something was the line, "four abreast," which they had hitherto kept. The field-path was narrow, and they walked along it two and two, and the two that walked first were Stanley Villars and his sister Florry.

——o——

CHAPTER XIV.

AN OLD STORY.

"Stanley, I like her so much."

"I thought you would like her, Florry. Ah! but you don't know her yet; you *will* like her by-and-by."

"What does Claude say about it all, Stanley?" She asked this rather hesitatingly, and with a confused expression of countenance. Claude's disapprobation, as manifested that sultry afternoon in her mother's drawing-room, had been a disheartening and a terrible thing. But now she was drifting under Stanley's influence, and it was disheartening to think what he might feel about Claude's disapprobation.

"Say about it all, my dear child! He admires her very much; but it is not even for Claude to say anything about her. I am very glad that you are come, dear," he added, kindly, for he saw that Florry was abashed by the veiled reproof he had administered to her in regard to Claude's possible opinions.

Florence was looking not so much abashed as low-spirited. She walked along the field-path with a very material decrease of that spring and elasticity which had marked her step when they were walking four abreast. On the face of it, it was the reverse of what "should have been," this progress home of theirs. The brother and sister were attached to each other, but their attachment was not of that ardent nature which makes other loves and anxieties seem of little worth in comparison. Each knew that the other had a dearer interest in life than him or herself. Each saw that the dearer interest elected to remain behind with another on this occasion, which was perplexing.

They were all going to dine at the rectory that night, and the rectory dinner had been deferred for an hour in order to favour this walking home scheme, which had fallen short of being the gay, enlivening thing it was intended to be. The order of procession which I described as being theirs when they got over the stile, was religiously observed during the rest of the way, and it was not the order of procession that Stanley Villars had contemplated when he had acceded to Bella's request that they should all walk up to meet Florry.

There had been, after that brief discussion about Miss Vane, a little family talk between the brother and sister. Georgina's marriage prospects had been alluded to in the calm, dispassionate way such unexceptionable, but by no means brilliant prospects would be alluded to, and then they spoke of the elder brother, Gerald, and of Gerald's wife.

"I hear of your being with her frequently in these days," Stanley Villars said, in relation to the reigning Lady Villars.

"Yes, we are with her a great deal; she is very kind, you know, Stanley."

"By Jove! kind!"

"Well, I mean that she is much nicer—I

mean different—to what she was at first. Gerald is always the same, you know."

The younger brother laughed. "Gerald was always a good fellow; but latterly there has been an air over him of scarcely feeling that he belongs to himself; at least I have remarked it whenever I have seen him. Is he so usually?"

"I don't know that it's that," Florence replied; and she looked puzzled.

"What have you thought 'it' then, Florry? You seem to have noticed something."

"Why, he is dreadfully afraid of putting Carrie out, you know."

Stanley laughed, and the colour rose to his forehead.

"Dear old Gerald! so he is," he said warmly. "I wish with all my heart 'Carrie' were not put out so readily. Does she bring her nerves to bear upon him as often as ever?"

Florence shook her head. "Worse than ever; and so much depends upon her keeping well, that we can't wonder at Gerald giving way to her in everything."

"So much, indeed," Stanley replied gravely; and then they changed the subject, for a little nephew, Sir Gerald's only son, had died but a year before, and there was no successor to him yet.

The pair behind had no such conversational safety-valves, no such neutral ground on which to meet. They had fallen into this line of march unintentionally, and had it not been for a wholesome dread of looking awkward, they would both of them have broken it at once. But the dread of doing aught with design that might be apparent, and so provoke suspicion, was upon them strongly—more strongly than the dread of something else which was upon them too.

For awhile they walked in the wake of Stanley and his sister without a word. Presently the silence grew irksome. Naturally the woman was the first to break it.

To break it with a little sentence—a few short words—a brief series of subdued tones, that would have been as nothing had they sounded on the ears of the great majority. The mischief was that they fell on the ears of the one who could interpret them aright.

"It was my wish that Florry should come. Did you know that?"

He nodded, and then again for a few yards they walked along without speaking.

"How heavy the air is," she said, abruptly. "Major Walsingham, do you know that I think we shall have a thunder-storm."

He looked up at the sky—at the cloudless blue sky—in which no trace of a coming storm was to be read. Then he glanced down to her and replied, "I think so too. Do you know that I wanted to leave Denham to-day?"

"No; did you? And Stanley said——?"

"That he wished me to remain, that was all," he answered. "Are you——" he was going to ask was she "glad or sorry" that he had waived his resolution, and remained. But good feeling intervened, and he paused. It would have been worse than unfair to his friend, he felt, to hold himself up as an object for which gladness or sorrow was to be experienced by this girl who was so prompt with either sentiment.

"Am I what?" she asked.

"Are you tired? these fields are hard walking."

"That is not what you were going to say," she retorted with true feminine pertinacity. "Tell me what it was."

"I really forget, Miss Vane."

"No, you do not. I see you don't forget. Say it to me; tell me, won't you?"

She said "tell me, won't you?" in small pleading accents that vibrated to his soul; but he would not, and his perseverance in keeping back that imagined speech did more harm than the speech itself could possibly have wrought.

For she clothed it with an importance that it never could have possessed had it been uttered. She deemed that it must be something very touching, very tender, very everything that it ought not to be when made by him to her. So she looked up at him half fearfully, and then gazed away into the bloomy haze that was hanging lovingly over the golden corn in the distance. Gazed away with eyes that, despite their earnestness, saw not that upon which they looked.

For Bella was thinking—thinking seriously of how, after all, she was only one among many who have made mistakes, and who must abide by the mistakes they have made, and seem to be happy in such continuance. For she was determined to abide and continue in hers, if it were one at this period. She was not prepared to quit the web and leave the loom, and take those fatal three paces, and compass that destruction which the Sir Lancelots, who ride by so gaily dight, are apt to bring to pass.

But still his uttered, and, worse still, his unuttered words sank into her soul, and filled it with a great delight, that she knew it would soon be a sin to experience.

There was a better division, or rather a far more satisfactory amalgamation, of the party that night. The two men lounged outside the open window and smoked cigars; and the two girls sang to them till it grew dark. Then they all gathered round the table and took tea, and talked on familiar topics until ease resumed his sway. Florence mentioned having seen Claude down at Richmond, with a blithe unconcern that robbed the mention of all bitterness to him; and Stanley, marking how fond Claude evidently was of Florry, in a quiet, half-fraternal way, hoped that much good would ensue from this meeting at dull Denham.

"What shall we do to-morrow?" is invariably the question raised by temporary denizens in a country place before separating for the night. It is imperative on those who would not die of the dulness of it (unless one is quite alone, when Time always takes care of himself) to map out a certain plan for the disposition of the next twelve daylight hours. They felt this, and therefore decided that they would go for a long drive in Claude's trap, and look at an old hall, the show-place of the county, by way of getting over the day, and duly fatiguing themselves.

Then they parted; and after they were gone up to their rooms, Bella went in and listened to a long exposition from Florence of the pleasure this engagement of her's (Bella's) with Stanley was to the whole Villars family. At hearing which Bella was very grateful and very sad.

Claude's trap was just the thing for the country. Of this there could be no doubt. More than that, it was the only thing for two gentlemen and two ladies to go out in. For in a phaeton—the ordinary "four-wheel"—the ladies are lost to view, and often to memory also, in the seat of honour, deprived of the society of both their cavaliers. In the order of things, when a man coaches his own cattle, his friend sits on the box by his side to see how he does it.

These dog-carts were well enough when they first came in; but, after all, a lady's voluminous drapery suffers sadly in one of them. Besides, the occupants of the back seats are in such a precarious position, that their enjoyment of the scenery through which they pass, and of the ideas evoked by that scenery in the minds of those in front, who have not to hold on all the time, is but ghastly. No, mere dog-carts are very well for mere men and dogs, but locomotives of the same order as Claude's are the only things for country driving when two ladies are of the party.

You sat back to back in it, as you do in the ordinary dog-cart; but the hind seat of this trap was broad and wide, and the foot-shelf projected afar, in a curve of beauty and comfort that was agreeable to look upon as well as pleasant to use. It was hung low, too, this vehicle, which looked like a phaeton in front, it had such a liberal allowance of seat and dasher, such gracefully sloping wings, and such an utter absence of anything angular or sporting about it. It showed the horses off wonderfully too, which was not one of its least charms, and its wheels were so close together, that it skimmed over the ground in the wake of the two horses lightly as a swallow.

There was a momentary hesitation as to how they should dispose of themselves in it, when Claude drove up to the door that morning. "Which of you girls will get up in front with Claude?" Stanley had asked with affected unconcern, and Bella had replied, "Oh! Florry will," and Florry had mildly hinted, "Won't Bella Stanley?" But when they had said that, they were no further on than they had been before, and it was left for Claude to make events march.

"Good morning, Miss Vane," he said, lifting his hat, "good morning, Florry; I always make both my sisters get up behind when I drive them. It's the best arrangement, I think, and it balances the cart better."

He had never driven either of his sisters in this trap yet, or any other woman for that matter; but this was a very white lie. He did not care to have Florry up with him, and he did not dare to have Bella.

The day was fine, and the greys were fresh and the pace fast. There is something in moving very quickly through the air behind horses that imparts a glow to the spirits. Perhaps it is that electricity conveys a something from the inferior animals—who neither lie nor plot, nor mingle sordid with the majority of their better motives—to the nobler animal, who do all these things. However that may be, the fact remains that he must be in an evil case indeed whose spirits do not rejoice, if but temporarily, when being whirled along at the rate of twelve or fourteen miles an hour.

The horses being entirely new to the rest, and nearly new to Claude, were a vast boon, in that they gave them so much to talk about. They had first to mark how cleverly the greys stepped together, and then to remark upon this fact according to their various lights. Then Bella, from her position behind, would glance at their gallant method of going, between the forms of the two men, and proceed to make brilliant discoveries relative to one or other grey "shirking his work" and not "pulling up," which discoveries resulted in Stanley being compelled to get down and take the offender up a hole or two, and brought condign punishment from Claude's hand once or twice on an entirely innocent horse.

Rollescourt was their bourn this day, and they reached it about one o'clock. Near all notorious show-places there is an inn, in which the weary who come to look upon the beauties of nature or art can take sustenance to keep up their stamina. Accordingly they found one here—the "Park Inn," it was called; and at the "Park Inn" they spent a pleasant hour in having luncheon, and wishing that the show-house was not so roomy, as they learnt from a loquacious waiter that it was.

A terribly grand old mansion this Rollescourt House was, it seemed to them, as they walked up a wide avenue and came directly out against its frowning massive front—a house that might well have been the prison of a monarch of the Titans, but that would never have been selected even by him as his residence in happier moments of freedom.

Up a broad flight of steps and into a large vaulted hall, in which there was nothing to be seen but size, but which nevertheless had to be looked at with marked interest by all who aspired to doing the place properly. There they were compelled to wait for a few minutes while the servant who had admitted them made a feint of going away into other regions to learn whether or not it was the good will of the housekeeper to come forward and graciously guide them. This ceremony lost what would otherwise have been imposing about it, through the fact of the visitors detecting the housekeeper anxiously peering at them through a little door to the left.

Eventually they were ushered through this same little door into an apartment called the "small prayer room," and the housekeeper's presence. She was not the ideal housekeeper of a grand old castellated building. She did not stalk in rustling black silk and the conscious majesty of being the chief retainer of a lordly house, which she alone had the power to show. On the contrary, she waddled wearily before them, as one who had done this same thing so many times for so many people, and seen the folly of it, would be apt to do in real life.

"Why the 'little prayer room?'" Claude asked, when the housekeeper had introduced it by name. It seemed a misnomer certainly. The adornments were not of a devotional cast, unless the house of Rollescourt was in the habit of offering up prayers and thanksgivings to a portrait of the restorer of the mansion, Sir

George Rolles—or to an inefficient representation of the Godolphin Arabian, who was curveting about on a large square of canvas in a marvellous manner.

"There *is* a chapel, which will be entered from the left when the visitors have passed through the saloon and yellow drawing-room," the housekeeper replied, in a tone that told them the nomenclature of the rooms was not to be idly questioned.

"They said their little prayers here, and kept the chapel for their big ones, perhaps," Bella whispered, suggestively. "What an old-fashioned horse he is!" she added, pointing to the famous Arabian. "We shouldn't think much of him in these days, should we?"

"No; we have improved our breed of horses, and our breed of men too, apparently. Look at the great gun, Sir George himself: his features all sit in the middle of his face, huddled up together in a most ignominious manner; yet he was a prime minister and a great architect."

The familiar sound of the list of Sir George's greatnesses caught the housekeeper's ear, and she immediately struck in—

"He commenced restoring the mansion in 17—, and it was finally completed as now seen by the visitor in 1856, by his great-grandson. Every door in the house is double, and is of mahogany, as are the sashes of all the windows."

They said, "Really now!" and "Ah, indeed!" in answer to this; and then, having taken their preliminary canter, and warmed to their work, went at full trot through about twenty rooms, till a chaotic mass of ideas—gleaned from faded tapestry, colossal velvet beds, gloomy portraits, interminable flights of stairs, gaunt furniture in ghastly shrouds, and marks of royal satisfaction, in the shape of flowered satins and false likenesses of themselves, that royal guests had left—oppressed their minds.

It was oppressive altogether—oppressive from its magnitude—oppressive from its wealth of art, from its poverty of life, from its grandeur and its gloom, its beauty and its barrenness—oppressive from the superbness of that solitude which could not be destroyed by such morsels of humanity as they felt themselves to be in it; above all, oppressive from its inutility. I am cursed with the modern mind, and I feel with my puppets here. They moved sadly through these long, solitary rooms, and listened sadly to the tale their guide told of how "the family" had never made this grand old place their home—how they had not even resided there temporarily—for upwards of fifty years. Half a century's desertion of a temple, on the part of those whose ancestors had lavished all that was their own, and much that was not their own, in its adornment! Fifty years of total abstinence from that which their founder had designed to be the glory of his race and age! We may entertain feelings of the darkest hatred towards the special white elephant whose requirements are sapping the foundation of our fortunes; but we experience sensations of tender pity for, and sympathy with, the one who is left quite alone by his prudent owners. Rollescourt would have ruined any resident under a royal personage—this was patent; nevertheless, it was pitiable to see such banquet halls deserted.

Every old house has its story. Rollescourt had a terribly sad one, and it was illustrated too. They came upon it—this party of young people whose fortunes we are following—suddenly; that is to say, they stepped out of the sombre chapel into a room that was small by comparison, and that had an air of being used, and not merely looked at, that struck home to their hearts at once.

On the walls of this room there hung four portraits. The first was of a gentleman of the period of billowing coat lappels and multiplicity of waistcoats. To judge from his appearance, as here represented, no one would have supposed that romance and himself could ever so remotely have come in contact with one another; yet he was the hero of the story, such as it was.

By his side—in a more prominent position, in a richer frame, and in a better light—hung the full-length figure of a woman—a tall, stately woman, whose velvet robe draped her form in most statuesque folds, and whose dark eyes gleamed out at you with a passionate vehemence that contrasted strangely with the firm, thin lips. A matron lady, obviously—for hers was a fully matured beauty, all perfect as it was. A matron lady—the mother of the boy who occupied the foreground to the left of the same picture, on whose head (the *fac-simile* of her own in bearing, form, and expression) one of her slender white hands rested lightly.

Opposite to these portraits hung a third—that of a young girl, who lived by the painter's art—the sweetest, fairest thing in all this grand old place. It was a bright, almost breathing beauty that dwelt on her parted full lips—in her laughing, unclouded eyes—on her sunny brow—on every feature, every portion of the vigorous young form that seemed to be leaning forward to look at you. She might have passed for a representation of the spirit of Joy. That delineation of careless, griefless, guileless, perfect womanhood, brought you up, and compelled you to gaze at it as unfailingly, as admiringly, as lovingly, as did that portrait of the Austrian Empress which we all knew so well in the gallery of the Exhibition of 1862.

This bright creature, who seemed to breathe; this embodiment of the spirit of Joy; this girl, whose cloudless brow bore no trace of even so much as a coming grief or care, was the heroine of the story, and the daughter of the stately lady in the velvet robe.

They knew the story already, but the illustrations were new to them; so they stood looking at them long and earnestly, with a certain sympathy in their breasts for the one who had erred most, and, unquestionably, not suffered least. Why they did so shall now be told.

The man was not a son of the house with whose traditions he was inseparably linked. He had come to Rollescourt in his earliest manhood, a stranger, to be tutor to the young lord of the house—to the boy on whose head the hand of the stately lady rested—to the only son of that lady who was the widow of the last lord of Rollescourt.

This man—his name was Ralph Crauford—had come there a stranger, but he had brought with him credentials that satisfied even the overweening care and pride of the lady, all of whose love and interest at this time were vested in her boy. So it came to pass that his services were accepted, and that he settled there as one of themselves.

In time the boy's sister shared his studies, and the tutor, who was young and handsome, then began to realise that he was not a mere machine for imparting instruction. She was so brightly, warmly beautiful that she lit up the dark, old library like a sunbeam, and after awhile the man forgot he was only an upper servant, and got dazzled by her rays.

"Then she forgot it, too! Forgot the claims she had as daughter of so proud a house; forgot how coldly her mother looked upon all that was not scholarly in this man—how systematically she sank him as a man, as it were, and recognised him alone in his official capacity; forgot that it would be hopeless, utterly, utterly hopeless, to do so, and like the true woman that she was, loved in the wrong direction.

About the same time that her fair young daughter let the man see that she had forgotten so much that was wise and well, the mother grew discreet. The stately lady—the proud matron, now in her best bloom of womanhood—swooped down upon them daily, and superintended their studies and many other things, and the sunbeam paled a little for awhile, and the tutor regained a portion of his memory.

By-and-by, the sunbeam faded still more, and this time it was with a terrible fear. Her brother's tutor began to be wise for her—wise in the way that it was an agony for her to watch. He ceased to woo her with the words and eyes and sighs of a love that had become a portion of her life, and at the same time her mother ceased to ice him by her bearing.

The lady and her daughter were rivals in fact; rivals in the heart of a man who "loved whate'er he looked on" in the shape of a beautiful woman, and who was determined to secure one of those women who loved him, at all hazards—at any cost to himself and her, and the other who should be left.

So he bribed the girl with gentle words and tender caresses, and vows of passionate devotion, to go away for a time, and leave all to his management. Then she, sorely fearing what might come of it, but hoping, trusting, believing still, went away, with a sort of vague impression (that both lover and mother had fostered) on her mind, that her mother was but seeming to frown upon her love till she might give way with grace.

She waited and waited till she wearied of waiting. She was patient till patience would have been mere torpor if longer indulged in. She stayed away, till each thought of what might be happening the while struck like a poisoned dart into her brain, and till the worst of all malarias—a feverish jealousy of no one in particular—enfeebled her mind. Then she went home and found her lover married to her mother.

She came home at night, and they could not stay her on her way to the room where the bridal pair sat hearing themselves wished long life and happiness by applauding friends. Her brother, roaming gloomily away from the festive scene, had met and told her the cause of it, so she understood it all when she entered, and they turned to her amazed.

It has been said that the worst of all malarias—jealousy—was at work in her system? All her joyousness, all her softness, all her love died out in the instant she beheld them—her tender lover and her tender mother—together; and she dealt her blow at him with the first thing she laid her hand upon, which happened to be a carving knife.

The man died—and went, let us hope, to the best heaven a poltroon may know. The girl lived—mad and immured—till her hair was grey, and the memory of her wrongs and crime faint in the land. The mother lived *sane*, which was the hardest fate of all, I think.

That is the story of the four portraits which hang in the cosiest little room in Rollescourt.

—o—

CHAPTER XV.

BELLA AT HOME.

THE interest of the place culminated in this room. It had been judiciously ordained that sight-seeing should end here, and the visitor should be let down from the heights to which his imagination had soared, by a flight of back-stairs.

So they went away fresh from it, and consequently full of it; but somehow or other it was the tenderest of the party, it was Florence alone, who could speak glibly on the subject.

"Poor little thing! she looks so very fair and bright after all these years. I can't help thinking of her, and loving her as if she had lived still. Wasn't it a cruel fate, Claude?"

They were descending a narrow stone staircase as Florence spoke—one of those winding, never-ending, brain-bewildering staircases that we do find in the back-regions of old mansions. Major Walsingham was just a step in advance of Florence, and he had taken her hand and placed it on his own shoulder, for the purpose of ensuring her safety in the descent. Bella had marked the action, the kind brotherly action, which showed regard for Florry's safety, nothing more, and Miss Vane felt nettled, for she thought she saw more in it.

"Pray, Florry, keep your love and pity for some more deserving object; those 'love and revenge' people are odious to me: she was little better than a wild beast."

Bella spoke very warmly, and her whole face was suffused with colour. The cause seemed insufficient for the effects, considering how long past those events of which they spoke were.

"She was sharply tried, you must remember, Bella," Stanley Villars replied; "the faith that was so basely broken was feigned to the last, remember."

"Poor Crauford! he paid a terrible penalty for trying to please her while he could," Bella said, with a hard little laugh. "You none of you seem to think it possible that he may have loved the mother better than the girl."

"He had given his love voluntarily to the girl."

"And he changed his mind. How could he help it—he was but human?" she replied, quickly. "How unsympathetic you all are with the one who erred most humanely, after all. Florry bestows love and pity upon the one who gave way to the lowest, most brutal feelings of revenge. But you have not a grain of sympathy for the one who gave way to the feelings of his heart when he found that he had been mistaken about his first love."

"People are not justified in making such mistakes," Stanley Villars said, quietly. He had waited for Claude to answer Bella's last tirade, but Claude had walked along, his hands in his pockets, and his eyes bent on the ground, without speaking.

"Not justified! No, I don't say they are justified, but it's natural; some people can't help it, and because it's 'their nature to,' they are to be murdered, and told it serves them right!"

"Worse than that befalls them sometimes," Stanley said, in a low voice.

"What? what can be worse?"

"The knowledge may force itself upon them that they have murdered another morally. Bella, why are you defending recreants from a freely-pledged faith?"

"Only because I hate injustice," she answered. "I like toleration in all things. One is not deemed worse than the beasts that perish if one finds a friendship a bore when once one thought it a blessing; but there seems to be no heaven and no hope in the minds of the majority for the man who breaks an engagement because he finds he can't fulfil it honorably with his whole heart."

"Is it to men alone you are so lenient? Would you not extend such liberty of action to women also, Bella?"

"The case in point was a man's; besides, Stanley, men are more generous than women" —she went nearer to him as she said this, and placed her hand within his arm—"they release and forgive."

An almost perceptible shudder ran through his frame. He loved her so dearly, and she seemed to be lapsing from him, and appealing to his manliness not to hold her back. How had this evil come to pass? How had Claude —for he could not doubt that it was Claude—gained this influence over her without an effort that had been apparent to him, Stanley. He had seen every look, had watched every word that had passed between his friend and his love since they had been together at Denham, and there had been nothing with which he could charge either. Yet the thing seemed to be growing, and he could not check its growth. "He was but human," as Bella had said about Ralph Crauford, and he was very miserable.

He resolved to speak to her—to ask her what this change that had come over her, which he felt and could not analyse, meant. Walking there by her side, while it was still impossible that he should do so, he determined on having an explanation with her, and of being magnanimous even as she would wish him to be, if his fears — his heart-subduing fears — were well founded. Thus he felt for a minute or two. Then he looked at her again, and saw her so fair, and knew her all his own as yet, and acknowledged that he could not tear her from himself without dying in the struggle.

They had loitered away many hours in that old house, which gave them another example of the old story of being loved, and left, and lost. It was evening before the "Park Inn" was regained, and the horses put in, and the start homewards made; and evening seemed to justify silence on the part of all, and smoking on the part of the men.

Claude was simply taciturn. Fascinated as he knew himself to his cost to be, by Miss Vane, he had felt her special pleading on behalf of faithlessness in general to be ill-timed, weak, and unnecessarily aggravating to Stanley. It had come to this that he saw it to be on the cards that Stanley might suffer largely through Bella and himself. But the loyalty, that was not dead yet, towards his friends, made him averse to small foreshadowings of that suffering being thrown over Stanley by Bella's hand when there was no immediate call for them. Being annoyed, and being "but human," he relapsed into taciturnity for the greater portion of the drive home. Even then, when he had no more cigars to smoke, and there existed, therefore, no longer any just cause and impediment why he should not speak, he chiefly addressed Florry.

This course of conduct of Major Walsingham's, which caused poor, weak, erring Bella much anguish, was dictated partly by prudence, partly by right feeling, and partly by a sore sensation that was something akin to jealousy. Prudential motives taught him that to throw off all disguise and devote himself to her, as he had it in his heart to devote himself, would be rash in the extreme in the case of a young lady so given to acting on impulse as was Miss Vane. Good feeling told him that Florry who had loved him so long, and shown, in her sweet, unsuspicious way, that she had done so—shown it freely, shown it purely—deserved something better at his hands than neglect. But more powerful than either of these motives for chilling Bella was the bastard jealousy that would obtain in his soul, of the authorised intimacy that existed still between the woman he loved and another man. It was not a noble, exalted, legitimate passion—jealousy very rarely is—but it was as strong as death, and cruel as the grave. He could not check it. Worse than this, he could not check the sights, the sounds, the thousand small causes which brought it into being. It was only right, and fair, and proper that Stanley should touch Bella's hand with a touch that told the man who was watching how dear a thing that hand was. "God of heaven! perhaps he kisses her when I am not by!" he thought; and as this not remarkably improbable contingency struck him, he would grind his teeth together, and but just refrain from stamping his foot with the cruel rage it cost him. So, as these feelings obtained more and more dominion over him, as he grew to love her deeper and deeper still, he could not resist the temptation to punish her a little, and make her miserable in a measure, since he was so himself.

Poor Bella writhed under the torture as soon as it was applied. Those words of Stanley's that report had said—"Claude was sweet on Florry"—were ever ringing in her ears; so at once, as soon as Claude looked at or spoke to Florry, Bella fancied that he was corroborating report. She ached at the idea, and nearly fell off the back of the trap with emotion, and hated Florry for her blooming unruffled beauty, and the happy freedom with which she was conversing with their charioteer.

Matters went on in this way for many days—days that seemed like weeks for three of them, they were so fraught with feeling and remorse, but that were but as hours, and those fairy-footed, to Florry, who took the top of things alone, and if the top chanced to be fine, never bewailed the possibly inferior quality of what was away at the bottom. She was very happy in Claude's presence, and in the receipt of Claude's somewhat fitful attentions. It never occurred to her to distrust them, or to dread a canker at the root of her brother's engagement.

Stanley had put off speaking to Bella indefinitely. He was far more chary of his reprehensions now, than he had been during the first days of his engagement. He was bitterly conscious, in fact, that if he strained this chord which was more than life to him, she would snap it and cast him adrift; and he clung to the hope of this being a mere fever for Claude, an illness of the soul that would pass away and leave her as she had been before. He had ceased from the folly now of pressing Major Walsingham to stay on, and he knew that he had erred in having ever done so. But still Major Walsingham did stay on, and the fever palpably continued, and there was no valid excuse for removing the cause of it.

August came at last, and with it an eager desire on the part of Miss Vane to go up to town to her mamma. "My mother wishes you to be her guest, Bella," Stanley said. "I should like you to go to her."

"But mamma wouldn't like it," Bella said, seized with a dutiful fit on the instant; "I couldn't think of leaving mamma for any one, for the little time I shall be a free agent" (there was still a talk of their being married in September).

Mr. Villars felt chagrined. He had grave doubts of the life Bella would lead under her mother's roof being the life he would desire his bride-elect to lead. With his mother and two sisters, Bella would have been better placed, according to his notions—left less to herself. He had hoped that Florence's companionship would have become sufficiently dear to Bella, during this time they had spent together at Denham, to make Miss Vane covet a continuance of it. Miss Vane, however, so far from coveting a continuance of it, never uttered a word which could be construed into the mildest desire for such a thing. There was no help for it. She was resolved to go to her "own mother for three weeks," and on the surface the resolve was all that was correct.

Soon Mrs. Vane reported herself established in her temporary town residence, and the Denham party broke up. The two girls went up to London, escorted by Stanley, and Major Walsingham started for the west of England, to spend a short time with his own family.

One of Sir Gerald Villars' carriages was at the station to meet his sister, with a note, giving them the information that there was an hour-old heir to the title again. "You had better go and see Lady Villars, Florry," her younger brother remarked. "Give my love to them, and tell them I'm delighted. I shall see Bella safely home."

Bella got into her mother's brougham after embracing Florence, and saying that she "hoped they would meet again in a day or two," and Stanley followed her, heartily glad to have her to himself again, and blindly deeming that all danger was over, since Claude had certainly had no plans of returning to town almost immediately when they parted. Stanley was only going to stay one night in London, and return to his duties on the following morning. He had, therefore, not too much time in which to say the many things he had to say to her; but he found that he was not to say them yet.

"My head aches from the train," Bella said softly, as soon as they drove off; "please don't speak to me till we get home, Stanley, or I shall be worse."

Condemned to silence, the way seemed very long to Mr. Villars; but he would not disobey her, for she was leaning back in the corner, looking very pale and weary, with her eyes closed, and one of her hands pressed against her forehead. The attitude betokened pain unmistakeably — wearing pain, either mental or bodily. He fondly hoped that it might only be the latter.

He beguiled the time by conjuring up a vision of a Mrs. Vane, for he had never seen Bella's mother yet. By the time he had arranged and draped four or five utterly different figures, the carriage stopped at the door of a house, with an awning stretched over a flower-laden balcony, and another over the steps, on which scarlet cloth was spread, and Bella Vane was at home.

"This must be wrong, Bella," he said, checking her on the step; "there are preparations for a party—it's the next house."

"No, this is right, Stanley. I forgot to tell you mamma has a few friends to-night," she said, hurriedly running up, and through the quickly opened door. "Come up at once, and let me introduce you to mamma before people come."

He followed her slowly, feeling annoyed and tricked in a small, low way. It was nothing to him, of course, whether Mrs. Vane saw "a few friends" every night—or every moment, for that matter—of her life. But it was much to him that Bella should make little concealments from him; it forced the unwilling conviction upon him that she was well inclined that way.

They found Mrs. Vane sitting in the drawing-room. She was very tall, very fair, very faded, very unlike her daughter in all respects; but there was something marvellously pleasing in her perfectly effortless manner. It was repose that sprang from the most thorough laziness—naturalism that was too indolent to be anything else. But it was pleasant to behold, and put you at your ease at once, it was so very perfect in its way. As soon as he saw Mrs. Vane, Stanley Villars understood how it came about that Bella was what she was.

The tall, fair, lymphatic woman rose up as they approached her, and kissed her daughter. Then she gave her hand to Stanley, and said, "You're to be my son-in-law, I find. I am very happy to see you." With that she sat down again; and while Bella made a rapid tour of the room, and buried her face in quick succession in several vases of flowers, inhaling their sweetness with a rapture that was partly real and partly put on to hide a trifling emotion she could not entirely subdue, Mrs. Vane looked at her hands, and smiled gently into space.

They were long, slender, white hands, that never writhed or contorted themselves. The most violent exercise they ever took, was when they inserted each other into gloves. Generally they sat upon her lap, resting one upon the other, with the taper fingers bent ever so slightly. Thus they would remain for hours with rarely a change in their position—never a change in their hue.

It needed but to see one of these hands of hers, and, without a glance at the remainder of the woman, all the weakness of her character might be read by those who ran.

"You won't dress till after dinner, please," Mrs. Vane said, looking from one to the other, appealingly, when Bella came back, after her inspection of the floral adornments.

"A great bore to dine in a travelling dress; one feels so dusty," Bella replied. "When was dinner to be ready, mamma?"

"Ten minutes after you came in," Mrs. Vane said, settling further back into her chair. "Have it your own way, dear—only order it yourself."

"Dine in your travelling dress for once, Bella, as your mother wishes it," Stanley whispered; "you will be obliged to make a wonderful toilet by-and-by, I suppose: but this dress will do to dine in."

In the Villars family the mother's will was law to her children—a law they loved to live under, and that they never thought of questioning. It pained him to see Bella put Mrs. Vane aside, weak as Mrs. Vane was.

"Do to dine in! It's not that; but I want to rest and refresh myself after that awful journey." Then she rang and ordered the dinner back half an hour, unceremoniously; and Mrs. Vane smiled perfect satisfaction at the alteration in her plans.

Stanley was dressed and down in the drawing-room again for some short time before the arbitrary queen of his soul. When she saw him come in by himself, Mrs. Vane appeared to feel that he devolved upon her, and forthwith she made conversational efforts.

"I am afraid the dinner will be spoilt, Mr. Villars; but it is of no consequence, as Bella wished it."

"On the contrary," he said, "Bella had no business to spoil your dinner; you must scold her if she has done so."

He saw that, even in joke, the idea of scolding Bella was a foreign one to Mr. Vane.

"Scold her!" she repeated; "really I shall not care about the dinner; and even if I did—" She paused for a moment, and then added, "Bella has so much energy; it is a great blessing that she has, for my health would never permit me to exert myself, so she has always pleased herself without troubling me, and I am sure no daughter could be a greater comfort to a mother."

Mrs. Vane was terribly afraid that Mr. Villars would be expecting her to control or direct Bella in some way or other. It was quite worth while verbally exerting herself to avoid such fearful labour as this. "No daughter could be a greater comfort to a mother than she has always been to me," she repeated emphatically; and then she tried to bribe him to let her suffer Bella to continue unmolested by maternal influence, by saying—

"I assure you, I don't think I could bring myself to resign her to any one but you."

Broadly speaking, this was sacrificing truth to politeness. Mrs. Vane would have brought herself to resigning Bella to any mortal man to whom Bella gave orders that she should be resigned. She knew very well that she would have done so; and, in a lazy kind of way, it occurred to her that most probably Mr. Villars knew it too. But she hoped that her little lapse from perfect veracity would sound pleasantly in his ears, and induce him to cease from troubling her about Bella's manners and customs, till Bella came down and could undertake the defence of them herself.

In due time Bella came down, and they dined; and Mrs. Vane awoke to an immediate sense of expecting people. "Bella has explained to you why we have friends to-night, Mr. Villars?" Mrs. Vane said to him about nine o'clock; and when he somewhat sulkily replied, "No, Bella had not," Mrs. Vane responded, "Oh!" in as thoroughly satisfied a tone as if her first suggestion had been founded on fact, or, which was more probable, as if it were not of the smallest consequence whether or not Bella had so explained.

To tell the truth, Stanley was feeling somewhat injured and neglected. Bella was taken up with a variety of matters with which she need not have been taken up during the few short hours he would still be with her. She was all the "daughter of the house," truly, but it was in an anticipatory sort of way that was not particularly flattering to him, the present guest. "I have something to say to you, Bella; come in here for five minutes," he had said to her, when they were journeying back to the drawing-room after dinner. He would not stay below and take wine drearily by himself; he wanted Bella to go with him for five minutes into a little room, through the open door of which he caught a glimpse of gleaming white statuettes backed against crimson velvet, and coloured wax candles cleverly interspersed amidst flowers in full bloom. He wanted her to go in there and hear the something he unguardedly confessed to her that he had to say, and Bella would not.

"I will attend to whatever you have to say directly, Stanley; but I must see to the guitar first. Mamma will expect me to sing, and of course all the strings will fly as soon as I touch them. I'll get that over first."

He did not relish this promise of attention being paid to him after the guitar's claims had been settled. But Bella, ensconced in her home duties, was unassailable. There was nothing for him to do but to wait her good pleasure.

Her good pleasure led her to make a very long and arduous business of that re-stringing the guitar, a business that it was irritating to him to watch. At the best of times, and under the happiest auspices, a guitar and himself were far from sympathetic. But now he was out of tune, and the guitar was the same; and he hated it, as an excuse, that was not even melodious, for lounging attitudes and languishing looks. Bella was employing herself with apparently laborious exactness about it now; but he felt that, when the few friends came, he should have cause to detest it and its blue ribbon.

Some of the friends came at ten, some shortly after. By eleven, at all events, Stanley knew the worst: all who were to arrive had arrived. Mrs. Vane was not that awful product of nature, a feminine seeker of celebrities. The class of women of whom Mrs. Leo Hunter may stand as the type are not indolent, let them be faulty in other respects as they will. Mrs. Vane was not one to assiduously look up the last living thing in literature, art, or the drama, and forthwith lure it into her web. But she was something almost equally distressing—a woman who took what came first, when it behoved her to take anything at all; and regarded all men (of her own class) as equal in mind, body, and social qualifications. Inertly amiable, and thoroughly well-disposed, she sat and smiled upon the people who came to stand about in the draught in her rooms, and eat wafer biscuits and ices; and never troubled herself to think whether they were amused or amusing. She invited them because, in the second year of her widowhood, the weaker-minded of Bella's two guardians had said to her, "My dear madam, you must keep up with the world. You must see people. Above all, you must see poor Vane's set, for your little girl's sake." She obeyed, because she saw no more reason for not seeing people than for seeing them. What good the vision was to do either herself or her child, or anybody else, she did not distress herself by attempting to discover. "Poor Vane's set" had been an elastic, not to say a limitless one. His widow was far from being sure where it began, or where it ended. This was of small consequence. There were plenty of people in the world, and she had no prejudices.

This being the case, it will readily be understood that her gatherings were variable in their nature. When Bella took the management of them into her own resolute young hands, salient points, in the shape of the best she knew, were put in, and their complementary colours provided for them. But when Mrs. Vane (as now) drifted into an evening party without her daughter's protection, the dull drab of inane mediocrity was apt to be over all things.

—o—

CHAPTER XVI.

JESUITICAL PRACTICES.

The best and bravest lose their individuality as soon as they find themselves at an evening party. The stoutest heart quails when its owner catches sight of himself in a glass with the remnant of the inane smile he called into being two minutes ago, when addressing some lady whom he did not want to address, and who did not want him to address her.

It is one of the absolute conditions that a portion of the "entertainment" shall be ghastly, even though it be held in one of the best houses in London. If you are in a proper frame of mind, that is to say, if you are honourable enough not to object to occupying a permanent position in the background, and healthy enough to dare to disregard the draughts which there abound, you may derive the finest enjoyment from an evening party; but not under any other circumstances.

What, for instance, can be pleasanter to witness, than the efforts a pretty girl makes to seem not to be trying to get away from some one who is boring her awfully? At the short distance of a yard and a half from said pretty girl, is a something else (probably an awful bore also in his generation), who wishes to say something to her which she wishes to hear, or thinks for the hour that she wishes to hear, which comes to the same thing, for all practical purposes. That girl is a victim. Her current shrine is an old lady perhaps, who only speaks to and detains her from bliss, because "it would look odd not to speak to her, having known her mother's uncle." Rest assured that the girl did not adorn for this sacrifice; but only see food for mirth in it, because it may save her from making a worse.

How nice it is, too, to witness the liberal manner in which people who give you worse than nothing, press you to take it. People who do this well, are really worth standing in the background in a draught for. They have an air of modest faith in themselves, and of wishing you not to over-estimate their little efforts on your behalf, that appeals to you as Genius only can. The hilarious manner is not a lasting one; it starts on a better foundation than the "liberal," but it is apt to break down on the first appearance of gloom amongst the guests. But the liberal manner, being founded upon nothing, flourishes to the last—a vigorous impostor.

Richer and rarer ("rarer" in the sense of "better") than all other spectacles that the evening party affords, is that one of members of the same family being driven up into a corner by the exigencies of fate, and there being compelled to talk company talk, with company faces and tones. Which is it?—sublime from its blind gallantry, or ridiculous from its foolhardihood, to hear a brother discussing the merits of "Faust" with his sister, or a husband giving and taking opinions with his wife about the last new novel? They only subside into these topics when any one approaches, and no one is blinded for an instant. One feels instinctively that there has been time enough at home for the question to be settled, and that it is only mooted here to avoid confusion. Perhaps we are all extra quick at this special bit of social detection, since we have all been guilty of the folly.

Mrs. Vane "saw her friends" in precisely the same way in which other people indulge in that spectacle. They came and stood about, and glanced furtively at the clocks, and addressed each other in vigorous accents whenever they fancied that either the hostess or her daughter, or any one likely to mention to the hostess or her daughter that they looked dull, were looking at them. In a mass they looked like other well-bred, well-dressed crowds. It was only when you analysed them that you found Mrs. Vane had omitted to secure one that was above mediocrity.

Bella was very weary of it all; in that at least—and to the eye of love it was very apparent—there was satisfaction. She glanced at the clock to the full as frequently as any one else, and in this there was joy, since she could not glance very often at him. "Do your best to make things go, Stanley," she said to him once. And he replied, "And people, too, if you like." At which she shook her head, and whispered, "You see my time in London won't be one of maddening excitement—will it? Dear mamma does ask the dullest people." After that she had not spoken to him any more, and he had borne his solitude nobly, partly because he did believe in her last assertion, and partly because he received no aggravation from the guitar. That instrument, after all the elaborate preparation that had been expended upon it, was left to its own devices in a corner, where it was gazed at fondly by a young man with tiny feet in cloth boots, with a big head, who wished the company to become acquainted with the fact that he warbled in Spanish whenever he was asked, and who found no good opportunity for telling them so in words that should induce them to ask him.

It was all very stupid, and superficial in fact, and no bewildering novelty from being these things. Very many things are stupid in this world; and the exceptional things, that we dare to like, break through quickly, and show us how hollow they are. There is nothing lasting save dulness and disappointment. Both Bella and Stanley Villars had come to the knowledge of the truth of this already, though old age was not their portion yet. But for all their knowledge of the truth, the special form their own dulnesses and disappointments took seemed exceptionally hard.

People went off as aimlessly, apparently, as they had come, about twelve. The only man who seemed to know what he was going to do with himself, or to have an object in life, was a stranger and a pilgrim amongst them. Stanley had, at an earlier stage, asked this man's name, of one with whom he found himself temporarily isolated, and he had been answered that "it was a man on the 'Extinguisher,'" a daily paper, the delight of millions. This man mentioned at large when he was about departing, that he was going to "do an article, and smoke with some other fellows at a tavern in the City;" and Stanley Villars gazed at him over his own white cravat with exalted contempt, and said a little sentence to himself respecting the prostitution of intellect, and the degradation of brains. He deemed that the man ought to have been ashamed of himself, and despised him for daring to be happy.

When every one was gone Bella portrayed intense sleepiness. "I, who have nothing more to do, feel such pity for myself for being tired," she said, when she had her bed-room candle in her hand. "How clever and wide-awake that man looked, who has been doing to the full as much as I have done all day, and who now has to go away and rack his brains to produce something that may be printed for us to read at breakfast."

Stanley looked down at her, superior as a god.

"Those poor fellows have a wonderful power of continuous work in them," he said, calmly; "but you must bear in mind that their productions are not meant to outlive the day. Feeling them to be ephemeral, they do not bestow the care on their composition that would involve much brain work."

"What is ephemeral in English, Stanley? Never mind explaining now. I am *so* tired, that I shall go off at once, and congratulate myself to sleep, on not having to write a given quantity in a given time, that I needn't bestow much brain-work upon."

"I shall see you before I leave in the morning?" he asked, anxiously.

"Oh, yes! of course," she replied, and then Mrs. Vane roused herself a little, and said—

"You won't go to-morrow, surely, Mr. Villars?"

"I shall leave you to argue the question with mamma," Bella interrupted. "Good night, Stanley."

She gave him her cheek to kiss, and he saw that it grew blood-red under his touch. Red with a sudden fire, that almost scorched his eyes to witness. Red, with a glow that scared certain hopes which were newly springing in his heart.

Miss Vane did not see Mr. Villars the following morning. He had arranged to leave by a certain train, and she knew it, and still did not find it convenient to rise in time to see him before he started to catch it. She sent down two or three delusive messages to the effect that she would make an almost immediate appearance; so till the last he thought she was coming, and drank his coffee in hope. But when the Hansom that had been sent for to speed the parting guest was announced, hope was extinguished by Miss Vane's maid, who met him in the hall, and told him the truth somewhat tardily: "Miss Vane had risen with one of her very bad headaches, and she (the maid) feared that there was no prospect of her being able to come down for an hour or two at least. Could Mr. Villars wait? Would there not be a later train?"

There would be a later train, but Mr. Villars could not wait. Unbelief set in strongly and submerged confiding love. He doubted that headache. It had come on rather too often lately for it to weigh with him as once it would have done. The truth, or rather a portion of the truth, struck him vividly. Bella did not want to see him, and listen to what he had to say, until the memory of Claude Walsingham had retreated further into the background. He thought that she craved time to restore her to her usual tone of mind. He deemed her semi-conscious of certain feelings which he accredited her with a desire to kill and have done with before she saw him again. That such feelings should have obtained at all was extremely undesirable, of course; but he was more lenient now than he had been in the first days of his engagement, the days of complete security and absolute faith, so he forgave her in his heart for evading him "for awhile," and went away sorry but not angry.

There were two flying visits that he believed himself bound to pay before quitting town. The one was to his mother, the second to his brother. They were necessarily brief; but during the first he had time to suggest to his mother and sisters that frequent intercourse with Bella would be desirable; and Sir Gerald found opportunity for telling him that the "affair," meaning the engagement, "was a source of great satisfaction to Carrie."

"She's very good to take such an interest in me," Stanley replied; and he could not help remembering, and allowing it to be perceived, that he did remember how very little interest his sister-in-law had hitherto taken in him. He also heard that the new son and heir was a young thing that they hardly dared to hope would live. Altogether, his latest London impressions were unpleasant ones; and still he felt no satisfaction in going back into the country.

It was now August, and in September the climax was to be brought about—so, at least, it had been ordained when this marriage prospect had been first started between them. But when he had been back at Denham a week, there came a letter from Bella pleading for a delay.

A letter that pained him, even more from its manner than its matter, though that was painful enough, heaven knows, to the man who wanted this woman for his wife! He had always marked with admiration, always loved to a degree, a certain fearlessness in Bella that led her to take the responsibility of her own opinions upon herself, even when she knew them unsound and antagonistic to his views. But now there was a touch less of this fearlessness. She pleaded for the delay in their marriage—"not out of the fulness of her own heart," she said, "but because the instincts of her friends were against such a short engagement."

Who were these friends whose instincts dared to step between happiness and himself? He asked this question fiercely of himself. He asked it little less fiercely of her by letter. He accused them of tampering with her with intent to wean her from him—of being false to him, whoever they might be, and untrue to her also, speciously as their counsels might be clothed. He told her that love such as he had offered and she had accepted and re-pledged to him, was a sacred thing from its intensity—far too sacred a thing for idle hands to play with, or put it aside for a time. He was far less of the good young priest in this letter, in fact, than she had anticipated; and she realised, with an aching soul, that he had the passions of a man, chilling as he had been to her sometimes at Denham.

She made no answer to those strong appeals of his. She wrote to him again after an interval of a few days, but she utterly ignored the subject—passed it over as though it had never been mooted. "I did not tell you when I wrote before," she said, "that I have my ponies; they are the chestnuts; and even Florence, who knows so little about horses, declares them to be perfection. You should see them step! They are quite equal to Major Walsingham's greys. I suppose Florence has told you that he is in town again? Mamma is much as usual, and I often wish myself back at Denham." Then she went on to speak of some new novel she had been reading, and new concert singer she had been hearing; and the letter drifted off into generalities.

But his eyes went back, and fastened themselves upon that passage in which Claude's name appeared in such a suspiciously casual way, before he read the rest that she had written. He gave no thought to the once-prohibited ponies. They were as nothing now.

His anger rose high against his sister as he read, "I suppose Florence has told you that he is in town again?" Florence ought to have told him, have warned him—ah! He shrank within himself as he thought of the word "warned" him. Of what should she "warn" him in relation to Claude, his friend, and Bella, his future bride? He killed the suspicion—or, rather, smothered it for a time, and finished her letter.

Then he turned to a heap of other epistles that were lying unopened on the table before him, and found that there was one from Claude.

"My dear Stanley" (it ran),

"I came up to town, unexpectedly, the day before yesterday. Curtailed my visit to them at home on account of a change in the regiment. I saw Florry yesterday driving with Miss Vane; this is the first I had seen of either of them since the Denham day. That affair which I spoke to you about is over. Be all your scruples set at rest: the lady wished to back out of it, therefore I had no appeal. Lord Lexley is the happy man who has superseded me. You wanted a dog-pup of that breed of red setters of my brother Jack's once I remember. Are you still in the mind for one? If you are, you will find one at your service any day you like to look in at my quarters and take him.

"Yours affectionately,

"Claude Walsingham."

Stanley Villars read that letter over many times, and, save in one small respect, it was entirely satisfactory. He could but feel that there was no desire on Claude's part to steal a march on him. Claude came back to town, on service, as he said, and immediately signalized that return frankly, and as frankly avowed that he had seen Miss Vane. There was no concealment, no evasion, no anything that there ought not to be. He had seen Miss Vane and Florence; and he mentioned the fact of having seen them, just as any other man writing to a familiar friend, would have mentioned it. So far all was satisfactory.

It was satisfactory, too, to know that the engagement Claude had entered into so lightly had been broken off in an equally airy manner—by the lady too! so that no blame could attach to Claude. It gave him great pleasure to read this statement, on the whole, though a portion of the phrasing—"the lady wished to back out of it, therefore I had no appeal"—grated on him harshly.

But what was not pleasant about Claude's letter was the manner in which he subscribed himself. The words "always truly" had been written first, but they had been dashed out with a stroke of the pen, and the word "affectionately" had been substituted. He asked himself, had doubts arisen in Claude's mind as to whether he should be "always true" to Stanley, and, with the doubt, some of the old schoolboy warmth of affection dictating the altered expression?

He wrote to his sister and questioned her guardedly, and felt like a Jesuit the while. Florence was so thoroughly true, so extremely unreserved, so entirely above suspicion, that he felt mean in being thus guarded. But then again he knew that whatever he wrote would be passed on to Bella, and this reflection induced him to couch the letter, whose mission it was to gain evidence about her, in very guarded terms.

Florence's reply came in due time. It was on rose-tinted paper and in rose-tinted terms; it was indited in a palpable tremor of happiness. "You ask about Bella's ponies; they are beautiful, and she drives them charmingly. We go into the park every morning—that is, we have been there three mornings and come back here to luncheon, and Claude comes too. He says if you won't come up for that puppy, that I shall have it. Do you consent?"

Stanley discovered little, save that Claude was in the ascendant with Florry, and that he had known before.

—o—

CHAPTER XVII.

A LAST FAVOR.

Have you ever felt a fever or an ague-fit coming on, and striven to cheat yourself into the belief that it was "only" a chill, or a heat, or a something which you knew all the while it was not? To the very last, till you are utterly worsted, till you are completely overthrown, till "keeping up" any longer becomes of no avail even in your own eyes, till Nature will not be lied to any longer, you deceive yourself, and say that it is not what you dread it to be.

As with the bodily ailment, so with the fever or ague-fit of the mind. We may feel miserably sure that by-and-by, in due course of time, we may be compelled to succumb to it altogether; but until we are so compelled, we affect extra health and security, and, alas! the affectation deceives no one, not even ourselves.

That August was a period of sultry, soul-subduing suspicion, of burning fear, of harassing perplexity and doubt, to Stanley Villars. He was very orthodox up to this date—orthodox in social as well as in religious matters. An engagement to enter, at no distant date, into a union for life, was no light thing in his eyes; and the one with whom he had entered into it seemed to regard it so lightly, so very lightly!

It will be well to record the events of this period briefly. It will be wise, if I would "hold my readers"—the novelist's proudest triumph!—to come quickly to that point from whence the chief interest of my story will flow—to pass on, without halting, to that time which passed over my hero's head in agony, and left him broken down.

During the greater part of that weary month he strove as hardly as man may strive to absorb himself in his duties, and be a priest of God. He was constant in prayer; he rang the villagers up at unheard-of hours, and caused them to be sleepily devotional at times when nought save their virtuous couches had known them heretofore. He was incessant in sickness; visiting, attending, relieving, in a way that brought down blessings that were heart-felt on his head. He would not relax in a single thing! He did all that was to be done in his vocation, and he did it thoroughly; and still he had time to think—time to be all a human being—nothing more.

Time was lightened and life brightened occasionally by letters from Bella Vane. He took such comfort as he might in them, marking how kind they strove to be, and how unconstrainedly Claude Walsingham was mentioned in them, and how regularly they came. The very thing that should have warned him lulled him into greater security; he had yet to learn that love has no routine—that there is no red-tapeism about real passion.

Time stood still, and life darkened to the darkness of death at last, one day when he received a letter from her, telling him that she could not keep the vow she had made. "He would hate and despise and forget her. For this she was prepared. She only craved his permission to go and bury her fallen head in freedom."

This was the whole purport of her letter, but he felt that there must be more behind it, and he cursed the cause of such a change in her, his cherished love. He knew that Bella Vane was not a girl to forfeit all that was sweet and warm and thrilling in life for the sake of going away to hide in solitude. What he had lost another had won—for Bella's heart was like Nature, in that it could not endure a vacuum. He knew this at once, and the knowledge made his heart stand still with a great rage that nothing could cast out; not even the recollection that he was a minister of that Gospel which inculcates forgiveness of our enemies, to say nothing of good-will towards all men.

He answered her prayer for release, and her supplication to be ignored by him, from that time forth for evermore, by going up and seeing her. This he did with no weak desire, no faint hope of turning her from her purpose, but simply because he burnt to learn from her own lips how that purpose had been born.

His going up at this juncture laid bare another misery to him; his life seemed full of gaping wounds, poor fellow! and he was powerless to stop the bleeding of any one of them.

Miss Vane had nothing to offer in extenuation of this change which had come over her. He asked for none indeed; he was only guilty of the minor folly of asking her "why she had not told him before?" She was a great beauty, and was in such a position that no one could say her nay; but for all that, she knew herself to be a pitiable spectacle as she stood before the man whose heart she had crushed, with so little to say for herself, which he could not read by the light of this new revelation.

The last few scenes in the first act of this drama shall be placed before you speedily.

There was a faint touch of ghastly humour over the final one in which he played a part when he went up to town. He was ushered unexpectedly into a room where the girl sat with her mother—the same room in which Mrs. Vane had seen her friend. His sudden appearance startled the quiet lady; she almost believed that he had come to put an end to all further discussion and doubt by insisting upon Bella's marrying him that moment. Almost believed, and quite hoped it; for, as she had plaintively remarked to Bella several times since the latter had told her that it was to be broken off, "What shall I say when people ask me about it? I would give worlds—yes, worlds—that this could be avoided, Bella!"

Thereupon Bella had told her mother somewhat peremptorily that it could not be avoided, and that therefore the best had better be made of it. "Besides, mamma, I don't see why you should feel bound to give an account of it; you were not the one who was going to marry him, and now you're not the one who is *not* going to marry him."

"Mrs. Melville has been so very much interested, that she will come to me about it directly it gets abroad; I know she will!" Mrs. Vane urged almost tearfully. "What will your guardians say? What will people think?"

"Really, mamma, I don't care what they think," Bella replied, coldly; "there is no sting to me in public opinion about such a matter as this—it is too entirely to ourselves."

"It's terrible—after all your things are made, too!" Mrs. Vane went on, not heeding her daughter's words.

"That's the least part of it, dear mother," said Bella. "Don't prick me with trifles! I am sorry enough."

"Then why break it off?" Mrs. Vane responded; "I hope you won't. I do so dread being questioned and having to tell the whole story, for I'm sure I don't understand it!"

"Then you can plead ignorance, and save yourself the trouble."

"That will strike people as being most extraordinary," Mrs. Vane replied, gently shrugging her shoulders. If mild advice, that she had not to move to offer, might possibly avert these evils, Mrs. Vane was ready to offer it.

"I do not care whether it strikes people as being extraordinary or not," Bella answered, speaking with a passionate energy, that came partly from the conviction that she was acting ill towards another, and partly from a suspicion that others had not always acted well by her. "If they knew," she went on recklessly, "it might strike them as a little extraordinary also, that you have never taken the smallest trouble to find out what I was doing or going to do all my life; you left me to get new toys for myself when I broke my old ones, when I was a child!—let me do the same now!"

"Really, Bella, I have no desire to interfere with you; but I shall *not* know what to say when people question me."

"Refer them to me for an answer, if you like." Then her face softened suddenly, and she added, "Oh, mother! I wish that what a pack of idle, curious, gossiping old women may say about it were the worst I had to dread! I do suffer, indeed I do; but it is about something so widely different. The common cry will never cut me—how can you care for it?"

Mrs. Vane thought she saw a good opening for the insertion of the small end of an argument, capable of overturning everything.

"Because I think it a most shocking thing, as does every one else who thinks properly. From the moment I was engaged to your father, or, at any rate, from the moment my trousseau was commenced, I no more thought it possible to break it off, than I would have thought it creditable to run away from him after I was married. If you could fulfil your engagement to Mr. Villars, it would be very much better."

"It would be very much better, but I can't," Bella replied, curtly; and she had hardly uttered the words before Stanley Villars came into the room.

Bella was not surprised to see him. When she wrote and begged him to forget her at once and for ever, she knew that he would not do so; she felt sure that he would come. She had seen, as in a vision, the very expression that was on his face as he entered.

They shook hands, and Bella found it so like the ordinary meeting of ordinary mortals who were not about to cut each other to the quick, that she commenced the conventional "I am very happy to see you." But she checked herself at the third word, and sat down with a trembling in both her tongue and knees.

"I was saying to Bella, just before you came in," Mrs. Vane began by way of putting them at their ease; "that I am very, very much concerned at all this, Mr. Villars; I hope, now you have come——"

"Mother! mother!" Bella interrupted, pleadingly, "don't say anything—there is nothing to be said."

He had seated himself also when Bella broke down in her welcoming phrase, and now he was resting his chin on his hand, leaning on the table, and looking at her fixedly.

"There is nothing to be said!" he repeated after her. "Yes, there is one thing to say; I have one last favour to ask of you!"

She made a deprecating movement with her hands. This giving-up tone into which he had fallen stabbed her more than reproaches would have done. She felt now how she had wronged him, when she supposed that he would strive to keep her to himself at any cost—to her.

"Don't speak in that way!"—she almost sobbed the words out. "Oh! if you knew—if you knew——"

There was nothing cruel or hard in her nature. She could stab, and wound, and wrong; but her heart bled the while she did these things. Her worst fault was instability.

"I will say it to Claude, then," he answered; "one of you must hear me."

At the mention of Claude's name, Bella gave a little, guilty, quickly subdued start, and Mrs. Vane asked, "Who's Claude?" in a tone that, miserable as he was, brought the advertisement "Who's Griffiths?" with which enterprise has adorned the walls of our metropolis, vividly before Mr. Villars' eyes.

"It is not his fault," Bella began; "if any one is to blame——"

"There is no one to blame in the matter," Stanley muttered impatiently; "no one is to blame—only I am damned unfortunate!"

She knew how she had wrung him then, when she heard him say that. She dared not reprove him for the force of that expression: she scarcely dared to look as if she had heard it. She trembled for him, and for herself, and above all, for Claude, should Stanley go to him in this frame of mind. Besides, she would be shamed by his going to Claude, for between Claude and herself there had been no words—no shadow of an explanation that could justify his being incriminated with her in this evil. Still, on such light accusation as Stanley had made, would she be justified in attempting to excuse herself? There was but one course for her to pursue; she was a woman, and she threw up her hand.

"Claude does not know what I have done—he would never have asked me to do it. Don't hurt him, Stanley. Don't blame him!"

She called him "Stanley" with all the tenderness she so well knew how to throw into her tone; but though his own name was uttered, the tenderness was for his rival now.

Disloyal as she had been to him, desperately as he had been deceived in her, he could but feel tenderly, pityingly towards her, as the pleading tones fell upon his ears, and the anxious eyes met his own. He forgot in that moment that soon tenderness and pity felt for her would be treading on dangerous ground for himself, and on treacherous ground as regarded the friend who had been treacherous to him. He forgot everything, even the presence of her mother, as he went up to her and held her in a strong embrace, from which she could not free herself.

"My love! I would hold you here against God, and the world, and the devil, if you cared to stay—if I could!"

The agony he felt in his full consciousness of his powerlessness to do it, came out in the hoarse fervour with which he uttered the last three words. She dared not struggle against that embrace.

"If I could, if I could!" he repeated hotly; and, as in a glass, she saw dimly a day in the far future when her heart should be chilled, and should yearn for a particle of that fiery passionate heart to which now it could not respond.

Suddenly he released her, and she staggered and sat down on the chair from which he had raised her, her eyes still fixed on his face apparently, but in reality on that visionary future day. By a strong effort he conquered his emotion presently—conquered it, that is, sufficiently to hear and comprehend Mrs. Vane's mild "Pray be calm, Mr. Villars!" and to realise that the effect of such an embrace on a woman who no longer loved would be to disgust her with him further. The thought, the possibility, struck him with a new despair; he could not be banished, be hated, be left in every way by this woman who had sunk into his soul!

"Forgive me!"—he asked it as humbly as if he had injured her. "Bella, let me be your friend and his, and I will never be mad or offend you again!"

She tried to smile, and the effort broke down her self-control, and caused the tears to flow out freely from the sweet, kind-looking blue eyes, that would always go on seeking, seeking still something more to look fondly upon. Then she gave him her hand, and, as he pressed it, and poured forth some incoherent words about being permitted "to watch over and guard her still," the black retriever, faithful Rock, came out wagging his tail, and almost smiling, and stood up against him, licking the hands thus linked together.

"Will you take Rock?" she asked in a whisper; "he's very fond of you."

He saw that it was some sort of poor salve to her conscience to give him the dog that was dear to her. He felt that she would be the happier for this poor bond still existing between them, and with that curious clinging to what might be left to him of the old—with a strange gratitude for such a man to feel—he took the crumbs that fell from the rich man's table: he accepted the boon.

"I will take your last gift; and now, good-bye. I shall not see you again till your wedding-day." Then he bent his head down and whispered, "The favour I shall ask of Claude is, that I may marry you to him!"

CHAPTER XVIII.

BROKEN OFF.

The light was dim, though not remarkably religious, in Claude Walsingham's quarters, when Stanley Villars entered them that night, some hours after that last scene with Miss Vane. An aromatic haze hung over all things, and through it the forms of three men loomed largely. "A smoking orgie," Stanley thought, with a momentary disgust: "it's neither the time nor the place to speak of *her;* and yet she must be spoken of before Claude and I part again."

He went in, and sat down in a low chair, at the end of the couch on which Major Walsingham had been lounging, when he entered, Claude meeting and greeting him as he came along, and noticing the dog Rock, who followed close at his heels, with an angry wonder that he (Claude) was unable to conceal from Stanley.

"Glad to see you, old fellow. Is this meant as a delicate hint that you don't want the setter pup?" Major Walsingham asked, patting Rock on the head; and Stanley answered—

"It is not meant as a delicate hint about anything—that you're not well acquainted with already." This he said in so low a voice that the other two men could not hear him. Claude heard him, however, and leant forward tendering him a cigar and a light from the end of his own, and asked—

"What is it, Stanley? speak out!"

Stanley gave two little puffs, and the cigar caught the spark from the end of the one that was a burning and shining light in the mouth of his friend. Then he leant back, saying—

"The dog is all that I'm to have: you won't grudge me that, will you?"

"They leave me at ten to see the last act of 'Fidelio:' wait till they're gone, for God's sake!" Claude replied hurriedly. He saw that Stanley Villars was in a humour to speak out and say rash things, perhaps, without a care or a thought of who heard them. Foreseeing the nature, in a measure, of those things, he was desirous to stay the saying of them till such time as they (Stanley and he) should be alone together.

The two men who were sharing in what Stanley Villars had declared to himself to be a "smoking orgie" when he entered, were two of the same men who had gone down to Richmond on the drag that warm July night, and congratulated Claude on his victory over many things. They were not gifted with extraordinary perceptive faculties, still they had marked that Claude seemed rather more than a "trifle taken with the girl who was going to throw herself away upon a country parson." They had seen him bring his greys up abreast of her chestnuts several times in the drive. They had observed him far back in her mother's box at the opera, even when Circe sang. They had seen him riding by her side in the Row, which last sight was conclusive evidence in their eyes that he was "going to try it on with her," his detestation of the Row being an understood thing. Stanley Villars' advent appeared to afford promise of a piquant study. They therefore resolved to forego "Fidelio," and abide the issue of said advent here in Claude's room.

The hour—ten—approached, arrived, passed: all four men began to get impatient. The old friends, who felt themselves, and were felt by these comparative strangers, to be rivals, wanted to be alone in order to say those things to each other which the interlopers trusted might leak out under the influence of wine, smoke, and excitement. Unfortunately, however, as far as their curiosity was concerned, both Claude and Stanley were gentlemen. No vintage so potent as to make them forget the respect due to a lady's name, small cause as one of them had for so respecting her.

Still their hearts, and heads, and thoughts, were all too hot for cool, sensible converse to be within the bounds of possibility, when they were finally left alone. The "good nights" of Claude's unwanted guests had scarcely ceased echoing in their ears when Stanley Villars commenced—

"I have seen Miss Vane to-day," and stopped abruptly, thinking over how he had sworn to himself not to see her as Miss Vane again till the day when he should unite her to his friend.

"Well!" Claude answered doggedly. He felt guilty, how guilty! True he had never spoken words to her that should not have fallen on the ears of the betrothed bride of his friend; but the manner of his refraining from such words had been fraught with a tender danger that no spoken words could have aggravated, and he knew it. I do not think that he felt repentant at that moment, but unquestionably he felt guilty; and feeling so, feeling guilty, and grieved for himself and for her, and for this old friend who had made the romance of his boyhood, he answered, doggedly, "Well!"

"Well!" Stanley repeated after him; "is it well? You shall hear and judge. She was to have been my wife, you know; she was to have been my wife this month! I loved her so—I loved her so, that I would have given my life, my soul, by God, for her! Don't look at the brandy, Claude; I'm not drunk! I'm not avowing a readiness to go to perdition under any other intoxicating influence than the intoxication of disappointment. 'Well,' as you said just now, the dog is all that is left to me of the dream. She can't keep her vow now her love has left me. Do you hear me, old fellow?"

He did not look in his friend's face as he asked "did he hear?" He sat down again, and covered his eyes with his hands, and the dog that she had given him stood up and licked away the tears that were oozing through his fingers. Thus he sat, thus Rock and himself grouped themselves for a few minutes, during which Major Walsingham went through the elementary white bear evolutions up and down the length of the room.

Claude was horribly perplexed. He did not know what to say; more, he did not know what to think: worse than this even, he could not decide on what it would sound well to say. The position was an awfully unpleasant one; for he had loved Stanley as warmly as he had loved any one till this woman with the flickering eyelashes and flickering faith had come between them. He could not deem himself wholly blameless in the matter either; and yet it would be a task of no small difficulty to say in so many set words how he had erred.

He brought his promenade to a termination at last, and stood close by Stanley's shoulder.

"I'd give half my life that none of this had occurred!" he said, softly.

"Too late! it has occurred!"

"It has, as you say," Claude went on, speaking in a firmer tone than the one in which he had uttered his previous words; "it has occurred; bear it like a man, old fellow!"

The other dropped the concealing hands—dropped them down on the honest head of the tawny dog who was standing close up to him, and raised his pale, pain-lined face. That's devilish easy for you to say, Claude," he said slowly. "In losing her I lose my faith in all I have had faith in hitherto—in God and man, and, worse than all, in myself; it has all gone at one blow."

"It will come back. We have all gone through this sort of thing."

"Have you? By heaven, *no!* If you had, you would never have put me through it," Stanley interrupted. It was the first allusion either of them had made to Claude's share in this disruption in the established order of things. Major Walsingham said nothing in reply to this immediately. He was feeling that if he noticed it and defended himself, it would have the appearance of casting the reflection upon Bella that she had been over easy to win, and this he scorned to do, though Miss Vane certainly had "had no cunning to be strange," as far as he was concerned.

After a brief period of silence he spoke—

"Why did you keep me at Denham, when I wanted to come away?"

"Don't speak about it!" Stanley said, miserably. Then he added, in that contradictory spirit which is so symptomatic of the disease under which he was labouring, "You have seen her here in town; leaving Denham would have been of no avail. Don't explain—don't excuse yourself by telling me how it has been done; why should you? all is fair in love or war."

"Stanley! on my honour, there has been

nothing premeditated! 'All is fair.' What are you thinking of? I would have cut off my right hand sooner than run against you in such a race. It's fate, old fellow—blind fortune. Don't you think I suffer as much in winning, if I have won, from you, as I should in losing to any other man? Can you not believe me? Is this thing to come between us and blot out the warm feelings and the confidence of years? By God, no woman's worth it!—no, not the sweetest and purest that ever stepped!"

"Don't undervalue what you have gained. There will be poor comfort to me in the thought that she may possibly be judged less highly by you than she would have been by me if she—could—have—kept to me." His voice faltered a little as he said this, and Claude turned away impatiently. Had Major Walsingham alone been concerned, he would willingly at that moment have restored Miss Vane to Stanley; he really did feel that no woman was worthy of this sorrow that could even temporarily subdue such manliness. The game was a pretty one enough, and an interesting one to play, but scarcely worth the candle.

But he was not alone concerned. Bella had put forth all her strength, and broken the bonds; or she had exerted all her feminine ingenuity, and wriggled out of them. It was out of his power to re-adjust them on Stanley's behalf. There was nothing to be done, save to make the best of it.

"Look here, old fellow, we only torture each other by talking about it; from the bottom of my soul I regret my share in the business."

"From the bottom of mine I forgive you," poor Stanley replied; "we'll have done with the topic for ever, if you will, when you have answered me one question—granted me one favour."

"Ask it."

"Let me be the one to join you to her when you do marry her?"

Claude moved uneasily; this request seemed to him romantic in the last degree—romantic, foolish, idle—everything that was most unlike Stanley Villars. He no more fathomed the motive which had dictated it than did the dog which stood gazing at him while he hesitated to answer it.

"I don't attach much importance to the 'holy ceremony,' you know," he said at last; "it's womanly, though, not to be satisfied with a civil contract."

"The 'holy ceremony,'" Stanley repeated after him; "at any rate, I may as well perform it as any other man. Do you say 'Yes?'"

"Yes."

"Agreed! And now we will never speak of these things again. Good night, Claude; be happy, old boy, and—and—don't think that I am not so too!"

Stanley Villars did not see his sister Florence that night, though he went to his mother's house, scandalising her orderly domestics by arriving at such an unholy hour, and slept through what was left of it. When he came down the following morning, Florence came to meet him as soon as he opened the door; and she looked so brightly beautiful, so happy and blooming, that it almost jarred upon him

"Dear Stanley, why didn't you let us know you were coming!" Florence asked.

"I dare say Bella knew," Lady Villars said, getting up to give her son a warmer welcome.

"No, she didn't. Where's Georgie?" he asked, rather absently. He wanted to tell out the truth at once; he wanted them all to hear it, in order that there might be no repetitions.

"Georgie is staying with Gerald and his wife."

"In Scotland, are they not?"

"Yes, Mr. Manners is with them. They hope that Bella and you will go to them when you come back from wherever you're going on the Continent. When is it to be, Stanley?"

"Never!" Stanley said. "Don't express surprise, or anything else, for mercy's sake, mother!"

Lady Villars controlled all expression, not alone of surprise, but of the horrible disappointment she felt at this downfall of her son's prospects. She had sincerely rejoiced in the contemplated alliance, for Stanley was her pet son; and, alas! he was the younger one.

"Broken off," she faintly articulated at last; "my poor boy! my poor, dear boy!"

"How, Stanley? why?" Florence asked, going up and clasping her arms over his shoulder, and leaning her head down upon his chest. "You haven't quarrelled—she loves you so! Can't it be made up?"

"Don't be a little fool," he replied, almost roughly; "it's all over, I tell you. Love me! that's absurd now. She is going to marry Claude Walsingham!"

This was the moment when that other misery, to which I have alluded in a former chapter, was laid bare to him. As he spoke in those rough accents, and accents that it went against his heart then, even in the midst of his own anguish, to use to Florence, she shrank away from him with a cry of "No! no! no!" and a shiver that seemed to wither, as it passed over her frame.

"My God! my poor darling! there's not *this* in addition to my own wretchedness?" he cried, taking her in his arms again. "He has not been a scoundrel to us *both?*" he interrogated, as his mother came up and kissed Florence on her now flame-coloured forehead, and sighed that "she had feared it all along; that she had always distrusted Major Walsingham, and enjoined caution on Florence."

"How should caution have availed her when he made her love him, as, to my cost, I know he *can* make a woman love?" Stanley said in answer. Then Florence shuddered and drew away from him, and played a portion of that little mock heroic part which custom commands that women shall play on such occasions.

"I was only the more sorry and surprised because it was Claude," she said, with a gulp over his name. "It wasn't for myself, Stanley. Don't think anything; don't! don't! Promise you won't!"

"The other I might have forgiven, but not this double treachery," he replied.

"There has been no treachery," Florence said, trying to speak firmly in order to carry conviction to her brother's heart.

"It is a folly that you will soon—that you *must* soon conquer, dear," her mother interposed. Lady Villars was a loving parent, tender and considerate to her children. But for all that tenderness and consideration, she could not suffer Florence to be encouraged to destroy her earliest bloom, and so injure her prospects, by weeping over the defalcation of one who, whether he had loved or not, had undoubtedly ridden away.

It was almost as if there had been a death in the house that day. The usual order of things was rudely interrupted. There was no future sister-in-law sending round an intimation of her intention to call Florence for a drive, as had been the custom lately. There was no Claude to be hoped for all the morning, and found at the luncheon table. Lady Villars, feeling that she could not assuage the sorrow which had come upon her children, retired to her own room and wrote a long account, or, rather, many pages of conjectures, as to the real cause of Bella Vane's change of faith, to her eldest son, Sir Gerald. It was a bitter grief to her that the girl whose money would have placed Stanley so well, whether he clung to his profession or not, should have turned round at the last and bestowed it on the man whose dallying around Florence had been for many months a source of annoyance to her. But though she lamented on Stanley's account, and censured Bella with a warm censure in which there was no toleration, she refrained from saying a word about either Claude or Florence. The mother remembered that her eldest son was a married man, and that young Lady Villars was one who would not suffer a telling story to die out for want of frequent repetition, even were it against her nearest. All she said about her daughter, therefore, was—"Florry feels this dreadfully, knowing (as I do also) that Stanley will never make another scheme of happiness. Miss Vane has wronged us all cruelly by being so falsely fond. He will never forget it; and while he remembers, his life will be barren."

For many hours after that disclosure Florence strove to avoid her mother, her brother, even the light of day. A sort of ague, that increased directly it was looked upon, seized her; and so she crept away to a corner of her bedroom, between the wall and the heavy masses of curtain that fell from a ring in the ceiling over her bed, the shade of which partially concealed her. She had neither been fickle, heartless, unstable, nor false. But she suffered as much pain and as much shame as though she had been all these things. When she thought of Claude she could scarcely lift her eyes from the ground. He had been the deceiver, but it was the deceived that was abashed, and suffered bitter woe at the memory of the deception.

Superadded to her own sorrow at losing the hope that the love which she thought a more glorious thing than God's sun would eventually be pledged openly, as it had been persistently proffered to her mutely for long, was the heartache she had for her brother. Hard as her own case was, his she felt to be an infinitely harder one. He was deceived by both friend and love; she by her heart alone!

So she told herself; for even to herself she would strive to vindicate Claude; even to her own heart she told the white lie that removed the semblance of dishonourable dealing from him. He had been kind, gentle, and loving to her in what she ought to have felt to be what it was, a brotherly way only. As she thought of some of his brotherly kindnesses she would break down for a minute or two with the sickening consciousness that they had clouded her life in a way brotherly kindnesses should never have done; and then she would battle with the external display of emotion and do away with the signs of it, remembering that she must see Stanley again at luncheon, when every tear-stain on her face would recall to him that which it behoved her to try and teach him to forget.

She was very loyal to her brother, but she was loyal to her woman's nature too. She wished to think of Stanley only, but some superior behest—whether God-given or not, who shall say?—made her think almost entirely of Claude.

She hardly dared to raise her eyes to Stanley's face when she found herself seated opposite to him again. She dreaded what she might see there. It seemed to her a sort of treason to be observant of aught that Stanley himself could wish unseen. When she did at last, in answer to some question he addressed to her, raise her eyes to his and nod assent, she found that he was looking at her very steadily, as though he desired to read all that she desired to conceal.

"You have been having a hard time of it this morning, Florry," he said compassionately; "don't try to tell me no, little one!" he added, hastily rising up and going round to her and clasping her to his heart, as a man would clasp the one thing he felt to be true to him when the one to whom he was most true had given that heart a deadening blow.

"I am so foolish," she murmured; "only for you though, dear! only for you!"

He tried to believe her, for he desired to believe her. If he did not credit this statement of hers, he could not ask her to do something for him which he wanted done. He was not that exceptional thing, an entirely unselfish man, therefore he strove to credit his sister's statement of her sorrow being for him alone.

"Will you do something that I would not ask another woman in the world to do for me, Florry; that no other woman, save my sister Florry, would be noble enough to do?"

"Yes, anything."

The love that not even perfidy and light regard of his mighty claims on her could quell welled up for Bella Vane and cast out his consideration for his sister.

"Be a friend to Bella should she ever need you, Florry. Promise me that you will not avoid her should she seek you. Promise me that you will never let her guess that you have cause for suffering in connection with her, independent of my share in this affair."

"You ask me, Stanley?"

"I entreat you to do this."

"I will, dear. But how should she want me? Why should she need a friend? Why should I trouble her, even? She will have Claude! She will be so happy!"

Not all her gentle sweetness; not all her love for her brother; not all her modest doubt of Claude's ever having entertained more than a brotherly fondness for her, could soften or subdue the sharp, poignant, bitter ring of genuine jealousy with which these words rang out. "She will have Claude! She will be so happy!" They painted vividly a whole series of pictures of Claude and Bella, happy and together, that were maddening to look upon. They brought with hideous clearness to the mind of the one who listened, Bella's caressing words and ways; and to the one who spoke, Claude's mighty power of tenderness.

"She will have Claude; but make her happiness while you may, for it will not last long," he said at last; and Florry sobbingly rejoined, "I promise; I promise."

——o——

CHAPTER XIX.

OVER THE PRECIPICE.

It can hardly be told how the fair and perfect understanding which it was necessary should subsist came about between Major Walsingham and Bella Vane. Their first meeting after that last scene with Stanley was very awkward, for not even to woman is given the exquisite tact to utterly ignore all that has been held most binding and most holy, in an instant. The next interview was less embarrassing, however; and the next (they were both so young, and were in such perfect health—the secret of more than half the joyousness of the world) was all that could be desired in the way of blest oblivion.

Bella stood to these newly-cast guns of hers stoutly; and she had some need for the display of all her strength. A great many wearing obstacles obtruded themselves, in the shape of irrelevant prayers from her guardians, and a lot of people who were loosely connected with her, to "be careful *this* time, and not to hastily rush into a *second* error."

But she was young, and her health was very perfect, so she stood to her guns gallantly, and never fired a shot in anger. Indeed, this period may be judged to have been far from an unpleasant one, for Claude was so devoted to her that they both forgot to speak of or to seek Florry Villars.

Miss Vane decided, on very good solid grounds, that she had chosen the better part, and been wise in throwing over the old love for this new one, who never dictated to her in arbitrary tones, or strove to rule her in right lines harshly. She contrasted Claude's non-exacting spirit with Stanley's slightly domineering one, and the contrast showed Claude off favourably. She began to bless that luckless ride which had brought Major Walsingham and herself together under circumstances that had proved so eminently conducive to feelings that it behooved them both in honour to have check. She sang full many an inward jubilate over that morning stroll under the green trees in the cathedral close, and gave the feelings which she had held in with a tight hand that day full play, now that she dared to do so.

It was a glorious time of triumph, and she thought scarcely at all of Stanley, and never at all of Florence during it. But they thought of her. With a feverish, incessant pertinacity, that would not be quieted, this brother and sister had the memory of this girl, and her pretty, pettish ways, ever before them. He, running the round of duties down at Denham, that had become not alone arduous, but odious to him, would wonder restlessly when he should be summoned to consummate the sacrifice, and mock his own heart by repeating the formula that he had once held holy; while Florence strained her eyes daily, when out for a drive with her mother, in order not so much that she might see them, as that she might see to avoid them.

Clearly Bella had no need of a friend as yet. Florence was not put to the sore test by which her brother had desired to try her. The girls had been very friendly, after the manner of girls; but when, in October, some of Claude's relations, amongst others one of his sisters, came up, and asked Bella, "How did she and the Villars' meet? She had had one of the girls staying with her, had she not?" Bella answered, with ever so little of a blush, and with no shadow of contrite embarrassment—

"Oh, yes! but that was long ago. We should be friendly enough if we met, I dare say, but we never *do* meet. I wrote to her once after *that* (you know), and she answered me very kindly. Don't speak about it before Claude, for he doesn't like it!"

This reputed prejudice of Claude's was respected to the letter by his own family; they none of them offended him by the most distant allusion to his predecessor in the heart of Miss Vane. He marked their reticence, and, half fancying that it sprang from some doubt of the prudence of his choice, he resented it by still greater reserve, which reacted upon them, rendering them more reticent still.

Bella herself would talk cheerily enough to him about Stanley. "He was too good and too hard for me. I never loved him really, I'm ashamed to say. What carried me away to the point of such forgetfulness of what I knew my needs to be, as to engage myself to him, I can't think. I wanted 'warmth and colour,' like Queen Guinevre, and that I found in you, Claude."

"If I have been Launcelot to you hitherto, I warn you I shall be Arthur henceforth," he said; and Bella replied, "Oh, yes! Arthur, without the unpleasantness."

It was not wholly disagreeable to Claude to hear that Stanley Villars had ever been cold and hard to Bella, even while betrothed to her. He did not entirely believe it, but still the hearing it was pleasanter than the hearing records of impassioned sympathy would have been. That Stanley had had hot love in his heart for Bella he felt firmly convinced. He also felt firmly convinced that Stanley had never suffered the utmost fervour of that heat to betray itself to her, for Bella sagaciously kept the story of that last meeting and parting embrace to herself.

It was in the last ruddy October days that the marriage was to take place, and a brief notice of this fact was forwarded to Stanley, according to promise, by the happy expectant bridegroom. The answer to this notice assured Claude that he (Mr. Villars) would be there at the time appointed. After it came they forgot, or seemed to forget him again.

Comparatively speaking, it was to be a very quiet wedding. They had erected this new fabric too quickly on the ashes of the old for it to seem well to those who had the organisation of it to bid many to the opening spectacle. But, quiet as they determined that the wedding should be, and few as were the guests whom they cared to assemble, it gave them a power of trouble.

In the first place Mrs. Vane, Bella's indolent mamma, unexpectedly roused herself, and declared that it would be an indecent exhibition of carelessness of what had gone before to allow Stanley Villars to perform the ceremony. It was in vain that Bella avowed that it was "nice and natural of Stanley to wish to do it, since he desired to be friendly with Claude and herself." Mrs. Vane could not deny her natural maternal instincts. She doubted the desire for future intercourse of a merely friendly order, and remembered that embrace which she had witnessed that day when the final blow was struck at the last contemplated alliance.

"You must argue the question with Claude, mamma," Bella said, at last; "he agreed to Stanley's request. That being the case, I do feel that no one else has any excuse for saying a word against it."

Even to this extent—the extent of arguing with Claude—did Mrs. Vane go, in her desire to avert this thing, from which she felt no good could accrue.

"It will be a needless trial to all your feelings," she urged, and Claude answered—

"No trial to mine; and if Stanley's half as sensible as I take him to be, none to his either, after this lapse of time. At any rate, my dear madam, if we are to be had up at all, like criminals at the bar, before the altar, for a mob to stare at, it must be under Stanley's auspices. I'd prefer going through some simpler ceremony —say jumping over a broomstick, or going to a registrar's office; but perhaps you would hardly feel satisfied about your daughter."

On hearing which, Mrs. Vane lifted up the hands of her soul in dumb amaze, and said no further words that were antagonistic to that plan regarding Stanley Villars.

After this a second and a mightier annoyance arose. It has been seen that some of Major Walsingham's relations had come up and made the acquaintance of the bride. But they were minor relations—sisters and younger brothers, and such small deer. Claude wanted his parents to come up and do honour to the alliance, and the woman with whom he was going to make it. He had asked both his father and mother to come, but he had been especially urgent that his mother should do so, and his mother steadfastly declined to pleasure him in this. She would not come. Worse than this, she wrote him four pages of reasons why she would not do so, and none of these reasons were soothing to him. She was ill pleased at his choice: a heart so lightly won and lightly lost, as she affected to believe Miss Vane's must have been, was not the heart that should have beaten within the breast of the wife of the hope of her house. She distrusted Miss Vane; she disliked that complete abnegation of all the old ties of friendship with her late lover's family, of which report said Miss Vane was now guilty. All this she said in so many straightforward words to her son, and the reading it was disturbing.

"It's devilish hard that because a girl can't control her affections she is to be regarded in this way!" Claude said to his sister, who had received a corresponding letter. "Bella is impressionable—a grave offence in my mother's eyes. I shall never take her down there."

"Oh yes, you will!—take her down and all will be well. Mamma is a little rigid, perhaps; but it all comes of her anxiety for your happiness, Claude."

"Bella will be awfully hurt at this definite refusal to come to our marriage," he said, rather sadly. "I thought my mother would have done me so much grace as that."

However, when he told Bella that his "mother found she could not come," he was surprised (he scarcely knew himself whether agreeably or not) to find that Miss Vane was most unfeignedly indifferent about it. "Oh! can't she, Claude? Let me see, that's one—two, indeed, for we counted your father—off the list, for sure!"

When her marriage morning came Miss Vane neither was, nor did she feign to be indifferent. She was as nervous, despite her experiences, as an author over a first review. She could but remember vividly—she could but feel conscious that others were remembering vividly—the widely different conditions under which, but the other day, she had thought to stand at the altar with Stanley Villars. For the first time she felt that her mother's objections to him as the uniting medium were good, valid, and reasonable. For the first time it struck her that Claude had been wanting in delicacy of feeling in acceding to a request that had been made under most disordering circumstances. It was all too late to alter things, however, so she kept her just awakened scruples to herself, and resolved to go through it all, as though it all seemed fair and smooth to her, as it did to the majority of the idle, unenlightened lookers-on.

But it was far from being fair and smooth to her. It was an awful ordeal to stand there, and hear the words that were binding her to another uttered by the man who had avowed the hottest passion for her when last they met. It was hard to know what he felt for her, and then to hear him asking her to vow, before God, to love, honour, and obey the one who had wrested her from him. It was hard to have him taking her hand and Claude's together! Thoughtless as she was, there was not one touch of baseness in her nature—her whole soul revolted at this. But harder than all else was it to hear him utter the final blessing, in tones that told her fully that he felt how idle the words were—how weak, after all that had gone before.

He meanwhile found himself marvelling, with a strange composure, whether custom had so monstrously distorted her naturally bright understanding as to render her oblivious of the ghastly incongruity which was the distinguishing characteristic of the occasion. In his presence could she possibly forget that at "the dreadful day of judgment, when the secrets of all hearts shall be disclosed," an "impediment" to so brisk an alteration as she had made in her scheme of life, should have to be confessed? Or had she thrown the pieces of the broken troth aside, as we do a shattered vase or a fractured glove, either of which may be replaced at our earliest opportunity?

He decided in favour of deeming her guilty of the utter oblivion. Because she, remembering all too well as she did, dared not permit herself to show that she remembered aught, he fancied her to be just thus much more thoughtless and careless than she was. A woman must always be misjudged in such a case as this: she is arraigned at the bar of individual opinion, and common prudence forbids that she shall attempt to offer evidence in her own defence to that special person.

It was over at last! The priest, the bridegroom, and the rest of the nobler sex stalked as majestically as the nineteenth century garb and circumstances would allow, and the bride and bridesmaids billowed like surging waves of tulle; into the vestry, where as many as were requested to do so, signed a something, and all wished the happy pair long life and happiness, hysterically. Then the church was cleared of the curious crowd, and the clergyman who had officiated of his canonical costume, and it was all over, all over!

Stanley Villars did not intend, nor was he pressed to go back to the nest from which the bird had winged her flight, and eat, and drink, and be merry. The man who had won and the man who had lost said their final say to each other, while the bride was drawing on her gloves (and trying not to look at them), after signing her maiden name for the last time. Major Walsingham put his hand out with a half uncertain air to his old ally, and asked, "It is all well with us, Stanley? We shall see you when we come back?"

"It is all well with us, but you won't see me till one of you need me, sorely enough to make me forget, which, God knows, I trust may be *never!*"

"It's been devilish hard on both of us, old boy," the other replied in rather a shaken tone, "but the worst is over now."

"Yes, there can be nothing beyond it in point of pain; but it's over now, as you say."

Major Walsingham turned to his wife as his old friend said this, and drew her by the hand towards them.

"Can you tell him, Bella, how warmly we shall always regard him—how cut to the quick we shall be if he can't come to us?"

"That I can," she said frankly. "Good bye, *dear* Stanley," she added suddenly, with evident symptoms of breaking down, and a complete confession in her eyes of inability to say that which she had but the instant before avowed her perfect readiness to utter. Then the newly-made husband and wife turned away, and when Stanley Villars raised his eyes (he had dropped them when the confession gleamed from hers) he was almost alone, and the shouts of the crowd outside told him that the bridal pair were starting on the journey of life.

CHAPTER XX.

"MY WIFE."

The first stage in the journey was over. They whom we saw last in the act of starting upon it had been man and wife for some months now when we are about to run up the curtain, and call them forward to the front of the stage again. It was in the ruddy, mellow, latest October days that they vanished; the season of their re-appearance is bright, clear January weather.

Major and Mrs. Walsingham had every reason to suppose that they had executed a grand success in thus joining forces for the purpose of together fighting the battle of life. They had been excellent travelling companions. Everything had gone smoothly with them: none of the wilfulness of old days had cropped up in Bella. She, with her bright, high spirit, was as easy to manage—Claude told himself—as the meekest woman would have been. Her will never ran counter to his, though she was as far removed from being a slave wife as the north pole is from the south. True, he had never "pulled against her" yet; but up to the present time a hair-rein and a finger were all sufficient to guide her.

Major Walsingham had long since forgiven his mother for disregarding his warmly expressed wishes, and refusing to come to his wedding. He had gone on excusing her so assiduously to Bella (not that Bella seemed to think excuses needed), that at last he fully excused her to his own heart. He was not unnaturally desirous of showing his wife to her—his wife whom he firmly believed to be as "game as she was mild, and as mild as she was game." His mother's quick appreciation would speedily show her that Bella would never mar the breed.

This being the case, he felt a little disappointed when Bella received the news of an invitation to spend Christmas with them at the Court, his father's place, with a blank look. It might be that she "was a little tired though," he said to himself, for it was the night of their return to town from their tour. Invitations to be off and doing again immediately do not fall refreshingly on the ear when one has just come off a long journey.

"I thought you would like to go," he said. "However, we will speak about it to-morrow."

"Go!—of course I shall like to go above all things, Claude. I have been looking forward to going there in March."

"Why more in March than now? What has March done to be specially selected for the honour?"

"Why, this is the twenty-third, you see, Claude. If we go down to-morrow, I shall absolutely not have a moment to spare for anything, and I have so many things to do."

"Do them when you come back."

"Of course I shall, if you make—if you wish me to start off at once," she replied.

She was bearing on the bit, but very lightly—only just so much as a well-mettled one would do when taken unexpectedly over a little bit of rough ground.

"Well, we will speak about it to-morrow,"

Major Walsingham said once more, after looking at her for an instant or two in silence.

"Perhaps it would be better to settle it to-night, dear," she rejoined, brightly. "If we *do* go, I must sit up and write notes to divers people whom I have promised to see to-morrow; if we are not to go, I will be off to rest my weary head at once."

Her weary head looked uncommonly graceful and pretty as she spoke. He saw that she was trying to have her own way in this matter; but she was trying for it so good-humouredly, so gracefully, that he determined to give way—the more especially as a country Christmas did not recommend itself at all too warmly to his sympathies.

"Then I will settle that we go down in March," he said, laughing; on which Bella got up and danced across the room to him, and kissed him.

"You darling boy! I would do anything in the world to please you," she said; "but I *am* tired, and writing notes to-night would have been rather hard work."

So it came to pass that it was not until the bright, clear March weather had set in that the eldest son of the house and his bride made their appearance at the Court. The whole family were then assembled there; the married sisters and their husbands, and the younger brothers and the distant relatives, who remembered the ties of affinity annually, had not departed when Major and Mrs. Claude Walsingham arrived. There were just precisely the same elements of agreeability present at the Court now as there had been present during the Christmas week. But Mrs. Walsingham could not quite forgive her daughter-in-law for not having clutched at the olive-branch immediately it had been extended. Therefore, she elected to believe that "things would have been pleasanter if they had come at Christmas," and to assert the same, not alone in so many words, but in her manner also. The most delicate bloom, in fact, was brushed off the welcome, in consequence of the delay they had made in coming.

Mrs. Claude was very happy, notwithstanding this. Claude had brought down his horses, and the lamented Vengeance had such a successor that Mrs. Claude marvelled much at herself for ever having been satisfied with that once prized mare. During the time they had been in London, Bella and her new horse had grown well accustomed to each other, though their only field for the cultivation of this understanding had been Rotten Row. She had found him free, light in hand, and though not a "grand," a remarkably swift and elegant goer. His temper, too, appeared as perfect as was desirable, and Claude declared him to be as safe and strong as a woman's horse should be.

But he had been found by his mistress to be worthy of a superior sphere of action than the Row, therefore he had come down with Claude's greys, for the purpose of being tried over the neighbouring country, when the hounds met near the Court. This, at least, was Bella's intention, and as yet Claude had said nothing antagonistic to it.

Major and Mrs. Claude Walsingham arrived at an inauspicious hour at the family mansion. There was a minute railway-station for the accommodation of the Court, just half a mile from the park gates. But Claude happened to be asleep when the train stopped there, and Bella did not clearly comprehend what the guard was talking about, as he ran along the platform, asking, "Any passengers for the Court?" Consequently they were carried on five miles further, and then had to drive over in their own open trap, instead of going up comfortably in admirable time to dress for dinner, in the Court carriage. This little oversight caused them to be late for dinner; there was gloom in the family mansion when they arrived.

Gloom that Bella's bright presence almost dispelled. "How many of you do I know?" she said, throwing off some of her wraps, as her husband hurriedly led her into the drawing-room, where a powerful party awaited her. Then giving a hand on each side to as many brothers and sisters as came across her in her progress, she made a swift descent upon Mrs. Walsingham, and held up her cheek to be kissed by that stately lady, to whom she took an immediate liking, because, as she said afterwards, "She was like Claude, in a bad temper and a cap."

Old Mrs. Walsingham was very tall and very stately, oppressively so until you got used to her. She had married when she was very young, and nearly the whole of her life had been spent at the Court. It was small wonder, therefore, that she should deem the majority of things that were not done by herself, or some other denizen of the Court, wrong. She had never been guilty of jilting a man, nor had she ever missed the Court railway platform. Bella had done both these things, and Mrs. Walsingham remembered them against her, even as she came up blithely, and held up her cheek to be kissed.

But the offender was Claude's wife, that the mother "could never forget," she told herself, even as the memory of those other things rankled. So the kiss that was expected was given, and given not unkindly.

"Claude is leaving me to introduce you to his father, my dear," she said, taking Bella's hand, and turning her round to where a handsome old gentleman, who looked like a king with no thorns in his crown, stood shaking hands with his son. "Having done which," Mrs. Walsingham continued, as the father stooped down with real old chivalresque courtesy to salute the young wife, "I will suggest that you go to your room and prepare for dinner."

Mrs. Walsingham made the suggestion as another woman would have uttered words of the most authoritative command. Mrs. Claude glanced at her mother-in-law with a glance that looked half careless, but that was in reality very keen, and she saw breakers a-head.

"Will you ever forgive us for being so awkward as to make this mistake on our first visit, Mr. Walsingham?" the new daughter-in-law asked, suddenly turning to her host. She lifted her hat, a fast-looking turban hat, with a ptarmigan's wing in it, from her head, as she spoke, and stood revealed before them all, bright in such beauty as might have been held to excuse worse things than she had ever done.

"I think I could forgive you anything, my dear." The words were very simple; he could hardly have said less under the circumstances, but his manner pleased both his son and his son's bride. He lifted her little hand up as though it had been the hand of a queen, and pressed his lips upon it as a father should on the hand of his child. Bella was quite satisfied. One at least in this house, and that one the head of it, was not slow to recognise her claim to universal consideration and admiration.

"Then forgive me when I say that I would rather stay here and thaw over this big fire, than detain you all while I dressed for dinner. Do let me stay?"

Claude saw his mother's lips form the word "whims," and on the instant he ranged himself on the side of his wife.

"It would be odd if you couldn't please yourself about it, Bella; stay here by all means and rest yourself. Here, let me take your hat and shawl."

He took the hat from her hand; he lifted the shawl from her shoulders; he looked down into her face admiringly while he did these things, and his mother felt unqualified annoyance. He had been all her own son to the best of her knowledge before this, and now this girl had him for her loving lackey, and she his mother was nowhere!

"Mrs. Claude must do as she pleases," the old lady said, dropping her words out with fatal distinctness; "the rest of us will go in to dinner."

"Come up with me, Jack, while I wash my hands," Claude said, turning to a younger brother; "in one moment, mother, I will be with you—unless my wife would rather I stayed with her?" he added, interrogatively, turning to Bella, who shook her head, and laughed a negative, and assured him that "his wife would rather he went in and enjoyed himself," crouching away into a corner of a couch as she spoke, and looking strangely pretty and defiant.

Shall it be written?—she shed a few scalding tears when they were all gone, and she was left in that room alone. She had come expecting, she hardly knew what; but certainly not to be scrutinised keenly, and caused to feel that she was to blame in ever so little, on the first moment of her advent amongst them. She had broken through a hedge of moral prickly-pears for Claude, and they were Claude's relatives. They should have remembered that she had done this, and their manner should have accredited her with it. Whatever her sins of omission or commission, Claude had been the sole cause of them. Tossing on the sofa there alone, while her husband was dining (hilariously perhaps) with his family, she remembered all things that were past and over—amongst others, how the Villars' had prized her.

How dared his mother glance thus coldly at her? She asked the question aloud almost, in her young wrath against injustice. To the one in whom old Mrs. Walsingham alone was interested, she (Bella) had been all that was loving, devotional, faithful, and discreet. That she had been the reverse of all these things to Stanley Villars, she acknowledged to herself there in her solitude. But it was not for them—it was not "for these Walsinghams"—to point the barb of truth and dig it into her breast.

"These Walsinghams," ah! she was one of them now, she remembered—one of them for good or ill—their glory would be her glory, their interests hers. This was a softening reflection.

Presently another arose. How kind Claude had been! That of course; he would always be kind, for was he not Claude, and she very dearly fond of him. But how thoughtful he had been, saying he would stay there with her instead of going in and being happy and hungry with the rest when she had avowed a want of appetite, and a desire to stay there alone and be quiet!

"Unless my wife would rather that I stayed with her!" She recalled those words. She muttered them over to herself. "As if his 'wife' would have kept him from dining for nothing, dear old boy!" she murmured fondly; "but how angry his mother looked at the bare thought that I might possibly do so." Then she thought afresh, how odd it was that they did not all immediately feel her to be the boon she was; and then she felt magnanimous, "they would know better soon," and then a little sleepy. Finally, she curled herself more closely in the corner, and slumbered soundly, in happy forgetfulness of all things that she disliked being reminded of in her waking moments.

She awoke to the whiz of voices, and the whirr of garbs feminine. Gathering herself together she sat up and rubbed her eyes, and one of Claude's sisters, a Mrs. Markham, came and sat down by her, and asked her, "Was she rested now, and had she had a nice sleep? Three times within the last quarter of an hour mamma has crept up to you with a cup of tea in her hand; she thought you would like it when you awoke."

"That's very kind of her," Bella answered; she was softened directly by this attention. She spang up with no signs of her late fatigue in either face or bearing, and went across to Mrs. Walsingham, and told her how much obliged she was, and how grateful for the tea, which she forthwith sipped, and found cold and too sweet; but it was well meant, so she drank it (and felt slightly sick) with sensations of gratitude.

She was still in her travelling dress—a dark cloth, with a habit top, and a little stand-up collar round her throat. It was an unexceptionable dress for the occasion for which it had been donned. But Mrs. Walsingham took exception to it and its horse-shoe sleeve-link accompaniments here at night in her drawing-room.

The stately old lady, who had adhered with pertinacity to so many of the fashions of her youth as she could do without rendering herself what her daughters called "an object," was no friend to the semi-boyish style of modern female dress. She glanced askance at Bella, not with ill-concealed dislike, as Bella at once imagined, but with more than a half dread that her son had married the type of the girl of the day—an uncommonly offensive genus in her eyes.

Mrs. Claude Walsingham rose refreshed, like a young lion, from her sleep. She saw a task before her, and she felt fully equal to accomplishing it. Her quick mind thoroughly comprehended the fact that, desirable acquisition as she was, the mother of the man she had married did not deem her such; "and though I won't cringe to her a bit, I will win her entirely," she said resolutely to herself.

"She did not sit down before the fortress at once, and attempt patiently to besiege it. She made light skirmishing attacks on the junior members of the family, and left Mrs. Walsingham free to think over her iniquities undisturbed for that evening. When the men came in she whispered to Claude, who came to her at once, to "go and talk to his mother," which Claude did to the best of his ability; but it was uphill work, as Mrs. Walsingham had observed the whisper, and had taken it into her head that her son's wife "was trying to keep him to herself."

The two members of the family that Bella liked best, as yet, were Mr. Walsingham and Jack, the owner of the remarkable breed of red setters, of which mention has been made in a former chapter. To all outward seeming, Mr. Walsingham was as dignified, stately, and determined a gentleman as was fitting in the head of the house. But straws show the direction of the current; and the reader will see in time, as Bella did shortly, that Mr. Walsingham's strongest characteristic was a deep reverence for his wife.

Moreover, though she liked him much, Bella did not care to battle with somnolency for his attention. With a very pretty air of dutifulness and gradually developing affection, Mrs. Claude sat on a low stool by the right arm of his chair for a few minutes, toning her speeches to the right family key as far as she could, and giving Claude the place of honour, in the brief tales she told of their tour, in a way that she judged would be as pleasing for his father to hear, as it was to her to speak. Still, though the air of dutifulness sat upon her very naturally and pleasingly, she was not sorry when sleep carried the day against her, leaving her free to cultivate one of the younger branches of this tree on which she was grafted.

The one to whom she turned was the aforesaid Jack, Claude's third brother, who was about her own age, as far as years went, and therefore considerably younger in some things. He had been to her wedding, and had then shown himself shy of her to a slight degree, as he would have been of any woman who was about to be married, and to whom he might be expected to speak respecting such intention. But now all the awkwardness was over—there was nothing more to say; he almost succeeded in answering her with as little embarrassment as he would have answered a genuine sister, when she left his father's side, and went and placed herself on a sofa by him.

"I was so glad to see your face when I came into the room. Claude had frightened me; he said 'Jack would be safe to be gone,' and I shall want you so much."

He fought with his youth, and conquered. She was only his sister after all!

"I am very glad that you have come now you have. I shall be off in a fortnight, and I want to have two or three days with Claude with Markham's hounds. We haven't had a day together for years—never since I was a boy."

Jack Walsingham was a handsome, fine, stalwart young fellow, with bright curly brown hair, and honest blue eyes, full of life and health and pluck and vigour, and with none of these things toned down as yet. The ardent-spirited part of her nature sympathised with him at once, so she checked the smile that began to quiver on her lips when he said he had "not ridden with Claude since he was a boy," and answered the boy animatedly.

"Is Mr. Markham, your brother-in-law, master of the hounds?"

"He has a pack—foxhounds, too. You must go and see them throw off when they next meet."

"Indeed I will! Where will they meet?"

"At Horsley Hollow, about two miles from here. We always have a good day when the meet is there; sure to find soon in Horsley Wood. And—— but do you care for hunting? Perhaps you don't; and if so, I shall bore you if I talk about it."

She shook her head. "Do I not care for it! You won't bore me, never fear; you must tell me all about the manners and customs of your —— shire hunting-field. Does Mrs. Markham ride?"

"What! Ellen?"

"Yes!"

"No; Markham wouldn't let her if she could, and she couldn't if he would. He hates to see a woman in the field."

Mrs. Claude looked at Mr. Markham as her young brother-in-law said this, and saw a stout, tall, heavy-looking man, with an impassive red face.

"Hates to see a woman in the field, does he? I can fancy it; he looks fat and selfish."

"The fact is," Jack replied, confidentially putting his arm along on the back of the sofa, and leaning nearer to Mrs Claude—"the fact is, Markham doesn't hunt them well at all; he can't ride a bit; he always keeps along on the roads, and creeps through gates. He's awfully afraid of coming to grief; so, if there's a lady in the field who does take anything, he is about the only man who dare not follow, and then he gets laughed at. He does all he can to stop it; says women override the hounds and get in the way. But it is all because it is awkward even for him to shirk what a lady goes at."

"It must be great fun to see him," Bella said, reflectively, looking across at the object of Jack's remarks once more. "Do you know that my riding-horse has come down with me?"

"Claude mentioned it at dinner."

"Look here, Jack, I will go out on him when the meet is at Horsley Hollow," she said abruptly.

"You will ride to see them throw off?"

"Yes, and then follow."

"By Jove, do!" he exclaimed, delightedly. He had to put a severe restraint upon himself in order not to risk offending her, by telling her that she was "a brick to think of it!"

"Hush!" she whispered, laughing, "don't say a word, or Mr. Markham will be raising objections to it, probably, and I could not set him at defiance. I suppose he might refuse to hunt them while I am down here, if he knew beforehand of my intention; but I don't think he will be silly enough to call them off when he finds me in the field?"

"No, humbug as he is, he won't do that. I shall go out and have a look at your horse presently. What has Claude done with the pup I gave him?"

"Kept it."

"I thought he wanted it for ——" The boy paused suddenly; he was going to say "for Stanley Villars." The name of Claude's old friend was a household word at the Court; but he paused, remembering what Claude's old friend had been to Claude's young wife.

"You were going to say you thought the puppy was for Stanley Villars," she said very gently, with a tenderness spreading like a film over her face as she spoke, which the inconsiderate Jack found most marvellously touching. "I gave Stanley a dog, and then he did not care to have the setter puppy."

"I beg your pardon," he began, "I didn't mean——"

"I know you didn't—don't say another word about it; I know you didn't mean it. I feel very sure of you, Jack."

She rose when she had said that, and went and seated herself by Mrs. Markham's side, leaving Jack uncertain whether she was more of a forgiving angel than he was of a "blundering brute." She was quite the ideal sister to so young a man as Jack Walsingham; she was interested in his breed of setters, and she purposed riding to hounds for the sake of putting "old Markham out!"

But she was not the ideal sister in Mrs. Markham's eyes. Claude's eldest sister had been mated with an uncongenial man from very early girlhood, and she had always deported herself admirably, and suffered no man to suppose from her manner that the uncongeniality was in reality a wearing sorrow to her. She was a remarkably undemonstrative woman, one who went on doing her duty in such a perfect way day by day that no one had the shadow of a cause to imagine that the shadow of a doubt ever crossed her mind as to this lot of hers being as blissful as it might be. She was good, just, and true as steel; but she was not a lenient woman. She would assist the erring, but she could not deal gently with them. She would bind up wounds with a strong hand if they came to her to be bound up; but she would not pour oil into them. She rather preferred treating them with balsam, which was wholesome, though it made them smart.

Mrs. Claude opened the conversation.

"What is that combination of glass and leather and wool to be when it is finished, Ellen?" she asked, looking at the work on which Mrs. Markham was employing herself assiduously.

"A sofa cushion."

"It will be uncomfortable, but pretty. I have not seen anything of the sort before. Leather for the grounding!—it's very pretty!"

"You are very good to admire it so freely; I should hardly have supposed that you had much taste for such things."

"Nor have I, as far as doing them myself goes; but I think some of them very pretty, though scarcely worth the trouble of doing."

"You are so much better employed now, for instance," Mrs. Markham said quietly.

Bella laughed.

"So I am; I am amusing you, or trying to amuse you, and that is a more praiseworthy occupation than studding a sofa cushion with beads and bright nails. How they'll hurt people!"

Mrs. Markham liked the unresentful tone. She had more than half expected that Bella would either have answered her in anger, or not have answered her at all. So she relaxed a trifle, and said—

"While you are staying here, you had better take to some such occupation as this. Days in a country house are very long and very dull very often in the winter, unless you can find pleasure in some such occupation."

"Oh, I'm never dull in the country—there's always so much to do—unless it pours with rain and one can't get out."

"Those are the liveliest days very often, I have found, for then the gentlemen stay in, and we are obliged to exert ourselves to keep dull care away."

"I was going to say that," Mrs. Claude replied; "even on such days we can act charades and play billiards, and do, oh! all sorts of things. I have a husband now; it will be his bounden duty to see that I don't stagnate; but I know" (and she laughed) "that I have never found it the least dull in a country house."

Mrs. Markham regarded this as an indecorous allusion to former experiences, which she shuddered in her soul to think her brother's wife should have had. She fancied that Bella was thinking of some of the many whom report said she had smiled upon. Such thoughts Mrs. Markham held to be fraught with danger, so she looked rather sternly at the offender as she said—

"Yes, you have a husband now; as his sister I must express a hope that you will not forget that fact when recalling bygone hours in other country houses, either for our benefit or to your own mind."

"Good gracious! there was no harm in them! What *do* you mean?" Bella cried. Then the recollection of Stanley Villars came over her, and she felt humbled and silenced. That episode in her life was known to Mrs. Markham, who, with such knowledge, might well deem her capable of further fickleness and faithlessness. Still it was hard to be distrusted by the friends of the one who had been the cause of that fickleness and faithlessness. Very hard, after all she had gone through for Claude—after all the misery her waning faith had caused her—after all those inward struggles to do right—after all the agony their failure cost—after a lifetime of complete exemption from blame,—it was very hard to be condemned and coldly regarded!

For a minute or two she sat, a prey to the throes of conscience. Then anger filled her soul. Then the pity for oneself that is born of bodily fatigue, and a consciousness of being just a little wrong and just a little wronged, overwhelmed her, and she dropped her face down upon her convulsively-twitching nands, and began to cry with passionate force.

In a moment Claude was by her side and the rest were round her, and in another moment she was alive to the full folly of her act.

"My own darling, what is it?" Claude asked. "What the devil has any one said to her?" he continued, looking angrily at each one in turn, but especially at Jack, who was looking conscience-smitten on account of that speech he had made about the setter pup and Stanley Villars.

"No one has said anything," Bella answered, striving to clear up. "Who should? Don't think it; I am a goose!"

"I am the culprit, Claude," Mrs. Markham put in quietly. "In all kindness I made a remark to your wife that seems to have offended her very much."

"No, it hasn't," Bella said promptly. "I'm not offended—I'm tired and a goose, as I said before."

"I cannot have my wife worried, or suffer remarks to be made to her that make her cry, whether she is a 'goose' or not," Claude said; and Mrs. Markham turned away to her leather and glass beads and wool again with a feeling that her brother's bride was a mistake, which it behoved her to rectify if possible.

——o——

CHAPTER XXI.

TOO IMPULSIVE.

It has been said that Claude found it up-hill work to carry on a conversation with his mother that evening. Mrs. Walsingham had started on the supposition that her son had sought her side in opposition to the wishes of his wife; and this supposition rendered her inaccessible, so to say. She was very curious—curious as only a woman can be—about this marriage her son had made, and its attendant circumstances. She longed to know how the other affair had been broken off, and how this one had come on. She also wanted to know the exact amount of Mrs. Claude's fortune, report having varied considerably on that last point.

Curious as she was, however, she would not take the honest and straight road to arriving at a knowledge of what excited her curiosity, by asking him outright the how and why of it all. She was too proud to seek a confidence that was not given. He was her own son, and too proud to offer a confidence that was not sought.

For the last six or seven years Mrs. Walsingham had nourished and cherished a scheme in her heart. It was a fair, bright scheme; and it was founded upon a fair, bright girl, whom she had designed, when opportunity offered, to marry to her eldest son. The girl was a Miss Harper, the well-portioned daughter of a neighbouring country gentleman. She had won upon Mrs. Walsingham when a mere child, and her growth in grace and guilelessness had been watched with loving eyes by the mother who meant her for her son.

It was the thought of Grace Harper that pointed the pain Mrs. Walsingham felt in this marriage Claude had made. On one or two occasions, when Grace had been spending long, dull days with Mrs. Walsingham in the solitude of that old west country house, the hostess had striven to brighten the hours to the young guest by talking about Claude. She had talked about Claude in that wonderful maternal tone which conveys to the listener the flattering conviction that she may not only speak, but may think, with affection—affection tempered with awe, of course, but still affection—of the spoken about. Worse than this: with even greater, more lamentable indiscretion, she had lately hinted, in unmistakable terms, that it was upon the cards that the glory of being Claude's wife should be Miss Grace's.

Then a rumour had been heard in the land relative to Florence Villars—relative to a "sort of attachment that, there was a sort of report," Claude had formed for the sister of his friend. On this Miss Gracie had gone into gentle melancholy, and red rims to her eyes; and Mrs. Walsingham had gone to her davenport, and despatched a searching inquiry into the truth of said statement to Claude. All this had happened about the period of the Richmond dinner, just previous to Claude's going down to Denham. The amiable nature of the reassuring negative he returned to his mother's question was due principally to his pleasure at finding her so far off the Circe scent.

During the few days he had spent at the Court before he went to town, and met Bella driving her chestnuts in the park, he had every opportunity afforded him of falling in love with Miss Harper. She had come, at his mother's special request, to stay in the house while he stayed; and Mrs. Walsingham sedulously eschewed other visitors, and went to sleep for a couple of hours every evening. But it was all of no avail. Miss Harper resembled a daughter of the gods, in that she "was divinely tall, and most divinely fair;" but Claude apostrophised Jove about her only when declaring her to be dull.

He had fully fathomed the plan that had been made for his happiness, but he had ever affected to be innocently unconscious of it, deeming it a pity to spoil the enjoyment his mother derived from perfecting and touching it up. Now, however, that all was at an end, and other topics appeared unmanageable between his mother and himself, he reverted to Miss Harper by asking—

"By the way, mother, is Gracie coming here? I thought she was always at the Court when anything was going on."

"I really don't know why you should have supposed so. Dear girl! no; she is not coming. She is in such great request that she cannot spare a day for us for the next month."

"I only know what she told me herself. She said, when I asked her when I should see her again, that she 'would probably be here when I came the next time, as she was always with Mrs. Walsingham when anything was going on.' Now there is even more going on than she could possibly have anticipated, seeing I have not come alone."

"Your wife would hardly care for Grace's society."

"Probably not; I found her the reverse of enlivening."

"My dear Claude, remember! she is a friend of mine!"

"She made tea very prettily, didn't she?" Claude asked, laughingly. "It was quite a study to see her poise her white hand on the teapot cover, and keep it there standing out in bold relief, while she debated with me circumspectly whether or not more water should be poured in!"

"She was a thorough lady," Mrs. Walsingham replied slowly; "a pure-minded girl, with nothing volatile in either manner or disposition."

Claude shrugged his shoulders.

"I hope she will be able to spare you a few days before we leave, mother."

"Extremely improbable. You will see her though, Claude; for her cousin and his bride are coming to stay with them, and we must ask them to dinner."

"Which cousin?"

"Her mother's nephew, Lord Lexley."

Claude started—inside, not externally. He had heard of Adèle's marriage when he came back to town, but he had little thought to meet her ladyship as a domesticated animal so soon, down in these pure-minded wilds.

"Oh! Lexley and his wife are coming, are they? Who's the lady, do you know?"

"An admirable young creature, an Italian countess, who went on the opera boards in order to support her widowed mother," Mrs. Walsingham replied. Then Claude said, "Ah! really!" and his mother went on to tell him much that was new about Lady Lexley, which did immense credit to her ladyship's powers of invention.

"I almost wonder you have not heard of her, Claude," Mrs. Walsingham said, when they had thoroughly talked through the topic. "The Harpers say that she regrets it very much, but that she has not been able to avoid publicity."

"No doubt she was desirous of doing so," he said drily; "opera singers generally are. I have heard of her, of course—heard her too often. By Jove! she will be an acquisition! I hadn't counted on this when I came down," he continued to himself, his eyes sparkling with excitement. Just then his wife's sobs fell upon his ears, and he speedily forgot the existence of Lady Lexley—speedily forgot it for a time.

The following morning Mrs. Claude heard with satisfaction that the hounds would meet at Horsley Hollow on the 12th. This was Friday, the 7th. Wednesday would shortly be upon them. So she resolved to go out daily on her new horse, and get him well accustomed to her hand and the country before the eventful day.

Claude was ready to go for a ride with her "anywhere at any hour," he said. When he said this, however, Bella noticed that his father looked a little disappointed, and she fathomed the cause of that disappointment at once.

"Unless Mr. Walsingham wants you to ride round the land with him, Claude."

"Oh! any day will do for that, my dear," Mr. Walsingham replied politely.

"Ah, but you would like him to go to-day; of course you would; how very natural!"

"Jack can go with you, Bella," Claude suggested.

"Or can't I ride with you and your father? should I be in the way?"

"Not in the way," the old gentleman explained with polite anxiety, "but it might be tedious; for we shall be standing about looking at improvements that don't interest ladies. Your horse is fresh most likely; he might give you trouble."

"He is fresh, and no mistake," Jack put in. "You had better come out with me, Mrs. Claude, along a good riding road. We will give him a breather."

"I think that will be the best plan. Won't you go with us, Ellen?"

Mrs. Markham shook her head.

"Jack and I had your horse out this morning before you were awake, Bella," her husband said to her. "He is too good at his fences for a lady's hack, Markham says."

"I thought a lady's horse couldn't be too good at his fences?" Bella said, looking at Mr. Markham.

"A lady's hunter cannot, but *you* won't hunt?"

"Why not?" she asked quickly.

"Oh! I know of no reason against it, if your husband does not, Mrs. Claude. He is a nice horse, a very nice horse," Mr. Markham continued, with the air of one who would change the conversation; "as sound before as he is behind. I see he touches his fences."

"Yes, he is satisfactory enough as far as he has gone yet," Claude rejoined. Then he gave his wife some cautions about her method of treating him at first starting. "Be very steady with him at first, and don't lose yourself with Jack as you did with Vengeance and Hill."

"Was Vengeance the name of the horse you were riding on the occasion of your first romantic meeting with Claude?" Mrs. Walsingham asked.

"Yes," Bella replied; and she blushed a little as she remembered what that meeting had cost Stanley Villars.

"What is your new horse's name?"

"Devilskin."

"A horrid name for a lady's horse!" Mrs. Walsingham remarked—superciliously, Bella thought.

"But *I* have given it to him; so whether it's 'horrid' or not, he will have to be known by it, I am afraid," Mrs. Claude rejoined. Then Claude got up rather hastily, and asked—

"When will you have your horse, Bella?—say twelve?" in a tone that showed his wife that his wishes tended to a subversion of the subject in dispute between herself and his mother.

Devilskin came round at twelve, Jack following on his own horse with that in his manner of following that would lead one to suppose that he desired to have it believed that he was there by accident, and was not at all desirous of escorting his sister-in-law. He was but twenty—he was very young—and his youth was apt to rise up in judgment, as it were, at unforeseen times, and convict him of having acted or spoken as it behoved "a man" not to act or speak.

He was but twenty; but he was honest and

handsome, frank and fearless, tender (when no one was by to see him thus tripping), and true as steel. These are qualities that tell on a woman, let the man to whom they belong be to her what he may—a stranger or one of her own kindred. These are qualities that must and do tell, and it is only fitting that they should do so.

"Take care of her, Jack!" Claude said, as he put his wife up, and Bella looked round laughing at her young escort in a way that caused his blood to seethe and bubble with a variety of emotions. His brother's caution implied a doubt, he fancied, and Bella's laugh seemed to cast a shadow of ridicule over his protectorship of her. He felt very young and very uncomfortable, but intensely loyal and devoted, as he rode down to the gate by her side.

Mrs. Claude saw the constraint that had come over him, and Mrs. Claude thoroughly appreciated the cause of it. He had been free and graciously unreserved with her last night, but in broad daylight he remembered that she was a stranger to him, and a young woman, and the freedom and unreserve vanished. The young lady looked at him cautiously now and again as she rode gently along by his side, and she pitied the boy on whose cheek and mind there still dwelt this delicate bloom.

She tried two or three topics which she trusted might induce him to forget himself—the scenery, the family, the Court, &c.—and all were of no avail. Then, she thought, "I have reserved my heaviest shot till the last; if that falls flat, Jack and I will have but a dull ride of it."

"Could you take me to Horsley Hollow, Jack?" she asked, in as confidential a tone as his constrained manner would permit her to use. "Could you take me to Horsley Hollow, Jack, and show what the land is like about it?"

The shot told instantaneously. He turned his head and looked full upon her for the first time since they had started.

"If I showed you some of the stiffest places you would know the worst Devilskin would have to do when the day comes—if Claude lets you ride—wouldn't you?" he replied.

"Yes. If Claude lets me ride! why, *of course*, Claude will let me ride."

"I will show you the way if you like, then," he said. "This old fellow"—he patted his horse as he spoke—"knows every stick, and stone, and drop of water about here: he's an awfully safe lead."

"Then I shall follow him: you won't be too rash, I'm sure."

"That I won't."

"Did you mean that you'd show me the way to-day?"

"I think———." He paused and faltered. His judgment told him that Devilskin had better learn more both of the lady and the locality before he was taken 'cross country. But his inclinations led him to please his brother's wife, and his own horse, and himself, by showing her the way without further delay.

"What, do you think," she asked, "that Mr. Markham would fathom my intention if he heard of our practising over the ground, and frustrate it?"

"Perhaps that: he would if he could."

"Ah! but he couldn't," she replied with a little decided laugh; "he couldn't. Who could, indeed, if I would go—if Claude did not object?" she added hastily.

"Markham would be making objections, and pointing out things to Claude that might make Claude object—if Markham knew of it long beforehand, that is; he's so slow that he can do nothing if you don't give him time."

"He wouldn't know anything about it, Jack," she said suddenly, as they came upon a short bit of road that led them right down to the side of a three-cornered well-wooded dell. "This is Horsley Hollow I'm sure. Now, when the fox breaks cover, which way is he most likely to go? Show me, and we will ride that way, and we'll say nothing to Mr. Markham about it we won't mention it at home."

Jack hesitated, and assoiled his conscience.

"I wouldn't be the one to take you along over anything if I hadn't seen what your horse can do, and if I hadn't heard Claude say that Devilskin was a clipper at his fences," he said slowly.

"No, of course not!" she replied with animation. She was eager as a child to try whether crossing the country was as delightful in practice as it was in theory.

"Then come along," he said, turning round and putting his horse to climb over a bit of a broken bank, with more a gutter than a ditch beyond it.

She followed on Devilskin. "He will creep over: it is nothing to lift him to," her brother-in-law cried, leaning round to look at her. Mrs. Claude relied on her horse's sagacity to do what was expected and prognosticated of him, and consequently received a slight shock. Devilskin elected to make a mighty leap of the gutter, and his mistress came forward almost on to his neck.

Mrs. Claude recovered herself in an instant—recovered her seat, that is, but not her equanimity. The leap, even as her horse had taken it, had been a mere nothing—a trifle suited to the meanest equestrian capacity had she been prepared for it. But she had not been prepared for it. She had, in truth, been prepared for something quite the reverse, and she felt annoyed with herself, her horse, and her companion.

The mighty leap over the tiny ditch—the much ado about nothing that Devilskin had been guilty of—had landed them in a pasture intersected with ditches. "The last time we drew the Hollow the fox made right away out there; over that corner, and along the road for a bit, and then across a field to that dark spot, do you see? Follow the direction of my whip. That's another cover. There we were at fault: and that Markham is such a humbug; he made such a noise when he was taking the hounds in, that he didn't hear a fellow halloo, or didn't know where the halloo came from, and so he rode a couple of miles the wrong way, and lost the fox."

This was a tremendous long speech, as the reader will doubtless have observed, to him or herself disparagingly. When he had communicated it, they found themselves near to the corner which Jack had indicated as the corner over which the last fox they 'had drawn in Horsley Hollow had made his exit from the pasture.

"Perhaps the next won't go over there," Mrs. Claude observed; "but still we may as well try it, may we not, Jack?"

"Yes, we may as well," he replied, dubiously. That affair at the other side of the pasture had rather shaken his confidence; he was not quite sure in what, though—whether in Bella's horse, or horsewomanship.

"Yes, we may as well," he repeated; they were nearing the corner now. "Look here. I'll tell you, it isn't much of a jump, only it's rather a drop into the road. Let him have his head when he's rising to it, and mind you have him well in hand when he's landing."

Bella listened with understanding. "I see," she replied; "all right; will you go first?"

He would go first. His steady old hunter went over like a bird, and as his heels vanished, Devilskin began to fidget, and wheeled half round.

"Keep him at it—come along," Jack cried from the other side; and Bella having pulled her horse round to it determinately, Devilskin went at it with a rush.

For a moment or two Jack experienced the sort of elation we are all apt to feel when we fancy that a thing of this sort is about to be done remarkably well. Mrs. Claude was settled well down in her saddle, he marked that. Her figure swayed as the figure only can when you have come down to it tightly, and are vibrating to the horse; but though she had come down to her saddle well, her seat was too forward a one, if not for the jump, at least for the way Devilskin was going to do it.

A moment more! Devilskin was over the hedge, and Mrs. Claude Walsingham was over the near pummel, upon the road, under Devilskin's forefeet, apparently.

What misery one moment of time is all-sufficient for! I am not about to moralize a long unbroken paragraph of my own; reflections would be as ineffably tedious to myself as to the rest of the enlightened reading public; still I cannot help marvelling at the muchness of misery which may be endured in a moment. It is so complete, so perfect a thing of its kind, that misery, that it might have occupied the best years of the life of a master in the art of creating wretchedness. There is nothing jagged or unfinished about it; it appears to be round and never ending.

Jack Walsingham had such a moment as Devilskin landed, and his brother's bride came off on the near side.

He was the cause of the catastrophe. That was the first thought that arose as he heard the dull sound, that, slight as she was, she made when coming down upon the ground with a crash. He was the cause; on him the blame would rest had aught befallen her. Then he sprang from his own horse and picked her up, and she was not hurt—not bruised and marred, as he had feared to find her.

The horse had not done that which had not been anticipated of him out of viciousness. It had been prophesied of Devilskin by the infallible Claude, that he would touch his fences—buck them, in fact; instead of which he had flown this, and thrown Bella "out" in her calculations, and off her saddle. But there had not been an atom of vice or of malice prepense in Devilskin's mind. He had flown his fence and thrown his rider, but now he stood looking down at the result of his unexpected act with much mildness in his eyes.

Mrs. Claude Walsingham, when she found herself sloping away down to the earth over Devilskin's near shoulder, did the wisest and only thing to be done under the circumstances—freed her foot from the stirrup, and so far ensured a clear fall. But she had held on to the snaffle-rein so firmly, that it was her elbow, instead of her hand and wrist, which came down upon the ground, and the elbow was saved from dislocation through the fact of the snaffle-rein being only just long enough to admit of her elbow coming into the barest contact with the ground before her whole body was there also to bear its own weight. But her hands got a cruel jerk.

Jack picked her up, and looked at her with a big, loving anxiety in his eyes, and a face paler than her own.

"How on earth did you do it? Are you hurt?" he asked, stammering, in his intense impatience to question and to hear.

"No, I'm not hurt. My arm is grazed, I think. But, oh! Jack, I wonder that not only my arm, but my neck too, isn't broken!"

Her hat had fallen off, and had got an indentation that might not be rectified by unskilful hands. She looked at it ruefully, as he picked it up, and said—

"I seemed to be falling down miles straight upon my head to the road that was rushing up to meet me. What *did* he do?"

"*He* did his part of the business all right enough," Jack said, dispassionately, looking at the horse. He had conceived a great love and admiration for his sister-in-law, and a vast pity for her tangled and torn condition filled his heart as he stood there by her side. But, for all that, he could not deem a horse who had flown a fence so cleverly deserving of aught but praise.

When the hat had been restored to something more like its original shape than had been its portion when first they picked it up, and some of the mud had been brushed from her habit, Jack proposed that they should re-mount and go home very steadily by the road.

She put her right hand on the pummel, and raised the other to his shoulder, but as soon as she touched him, she suffered her hand to fall away down by her side, with a little cry of pain.

"What is the matter?" he asked it with a prompt and complete return of the big, loving anxiety in his eyes, with such tenderness in his tones, that the tears glistened up between her lashes in response.

"I *am* hurt—my wrist—"

He touched her hand, unbuttoning her glove, and baring the delicately-veined wrist with a deft gentleness that was a newly-born thing in Jack.

"Your wrist is strained! Don't cry, dear Bella!" he said, half sobbing himself, as she heaved, and panted, and wept, partly with pain, and partly because she was afraid Claude would disapprove of the steps she had taken unknown to him to improve her acquaintance with the locality, and strain her wrist.

"Don't cry, dear Bella!" he repeated, with imploring eyes and tones; and then—he was very young, and true as steel, as I have said—he put his arm round her, and stooped his honest young head, and kissed her on the mouth, in attempted consolation. It was a gesture that was more like the impulsive, awkward, protecting fondness of a big Newfoundland dog than a mere man's salute. She could not help regarding it with the same sort of grateful toleration she had experienced in former days when Rock had striven to console her in some sorrow, by nearly knocking her down.

"You dear, good-natured boy, I'm not hurt much, and I won't cry!" she said, smiling at him; "give me a hand up, and we'll go home by the road, as you say."

They mounted and rode along in silence for about half a mile, when she broke it by saying—

"Don't tel' any one about my bungling over that hedge, as I did, Jack, or I shall not be let ride on Wednesday."

"I won't, as you wish mo not."

As he answered her, a gentleman and lady rode past, and Bella recognised Lord Lexley.

——o——

CHAPTER XXII.

LADY LEXLEY.

It must be confessed that Mrs. Claude Walsingham took ignominious precautions to gain ingress to the halls of her husband's fathers unobserved that day, on her return from the unlucky trial trip with Jack and Devilskin. She was shaken and very muddy, and she had a keen desire to keep these two facts from the eyes of the Markhams. "Can we not ride into the yard, and then can't I get into the house through some side door, Jack?" Bella said to him, in the confidential tone that is frequently adopted by women when designed to fall upon very young masculine ears. "Oh yes; but why?" Jack had answered; and then Bella had explained to him that the most casual glance from the least observant female eyes would be sufficient to enable the possessor of said eyes to glean from her (Bella's) appearance all that she most ardently desired should not be gleaned.

But there is no such thing as gaining quiet ingress to a country house from the stable-yard regions. There were no less than three dogs chained up in the yard, and these all plunged cut of their kennels, and greeted her first with ferocious barks, and presently with servile whines and yells to be let loose. The tramp of the horses, and the rattling of the chains, and Jack's cries of "Down, Rose, old girl! What, Nep! do you want to be loosed?" brought heads, or, at least, a head, to every window from which a glimpse of the most remote portion of the yard could be gained, and while the heads were at the windows Bella would not brave discovery by approaching the house in her mud-spattered habit. So she stood away at the extreme end, playing with Neptune and a couple of Jack's red setters, till her feet got cold, and it was opined by her patient watchers that she "seemed wonderful fond of Master Jack, that she did, letting them great, big, ugly dogs of his put their dirty paws on her shoulders."

Finally she went in through a side door, as she had said she would do, but the splashes of mud did not escape detection. In the hall, just as she was about to flee up stairs, followed by her own maid, she met Mrs. Markham.

"What a dreadful state Jack's dogs have made you in, my dear Bella! I hear you have been playing with them for the last hour," Claude's eldest sister said.

"More or less," Bella replied, catching at the excuse for her having such a liberal portion of the soil about her, eagerly. "I'm so fond of dogs, you know, that I never care a bit what they do to me."

"Luncheon is still on the table; won't you come in as you are?"

"No, thank you; I'll go first and take off my habit," Bella replied, colouring vividly. She was annoyed at being detained, and her wrist was paining her.

"Oh, very well," Mrs. Markham replied, standing aside elaborately to let Mrs. Claude pass. "You will find Miss Harper with us when you come down. Claude has been in a long time."

It is not a nice thing to have a sprained wrist, and to feel morally certain that unless you keep your sentiments respecting it to yourself, that condemnation, instead of pity, will be your portion from the unsympathetic masses. Bella's perfect love for Claude by no means cast out her fear of Claude's family developing unpleasant traits towards her on the first opportunity. Therefore she resolved upon making a small secret of the dilemma into which she had fallen, through Devilskin's change of purpose, on account of the mighty and most reasonable dread she had of aught being said which she might not like to hear.

She was pale with the pain when she reached the dining-room at last, after laboriously dressing, and striving (ineffectually) to keep back the swelling in her wrist, simultaneously. The ruins of the luncheon were on the table still, and by it was one who had materially conduced to this ruin—a great, fair girl, with a wealth of hair, and colour, and flesh, who was introduced to the bride as Miss Harper.

It only speaks well for the breed, and is by no means derogatory to the individual, when I say that Miss Harper was the very usual type of big, blue-eyed blondes. You will see one or two, at least, resembling her, in every ball-room, Tall, with an immense amount of back; oval faced, yet inclining to be thick about the jaw; large limbed, with luxuriant hair that was too dark to be called yellow, and too light for brown to be its fitting appellation; luxurious rather than loose or even easy in action; young, healthy, and animal, in a quiet, unobtrusive, voluptuous way that a painter would have loved to look upon, it being entirely harmonious with her beauty, Grace Harper impressed Mrs. Claude Walsingham on the instant as being a well-bred, well-fed nonentity.

"Where have you been, Bella?" Claude asked. "Jack has made a rambling statement as to where he took you."

"Mine will probably be still more rambling. How should I know the names of your roads? We tried three different roads; and oh, Claude, I saw Lord Lexley riding with a lady!"

Claude leant forward a little more before he replied. He was sitting lounging forward with his arms on his knees, before Miss Harper, in a semi-devotional manner, that angered his mother to the full as much as it would have pleased her in former days.

"That's his wife," he said, when he did answer Bella's remark relative to Lord Lexley.

"I didn't know he was married. How strange! Whom did he marry, Claude?"

She asked it eagerly. She was naturally interested about the man who had fancied himself—and caused her to fancy him—in love with her once.

"You had better ask Miss Harper; he is her cousin; she can give you full information—can't you?" he added, looking up at Miss Grace with eyes that made her feel Mrs. Claude to be a thorn in her flesh.

"As full information as any stranger can care to have, I suppose. Lord Lexley married two months ago. Lady Lexley is a delightful person; not an Englishwoman."

"But Lord Lexley is not a stranger to me by any means, Miss Harper. (No, Jack, I won't have anything more; thank you. I don't like eating by myself.) He's not a stranger to me, as you will find, if you ask him."

Mrs. Claude was colouring and flashing, and speaking as she was wont to look and speak when angry. Claude felt annoyed; trifling as the storm might be, it would probably interfere with his massive flirtation with Miss Harper.

"You shouldn't have let Jack lure you away so far if you dislike eating by yourself, dear," he said quietly.

"We have not been far."

"Then what the deuce—beg pardon—what in the world have you been doing? You have been out long enough. Was your horse troublesome?"

"Not a bit—was he, Jack?" Bella replied, confidently.

"Not a bit," Jack answered, with an alacrity he had not displayed before. There was truth, to his mind, in the statement as to the horse not having been troublesome. The horse had done all which may become a horse, all which could be expected of the best known and best conducted animal. Jack rather hoped that the conversation would not quit the field of Devilskin's worthy merits. If it did, and wandered off into riding experience generalities, and so provoked further questioning and cross-examination as to what had befallen Mrs. Claude and himself this morning, he would be in a sore strait. His newly-born loyalty towards his brother's wife would rise up in arms against his normal loyalty towards the truth, and maybe conquer the latter, for Bella's charm had worked.

Mrs. Claude had contented herself with the mildest viands up to this juncture—contented herself with viands to which she did not ordinarily incline, such as sweet soft puddings that permitted themselves to be eaten with a spoon. Just now it occurred to her to try something else—something which necessitated the use of a fork, and as soon as she took the fork in her hand, she gave a little exclamation and suffered the fork to fall on her plate with a heavy clatter.

Her strained wrist could be kept a secret no longer; she was holding it away from her with her other hand, and saying, "Oh, how it's swollen! what *shall* I do?" when Claude looked at her. He ceased seeking to improve the shining hours with Miss Harper in an instant, and went over to his wife's side.

"What is it? How did this happen, darling? You are hurt?"

He was leaning over her with a tenderly-protecting air, that almost made her feel that it would be well to confide the cause of this accident to him. However, second thoughts arose and checked her. It would not be confiding it alone to Claude—that she would have done at once—but to Claude's family, who might interfere, on the strength of this accident, and persuade him not to let her have a run with the hounds on Wednesday.

"My wrist got a little jerk," she stammered. "Don't touch it so—take care," she cried, as Claude manipulated the swollen wrist.

"How did it get a little jerk? the horse has as good a mouth as need be. Did you get it while you were out though, or after you came home?"

The husband asked these questions gently, and Bella once more felt disposed to make a clean breast of it.

"Well, it was——" she began, and then Mrs. Markham interrupted her to say—

"Most probably it was the dogs; they are such rough brutes that no lady should venture near them when they are chained."

"If it had been Devilskin's doing, you should never have ridden him again," Claude said. "It isn't a sprain, though; it's only a tendon that is strained a little. Did old Nep throw your hand up while you were patting him?"

"Yes," Bella answered, colouring vividly; but telling her story without hesitation, nevertheless. Then Claude carefully bound the injured wrist with a broad piece of ribbon, and, greatly to Jack's relief, the subject dropped.

"I got over it well, considering all things. It is impossible for me to avoid blundering, if I prevaricate ever so little," Bella remarked to her brother-in-law that evening.

"Why did you?"

"Why did I what?"

"Humbug about it. Why didn't you out with it—Claude couldn't have said anything—instead of laying the fault on the poor innocent dogs?"

"The poor innocent dogs are and will ever be in happy ignorance of the evil that is laid to their charge!"

"That doesn't make it one bit the fairer."

"Jack, I won't be reprimanded by you. I look upon you as my sworn ally; you mustn't turn against me, and go over to the enemy, on account of that tiniest of white lies that I told about your dogs. It would have been too much to have had every one up in arms against my plan of going out next Wednesday."

"So it would," Jack said frankly. "Well! looked at that way, perhaps; only——"

"What? give me the benefit of these profound reflections."

"They are not 'profound'—I know that very well," Jack said, rather hotly. "I only mean that it's pluckier to tell the truth: you *are* plucky enough too."

"That I am, in big things; but I am a very coward in facing fuss. They don't like me here, Jack; your mother and Mrs. Markham have mounted a sort of cold, polite guard over me, that I feel, though it's not tangible; they would be disposed to take a severe view of every little misfortune, horsey or otherwise, that befell me."

"If they found it out, but not if you said all there was to say about it yourself. You will after this, won't you—whether Devilskin flies his fences or not?"

"Yes, I will after this," she replied—"I will indeed, if you will only keep this one first little experience quiet."

Which Jack promised to do in accents so firm that Bella deemed the matter dead and buried beyond all possibility of resuscitation.

Miss Grace Harper was endowed by nature with a good memory. She was one of those people who can remember and reproduce for the edification of others what she said to him, and he to her, and what they were both doing at the time, together with what other people appeared to think about it. This last was the wildest conjecture; but the matter she conjectured, taken in conjunction with her manner of giving it forth, imparted that air of truth and reality to what she said which is apt to hover over dull thoughts dully worded. There was a vast appearance of sober reflection in the sentences in which she accredited So-and-so with having thought such and such. One forgot that truth is beauty when listening to her surmises, and only felt the improbability of any one having the bad taste to conceive so plain a fiction.

Miss Harper went home from her visit to the Court, and her interview with the heir and his bride, not at all indisposed to cry havoc and let loose the dogs of war upon the latter. She had been carefully trained to love and look up to Claude Walsingham, and she had a good memory, and could not forget that she had been so trained. She had a great gift of patience, and there had been no suffering to her in that waiting for him which his mother had tacitly enjoined of late years; but when the waiting was proved inefficacious, she began to bewail herself in her silent soul, and lament her lost time. She felt injured; she felt that Mrs. Claude had reaped the result for which she (Grace) had not "striven," but waited. Therefore, as was wise and womanly, she hated Mrs. Claude, and marked a mighty mote in Mrs. Claude's eye.

She had listened attentively to every word to which each member of the Walsingham family had given utterance on Mrs. Claude's return that day after luncheon. She had listened attentively to every word, and she was in her usual position of being able to repeat every word with wordy accuracy should occasion for doing so arise. According to her wont, also, she had not drawn any remarkably clear deductions from what she had heard, but had just suffered it to sink into her memory for reproduction on the earliest opportunity.

She found that her cousin, the great relative of her house, whose sins of omission (he had been guileless in act, and was only guilty of forgetting smaller people than himself) had been sedulously blinked by her whole family from his earliest childhood—she found, I say, that her great cousin Lord Lexley and his wife had been back from their ride for some time when she reached home. Lady Lexley was in her dressing-room. Lady Lexley had made known before retiring thither that she would be glad to see Miss Harper immediately on her return.

The Harpers had taken Lady Lexley on trust, in a measure—more than in a measure, indeed—they had taken her completely and entirely on trust. This they had done, partly because Lord Lexley's social countenance was loved by them as the sun is by its flower, and partly because in their hearts they did believe him to be incapable of folly or vice. Wishing him to continue to shine upon them, they argued warmly against nothing—for no one had to them breathed a word in disparagement of the new Lady Lexley—argued that "if Lexley were satisfied, it would ill become them to question the antecedents of a lovely Italian countess, whose filial feelings had subjected her to the agonies of publicity." So they took her upon trust, and gave her their best rooms, and were grateful for all the trouble she gave, as became worthy, kind country people, who liked their neighbours to see how well they stood with their grandest connection.

Lady Lexley was very anxious to hear of Claude, and she was even more anxious to hear of Claude's wife. Lord Lexley was one of those nice-looking, cool, crisp men, who never say clever things, but who never do foolish ones in everyday life; his marriage had not been all that was wise and discreet, perhaps, but it was the exception to an otherwise unvarying rule. Lord Lexley being this, his wife (she was only a woman) did sometimes remember that summer night at Richmond; and remembering this, she felt anxious to hear more of Mrs. Claude.

Lady Lexley, clever, designing, well used to conceal and to affect as she was, was a more legible book to the unsophisticated country girl, Miss Harper, than was the unsophisticated country girl to her. She had not found out that the great "what might be" of Grace's life had been her possible union with the son of her father's most important neighbour. But Grace had fathomed that the light which ne'er shall shine again on life's dull stream for Lady Lexley, had been a "something" which she had known, had felt, had looked, had sighed with, and for, and in the company of Claude.

Grace Harper did not love Lady Lexley the better for this discovery. No woman does feel better disposed towards the possibly favoured sharer of her feelings than towards the rest of the world. But she liked the idea which suggested itself to her of making Lady Lexley's hand administer a depreciatory pat on the head of Claude Walsingham's wife.

Miss Harper told the story of Mrs. Claude's ride, and Mrs. Claude's return, to Lady Lexley, while Lady Lexley was being perfected and prepared for the full light of many candles below. Miss Harper told the story in the minute, careful, laborious, truthful-upon-the-face-of-it way in which plump, lymphatic, fair women are apt to tell things when a listener is their portion. And Lady Lexley brightened through the deftly-applied rouge as she heard, and her flexible lips quivered!—quivered even under the liberal application of Chinese pink —and her form appeared to expand, and her luscious dark eyes kindled, and she was all the Queen of Song in a lyric rage of excitement, instead of being merely the well-established English lady, earnest only on the one point of refraining from betraying aught that might be used in evidence of her ever having known another calling.

"And this brother! what is he like?" she asked, with ill-subdued eagerness, when Grace had brought her narration to a conclusion.

"Oh, Jack?—well, I can hardly tell you what Jack is like, really; quite a boy."

"Quite a boy is he? too young to be deserving of a description?" Lady Lexley said with a peculiar little laugh, conjuring up as she spoke a vision of a vaulting horse, and a falling woman, and of a fair, flushed, young, honest face, bent on both these things in anguish.

"Yes, a mere boy," Grace replied. "If you ask men about him, they will tell you that he is a crack shot, and a first-rate rider (daring and judicious, you know—they say no one rides straighter than Jack Walsingham), and a good cricketer; but I don't care for such things. He is not intellectual, like Claude."

"I can fancy intellect appeals to you more unfailingly," Lady Lexley said, with what would have been a sneer had not Grace glanced at her, but which, as Grace did glance at her, she changed at the birth into a smile. "How good and kind of Major Walsingham to give his brother, his young guileless brother, such opportunities of improvement in the ways of this wicked world! No one knows them better than Mrs. Claude, I fancy; at any rate she has experience."

"Has she?' Grace asked, pricking up her ears. Lady Lexley laughed.

"Tolerably extensive experience, I should say, as would any one else who knew that she was so compromised with one of her old lovers, that she was obliged to agree in taking a part in the absurd farce into which he turned her wedding. They say she only submitted to Mr. Villars' plan of tying the holy knot under fear of exposure."

As she said this, Lady Lexley grew more bloomingly vicious; and, despite the opaque whiteness of Miss Harper's skin, a shade of green shot across her face.

"Oh! 'exposure?' I should doubt the possibility of that," Miss Harper remarked, with that stolid air which is the most wary of all manners. "Nothing could ever be said about her, I'm sure; she's too frank a flirt to be a bad one."

Lady Lexley was deceived by the stolidity, deceived even to the point of showing her highest trump to the unsophisticated cousin of her husband.

"Far too frank a flirt, Grace; far too frank to be let ride about with that handsome booby of a boy, even in these secluded country lanes."

"Oh! no; Jack is quite a boy."

Lady Lexley laughed out, and threw her head up; and the full blaze of the lamp that hung over her dressing-table fell down upon the rich yellow efflorescence that bloomed upon her face.

"Not too much of a boy to neglect tasting what lovely lips are near, whether they may ever be his legally or not. 'Quite a boy!' 'a mere boy!' What a child you are to sing to so old a nursery tune as that. *I* saw them out this morning. *I* saw her fall from her horse, and then he solaced the pain that strained wrist caused her by the tenderest caresses!"

"Did he? how very funny!" Grace said, quietly rising up, and keeping her big blue eye on the rich yellow efflorescence the while. "I must go and dress now, dear; you will be ready for dinner so long before me."

Then she went away soberly and slowly, as she was wont to go and come; and Lady Lexley watched, with her head turned with an eager, inquiring strain over her shoulder, the egress from her room of the girl to whom she had told her latest-seasoned secret. "I wish I had held my tongue," Lady Lexley said to herself; "but she will forget it; she is dull, dull, *dull*, as are the loves of her land."

It was the old story over again of the sharper-witted woman being deceived and outwitted by the more stupid one, who saw, and said, and suffered too sometimes, and still made no sign. The tortoise is perpetually winning victories over the hare. Let us, who are tortoises, be merry and rejoice, and hymn to the best of our ability the praises of stolidity and sober slowness.

"He shall be sorry yet that he has made me wait all these years for nothing!" Grace Harper said to herself while she was dressing. "I wonder how he will like hearing what Lady Lexley saw, and that, if *I* don't keep her from speaking of it, his wife will be talked about."

The wonder imparted an extraordinary zest to her toilet.

——o——

CHAPTER XXIII.

FALSE IMPRESSIONS.

On Tuesday morning—the morning before that day on which the hounds were to meet at Horsley Hollow—Mrs. Claude broached the subject of her design of following them to her husband. "What shall you go down on, Claude?" she asked—"your father's old cob?"

"I shall not go down 'on' anything; a fellow is one splash after ten yards of these roads. I shall have my mother's brougham."

"Then I'll have Devilskin led, and go down in the brougham with you," she said, in as quiet a tone as if she were making the most commonplace arrangement.

He looked up with a quick wonder. "Jack will want to go with me," he said, in a way that reminded her that there were but two seats in the brougham.

"Jack is too young to be a sporting dandy yet, I'm sure, Claude; he will follow with just as light a heart if he has got splashed before the hounds find, as if he's spotless till then!"

"But why have Devilskin led? What the deuce is the good of *driving* down in your habit to see them throw off?"

"I want to keep free from splashes, too, Claude. I want Devilskin to be fresh when we start," she said, with a little assumption of defiance dashed with deprecation.

"Do you want to ride with us?" he asked, suddenly.

"Oh, Claude, I do!"

"Well, I don't see why you shouldn't, if you like. You know your horse now, and Jack knows the country, and can look after you."

"You can look after me yourself, Claude."

"Certainly, only I am unacquainted with the country—comparatively unacquainted, that is —however, you'll be all right. Why have you made such a mighty mystery of your intention?"

"I didn't want it talked about."

"Does Jack know you mean to ride?"

"Ye—es," Bella said, hesitatingly.

"And he has kept his tongue between his teeth? That's wonderful for Jack!" Claude remarked, carelessly.

"I entreated him to do so; I felt convinced that my plan would be opposed."

"Nonsense! By whom?"

"Your mother won't like it—or the Markhams."

"Nonsense! Don't affect to be a martyr to old-world prejudices; they interfere with you very little, as far as I can see."

"Ah! as far as you can see!" Bella repeated, bitterly.

"Well, don't I see far enough? My dear Bella, this is childish! You imagine all sorts of things that have not the smallest foundation in sober fact, and then you fancy yourself injured."

"I'm sure I'm not litigious and quarrelsome."

"There you go, lovely woman—'litigious and quarrelsome!' Anything else? Can't you assure me that you are not a murderous miscreant, and that my mother believes you one?"

"Claude, I am not unjust to your mother."

"My dear child, I know it; nor is she to you, only you have taken it into your head that she either is or ought to be. The fact is, you have conceived parts for her and yourself, and you are determined to believe them played."

Mrs. Claude clasped her hands more firmly as they rested together on her lap, and restrained her desire to speak hard words.

"Well, never mind, dear," Claude said, presently; "you shall ride to-morrow, whatever my mother and the Markhams say or think about it. Will that content you?"

"It must—I mean, of course, it will; and I am satisfied and delighted, and all sorts of things."

"That's a pleasant frame of mind; I wish I could say the same of myself. Do you know we are to be bored by being carried off in triumph to luncheon at the Harpers' to-day, to meet Lexley and his wife?"

"It won't be much of a bore; I shall not in the least mind going," Bella replied, with a prompt amiability that arose from that craving for change which is apt to come over the spirit of a temporary denizen in a country house.

"I thought you would hardly care to go so far for so little as luncheon and Lexley," Major Walsingham observed, rather sulkily. "Odd it is—devilish odd—to see how eagerly women grab at everything that promises the meagrest excitement!"

"Are you not going? would you rather stay at home, Claude?" she asked, bending her brows upon him, and suffering a line that a foe might have termed a frown to come across her forehead.

"Oh, yes; I am going! that is, I suppose I shall not be let off if my mother and you go. Curse these country hospitalities! Why to God can't they let a fellow enjoy the brief peace that might be his when he has time to come down to these places!"

"Then, if you're going, why should I stay at home? I may wish to cultivate Miss Harper, for aught you know—or to see Lord Lexley under altered circumstances."

She laughed as she said this, and Claude got a bit of his moustache between his teeth, and gnawed it.

"I have no doubt but that you do want to see Lord Lexley: you have a sort of yearning to look upon the joys you have lost, I suppose? Just fancy!—you might have been Lady Lexley, had you played your cards properly, instead of being only Mrs. Walsingham!"

"Played my cards properly? How can you speak in such a way, Claude?—as if I had been hacked, and hawked, and offered about! You're partly right though in what you said, though you didn't mean it:—I *might* have been Lady Lexley."

"My dear Bella, really this confidence is most uncalled for! I thought you held that there was something unseemly, not to say unwomanly, in giving forth the name of a man who has been refused by you, with a flourish of trumpets."

"Now, Claude!—but I won't argue with you, for you're cross and unreasonable about something!"

Major Walsingham knew that the charge was just. He was cross and unreasonable, and he felt that the cause of such crossness and unreasoning ill-temper might not be given publicity. He was annoyed with his wife for her determination (all unconscious as she was) to go and witness the first post-nuptial meeting between Lady Lexley and himself; and he was annoyed with himself for caring to meet Lady Lexley at all. This latter annoyance, however, was swamped in the former one.

"Do you care much about seeing more of Gracie Harper?" he asked, after a time.

"Not a bit, in reality; I think her an uninteresting noodle."

"That is a very lady-like expression, upon my soul!"

"Oh, Claude, do you really correct me for such a trifle? I wouldn't have said it before any one else, dear, however much I might have thought it."

"I should hope not, indeed."

"Don't you agree with the matter, though the manner may be offensive to you, Claude?"

"No; I do not. She is not sharp and she

is not that worst of all feminine mistakes—a sayer of would-be-sensible things; she puts out the ideas God has gifted her with, in little, simple words, that you feel you need not listen to unless you like."

"God has gifted her with uncommonly few, according to my judgment. I wonder if you so prefer a fool, that you didn't marry one, Claude?"

"I might say something very invidious, if I pleased now," he replied, lounging up, and leaning his back upon the mantelpiece, and looking down on the flushed face of his young wife.

"Ah! but it won't please you to say it:—*don't* say it even if you think it," she cried, quickly springing up, and putting her arms round his neck. "Just think, Claude — I haven't been your wife six months yet, and I'm alone with you here amongst your friends, who don't like me too well. *Don't* say it."

"Nor do I think it, my darling — my darling!" he said, with a complete return to the old tones and old winning ways that had appealed to her with such thrilling force when they ought not to have so appealed, at which Mrs. Claude was intensely comforted.

Comforted to the degree of enlarging to her husband upon her intentions to-morrow. "I shall have the third crutch in, Claude," she said.

"What for? Doesn't he give you pull enough when he trots? I dislike your using that third crutch."

"I didn't require it for his trot at all."

"What do you require it for? It is so unsafe in my opinion; pins you in completely."

"It will prevent my being shaken forward when he is going over anything."

"But you can't go forward; how should you go forward if you have a commonly decent seat, as I believe you to have? I am not going to have you attempting a five-barred gate; and as to fences, he just jumps on to the bank and then jumps down the other side in a way that wouldn't shake an infant in the saddle."

"He might fly a fence by mistake, Claude."

"Preposterous nonsense! Don't have the third pummel, dear."

"Very well, I won't," she said; "I am so glad you see nothing against my having the treat of a run with Markham's hounds, Claude."

Then he assured her with a big air of magnanimity that he did not see anything against it, "if she would promise to be careful, and to rely upon Jack." Which Bella promised.

The luncheon to which the Walsinghams were invited, in the friendly unceremonious way indicated by the manner of Claude's mention of it to his wife, was in reality a well-matured plan. Mrs. Harper had inclined kindly to the idea, which she entertained in secret in her own mind for many days, before any one else spoke of it. Suddenly the gates of speech were opened, and both her daughter and Lady Lexley put the thing before her, as to be done. Accordingly, she contemplated it kindly for another day or two, and then did it, or, at any rate, put it in training by inviting Mr. and Mrs. Walsingham, and such of their friends then at the Court as liked to come.

When the day came, Lady Lexley commenced *her* preparations towards that reception of Claude Walsingham's young wife which it was well his old friends should offer her. In the first place, she refused to go out for a drive with Grace. Grace's opaque skin could stand the biting March air and wind. Her own susceptible epidermis could not, and she knew it. She had no intention of being spotted crimson and yellowish white in the wrong places, on the occasion of her first interview with Mrs. Claude Walsingham.

Lady Lexley had a good surface to work upon, and capital outlines to fill in. As a rough sketch from the hand of nature early in the morning, she was very striking. You would have said so, had she individually permitted you a glimpse. Later in the day (when she had an object in view) she was charming as a work of art.

What she did to herself she did well. She never looked fluffy! You had to glance very much athwart her skin in order to detect the bloom that God had had less to do with than Piesse and Lubin. And though (late in the day) her eyes were not so much "put in" as brought out "with a dirty finger," the under lids never looked bruised, as is the habit of artificially darkened eyes usually.

In fact, she was an artist who had never wasted her powers on any canvas save herself. This being the case, the surface was, at the time of our making her acquaintance, in excellent order: it was so thoroughly well mellowed that it would "take" the smallest and most delicate hues and touches.

Lady Lexley was down in the dining-room at two o'clock that day, standing about waiting for the people from the Court, with the rest of the Harper family and her husband. This latter never looked out of place in the house in the country in the daytime, as the majority of men, Englishmen at least, do in the shooting and hunting seasons. He looked fair, cool, and crisp, as it was usual with him to look externally. Inside, he was in a rose-blush of satisfaction, and a delicate tremor of delight at seeing how well his wife would look before the woman who had refused him.

They came: Mrs. Claude a trifle wearied by the drive, but supported wonderfully by the prospect of to-morrow, and Major Walsingham rather curious and rather dubious about the meeting between Lady Lexley and his wife. "I shall tell off that good-natured Gracie to Bella for the day," he thought; "she is stupid, but she has no sting."

But he was not suffered to carry out his idea, though Lady Lexley was as well inclined to the plan, which would have left her free to fan the flame of the fancy of the man who had liked her once, as was that man himself. Claude was clever, and Lady Lexley was adroit, but Grace Harper's stolidity defeated them both, without either being conscious that she was the defeating cause.

On their arrival Claude had been somewhat impressive in his manner of introducing his wife to his old acquaintance, Lady Lexley. He had prepared Bella for it in a measure, and had assigned a mean motive for doing so. "For God's sake, don't be distant or constrained in your manner towards Lexley's wife, or she'll think you are so because you lost him yourself, Bella," he had said; and when Bella had defended herself from the imputation of such manner ever being hers, he had made it a particular request that it should not be so, at any rate, or any cost of trouble, in this instance.

Mrs. Claude had promised promptly to comply with this request on its being made—had promised promptly, and without the faintest tinge of suspicion shadowing her mind. As the carriage rolled on, however, and Claude kept his mother and Mrs. Markham company in a sombre silence, Mrs. Claude began to turn the subject over and over, and look at it in every possible light. After a time she fancied that an elucidatory ray fell upon it. Claude had known Lady Lexley before! Who could tell but that Claude had loved her before, and had lost her to Lord Lexley, even as Stanley Villars had lost her (Bella) to Claude! Well, no good could accrue from speaking of it, or from endeavouring to find out what had been; but she would be on guard against Lady Lexley; on that she was resolved.

Feeling thus distrustful and jealous of Lady Lexley, it was only natural that Bella should essay to throw observers off the scent of such sentiments being hers, by devoting her attention almost exclusively to her ladyship; thus leaving Claude to fall a prey to dulness and Miss Gracie. Mrs. Claude simulated pleasure at making the acquaintance so prettily, that Lady Lexley, who was good-natured and well-disposed to so much of the world as did not appear likely to become a stumbling-block to her in any way, liked her, and felt almost sorry that the lapse from propriety which she had witnessed when Devilskin flew his fence down by Horsley Hollow, should have been recounted by her to Miss Harper. Not that Lady Lexley deemed Grace capable of meanly animadverting in an ill-natured spirit on the little occurrence to either friend or foe of Mrs. Claude's. She only felt sorry now that she should have, to one who was soberly correct and proper in all things as was Grace, said aught derogatory to the more impulsive woman, who was far more fascinating, and far less (probably) proper and correct.

In fact, since Lady Lexley had achieved such a much more decent destiny than her wildest hopes had ever led her to believe she should attain, she had become tolerant and tender to very many things. She had been dancing on a moral tight-rope for any number of years, and it was just an even chance, till the other day, whether she should remain aloft, or come down with damning violence into the mud. Now danger was over, and she was very safe. With the full knowledge of her own safety, there came upon her a good deal of loving-kindness towards those who might need it, which in former days she would have thought too unremunerative a quality to indulge in. She was prepared to be very tolerant indeed to Claude Walsingham's wife. Her sole mistake consisted in her belief that Claude's wife stood in need of such toleration.

So she responded to the advances Bella forced herself to make in a way that gave Mrs. Claude a rare idea of her duplicity. "She doesn't like me—of course she does not," Bella thought, though why "of course," she would have found it hard to say. Bella had only surmised that Lady Lexley had been loved by Claude in the long ago, before he had come to Denham. Out of this surmise grew another, viz., that now Lady Lexley was jealous of and did not like her. And this second surmise strengthened the first; gave it bone and substance, in the usual inconsequent feminine manner.

After the luncheon was over there was a conservatory to be looked at—a conservatory that caused you to stagger with surprise when your vision first fell upon it. God's beautiful flowers may be grouped together inartistically very often, but this generally occurs when they are gathered and put into vases where those blooms droop that should stand erect, and those stand erect which should droop. It is very rarely that they look hopelessly vulgar when they grow, especially in the country.

But they did look so here. They were about in large pots that wished to be considered majolica, and were not—in pots that it was evident were not there for the flowers, but that betrayed an oppressive consciousness that the flowers were there for them. It was an orderly conservatory—a conservatory with a pot and a plaster-cast placed around it in odious uniformity; with a lot of looking-glass in it also, as was meet and right and well, and an unfortunate air of being all ready prepared for the advent of a solemn-faced man, in seedy black and spacious collars, who would favour the company with a comic song, or of a young lady in white, who would warble something dubious, more dubiously still. It was a small bit of Cremorne by daylight, in fact, this combination of art and nature which the Harpers' wealth had effected down at their west country family seat.

Mrs. Claude Walsingham walked through this conservatory, avoiding a votary of Terpsichore who was bounding forward on the extreme tip of a lamentable slender foot, with a candle support in her hand, on the one side, and a bowl of bloated gold fish on the other—walked through with an elaborate air of "not wishing for any one's attention, thank you," and being perfectly satisfied that Claude should talk to Lady Lexley. Which manner was not lost upon Lady Lexley, who pitied the feeling that engendered it, and with mistaken mercifulness kept her brilliant self closely to Bella's side, leaving Claude to founder on the big, fair rock on which his mother and himself had nearly split.

The big, fair rock—in other words, the usually stolid Miss Harper—was happier than the rest of the party, in that she appeared to have something to say to the one with whom her lot was currently cast. She was talking—really talking—not with animation, or rather not with what would have been called animation in another woman, but with what almost deserved to be called so in her case, in comparison with her normal manners. She was making a series of coherent remarks apparently, and "what on earth about!" Bella thought, despairingly, as she felt keenly her own inability to originate an idea that should not die and leave her conversationally weaker than before, the moment it was born.

Not only was there a severe physical strain

on Mrs. Claude in getting through that conservatory, but there was a severe mental one also. Not only had she to serpentine, in a graceful but fatiguing way, through the mazes of the pots, and bowls, and statues, but she had to think perpetually of something to say that would not bear, ever so remotely, on what might have been in days of yore between Claude and Lady Lexley. She sought information laboriously. With the best intention in the world, she bored Lady Lexley to tell her the name of every stick and every leaf that emanated from the mighty pots. And though Lady Lexley was bored at being questioned, not alone about what did not interest her, but what (far more damping reflection!) did not interest the questioner, she strove to respond, strove to be hearty and sympathetic and genial to this young wife, who showed so freely to friends and foes what she felt and thought and suffered.

But they were all very glad when the investigation of the small bit of Cremorne by daylight had come to a conclusion.

——o——

CHAPTER XXIV.

A THORNY PATH.

STANLEY VILLARS was not the man to go to the dogs decorously in full canonicals. He had lost his hope in all things—he had lost his trust and faith in all things, since that day when Bella had stood and listened, passively apparently, to the false words, with a falser meaning, when falling from *his* lips, which he was tacitly suffering people to suppose he held to be uttered through himself "by the grace of God." As soon as he lost his hope and faith, he threw off the cloak which many continue judiciously to wear in order to conceal such loss, and quitted the Church.

We saw him last on that ruddy October morn, when the friend of his youth took from him the woman he loved. We meet him again on a bright March day, the day after the meet down at Horsley Hollow, of which frequent mention has been made.

He had given up his calling, he had quitted his profession; in their horrified hearts his family believed that he had abjured his faith. On this latter point he was silent to them; there would have been no pleasure to him, no good gained, in showing them how utterly his rock had crumbled, and so causing them to feel that, as they were but human, so theirs might crumble too.

In giving up his calling, in drifting out of the executive part of that Church, in the letter or the spirit of whose services he could no longer take a part, he had given up (and he knew it well) everything. The black coat and white cravat cling like a stigma to a man in such a case, honourable as they were formerly. Literally he could cast them off, figuratively they clung to him, and checked the possibility of another professional career.

On this bright March day on which I reintroduce him, he was sitting in a room into which its brightness could not penetrate, by reason of the heavy curtain of dust which clung to the window. A disconsolate room, though it was neither a small nor a badly furnished one—a terribly disconsolate room, with that compound air of utter neglect and laborious work about it which is always depressing.

The room was the first-floor front of a large lodging-house in a west-central street. "A house that was three minutes walk from Oxford Street, two minutes ditto from the Strand, and within an easy distance from the Bank," according to the advertisement, which embodied the sentiments of that great majority who regard Oxford Street, the Strand, and the Bank, as the great goals to be gained. There hung over all things a strong odour of smoke, and, littered about on the table, on sundry chairs, and even on the floor at his feet, there were lying a multiplicity of tale-telling slips.

Stanley Villars sat by the table writing. We saw him writing once before, if you remember? down in his Denham study, at his gentlemanlike scholarly ease, before he had outraged his family by flinging free of what he had come to consider his fetters. Since then he had outraged his family; and being only a younger son, and too proud a man to take aught that was not freely offered, he was now writing for dear life.

His losses had come upon him with a desperate, unrelenting force and haste. Soon after he had lost Bella Vane, and with her his hope and faith and youth, his mother died, and her death left him poor indeed.

There was no home for him in his brother's house. Gerald himself was kind and brotherly enough; but Gerald's wife was as hard as only a woman can be. She could not forget how sickly her child, the little heir, was. She could but think the worst of the man who stood next in succession. He was a hateful thing in her eyes, now that he was professionless and poor, and to be put upon with impunity.

There had been anger (this was one of the sharpest stabs that were given him) in his mother's heart when he first renounced all that that high Tory and thorough church-going heart held dear. The son she loved best appeared bent upon going to perdition in the most unorthodox way. It made her ill and angry when first she knew that he had given up his profession, and the prospect of a fat living that a friend of hers had promised in secrecy "should be Stanley's, when Stanley could take it."

It made her ill and angry, and, worse still, it caused her to alter her will.

Great consolation, to be given surviving friends after her demise, in the shape of well-proportioned legacies, it was not in her power to provide, for Lady Villars had for the last three or four years lived but to marry her daughters—an expensive motive which had rewarded itself in Georgina's case. Still she had designed a certain sum for Stanley; but on Stanley electing to kick over the traces of the harness in which she had willed he should wend his way to heaven, the Christian conquered the mother, and she made over the sum in equal portions to her two daughters.

It had been but trifling—not enough to make or mar him—still it marked sufficiently to pain him what his mother had felt, even if she had felt it but for a brief space. It marked a certain difference in his sisters also. Georgina took hers, or rather Mr. Manners did for her, with an effusive woe for the cause of the change that made him regret, less than he did previously, his scanty prospect of meeting with them in the celestial regions for which Manners and the rest of that ilk regarded themselves as booked

But Florence had been what he had always known she would be when tried—true, and lovingly generous, and gentle to him, and pained far, far more at the preference shown to her than he was himself.

Florence wanted him to take all she had, and "let her go and live with him" anywhere, any way in which it might please him to live. But his honour negatived this as sternly as did his brother's wife, when she heard of Florence's rash proposition.

"People don't think the better of you, Stanley, for leaving the Church in the way you have; that's only natural, even you must allow. Where would Florence be, if you took her away?" Lady Villars had said to him.

"Where, indeed!" he replied; "you're quite right, Carrie; my leaving the Church, as you say, is worse than a crime, it's a folly. Now if I had left it for something better, it would have been all right; but for nothing!—only because I couldn't live a lie!—it must strike the better portion of the world as idiotic.".

"You are quite right, it does," Lady Villars replied, coldly. "Florence is still to be married, remember, and men don't care to invest in a wife with as few religious principles as she has thousands; you would compromise Florence in *our* set now."

This had been quite enough to determine Stanley Villars. Hard and cruel as it seemed, awfully as it sounded, he knew that it was true, or at any rate that it would be truth to those whom Lady Villars called "our set." So he wiped off the last bloom that was left to him in life, and drew a broad, hard, black line between himself and the sister who loved him.

She, Florence, was very miserable at parting with him, and very helpless. The helplessness carried the day, and they were parted.

Sir Gerald Villars offered him "his interest" and an income—an income larger than Stanley's deserts, perhaps, but smaller than his brother's love for him. Stanley refused both. "Let me go my own way, for God's sake!" he said, after his mother's funeral; "it's no use telling you what I am feeling, but if you don't let me go and feel it out by myself, old boy, I shall go mad!"

Other careers were closed to him, and "men must work," or, rather, they must live. This is the sole excuse that can be offered for Stanley Villars casting himself adrift on the wide treacherous ocean of daily, hebdomadal, and other literature.

His early experiences on this ocean were not nice! Whose are? Still, bitter as they were, they were better than the necessity of evincing gratitude which he did not feel to outraged relatives and injured friends. His troubles, his disappointments, his time, his normal misery, his chronic excitement, the paltry sums these things gained for him—they were all his own—all, utterly, entirely his own!

I have told how—back in the old Denham days—he wrote grammatical dulnesses fo. journals that had such big names on their respective staffs that remuneration might not be mentioned. Well, those journals dropped him now that he really wanted them, for which prudential move he admired them immensely, as being on a par with their age—a fact their staff of *savans*, and dulness generally, had induced him to doubt before.

So to him, at last, there came a day in which he, too, bowed to the great galling necessity of sitting down to write what would sell. He was living like a gentleman in chambers in the Temple when he first took to the trade,—it was before he had made the discovery that money, like happiness, is a very fleeting thing,—and had come down to the grimy room, in the gaunt house, in the grim street, in the west central district.

He did not fall upon the awful evil of second-rate daily press work all at once. He came upon that by gradations—those ruinous, flattering, exciting gradations by which men do come to it. The boat in which he placed himself when first embarking upon the literary ocean was a monthly magazine with a good name. Casual reader, do you care to learn by what muddy paths the unknown, unwanted, walk into a monthly magazine?

He, who had never written aught but learned dulnesses before—learned dulnesses which elucidated mysteries which no one cared to have cleared up, or made "vulgar," buried and decomposed tongues—he wrote a popular article on a popular subject in terse sentences that told. He was very much ashamed of himself, but he could not help it! He went in for the people and general advancement!—just as though he had been a stump orator, or a penny-daily-paper man, or a Transpontine stage-manager, or anything else that sold himself to the times in order that the times might pay him in return.

His article was a very taking thing, even in MS., when he had finished it, a very taking thing indeed, for he had broken it up into the briefest paragraphs, and elaborated all his corrections in a—way he would cease to do when the P. D.'s were howling for "copy" on his door-mat. He treated of current literature in this article; and as he wanted to get it into a magazine that circulated well, he made believe to think ours the golden age of letters—especially of fiction—in the most obliging and popular manner.

When he had written it, the result was readable, and there were about twelve pages of it. It was an immense quantity for an unknown, unwanted man to get into a good, well-established magazine. But he was living like a gentleman at this period, as I said before,; he was wearing good broad cloth and pearl grey gloves stitched with black. And he was espied by the great man—by the editor himself—descending from a Hansom.

In short, he did not look like a man who wanted money; therefore, instead of being snubbed, and his article being rejected, the latter was accepted, and he was given twelve guineas for it, and altogether courteously entreated.

This editor was just the man to give a tyro heart to struggle on. He had a hopeful bearing and a buoyant voice, and the face of a huge, amiable, parboiled baby, or say, of a scalded cherub—it was so large, red, smooth, and hairless. His suave, considerate, promising manner sent shoals of aspiring young creatures away happy, even though they were laden with rejected MSS. He would not take what they offered him, or if he did take it, he paid them more in politeness than in coin of the realm. Still he had a cheery way of prognosticating a "brilliant success" for one of their still-to-be written efforts—a brilliant success, and fifteen thousand pounds at least, which was vastly encouraging. Neither were ever realised, the success or the fifteen thousand! Still, who can say that he did no good in his generation, when it is remembered how many hitherto despondent ones he had made wildly happy—for a day?

When Stanley Villars wended his way the second time into the Presence, things assumed a darker hue. "You must know, Mr. Villars," the mighty man said to him, "that I acted with more generosity than wisdom in giving your article such a prominent place in last month's number."

"It rested with you entirely to take or refuse it," Stanley replied rather gruffly. The round, red, kind, fat face was rounder, redder, kinder, and fatter than before even; but Mr. Villars began to distrust it. He began to do something else, also—which was to detect a certain assumption of mental superiority in the manner of the guiding star of that magazine's destinies. It struck him with vivid force at once, that if he remained, and sought to continue the connection, that the editor would, in the interests of his employers, cause him to pay a pretty severe penalty for what was averred to have been an editorial lapse of judgment. However, he had another article to sell, and he wanted money; therefore he remained.

"It rested entirely with you to take or refuse it," he had said in answer to the great man's soft reproach; to which Mr. Bacon replied—

"Gently, my dear sir! I am fully aware that it *did* rest entirely with me whether that paper, in which, despite its crudeness, I was *delighted*, delighted to recognise evidences of great power and merit, should go into the Mag. or not. I decided in your favour, wishing to encourage young talent. I decided in your favour; but the risk was very great, the sum paid *unheard* of for a beginner. When you have made the march in literature, which I feel sure you will eventually make, you must remember your first friend!"

Stanley was externally grateful for the kindly prophecy—internally, indifferent as to whether it were ever realised or not. He had no motive for making a name. Bella was lost to him—stolen from him by his friend. But men must live, therefore they must work.

"You will find this better suited to the character of your Magazine," he said quietly, touching his roll of slips; "it's not written with the almost pedantic care of the last; it treats of a popular subject, and is a devilish deal more readable. Will you have it?"

Mr. Bacon took it in his hand, glanced through it hastily, pursed up his lips (they were small lips, that crumpled up into a semblance of the most profound disapprobation on the smallest occasion), and shook his head. "You've worked it up very well to about the middle of it, but the end is vapid, dull, and flat in the extreme."

Mr. Villars grew red to the roots of his hair. This was free criticism, and no mistake, from a man to whom he had not sold his brains and soul yet.

"You will be good enough to return it to me," he said coldly, holding out his hand for it. Then Mr. Bacon gently smiled, and softly tapped the table with a large plump forefinger.

"Impetuosity is fatal to a man in literature, Mr. Villars. I have never before taken so strong an interest in a young author as I find myself taking in you. I shall *not* allow your impetuosity to come between us. I see before you a most brilliant future; you are a rich mine of gold, which only requires to be worked properly to make, not alone your own fortune, but the fortunes of the firm; and, by God, I will work it too!"

He seemed very much in earnest. Mr. Villars was conscious for a couple of moments of a thrill that would have been ambition, had he not lost Bella.

"You think then," he commenced—but Mr. Bacon interrupted him.

"I think—I know, indeed, that if you will only exercise patience, you will achieve great things. I am a practical working man, and I know what is to be done if you farm yourself out properly. You must not make yourself too cheap, and you must not diffuse yourself too freely. Now about this little thing," and he looked at Stanley's article; "it's not worth anything—scarcely worth the space it will occupy in the Magazine. Still I shall insert it, for the sake of familiarizing the public with your name: writers are like actors, they must be kept constantly before their great supporters, or their great supporters will soon cease to support them. 'The world forgetting by the world forgot,' is a natural, inevitable sequence in literature."

"I am quite willing to be kept before the public, since I have no alternative," Stanley said, moodily. "What will you give me for this? There are about three pages more than in the last article, but I shall take the same sum!"

Mr. Bacon shook his head and crumpled up his lips. "I will speak to my sub-editor," he said, "a man on whose opinion I firmly rely; you will then hear what we can do, and feel satisfied that we can do no more!"

Mr. Bacon awaited the advent of his sub, with a beaming brow. He accredited Stanley Villars with the guileless unsuspiciousness of the babe and suckling; he thought his new contributor had faith, when, alas! he had only despair. Mr. Stanley Villars felt that he was being done—but so he would be, go where he would, he told himself.

The sub-editor arrived, and looked at his great colleague with the inquiring eye a faithful terrier turns upon you when he is desirous of ascertaining what particular rat is to be worried for your delectation. He was a grimy little man with wild hair, which he tossed with both hands frantically, at such odd moments when his chief was not looking at him.

"I have been telling Mr. Villars," Mr. Bacon commenced, oratorically, "that in our anxiety to help him, we were guilty of a little error with respect to his last article; you can bear me out in this statement."

The sub. evinced the greatest desire to do so, but a trifling inability to comprehend the precise way in which it would be well to do it.

"Mr. Villars will be shocked to hear, that through the injudicious prominence we gave to a paper that was full of genius, and also full of the faults of a beginner, our circulation has decreased in a manner that is truly marvellous! marvellous!"

Mr. Stanley Villars expressed himself shocked, but unbelieving.

"This, though, I can show you by our books," the editor went on glibly—not offering to produce a single book, by the way, but speaking in a convincing tone that rendered ocular demonstration unnecessary. "However, this is not to the point; what I propose to Mr. Villars is, that we give him another chance in the Mag. as an essay writer, but that he does not rely on that chance; in short, that he gives all the powers of one of the most gifted minds" (here he bowed the plump cherub vision graciously towards Stanley) "I have ever been fortunate enough to come in contact with, to fiction."

"You will take the article then?" Stanley asked; the long, pompous speeches were wearying things to which to listen, despite their encouraging flattery.

"We will take the article—*I* will take the article, convinced that the firm, in whose interests I am acting, will have cause to extol that foresight on my part, which now they might be disposed to denominate rashness."

"What will you give me for it?"

Mr. Bacon glanced at his satellite; his satellite glanced at him in return.

"It would be impossible," they both began, and both paused, politely ceding the right of speech to the other.

"Pray proceed," the suave chief said. Accordingly the grimy sub. proceeded.

"It is against the rule of the magazine to pay anything for casual articles. Authors are too glad to see their names in it at all; it makes the running for other and more important works, in a way that is invaluable to fresh starters in the great literary race."

"You see, Mr. Villars?" Mr. Bacon observed.

"I see that you don't think my wares worth anything, so I must take them elsewhere," Stanley Villars said, in a disappointed tone. He saw that he was being done; he felt that they were merely trying how far undervaluing him would benefit themselves. Still he had not the heart to combat the palpable chicanery—he had not the spirit to risk a failure on the chance of making some better success. He "feared his fate too much." In fact, he dreaded a dull thumping fall down into utter poverty, utter distress, and despair, all at once. So, though he said "I must take them elsewhere," he said it in a tone that told plainly as possible how dreary their chances of being "accepted elsewhere" were.

"You will take them elsewhere?—good," the editor replied, grandiloquently. "Now, my dear sir, before we separate and you go off to certain disappointment, allow me to ask a very delicate question—a very delicate question, in deed?"

"Ask it," Stanley replied.

"Is the insertion of this article—the *immediate* insertion—of monetary importance to you?"

"What the hell difference does that make to you?" Stanley answered hotly. "I have offered it to you for a sum that's paltry enough, God knows—if He cares to know aught of my affairs any longer, which I doubt—and you have refused it. Let the matter end there. Good morning."

"The matter shall not end there!" the editor responded, hastily. He had no intention of permitting this fly to escape his net. "My dear sir, suffer me to speak; I cannot see such brilliant abilities founder close upon the starting shore, for want of a few favouring breezes. We will take your article; draw upon me for what sum you require, since unfortunately the usual want of money in the world is oppressing you. Draw on me for what sum you may require—say a hundred pounds—and work it off, write off the debt as occasion serves. Do you agree?"

"If my writings are worth nothing, how may I ever hope to work off the debt?" Stanley asked.

"Their value will be increased prodigiously after this article has appeared in the place I shall now assign it in the Mag."

"Then if you can venture to assign it a 'good place,'—whatever that may mean—all the pages of a magazine seem of equal merit to me—why can't you pay me for it? It must be worth something."

"In itself, no!" the gigantic cherub replied, decisively; "but we shall now have a motive in giving it an adventitious importance. You *shall* be successful, Mr. Villars, and when you are we should like something beyond your mere word to assure us that we shall not be unrewarded. You will not forget first friends?"

As Mr. Bacon accompanied this remark with a cheque for one hundred pounds, and as Stanley Villars sorely needed the money, the latter answered somewhat effusively that he would not object to giving some pledge more tangible than his mere word as to his readiness to supply "copy" till the debt should be worked out. Accordingly Mr. Bacon daintily prepared a little paper which Stanley daintily signed, which committed him to write for the firm, and the firm alone, under divers heavy penalties, for the term of three years.

"By that time you will have taken your stand in literature and will see what you are about," Mr. Bacon remarked in a gaudy manner. "You will see what you are about, and we shall see what you are made of. Never before have we taken a young author so enthusiastically by the hand; do not disappoint us."

"God of heaven!" Stanley thought, "has it come to this already; to be patronised and protected, to be 'taken in hand' by such a cad as this!"

However, though he thought thus, he pocketed the cheque for a hundred pounds, and Mr. Bacon held the "little formula" which bound him to do their bidding for three years! The business had managed itself marvellously!

After this second interview and marvellous management of the business, there were no difficulties intervening between Stanley Villars and publicity. He was incessant in the magazine which had been the receptacle of his first attempt at popular writing; and not alone in that magazine, but in others which emanated under apparently different supervision from the same source. The initials, "S. V.," came to be well known. More than that, they came to be eagerly looked for. Better still, they were missed when by chance absent. On the whole, in fact, they were liked!

The bar between publicity and himself was broken down in fact, and Stanley Villars had no cause to be ill pleased with the manner in which that "many-headed pig, the public," as he called it, grunted forth its satisfaction at his efforts in its behalf. He was well received. Benighted outsiders, who were happily ignorant of the backstairs work that is going on, regarded him as rising, prosperous, wondrously lucky. His sister-in-law heard of him from unconscious friends, who liked to sting her with civility, not so much as *a* success, but as *the* success; and Lady Villars repeated these sayings to Florence, winding up with a scoff at that perverted state of mind "which kept Stanley in the purlieus of low Bohemianism when he was doing so well and might escape from them, and live like a gentleman, *although* (with bitter emphasis) he wrote." She—that stern young judge—was as ignorant as was poor Florence of that little bond he had signed, which held him closely in the meshes of the enterprising firm who were reaping the benefit of his brains.

The £100 for which he had gone into this ignominious bondage, were long spent when we meet with him again, on the bright March morning—the day after the "meet" at Horsley Hollow. He was going on now, day by day, spinning off yards of slips with the velocity of despair; writing "to order" generally, and selling his copyrights for the most beggarly sums. He was kept before the public with a vengeance; but his brain was often likely to burst in the attempt to meet the demands made upon it. He was writing to live now; he had hired out his mind!—he had drawn in advance on the obliging firm who were never "hard upon young authors!" he was the veriest slave in the cursed trade that men drive in the noblest of all professions.

On this special morning he was very hard at work. He was striving to work himself free of his debt by supplying a novel for one magazine, and a series of articles on the "Early Fathers" in another. The price given for both these performances was of such delicate dimensions, that it would be but a drop in the ocean of his debt. But he had no appeal; he could not carry his wares elsewhere until the term of bondage had expired.

Have you ever seen this mental hemlock growing up and threatening to overshadow and poison a man's life? You can only act the part of the Levite; there is nothing that you can do, for rest assured that the man who is in such a plight, and who feels it as Stanley Villars did, will not howl his grievances aloud. There is nothing to be done, so pass by circumspectly on the other side.

The wild old legends of men who sold themselves to the devil for gold in olden times, are paralleled in these latter days. Only instead of selling themselves for much gold, they sell themselves very often for a mess of pottage. The Moloch of the press is insatiable—and very mean.

He had fallen away from the haunts and the friends of his youth. He had cut himself off from all, in his first dull agony of rage against the false love, and the false friend, and the frail faith; all of which had deserted him, and proved weak when tried. He had cut himself off from these, and had only replaced them by acquaintances of the hour. As his strait grew sorer and sorer, he felt that there was not one to whom he could apply—no, not one!

For he would not cloud what might be bright in Florence's life by allowing her to know how utterly his own was blasted. "Let her be happy, if she might and could be," he said to himself, as if the poor loving child could be happy while he maintained this miserable silence. He made no sign to her, and so she could only lament him in uncertainty and darkness.

He was working very hard this morning, and he had been working very hard all night. "They were going to press the following day," an imperative missive from head-quarters had informed him the previous night, and the second of the two chapters of the novel that he was bound to supply was still unwritten!

Oh! the folly of it! The almost awful folly of sitting there through long weary hours writing what his judgment declared to be twaddle. The miserable littleness of doing a dialogue that was as utterly unlike anything human beings would have said to one another under any circumstances, as were the circumstances under which it was spoken unlike any combination that could possibly have taken place in real life. The awful folly of it!—the ill-paid folly of it! But it was to be done, so he went on doing it.

I presume that the profound conviction of the game not being worth the candle is apt to oppress the mind of every writer with more or less frequency. That we who are still on the lowest round of the ladder suffer from it acutely very often, I can testify. But in the lives of all there must be many hours of that intense, indescribable anguish of fatigue, which can only be tasted to the full by those who, while worn out mentally and bodily, with a perfect completeness that appears to admit of no increase, are compelled to still hold a pen, and go on staining the paper with what might be their heart's blood by the hurt it gives them.

There was a chalky look around his lips, his eyelids were swollen, and his eyes red and sunken at last when he laid the pen down, and commenced gathering up the sheets of copy, taking a note of the MS. when he came to the last, and writing down in his note-book the last few lines in a way that plainly told its own story. He would go off when the time came to supply his next instalment, with just those few lines as a guide for the future, and a reminder of what had gone before. As he did so, the postman's knock sounded sharply, and before he had time to give a sigh to the times when his work had been conducted in so widely different a way, the servant came into his room with a letter; and, for the first time since she had sent him his dismissal at Denham, he saw the handwriting of Bella Vane.

—o—

CHAPTER XXV.

"THAT WOMAN."

Major Walsingham sat speechless in the corner of the carriage during the whole of the drive home after that pleasant luncheon at the Harpers' at which Lady Lexley had conceived such a vast toleration for Bella. He sat speechless—a bad sign in itself. Worse than this, he looked what Bella emphatically termed "glum."

Mrs. Claude left her husband to the undisturbed enjoyment of his silence and glumness till the carriage drew up at the hall door of the Court. Then, when he was handing her out, she said—

"I'm so cold, Claude; can't we go for a run before dinner?"

"You can go for a run if you please, I suppose," he replied grimly.

"Blessings on you for the gracious permission; I know I can go, but I want you to go with me."

"Then I am afraid you will not have what you want in this instance," he said coldly, and Bella saw that the red spots were very visible in his eyes, and that he looked stern and cold.

"Claude! what is the matter?" she asked, following him into the hall, and laying her hand on his arm. "What *is* the matter?" she repeated eagerly. "Come in here;" and she pushed the library door open and went in hastily with him.

"The matter! the matter is that I am very much annoyed," he replied, while Bella stirred the dully burning fire fiercely, causing a large blaze to leap up and show how flushed her cheek was, and how brilliant her eyes.

"What are you annoyed about?" she asked, standing right in front of him with her hat in her hand, and her face upturned to his gaze frankly. "What are you annoyed about?"

"You."

"What have I done, or left undone? What is it, Claude?"

"Don't speak in that peremptory tone to me!" he said coldly.

"Ah! think a little of what *I* feel at *your* tone! What have I done; tell me?"

"Made me a laughing-stock for the neighbourhood as well as yourself."

"Claude!"

"You have; don't deny it, Bella: were you not thrown from your horse the other day? You may as well tell the truth, for I know it."

She laughed out. "Is that all? Yes, I *was*, only I wouldn't tell for fear of your not letting me ride Devilskin to-morrow."

"I shall not let you ride now, you may be very certain; not because you were awkward enough to come off, but because of what followed. Really, madam," he began, walking up and down the room with hasty strides, for the purpose of getting his anger up to the proper pitch, "I think you might have a little more respect for your husband than to—to—heavens! I can hardly express myself about it—conduct yourself in the way you did!"

"In what way?" she asked, wonderingly. She was pallid with anger. Major Walsingham imagined her to be pallid from fear. She had entirely forgotten Jack's cubbish salute.

"In what way, Bella? Don't affect to have forgotten, or to regard the occurrence as one of no consequence. Jack is a young fool; but I don't choose to have a young fool, simply because he is my brother, treating my wife as he would any woman for whom he'd no respect."

"Claude! you don't know what you are saying."

"Don't I, faith! I know very well. Now I'll have no more of it, Bella; I'll have no more of it."

"Of what?"

"Of this cursed philandering with Jack!"

"How can you—how *dare* that woman accuse me of it? I saw her that day—that unfortunate day."

"What woman?—I mean you're quite mistaken," Claude said confusedly. "I have heard of your conduct, and I'm very much annoyed. Why you should imagine Lady Lexley to be my informant, I don't know."

"It *was* Lady Lexley—she passed me afterwards. Let me tell you now how it happened, Claude," and she proceeded to attempt to explain.

But Major Walsingham would not be a patient listener. He was angry—I may almost go so far as to say he was infuriated against his brother and his bride for having placed him in such a position that he might be laughed at. He did not want to hear Bella's explanations, therefore he would not listen.

"I shall put a stop to these long lonely rides with Jack. Your cursed vanity has led you into the coil. You have nothing to do down here, so I suppose you thought you would get Jack in your train—a grand triumph!" he said mockingly.

Mrs. Claude turned to leave the room. When she reached the door she paused.

"Will you speak reasonably about it, Claude? Don't accuse me of entertaining such a puerile motive: you know yourself that it is false."

"I know nothing of the kind. Judging from your antecedents, I should say——"

She was back by his side like a flash of light.

"Don't say those words, Claude!"

"That you were not the one to evade a flirtation if it came in your way. Now, don't treat me to hysterics or asseverations of innocence. The boy is a booby; but as he didn't know how to treat you with fitting respect, you ought to have taught him."

"Fitting respect!—your own brother!"

"Good God, you don't mean to tell me that you would smile and be happy if all my brothers took it into their heads to kiss and caress you! If you don't learn greater prudence and circumspection, we shall both have cause to rue the day we met."

"I think we shall," she said, sadly, and then she went away with a sober face, and step, and heart.

She was sure of it! That woman—that dark winsome woman, who had been so smiling and so suave to her—was the one who had given Claude the dagger, and shown him where to strike. Bella saw it all. The old love for Claude, and the animus against herself, Claude's hapless wife. "I must be on guard against her, or she'll poison my life," Bella thought. The idea, the wild idea of it's being the fair, placid Miss Harper against whom it would be well to be on guard, never struck her.

Sitting there, in the solitude of the big, state bed-room of her husband's father's house, she began to feel alone, friendless—very, very desolate! Claude had repulsed her. He had been hard, and cruel, and rude, at the instigation of "that woman!" It was wonderful the way in which she hated the woman who had done her no ill. It was wonderful that no instinct led her to beware of the one who was ready to strike her down with a stunning force, should opportunity offer.

Her desolation grew upon her as she reflected that the harmless bond which had existed between Jack and herself was to be snapped. She felt desperately ill-used, and desperately ill-tempered, as one is apt to feel under such circumstances. They were all cold and hard to her down here—cold, and hard, and horribly unjust! Claude was these things to an even stronger degree than the rest of his family; and that he was so at the instigation of the handsome, not too well authenticated Lady Lexley, she felt firmly convinced. Bella sat down, and hated Lady Lexley vigorously for a few minutes—hated her for her florid manner and those witching ways which had failed in deceiving her, Bella, but had done their work so well upon Claude—hated her for being the indirect cause of putting a stop to that run with Markham's hounds, the prospect which had made things endurable for the last few days,—hated her, in fact, as only a woman can hate the one whose influence over the man she loves, she fancies to be stronger than her own. After hating Lady Lexley vigorously in inaction for a few minutes, she rose up and bethought herself of Stanley Villars, and resolved to write to him, telling him how that she wanted a friend and adviser, and entreating him to be the former to her, and give her the latter for the sake of the old days that her heart now ached to recall.

She wrote her letter, but she did not say quite all she had intended saying when she first thought of writing to him. Her heart yearned for sympathy, and so she sought it from him in a roundabout way, since her husband appeared bent on refusing it to her; but she did not tell him this. She only told him that Claude and herself were going back to town early in the following week, and begged that he would come and see her at once. "You have shown yourself capable of so much, that you will give me this great pleasure," she wrote. "Besides, you promised to come to me did I ever need you. I need you now; and I know that you are not one to break a promise."

Her sole motive in applying to Stanley Villars was that he might come to them, and when he had heard a bit, the merest bit of the story of her venial error, and Claude's virulent denunciation of it, that he might "speak to Claude," and impress upon him that so long as the guiding hand was heavy she would jiffle. "No one knows that better than Stanley," she thought, "and no one can impress the truth of it so vividly upon Claude. *Some one* ought to tell Claude that he is going the way to alienate me; and I'm sure mamma can't."

However, when she had enclosed her letter and directed it to Mr. Villars, at the office of the magazine in which she had marked, with a very lax interest, for some two or three months past, that he wrote, she thought she would try another plan first. Claude had been rash and rude in not hearing her spoken words, but surely he would read a written appeal.

Her letter to her husband, the whole of which I shall not transcribe, was a trifle high flown, perhaps, but it was thoroughly meant. She told him how well she knew her own faults, and how she lamented them, and she implored him not to urge her on to any display of wilfulness by judging her over-harshly, and rebuking her at the instigation of any one. She told him how she had married him, firmly intending to be led and directed by him in all things, honestly and sincerely wishing to bow her will to his. "But"—the old defiant spirit would crop up, humbly as she strove to write—"I must be led and directed, not driven. Dear Claude, say to me kindly that you wish me to give up anything, *everything* in the world, and I will do it without hesitation; but do not order me with anger on your brow and in your tones, as though I had been a grievous culprit, and you were a stern judge, instead of a loving husband. Anger is as a blight to me—God knows *what* may wither under it. Let me feel that I may turn to you without the dread of a rebuff, and then I shall turn to you on all occasions."

There was a little more, but it was all in the same strain. It was a warm, loving, earnest, illogical plea, and her heart beat high as she carried it into her husband's dressing-room, and placed it on the table before him. "Will you read this, Claude?" she asked, timidly, and he (almost dreading that it might be some rash declaration of an intention to do something the mere thought of which made his heart stand still) said, "Yes, he would."

He read it. She, standing just inside the door, waiting for him to turn and take her in his arms, and pet and caress, and "make it all up with her," saw him read it through without pausing once. It was so much better, so much more conciliatory than he had anticipated, that he reminded himself that *now* was the time to teach her to have done with her old rebellious habits—that nonsense could be safely put an end to at once and for ever.

"My dear Bella," he said, tearing the letter in two and throwing the pieces away from him carelessly, "you might just as well have said all this (or rather have left it unsaid) as have written it: it is not a very sensible or pleasing way of taking a reproof that was as mild as any man who cared a rap for his honour could have administered."

"Is that all you'll say to me?"

"That is all I have to say. Perhaps you will be good enough to go and get ready for dinner; my mother will hardly appreciate the reason of your being late."

"That I am sure she will not—you needn't impress it upon me," Bella said. Then the tears started into her eyes, and she got away out of his presence hastily, with a big strong feeling in her beating heart that he was hard and callous—he, the man for whom she had jilted Stanley Villars. The letter should go to Stanley, after all. She needed kindness, she needed a friend, she needed and was justified in seeking one, for her husband had repulsed her.

So the letter went to Stanley Villars; and, to Claude's surprise, that night Bella was as glittering and as cold as steel.

—o—

CHAPTER XXVI.

A RUN WITH MARKHAM'S HOUNDS.

THE following morning was as trying a one to Mrs. Claude Walsingham as the most determined advocate of her being "kept under," and taught to submit her unruly desires to the wiser ones around, could have wished. Claude and Jack breakfasted with them in pink. Mr. Markham had started off at an earlier hour to interfere with his huntsman as to the hounds which should be drafted off for this day's sport. So all that Bella saw was gallant, dashing, and gay. Mr. Markham might have marred the harmony both of colour and proportion, for his coat was time-worn and faded, and he was heavy and fat.

Claude was a bit of a dandy—the majority of men who have well-balanced souls and a proper appreciation of the beautiful are. No more daring rider could be found in any hunting-field than Major Walsingham; no man had ever seen him swerve or hesitate, no man had ever seen him blunder or blench, no man had ever seen him quit the saddle without good cause. But he always came to the meet neat and trim, spotless, free from travel-soil or splash, unheated, unwearied, in a little brougham and a big grey wrap that covered him from head to foot.

To see him step from the little brougham, and the next moment settle to the saddle, and the stride of his grand grey hunter, was a sight that women congregated from far and near to witness. He had just that happy mixture of power and refinement that women love; he could button the tiniest glove round the tiniest wrist dexterously in one moment, and dash at the most tremendous fence with equal dexterity in the next. Claude was a man to watch in the field, whether it were of sport or love; and this morning, as his wife sat at breakfast with him, and saw him for the first time in "pink," she felt that he did not care for her to go and watch him.

Up to the very last, up to the moment of his donning the big grey wrap, up to the moment of the little brougham coming round to convey this dainty Nimrod to the field, she hoped that he would "make friends" and order Devilskin; or at least tell her to be happy, and graciously invite her to go and witness the glorious sight he would presently offer. But he did not do so; partly because he thought she had been wrong, and that it behoved him to teach her that she had been wrong, and partly because he did not know how hotly her heart was set upon going.

When he was gone, when the brougham had rolled out of sight, and she was left alone with the stern matrons, his mother and sister, neither of whom had hunting or any other fast propensities, the devil of defiance rose in her breast, and she went and rang the bell resolutely.

"I want my horse, Devilskin, round directly; and Hill must take something and go with me," she said when it was answered.

"Are you going out for a ride already?" her sister-in-law asked.

"Yes," Bella replied, somewhat shortly. "I feel like myself when I am out with my own horse and my own man."

"Terribly wilful! She must be a fearful trial to poor Claude," his mother remarked, as Bella left the room.

"Yes. I can't make her out," his sister, Mrs. Markham, replied—"I can't make her out at all. I believe she's trying to coquette with that poor boy Jack."

"I do not believe it."

"My dear mother! Well, be happy in your unbelief, for it wouldn't be pleasant; but you *know* what we have heard of her; *you* know what a shameful unblushing flirt she has been. For my own part, I would rather Claude had married the most stupid woman in the world, than one whose insatiable love of conquest leads her to pursue it in her husband's family."

"I think you are a little hard on her, Ellen."

"Hard on her! Hear what your favourite, Gracie Harper, says of her, then, mother, if you doubt me—'I know something about her that I would rather cut my tongue out than repeat, Mrs. Markham,' she said to me, yesterday; and when a quiet, amiable girl such as Gracie says that, one does feel doubtful."

Old Mrs. Walsingham shook her head.

"Very doubtful indeed; but not of poor Bella," she said, tremulously. "Leave the subject, dear; I may have done more harm than good in striving to win a fitting wife for my son; but you *do* think Gracie amiable and true, don't you; she would never———"

"Say a word against any one—oh, *no!* I'm sure of it," Mrs. Markham replied. "She has far too much stability, and is far too well principled for that; she would never hint a word in disparagement of any one without good cause."

"I have hoped that she would not do so, even with good cause," Mrs. Walsingham said, meditatively; "but one never knows what people are—never! does one?"

"Oh, mamma! I can't agree with you there. Look at Claude's wife, for instance. I read her as I do my alphabet—a wilful, thoughtless flirt, who will cause him some awful pangs, poor boy, unless he asserts himself, and breaks her in at once."

The wilful, thoughtless flirt, meanwhile, had arrayed herself in hat and habit with trembling fingers, and a heart that was beating in a way it had never beat before. She was going out to do a thing on which her wishes were no longer fixed, in direct defiance of her husband, in open opposition to his will. Let Devilskin carry her gallantly as he might, the bloom would be off the performance. Still she would go now, because Claude had never asked her once kindly to give it up, but had ordered her offensively, at the instigation, she supposed, of "that woman."

Her horse was very fresh that morning. He seemed to scent sport afar; and he carried her along to Horsley Hollow in such a short space of time that she had no opportunity of thinking better of it. They were still drawing the cover when she arrived at the scene of action. There was a good field assembled; and at a little distance, drawn up on an eminence that commanded a wide view of the country on all sides, there were a goodly array of carriages. In one of these Grace Harper sat, looking plump and placid as usual, with her mamma; and she nodded in a friendly way to Mrs. Claude—nodded with a kind smile on her lips that blinded Mrs. Claude to the peculiar nature of the glance that lived in Miss Grace's eyes at the same moment.

"Lady Lexley was just asking Major Walsingham if you were coming, and he said 'No,'" Grace said, leaning out of the carriage presently, and addressing Mrs. Claude, who had pulled her horse up in close proximity.

"Did he? he was mistaken, you see. Is Lady Lexley here?"

"Yes; she means to follow, I believe. Your husband has promised to take care of her."

Bella shook in her saddle, for the first time n her life, on small provocation, as Miss Harper aid those words. *This*, then, was the reason Claude had not wanted her out this day; he intended charging himself with the care of that woman!

Grace Harper saw that momentary falter, and the cause of it at the same moment, and pleasure dawned upon her soul. She had no settled plan of action. She was malicious, that was all; and if it came to her easily to sting, or even to stab, Mrs. Claude Walsingham, to whom she for divers reasons had conceived a dislike, well and good! she would so sting and stab. But she had no deep design in the matter—no fixed, unalterable purpose—no determination to pursue her unconscious rival to some unpleasant "inevitable end." She was as guileless of profound plot and elaborate scheme as are the majority of commonplace spiteful women, who will deal a death-blow to a sister as much in ignorance as ill-temper. Grace Harper would do the ill-natured act that came in her way, and that she had to use no exertion to achieve; but she was no modern Borgia, no female Machiavelli; she could not look through a long vista of cruel acts to be done by her, and refine upon each with subtlety. Thank God, the women who can do these things live only in novels that we in these latter days look upon as over-romantic!

But, though no modern Borgia, no female Machiavelli, she was quite dangerous enough, blonde, bland woman that she was, or looked. She was always counting so many years of her life as gone, utterly gone and lost, in consequence of her having waited on the chance of Claude Walsingham making her his wife; and though no more eager-minded ones had sought her in the interim, she held him responsible for her being Miss Harper still, and entertained feelings of sore spite against the woman who had won the post for which she (Grace) had waited.

When Mrs. Claude Walsingham had entirely subdued the sensations which caused her to shake in her saddle, she resumed the conversation, leaning forward a little on the pommel, and switching her whip in a way she would not have done, had she been all herself on the occasion.

"Oh! she means to follow, does she? Does Lady Lexley *ride*?"

Bella asked it in the tone one who believes herself to be a proficient in the art is sure to employ about one of whom a doubt may exist.

"I believe she does, well," Grace replied. Miss Harper was not too fond of her cousin's flashing wife herself, but she was prepared to extol and exalt her if the doing so could be proved to be disagreeable to Mrs. Claude Walsingham.

"Besides, your husband has promised to take care of her, and he is so careful. He's such a splendid rider—such a *judicious* rider—that she is sure to come out of it well."

"When did he promise?" Bella asked sharply.

"Yesterday," Miss Harper replied languidly. "What a time they are finding to-day!" she continued hurriedly; for as she had asked Claude to "look after Lady Lexley" the day before, she was anxious to change the conversation.

"That accounts for his being so cross, and for his not wanting me to come," poor Bella thought disconsolately. "The reason he gave, his annoyance at my tumble, and his jealousy of Jack, were all assumed as a blind."

For a few moments her colour and heart sank very low; and had it not been for very shame, she would have turned away from this enterprise, in which her heart no longer was—have turned away, and ridden home to the Court, and bewailed Claude's defalcation in secresy and silence all day.

At the expiration of a few moments, however, her colour rose, and her heart too; and she told herself that she could not go back, that it would not be compatible with her dignity that she should flee the field literally as well as figuratively before that woman.

"Do you know where Major Walsingham is planted? I must go and find him," she said to Miss Harper. "He may look after Lady Lexley, but he will also have me to look after now."

"He's down at the cover side with the rest," Miss Harper said, shortly.

"I wonder is he with that group?" Bella said, pointing to a party of men whose heads were just visible over a fence a little to her left.

"No; he went over there almost into the

wood just now, after Lady Lexley, who won't wait quietly. but will keep on riding about in the most irritating way; at least, it appears to be irritating to the rest."

Bella touched Devilskin, and went off in the direction indicated. "Irritating to the rest," but not to Claude apparently; yet who, as a general rule, could be more intolerant to unsportsman or womanlike conduct than Claude. The glamour must be over him, his wife felt; and she also felt that ill as she had behaved to another, she had not deserved this—"this open neglect," she called it—at his hands.

She came upon the group in the midst of which her husband was, very quietly. Two or three men made way for her, and recognised her at once; but Claude, who was talking to the sole Amazon, Lady Lexley, did not see her till Devilskin's head came in a line with his own hunter's, and her voice said close to his ear, "Claude, I'm come, you see; will you take care of me too, as well as of Lady Lexley?"

She gave a well-intentioned bow that lacked all graciousness to her imaginary rival, as she spoke, which Lady Lexley acknowledged vivaciously enough. *She* had no feeling towards Mrs. Claude. *She* had never been foolish enough to wait on an uncertainty.

"I see you are; but that horse won't carry you safely, Bella," Claude answered, as steadily as his anger would admit of his answering. He was very much, very seriously annoyed with his wife. He thought that this freak of hers would tell the whole story to the whole field. The whole story of their conjugal differences—of his manly wrath and her womanly weakness. He was very much annoyed.

"I know my horse's manner now, and I feel sure he will carry me safely enough. Any way, I shall try him—unless you have any particular feeling against my going so."

She looked at him with her eyes—those lovely eyes that he had loved so well when their softest glances belonged of right to Stanley Villars, not to him. She looked at him with her eyes sparkling with wrath—with wrath that had more love than anger in it, after all. But he could not read the glance aright. He thought that she was defying him, and, "by Jove! I'll teach her a trick worth two of that," he thought, pulling angrily with one hand at his moustache, and with the other at the grey hunter's curb.

"I have a particular feeling against it," he replied aloud, coldly, and as he spoke his horse, resenting the heavy hand, plunged, then reared, till he almost settled back on his haunches.

"Oh, Claude, be careful!" Bella cried, all thoughts of annoyance vanishing in an instant, as she saw him—or thought that she saw him—in danger.

Major Walsingham brought the loaded end of his hunting whip down between the grey's ears. He was displeased with his wife. It seemed to him well to let off a little of his displeasure on his horse, since the latter had given him such a fair opportunity.

"If I were your wife I would not let you ride a horse who looks so viciously out of the corner of his eye for nothing, in that way," Lady Lexley remarked, getting herself and the even-minded bay mare she was riding well out of the orbit of the grey hunter's heels.

"The horse is quiet enough. Claude is teasing him now because——" Bella stopped there. She had been about to add, "because he is angry with me," but she saw Claude scowl, and fancied that she heard him swear.

"Whether the horse be quiet or not, I can get him under," Major Walsingham replied; "he's spirited, but he is not an obstinate devil, always desirous of doing that which I want him not to do."

The two ladies, his auditors, heard him distinctly. Some men, who were waiting quietly near, heard him also, and they laughed and looked at one another, for they had heard the words which had passed between husband and wife when Mrs. Claude rode up. Bella marked that they thus looked and laughed, and once again she shook in her saddle. Had it come to this! that Claude should think her "an obstinate devil," and imply before men—strange men, and above all, before that woman, that he thought her so? Was it for this, to be rejected and despised by him, and looked and laughed at by his field friends, whose very names were unknown to her, that she had braved so much for Claude Walsingham? She could not bear it. She could not be bright and brave any longer. Since he wanted none of her companionship, she would go back again. Her heart was bowed down by those last words of his, and she no longer cared to do battle for an idea. She would beat a dignified retreat at once, before he had time to say anything more that could be construed by these people into matter for her present and his future humiliation.

Some such little phrase as, "Then, Claude, as you would rather I didn't ride I will go home," was rising to her lips, when an energetic man about ten yards to their right gave the view halloo, and presently the hounds came out and swept steadily across the road and over the opposite hedge, and Markham and the whole field followed. The sight was too much for her. She could not say her little phrase. She could not turn from the hunt now that it was fairly up.

Lady Lexley rode bravely enough up to the fence that had been already taken by a goodly number, but her heart baulked it, and her mare, the even-minded bay, speedily followed the example of her heart. "Hang these women!" Claude thought, impatiently, as he restrained his own hunter while he addressed encouraging words to the winsome woman with whom he had charged himself on the strength of the vast courage she had displayed in the field while it had been one of imagination only. "You'll find it a mere nothing. Bella, *you* go over and show Lady Lexley the way; the mare will follow Devilskin. *So!* well done!" he cried out heartily, as Bella triumphantly rose and landed without so much of a swerve as would have spilled a drop of water, had she carried a cupful in her hand. Mrs. Claude was brightly happy, brightly herself again all in an instant, as her husband gave that tacit permission for her to accompany him, even though it was at the cost of rendering herself useful to "that woman," she presently remembered.

The even-minded mare saw the folly of holding back the moment her rider saw the folly of flinching at such a trifle. She clambered up the bank, made a faint, small jump through, rather than over, the fence, and came down safely with a sigh into the field where Bella sat, her hand on Devilskin's back, turned round in her saddle to look at those who were coming. In a moment Claude came thundering over—the grey with his legs gathered well up under him, his head stretched out, and his nostrils blood-red from excitement at having been held back in such an unwonted way, the very *beau ideal* of a flying leaper; while Claude—Claude, who came to the hunt in a little brougham and a big grey wrap—Claude, who indulged in the dandyism of making it an important article in hunting creed that he should start spotless—sat with his hands low and his legs grasping the grey hunter's barrel as though they had been of iron; a sight, as his wife thought, to wonder at and admire with a larger wonder and admiration than a centaur could have claimed!

It was a magnificent leap, magnificently taken, and Bella's heart bounded with pride, for that he who had taken it was all her own. She forgave him his brief injustice; she forgot his temporary neglect as she had deemed it. She only remembered that he had gone over his first fence grandly, and that he was her own husband, and Lady Lexley's cavalier for this day only.

The grey hunter had come over gallantly, but the grey hunter had a temper of his own, and it had been sorely tried before he had been suffered to come over. He was a horse who would always be first if he were allowed to have his own way, and who, if he were not allowed to have his own way, went straight off into a strong fractiousness that required the subtlest management. Major Walsingham was not in the humour to bestow subtle management upon anything this day, for he was put out with his own wife, and with Lord Lexley's wife also. He had not been a free agent precisely in this matter of having her ladyship left upon his hands; she had been foisted upon him by the judicious Miss Harper. Foisted upon him so cleverly, that he could not say for the life of him how it came about.

The whole field were ahead of them now. These women! these women! what they were costing him! Through them he might miss the rare felicity of catching sight of the extreme tip of the brush of the fox. "I wish to God you had stayed at home, Bella!" he said, riding close up to her; "can't you propose to *her*" (he indicated Lady Lexley by a movement of his head)—can't you propose to her, presently, that you two go off back, and see what you can of it by keeping along the roads?"

"I hate keeping along the roads," Bella replied, shortly, "you needn't lag behind for me, Claude; don't be afraid for me, I'll not go at anything I'm a bit doubtful of."

"But I'm doubtful about her," Claude replied.

"Then let her go back," Bella said scornfully; "but I'm not going back with her!"

"Come along then; we shall catch them up at the brook—half of them will fall away there," Claude said, testily touching his horse with the spur as he spoke, and they all three went along accordingly—the grey, despite Claude's strenuous endeavours to keep him in, a good length ahead.

They were riding pretty well, at racing speed, and the pace soon brought them close upon the brook to which Claude had alluded. It was a brook so broad that it would have been called a river in some counties that are not too well watered. Where the fox had crossed, it was from eighteen to nineteen feet wide.

Mr. Markham himself had ridden along the bank on the left-hand side to a spot where the brook narrowed itself to a mere ditch for a couple of hundred yards, and thither all the more precautious spirits were following him. But Jack, and two or three others, had gone over without hesitation at the part where the fox had crossed, and Claude, after telling his wife and Lady Lexley to "follow Markham," went at it without hesitation too.

An ugly spirit had taken possession of the grey. He had tasted freely of the whip and spur this morning, and he had been held back and otherwise maltreated. He was one of those horses with more white corner than pupil to their eyes, who are prone to lose their tempers and not recover them again speedily. He had also had a bad example set him just now by the even-minded mare, whose quick sympathy with her rider had induced her to baulk her leap. Horses follow a bad example with as fatal a precision, very often, as the most intelligent human being can do. The grey hunter did now. Claude rode him straight at that portion of the brook over which the pluckier portion of the field had crossed in the wake of the fox and hounds, and when he seemed to be about to rise to it, he baulked, wheeled round, and burst into a gallop.

Only for a moment. Claude had him in hand, and he was brought round and put at it again with a deep dig from the spurs on either side, and a swift shower of blows on his near shoulder. He was put at it, and held to it with hands of iron, with hands so firm, and strong, and hard, that though he would have burst his heart to baulk again, he could not.

Major Walsingham had the satisfaction of feeling during the two or three seconds that he was riding at, and then rising to the leap, that he had conquered the grey's set purpose not to take it. The horse rushed at it with fury, rose at it like the very demon of strength, fell short of the bank on the opposite side, rolled over, and—whirr-r-r! there was a wild singing of waters in Major Walsingham's ears—a horrible rushing up of mud, and crushing down of horse and saddle upon him—a maddening entanglement of his own with a horse's limbs, with a hundred horses' limbs, all kicking and plunging and bruising him most horribly—a moment of wild joy as he came out of these difficulties, and breathed, and saw, and realised what had happened—a sinking back again, and then a blank. Claude Walsingham was at the bottom of the brook, held down there, entangled with one leg under the body of the grey hunter, who was writhing in the death agonies caused by a broken back.

He was lying there, senseless, incapable. The hunt meanwhile was streaming on, unconscious of that which had befallen him.

CHAPTER XXVII.

LITERARY LIFE.

MR. STANLEY VILLARS read Mrs. Claude Walsingham's letter carefully and thoroughly. He read all that she had written in it, and a great deal more besides.

So! it had come then, this hour which he had dreaded in his better moments, and half hoped for in his wilder ones of sorrow and despair. She had found out that old things are best. She had turned from her husband to him—her first love—her true friend. All the anguish had not been his, as he had thought that it had been when sitting, working wearily hour after hour, with no heart in the work he was engaged upon—no heart for *anything* that was not past and gone. The anguish had not been all his. That poor girl, who had been taught by a traitor to wrong him, had had no small share of it before ever she penned a letter bearing the faintest semblance of an appeal to him. This he knew—of this he felt sure from the bottom of his heart.

Thus his mind ran on from selfish sorrow to selfish triumph for "that he had known so well how it would be," for a few minutes. Then the better spirit—the normal spirit—resumed its sway, and he put the dark distrust away from him, and told himself that there was no more in the letter than was down in black and white, and that he was a hound to have hoped that there was for a moment. It was what it purported to be—a glad reminder to him that Claude and Bella remembered him, and wished to see him once again.

He sat twirling it between his fingers—that little letter that had been written in such pain—picturing the scene to himself in which it had been penned. It was from the country house of Claude's father. Ah! doubtless all the family were about her as she wrote, hearing any phrase that occurred to her as "neat," for Bella was wont to review herself favourably as she indited an epistle, and to make all present sharers, as far as their lights would lead them, in the satisfaction she derived from the turning of any sentence. Probably Claude had been sitting by her, too, in the spoony way young married people have. This was a remarkably pleasant part of the picture. He looked away from it back into the letter.

No; the letter had *not* been penned blithely in family conclave. There were no remembrances from Claude, and meaningless as remembrances ever are in epistolary communications, still he knew they would have been sent had Claude been cognizant of her writing. That expression too—"You promised to come to me, did I ever need you. I need you now, and you are not one to break a promise!" For what could his lost bride—the young wife of his friend—"need him," if her husband were the friend and fastness, the succour and support to her, that Stanley had always feared Claude would not be?

It was a dangerous subject to think out. The man who had lost faith, friends, and love at one fell blow, had not lost a jot or tittle of his honour. Still it was a dangerous subject to dwell upon, for unruly ideas respecting "what might be going on" would obtrude.

At first he decided upon not answering her letter in any way. Situated as he now was, he could not befriend her, and his struggles would only pain her. But this decision lasted only for one day; at the end of which he resolved that, though he would not write, he would call when they came to town. On this resolve he tried to put aside the subject, and work; but he found that he could not work on it; so after a while he came to the conclusion that early next week he would write, and then call. Having definitely fixed on a plan of action, he went to work with a will again; for the conviction smote him that next week would find him very restless, and incapable of running in harness; so he went and ground away at his popular "Early Fathers" series, till he had the satisfaction of feeling that he was at least two weeks in advance of the printers.

In addition to his serial labours, he had been engaged on a novel—a regular, orthodox, three-volume novel—to the last pages of the last volume of which he was putting the finishing strokes. As it was to be published without his name—as "by the author of" some great success could not stand on its title-page—as it had no "plot" properly so called—as there was no one prominent male or female figure in it—above all, as it was uncommonly like real life, and not at all breath-catching—his publisher was very despondent about it; and so in the nature of things Stanley Villars was rather despondent too.

Still it was one of those things which, when commenced, must be concluded. Like Frankenstein, our own creations continually overcome and rule us absolutely with an iron sway, that we cannot rebel against. We gloat upon them unctuously at first, in joy at having conceived them at all; and in return they loom upon us at all sorts of unexpected times when we do not want them so to loom, and frighten away all peace, and shadow over every moment of what would otherwise be relaxation.

Stanley was putting the last strokes to his first novel in the days when we meet him again; and how he hated his work! The darkest detestation for it had obtained possession of his soul, and had it not been for the money that he was to get upon it, and for the money that he had had upon it, he would have put every page of it in the fire, and felt himself the better for having done so. As it was, the unfinished work was another man's property—paid for in coin of the realm; therefore, Stanley knew that he must finish it.

He had no particular hero in it, and no particular plot, as I have said. It was more a series of society scenes, strung together on a loose kind of thread, that ran through the volumes, and that might as well have been absent for any intrinsic value that it had, than a novel, as a novel is generally understood. He had been a sharp observer of men and manners, of women and the ways of the world, from his boyhood. His sharp observations were useful to him in a measure now that he was thrown upon his own devices, but the power of stringing incongruous impossibilities together euphoniously would have been more useful still.

His characters were very unmanageable after reading Mrs. Claude Walsingham's letter. Previously he had been going on without hesitation, causing the evil to flourish like a green bay tree, and making virtue its own and sole reward in the gloomiest and most cynical manner. But he felt a better man himself after reading that veiled appeal that she whom he had loved so well and so unwisely had made to him. He felt himself to be a better man; consequently he desired to put better thoughts into it, to attribute better motives to the children of his brain.

He desired to do this—earnestly he desired it. Trivial as the matter may appear to those who have never sought to give publicity to the creatures of their imagination, the things we create—the things to which we endeavour to give form and substance—are not trivial to us. We put a considerable portion of our current hopes and fears, sorrows, despairs, aspirations, into them. They ebb and flow very often with our own life-tide in a way that the casual reader, who knows not—who thinks not—who cares not—how books are "done," no more understands or appreciates than does the dog who lies beside me at this moment; or than Rock did—solemn-faced, faithful Rock—who had remained with Stanley Villars through weal and woe, and certainly not suffering in the flesh yet through his fidelity.

For days after the receipt of that letter on that bleak March morning, Stanley Villars devoted himself to literature unceasingly, exclusively, with a sore foreboding that disturbing, distracting elements were about to arise and mar the unvarying obnoxious routine of his life. We all—or, at least, most of us do—conjure up a picture at the sound of those words, "a life devoted to literature." A charming one was mine for years—painted in the glowing tints of youth—a hero-worshipping temperament, and an imagination unspoilt through being untried. It was gorgeously framed and glazed. It was something like this to look upon:—

He (the *littérateurs* of my imagination were always men—my mental vision of women "who write" was not a pretty one) was usually in a study; if he was not in a study, he was away in the country, in a leafy alley of a large forest, where nobody had ever been before, on the back of a tall, black horse, with fiery eyes and flowing tail. I was very particular as to the fiery eyes and flowing tail. Common mortals, to my certain knowledge, rode horses who were not possessed of these luxurious attributes; but I never mounted an author on anything more possible than a jet black steed, with glowing orbs, and a tail like a pennon, always flying out gallantly, not to say wildly.

He was pleasanter in my eyes in a study, though—a study that contained all the books in the world (which, in those days, meant only all the books of which I had heard—the library would not have been extensive by any means). He was rarely reading those books. Ordinarily, I painted him holding a quill pen with an unsullied broad feather handle, such as Charles Dickens is represented as holding in one of his earlier portraits; and he was often giving audience, with indifference on his noble brow, and suppressed scorn on his haughty lip, to the grandest of earth's creatures!

If he was not giving audience to these kings and queens, and such like, who I always depicted prostrate before him, and deferentially delighted at being there at all; if he was not giving audience to these, he was surrounded by the loftier creatures of his own ilk. This last was the most glorious canvas I ever covered—a chaos of mighty writers, of books, of statuary, of pictures, all in the widest frames, and all, I believe, by Leonardo da Vinci, I having read a story of that master in my earliest childhood, which took my fancy much.

I never imagined such men marrying, and going out to dinner, or doing anything in fact as common mortals do. They were gods to me, and what a world my worship for them made. What a golden land I discovered and peopled—how largely I travelled in it, crouching over a fire in the semi-darkness of full many a winter's afternoon—lying under the trees in the sunbeams through many a long summer day—in that by-gone time when I bent the knees of my heart in unfeigned homage to those who led "a literary life."

Idle dreams! Unreal scenes! A sad wasting of the time God gave me to apply to some better purpose! Maybe they were all these things; but they gave me hours of such joy that not the knowledge of the mad ignorance which gilded them can tarnish now. Nor were the dreams more idle, the scenes more unreal, the wasting of time more reprehensible, than are the dreams, and the scenes, and the time that are paid for and read in post octavo now.

For days after the receipt of that letter from Bella, Stanley Villars devoted himself to literature unceasingly. The bleak March wind howled melodiously past his windows, and the hot March sun streamed through the same, and still he would not quit the task he had assigned himself, and go out to breathe that air and take that exercise which the habits of his former life rendered a necessity for him. He wrote on and on till deep marks came into his face, till his temples grew pinched, till his mouth took that hard line which speaks more frequently of ill-condition than ill-temper, till his blood-shot eyes almost refused to recognise the faithful dog who, on his part, looked at his master with the trembling of fearful love.

He had not taken any account of time lately. He had gone on hour after hour, till his fingers had stiffened, and then he had thrown down his pen, and bent his head down upon his arms on the table, till his hand could regain its cunning. He had not taken any account of time. His head and his mind were hot and weary, when at last his landlady came to him and told him that "such goings on she had no patience with; he had not been to bed for a week, nor eaten sufficient to keep the breath in the body of an infant."

"I am going to give over work for a little time—for a day or two," he replied; "and I think I will have something to eat now before I go out."

There was a singing in his ears, and a pain in the back of his head, to say nothing of a cord of blood behind the ball of each eye. The world appeared to be contained in his brain, and all its business to be transacting there. In a word, the man was nearly broken down. All you who can write can comprehend his sensations.

His landlady was a kind-hearted woman, blessed with a healthy appetite for animal food. It was about two o'clock in the middle of the day when she came to him, remonstrating with him on his state. At half-past two she brought him viands that she judged would improve the same—a large beef-steak that was very red when cut, floating in a red sea of gravy. A fine high-flavoured cabbage, and a couple of smiling potatoes, reposed on another dish. Altogether it was a dinner that her experience of former hungry lodgers taught her to believe would be most acceptable. She smiled as she uncovered it; and then a certain aching something in his chest sank lower; more business was transacted in his brain, and he moved away in loathing. Like a worn-out hunter, he was turning his nose up at his corn.

"I couldn't touch a bit of anything, Mrs. Green, to save my life," he said, deprecatingly; "it's very nice, I am sure, but do take it away. Rock and I will go out and see what the air will do for us."

"Going out on an empty stomach is digging your own grave, Mr. Villars, in your state; it is, sir," she remonstrated.

He was very weak. He felt miserably that he was very weak indeed, as he rose up and got his hat, and threw a plaid over his shoulders. Still he could not eat. There was something very wrong with him, he feared, for he could not recollect clearly whether or not the time had arrived when he was to call on the Walsinghams.

His landlady, watching him with pitying eyes, saw him catch sight of himself in the glass, and start. Small wonder that he started. The face of which he caught a glimpse was so haggard, so altered, that he did not know it for his own.

"I think if you would give me a little brandy, Mrs. Green, it would string me up for a walk," he said, trying to smile, and failing, as business was transacted faster and more furiously still in his brain.

Mrs. Green made some shadow of a protest against the brandy being taken on an empty stomach, but he overruled her, and took it, and then went out, Rock at his heels, with the pain in his chest slightly heightened, and the panic in his head increased.

He was careless as to whither he went. What matter where, so long as he got air to lighten that oppression which had come over him! He did not want to go to "Oxford Street," "the Bank," or "the Strand;" in vaguely avoiding either of these three places, he got away somewhere near the Regent's Park —not into it, but amidst those pretty Swiss cottages that line some of the streets in the vicinity.

He became conscious of a great lightness—a lightness that seemed to be lifting him from the earth. Trouble and the ground fell away from him at the same moment; the next, Rock stood whining piteously over the fallen form of his master.

About the same hour that he fell, crushed by the weight of so many things, Florence rose superior to her surroundings, and fought her way to her brother's lodgings. She found out his address from a clerk at the office of the magazine for which he wrote, and then wended her way there to see him, and tell him that she "had stood it long enough; that the dull void his absence had made in her heart must be filled up; that he must not cut himself off from her at any rate any longer." She listened to the pitiful tale his landlady told of long hours of unceasing toil, with tears in her eyes. She read the pages of MS., the pages of that novel over which he had broken down, with avidity and pride, tempered with reverence and awe, for it seemed to her a stupendous work of genius—a thing to be eulogised in reviews, and read by the world, and to remunerate the writer thereof at such a rate as should ensure him silken splendour for the rest of his days. She waited less impatiently after reading these. She imagined the landlady, with the tales of his pallor and weakness, to be merely a croaking old woman. She went away even happily at last when it was time for her to go back to dinner, firmly convinced that Stanley was only dwelling in seclusion till he should shine out the star of his family. Went away, leaving a tender little note for him, beseeching him to write to her, and say when she might come again, and that he was not angry with her for having come once. Went away home and made her sister-in-law prick up her ears by the rapturous way in which she gave selected sentences from those pages which she had read surreptitiously, just about the same time that Rock stood whining over her fallen brother Stanley's body.

He had staggered and fallen in a secluded spot. That is to say, in comparatively a secluded spot, for one that was so near—more than that, that was a portion of—this, the modern Babylon. It was a raised footpath—an unpaved footpath—on which the worn-out man of letters had laid him down low in a swoon, from which he might recover if promptly discovered, or out of which he might ebb into eternity without pain, if mercifully left undiscovered by fate and a passer-by.

It was a pitiful position! Pitiful, that is, to recount and think about. He had been so petted a son, so worshipped a brother, so once favoured a man, in having the love of Bella Vane. Now he was alone—down, half dead, on the cold, dusty ground—uncared for, as any tramp might have been, with none near that was dear to him—none to whom he was dear —alone in the world, and liable, to all appearance, to drift out of it without much further notice.

Stay! I wrong one grievously in saying that he was utterly alone and deserted, far from every one who was dear to him, and to whom he was dear. Rock was left to him, and there was love—love that may not be passed even by the love of woman, in the way in which Rock lifted up his voice and wept.

With one massive paw laid with the lightness of love, or a feather, on the chest of the prostrate man; with one eye's soft intelligence bent eagerly on Stanley's face, and the other glancing away earnestly on the road by which succour might perchance arrive; with his long thoughtful nose elevated, ready to sniff the first arrival; with the deepest notes of which his mighty chest was capable, brought into play for the purpose of arresting any who might pass by, Rock waited, waited, as only a dog or a woman can wait—hoping for no praise, expectant of no reward, anxious only to serve the one to whom he paid glad tribute of loving duty. There was no motive beyond the pure and simple one of striving to save. He was only a dog!

So Rock, in common with several others of the characters of this poor story, was on guard, where we leave him for awhile, to go back to the brook, at the bottom of which his former mistress's husband was lying when last we saw him in these pages.

CHAPTER XXVIII.

VARIOUS TYPES OF MINISTERING ANGELS.

It was a mere ditch, and Devilskin had taken it easily in his stride. Mrs. Claude Walsingham checked him when he was over, in order to look round and see how her companion came off. While pausing, she leant back with her hand on her horse's near flank, which position enabled her to command the brook along to the spot where Claude should have crossed.

The bay mare got over somehow or other, and Lady Lexley was still in the saddle—or rather was still on high, between the crupper and the mane. Bella did not stay to criticise the way in which "that woman had sat it." She had missed Claude.

"Where can he be?" she cried, as Lady Lexley came up.

"Whom do you mean?" Lady Lexley asked, adjusting herself as well as she could to the intricacies of the pummels again, and trying to persuade her habit to fall in classical folds, which it would not.

"My husband—why——!" Bella did not stay to finish her sentence; she was off along the rough bank of the brook, for she had seen something come up to the surface that might be a horse's head, or a man's hat, or anything in fact; all she knew was, that it was quite enough to alarm her.

As she galloped down to the spot—blessings now on that long stride of Devilskin's that covered so much ground!—she caught sight of a straggler, a man who had been thrown out through his horse falling lame, within hailing distance. She hailed him accordingly, and he knocked out what little wind there still was left in his horse, and reached the place where the broken bank and the turbulent waters told their own tale—reached it as soon as Bella herself.

It all happened very quickly. Lady Lexley, riding gently in Bella's wake on the even-minded mare, saw Mrs. Claude slide down from her saddle, rush to the brook, and feebly dabble her hands in it in a frantic manner. Poor Bella! she knew her husband was there, and in some wild way she entertained hopes of fishing him out herself.

Then the straggler, who had been thrown out, came to the aid of the unpractical wife, and at the cost of spoiling his "pink" for ever, and of dimming the polish of his boots for a while, went in, with the greatest gallantry, up to his waist, and after two or three slippery efforts that were failures, succeeded in bringing a very sodden Claude Walsingham to the bank where Bella knelt, with her face white, and her eyes protruding from their sockets, in an agony of excitement.

There was help to be had at no great distance, for the brook was not far from that elevation of the road where the carriages were, and thither Lady Lexley rode to ask assistance of the Harpers. While she was away, Bella knelt very quietly by the motionless form of the man with whom she had been so angry but a short hour before—of the man she loved so well—of the man who might be dead.

She knelt by him very quietly, making no moan that sounded beyond the immediate precincts of her heart—touching the straggler immensely by the intensity of her silent sorrow, as well as by the futility, not to say imprudence of the attempts she was making to resuscitate the man whose place that warm-hearted straggler would have taken to spare that lady pain. Wiping his brow, and kissing his hand, and looking down! down! upon those closed lids, in wild desire to know whether still a soul was there to animate the eyes those lids concealed?

The time—it was very brief—during which Lady Lexley was away seeking for help, seemed an eternity to Bella. When the help came, it was in the person of the placid Miss Harper, whose mamma, having a horror of "corpses, and accidents, and such things," had discreetly vacated her seat in the carriage, and deputed her daughter to do all that was kind to any one who might be hurt.

Miss Harper's face lost its placidity when the carriage stopped, and she, leaning out to look, saw the face of the man to whom this hurt, that they could not gauge, had come. It lost its placidity then, and it gained another look—a spiteful look, that was still dashed slightly with sorrow—when she caught sight of that man's wife. So, but for that wife, might *she*, Grace, have knelt and sobbed and suffered with a right! She could not pity Bella for her agony; she could not sympathise in Bella's sorrow; she could only feel sore and partially avenged. Sore, that another woman had the better right to betray grief than herself; avenged, by cause for that grief being given.

They lifted soaked, insensible Claude into the carriage, and the two women, Grace Harper and Claude's wife, stepped in after him, and put themselves into impossible positions in order that he might rest softly and well. Lady Lexley proposed getting in too, and "holding his head steady, poor fellow! or doing anything you tell me, dear!" she said to Bella. On which Bella roused herself abruptly from her silent grief, and snubbed Lady Lexley ruthlessly; then turned, with the acumen women are apt to display on such occasions, to the big blonde whom she did not distrust. So Lady Lexley rode behind them, sorrowfully and sympathetically;

endeavouring not to cry herself, and to make the gentle straggler who had rescued Claude do so, by the way in which she praised Claude's past, and prognosticated all sorts of joys for his young wife and himself, did he but survive "this." Despite the way in which she had looked into the water that night at Richmond—despite the way in which she had thrown over the result of that sagacious look when a brighter star promised to shine upon her—despite divers dubious deeds, that some women, who had done ditto in the dark, were very hard upon, she had a heart, and it was larger and more loving than Grace Harper, whose conduct had always been immaculate, possessed. The woman who had erred and been sorry for her sin, and succeeded brilliantly, as success goes socially, after it all, saw how keenly jealous the hot-hearted young wife of the man who had loved her (Adèle) once, was of her. She forgave the jealousy freely, knowing that perhaps, if Bella knew all, still stronger pangs would have assailed her. She forgave it freely, not in an obtrusively magnanimous way that is far harder to endure than outright open antagonism, but with a quiet, hearty thoroughness that, could it only have been made patent to Bella, would have won that misguided individual's suffrages at once.

The fine, fair, generous-looking creature in the carriage—the bonnie blonde whom Bell trusted—would have been a far more dangerous rival, even in a legitimate field, when once her pale envy, her rancorous spite, was roused. There was something broad and smooth and quiet about her, something fair and fleshy, somnolent and soft, that was very disarming. She was just the woman to whom a tired man would turn—on whom a deceived man would rely. You could not look upon her placid, fair face, and fear that she would ever plot and intrigue ever so innocently. "There was such a lot of the animal and so little of that beastly dangerous intellect about her," as an artist once said, that she lapped all suspiciou of everything not being all fair and above-board, to slumber. She would develop into a glorious specimen of English motherliness and matronhood, men's eyes and tastes told them. But somehow their instincts whispered a different tale, and very few of them had given her the option of so developing yet.

There was this peculiarity about Grace—about the woman who looked so unimpassioned—who seemed, to casual guileless observers of her own sex, so uncommonly hard to move,—there was this peculiarity about her—she liked this man less now that he was insensible, helpless, incapable of looking hot things hotly, whether he meant them or not, at her. She liked him less; she was far less moved towards him than she had been inwardly in his hours of strength, albeit in those hours he had overlooked her. She was devoid of that generous womanly instinct which is usually attributed to women. Look in her face, and you would at once imagine a sister of mercy in the widest sense of the phrase. Look in her heart, and you would perceive, equally at once, that the man's powerlessness wiped off all his claim upon her. She had no feeling, no pity, no tenderness for incapacity. She revolted inwardly from all that was weaker than herself. She had none of a woman's pride in being, even for the briefest space, a protecting power. She was not adapted for the part of a ministering angel.

Still she, being a well-trained, well-brought-up, discreetly-nurtured, nineteenth-century young English lady, said and did all that was becoming, and left unsaid and undone all that might have been construed into unbecoming, on this occasion. She was a large, soft, apparently trustworthy "something to lean upon." Accordingly misguided Bella leant upon her morally and physically during the sad hours that ensued while Claude's case was still one of doubt.

Leant upon her, and confided in her in a measure, and utterly scorned Lady Lexley, and turned away resolutely from all poor Circe's efforts at consolation. Lady Lexley sat and shed genuine tears of genuine sorrow for this thing that had come upon the young man around whom she had thrown her spell once. She was heartily in earnest, and she did not care a bit for the tell-tale marks those tears left upon her prepared cheeks. What though the rouge were obvious, and the yellowish powder removed with irregularity? She had tears in her heart, and she would shed them out, little thinking that the truth those tears made manifest rendered her more odious still in the eyes of the wife of the man for whom she wept.

They carried Claude up-stairs, and laid him on the big hearse-like bed—the bed of state, and dust, and black velvet, and plumes, and all the other abominations that go to the making up of the couch of importance in the home of antiquity—and stripped him of the gay and dainty clothing that he had carried so spotlessly to the cover-side that morning. Then the doctor, whom they had summoned with a speed that still seemed slow to Bella, came; and then—then her heart, and her horror, and her huge love for her husband, and remorse that she had permitted anger to obtain in her soul for a moment, overcame her, and she went and crouched away and drank water in a corner in order to save herself from fainting, and so distracting an atom of attention from Claude—from the one whose state called for all that could be given.

Went and crouched away in a corner, gasping for breath and gulping down water, with a terrible undefined feeling that all misery was immediately about to crush down upon and destroy her. It was not her nerves or her heart that failed her at this crisis. It was simply that she, not having the muscles of a bison, became physically incapable of standing by, now, alas! when Claude most needed her. But they—those others that loved him well also—saw all that she did in a distorted mirror. So they cast oblique glances upon her in her unconsciousness and corner, and were obtrusively strong-minded and "incapable of considering their *own* feelings at *such* a moment," on the spot.

I wrong his mother, though, in including her in this somewhat sweeping assertion. No; there was nothing obtrusive in the way in which she came up, without words, and just looked her resolve to stand close to her senseless son, and hear the verdict as soon as it might be given, and know the worst as soon as it might be told. Be it told, too, that though there was all this in her look, there was not a trace of aught that might be construed into censure of her son's wife in it. All her silent eloquence was expended in asking and hoping that all might be well with the hope of her house, and wildly fearing that it would not be so.

But Mrs. Markham made up amply for her mother's generous abnegation of the bliss of blaming. She was considerably "upset"—that was how she phrased it herself—for her love for her brother was an honest love, albeit somewhat of an exacting one. But she was a woman who was never distraught to the point of becoming oblivious of the shortcomings of those around whom she did not like. It is perhaps well for the better ordering of the social state that this type of woman should be lavished upon a miserable and erring section of humanity. I can only say, thank God, that such an one does not dwell in the tents with me!

She was an admirable executive power, though—especially at such a time as this, when to be prompt was the first condition. No other woman would have had up boiling water and an unlimited supply of the softest blankets, to say nothing of the stomach-pump, and a bottle of the best brandy, into Claude's room, in such a short space of time. Servants never stayed to ask her irrelevant questions, and she had the art of causing them to comprehend, in the fewest words that a woman can bring herself to utter on an emergency. They did not like Mrs. Markham, those obedient domestics, but they did what she told them, which was far more to the purpose. On the whole, then, it will be perceived that she had her good side. Her good side, indeed! the most tedious thing to be endured about her was, that even her most aggravating side was not "bad"—was not a thing to be justly hated, though heartily hated it was.

On this occasion executive power, and forethought, and a knowledge of what "would be wanted next," was much needed, and was, in truth, invaluable. "I shall retire into a corner and cry when my brother is better, or——" She did not finish her sentence, but she jerked its meaning emphatically towards poor Bella, who did not hear her, or anything else, in fact, save the maddening throbs of her heart and the jingle of her teeth against the glass, with which she could not avoid coming in contact through agitation. Mrs. Markham made her speech to Lady Lexley and Miss Harper, both of whom were standing about aimlessly in the dressing-room, and Miss Grace whispered to her companion that Mrs. Markham was always "so collected and so *good;*" whereat Lady Lexley looked at Mrs. Markham, and thought that it was almost a pity that her well-ordered wits did not impel her to say a kind word, or give a gentle touch, which would not have occupied a moment's more time, to the player of the voluntary on the glass in the corner. Of course Mrs. Markham was doing her duty most perfectly; her conduct was flawless, and her heart was sincerely in her work. But she was not moulded out of soft stuff. She could not deal gently with the erring, and she thought her brother's wife was erring now. The very atmosphere, which always seemed so hazy about her presence, expressed this thought—that was all.

Never having been half-drowned, I feel that failure ignominious and total will be my portion if I attempt to describe the sensations which swept through Claude Walsingham during those few first poignant moments when the partial restoration is hovering between the black "all being over" and the dim grey of possible recovery. But from the period of the dawning of that dim grey I will venture to take up the theme.

His heart had given signs, so had his pulse. These signals were responded to speedily by his blood, which proceeded to diffuse itself, and gradually dispel that awful livid look which had reigned all too long in his face. He breathed—he opened his eyes—he was living. "He will live," his mother said, turning round and sending her voice straight, soft, and low, to the corner in which Bella was crouching. The sound fell upon her ears—her heart: it drew her up, and threw the glass down, and brought her to the side of the bed just as he turned his head and murmured, "My poor girl! have they got the grey home, and——" But he could say no more just then, on account of a certain looseness of tongue, and difficulty of definitely deciding on an idea to which he desired to give words. But for all this looseness and difficulty they knew that he was safe: he—the pride and hope of the house—the true English gentleman—whose first thought after a mighty danger was for his wife, his second for his horse.

There being nothing more to be done, the doctor promised to "look in" at brief intervals, and soon the incidentals removed themselves from the vicinity of his room, leaving Bella and Mrs. Walsingham in possession, subject only to occasional raids from Mrs. Markham. Lady Lexley and Miss Harper had agreed to remain till late in the day, in order to see "how he went on," and to take away the latest intelligence for their own dinner-table. They were very cosy and comfortable down in the drawing-room with Mrs. Markham, on three couches drawn up close to the fire. Miss Harper was specially so, for she let off a lot of judicious laments about Mrs. Claude; laments as to her frivolity, and allusions to her notorious love of flirtation, and she had the satisfaction of seeing that few, if any, of her shots missed fire on the sister of the man about whose wife she was saying insidious words, that might neither be verified nor refuted.

"I am sure there is not a bit of harm in her—but—well, Lord Lexley isn't one to say a word about a woman, is he now, Ellen? and even he looked rather queer, and said something, I can't remember what; but that I was *very* sorry to hear about your brother's wife."

"I am certain Lexley never said nor looked a word against her," Lady Lexley exclaimed. "More than that, I'm very certain he has nothing to say. I should think I ought to know as much about my own husband as you do, Grace."

"Oh! of course it's nothing," Miss Harper responded, hurriedly; "at least, I think nothing of such things; but then, some people do, you know."

"Well, what is said? You're making a nice impression on Mrs. Markham. What 'is said' is better than what you imply."

"Only that she has flirted. I tell you that I think nothing of it."

"Then why do you talk about it? Let us talk of something else. How jolly this tea is. That poor girl upstairs would like a cup, I have no doubt. Stay! don't send; I'll take it to her."

So Lady Lexley ran upstairs with a cup of tea for Bella, and while she was away Miss Harper generously remarked that—

"Professionals naturally get looser notions, don't they? Not that I would breathe a word against Adèle, as far as she goes herself; but she has lived in a world where there is a good deal of freedom, among people who think nothing of a kiss on a lady's hand, more or less; but then we do."

Miss Harper said "we do" all in capital letters, in a way that drew the line at once between that world of which she spoke and the guileless one in which Mrs. Markham and herself had been nurtured. Her tone, her voice, her words, all had the true "county persons" ring about them, just rendered a trifle less harmonious than they would otherwise have been, by a dash of spite.

She hated Mrs. Claude Walsingham. Hated her not alone for being prettier and wittier than herself, and for that winning for which she (Grace) had waited—the winning of Claude, namely; but also for that nameless something which may not be defined, which we call "charm" and "fascination" for want of better words, and then, to ourselves even, utterly fail to express our own meaning. Miss Harper would have given much—say the peace of mind for a month of her nearest relative—in order that she might have seen Bella even temporarily abashed, discomfited, or lightly esteemed by one in whose estimation Bella might be supposed to desire to stand well. Apparently there was a lack of all motive in this desire to under-rate; but in reality the motive was powerful enough. Another had been preferred before her!

There was nothing chivalrous in this girl's nature. She would strike from behind, and feel no shame in so doing, provided no one were by to see the blow dealt. She had never in the course of her life been guilty of a single action that could have been stigmatised as "unladylike" by the most severe of critics. But had she been a man, one could not have applied the title of "gentleman," in its proudest, fullest meaning, to her.

Now that she was left alone with Claude's rigorous sister, she sat and said a lot of little things that are extremely difficult to set down in black and white, and that nevertheless leave a bad impression on the mind for whose benefit they are uttered. Taken by themselves, looked at separately, each sentence that she spoke was harmless and of little consequence. But the dangerous thing about these sentences of hers was, that one could not gaze at them separately with the calm eyes of cool reason. One could but gather them together, so subtly were they linked, and find them uncommonly unpleasant in such union. One could but mark, the while these words were being said, how soft was the face of the speaker, and tell oneself that from so genial a soil nought premeditatedly evil had ever sprung. It was such a tenderly tinted face! It was so innocently plump! It had such gentle lips and cloudless eyes! Not of such materials are formed the Iagos, male or female, surely?

"I like her so much that I am sure you won't wrong me by thinking I have said a word of this in unkindness," Miss Harper said, in reference to Bella, when they heard Lady Lexley's footfall outside the door.

"My dear, I know you too well!" Mrs. Markham replied, earnestly. "In unkindness, indeed!"

"And you must promise me that you won't think about it at all? I have been carried away into telling you little things I have heard, which, very probably, have but small foundation in fact." This Miss Harper said in a very low voice—almost in a whisper—as Lady Lexley strove to occupy herself with something else at the extreme end of the room, in the way people do strive to occupy themselves when the discovery dawns upon them that their advent is inopportune.

"Oh, of course not! of course not!" Mrs. Markham replied, glibly. But she did think about it for all that glibly given promise; and she resolved that for his good, when he came out of his present danger, her brother should think about it too.

Jack came home about half-past five, in a terribly cast down condition. He had been very high-hearted all day, for the brown hunter had faced all things that came in his way bravely, and had been in a very good place when they found. Wearily jogging homewards, however, he had been met with tidings of Claude's accident, and Mrs. Claude's distress; and his heart was very sore for those things, though Claude had snubbed him ruthlessly this morning, and Mrs. Claude turned upon him glances of constraint. He had no idea, poor boy! that he had been the cause of Bella being made to feel that the bit was in her mouth with some severity.

He went up in his hunting garb to his brother's dressing-room, and poured out poignant inquiries through the key-hole as to how Claude was progressing. Inquiries that caused Bella's hair to stand aloof from her head, in that they were uttered in accents unmanageable through emotion; commencing in a husky bass and terminating in a shrill treble, that sounded like a whistle in the ears of the dozing invalid.

"You go to bed, and I'll sit up with him," he suggested, earnestly, but inconsequently, there being no question as yet, in the broad daylight, of any one sitting up with Claude.

"No, no! hush-h! do!" Bella implored, in a series of gasps that came from her gratitude to Jack for this devotion to her bosom's lord, and her great dread that the expression of such devotion might awaken said bosom's lord.

"Then I'll sit here, and you shall call me if you want me; will you?"

Bella went to the door, opened it a tiny bit, and extended her hand to him through the crevice.

"Yes, I will," she said, looking up with a

loving thankfulness, that grew out of her great love for his brother, into his agitated, frank, loving young face. "Yes, I will, Jack."

She was so pale, so worn, so miserably anxious. These hours of watching—they had not been many—had toned down so much of that brightness that had been so beautiful in his eyes. Much of her vitality had vanished, and there was a sorrowful soberness about her that touched him inexpressibly. He loved his brother well, too. Altogether, the great wish that he could have taken Claude's place and spared her pain made itself manifest in his face, as he stooped it over the little hand he had clasped through the crevice, and kissed it.

"Jack, you had better go and dress for dinner; you're merely detaining Mrs. Claude," a cold voice said behind him; and he looked round, and Bella looked up through the tears his brotherly sympathy had brought into her eyes, to see Mrs. Markham and Grace Harper standing in the doorway of the dressing-room.

"Grace has come to hear the latest bulletin. From your not being with him, Bella, I conclude my brother is better," Mrs. Markham said, reproachfully, as Jack got himself away out of their presence, with a gait to which he could not impart an atom of dignity, or render aught but slinking, for the life of him. He had kissed Bella's hand as reverentially as he would have kissed the hand of the queen. But he had his instincts, and they led him to feel how much better it would have been had that special evidence of his reverence for her not been visible to the eyes of such beholders. So he dressed in discomfort, and ate his dinner with a heart that was heavy for his brother—and for something else.

Bella was troubled with no foreboding unconnected with Claude's physical state. Very frankly did she make a statement of all the symptoms that had intervened since Miss Harper had been there last, up to the present time, to that young lady. She almost felt sorry that the fair, remarkably womanly-looking girl was going away from the Court. The matrons who remained were so much harder than the maiden who was leaving it appeared to her. In perfect trust and confidence she would, had opportunity offered, have laid her head down upon the buxom white shoulder, and breathed out a portion of her anguish and anxiety respecting Claude, and her remorse touching that letter she had written, and her defiant determination to ride Devilskin. The opportunity not offering, however, she did not do it, which was, perhaps, just as well.

Late in the night, or, rather, early in the morning, Claude roused himself a little, and the untiring watcher by his side leant over and heard him speak coherently once more.

"You poor, little, weary mouse! this is a great deal too much for you," he whispered faintly, putting his hand on her head with a touch that told better even than his loving words how dear her presence was to him.

"I'm not weary a bit," she said, softly; and then some tears rolled down on his face before she was aware that they were springing from her eyes, as she went on to tell him how tender Jack had been about him, and how anxious to help her in her vigil. Claude lay listening thoughtfully to this communication for a minute; then he smoothed her hair again, calling her "darling" and "pet," and bidding her forget that crossness of his as to Jack and other things which had been so grievous to her. He declared that he had been "simply brutal," and this was more grievous still to hear in his present state. "But you'll never distrust me again, Claude?"

"Never; not even if you compare me with dear old Stanley, who was an infinitely better fellow than I shall ever be," he replied. And at that reply Bella blushed hotly in spite of herself, for had she not already compared them?

—o—

CHAPTER XXIX.

"ONE MORE UNFORTUNATE."

THIS life to which Stanley returned was not one with which he was acquainted. The scene upon which his eyes opened had never been gazed upon by him before. It was all strange and disturbing—disturbing by reason of its extreme peacefulness.

It was useless to try and remember where he had been and what he had been prior to this existence. There was warm sunshine around him now; there were tiny rosebuds—or were they fairies' faces? blinking at him from the curtains and the wall.

The peacefulness of it, and the prettiness of it, the beauty of the rest he was enjoying—was it all a dream? Was it entirely the creation of that burning spirit of inspiration he had begged as a boon of his landlady but an hour ago, as it seemed?

He closed his eyes as his reflections reached this point; the lashes trembled down and lighted upon his cheeks, and as they touched he went off into blest oblivion again, and a watcher by his side stifled a sigh for that the flicker for which she had wearied so long had been so brief.

The lamp of life in this stranger—this waif and stray, cast up by the tide of human events to her very door—had been so faint, so feeble, for many days, that the torch of hope had been sympathetic. But now, for a few minutes, the light of life in his had kindled that of hope in her eyes and heart, and now it had gone out again.

We saw Stanley Villars last, prostrate, fallen down upon the raised foothpath, with the tawny setter howling over him. The battle for life had been a little too strong for him; he had been overtaken and routed; he had broken down while making a late feeble effort to regain that best of all allies on any field—health.

His case was widely different now; widely different and far better. The scene on which his eyes had closed was all the more unpleasant by contrast with that one on which they opened.

For they opened again in about an hour after the flickering up and fading away which was alluded to at the commencement of this chapter. The watch had been weary, sad, disheartening; but the watcher was well rewarded at last.

The peacefulness of that scene, and the prettiness of it! These were the influences which had been most apparent to him when the light of reason first came back to his eyes and to his soul. These were the influences that soothed him more and more, as such light grew stronger.

The rosebuds that had looked to him like the faces of kind fairies when he gazed upon them first, were on the walls, and on the curtains of the bed. The windows were shrouded with white muslin, and there was delicate feminine craft in the broad blue ribbon bows which held those curtains back.

It was a pretty room, fresh, sweet, and simple. From his bed in the corner he commanded a good view of the toilet table in diaphanous drapery, with a tall vase of early roses upon it, standing by the side of a large glass, in which was reflected a face.

The peacefulness of the room and the prettiness of it, these had been sufficient to arouse and enchain his attention before. But now, when he saw that vision in the glass, he looked no more about him.

It was only the head and a portion of one of the shoulders that he saw. From the position, he judged her to be reading, though he saw no book, and heard no flutter or rustle from the leaves.

There was a red glory—not a golden one, but a dark red glory—in the hair that crowned that head. It was massed back from her brow, and arranged behind in two big loose knots, that were kept in place by a net; and from the depth of its colour, and the massiveness of its arrangements, it had the effect of being too rich and too heavy for the head on which it grew.

He got a three-quarter view of her face in the glass, and it was such a tiny face, and it had such a confiding brow, and such a rosy, dewy mouth, and such a very, very young, innocent, almost babyish look altogether, that he began to pity it, he knew not why.

Do you know that nose that stands out well from the face, and is still straight?—well, she had it. Do you know that mouth that springs like a rosebud with the morning mist upon it from immediately beneath this nose?—she had that too. That style of face to which this nose and mouth belong is far more perfect in expression than in feature. Yet the expression is no more intellectual than the features are perfect. The face is mobile, sympathetic—a thing to love and be sorry for—to kiss and to leave!—so God help the possessors of such!

It was sweetly pretty this face that he saw in the glass. Sweetly pretty by right of its babyishness, of its plaintive sweetness. It stirred him by its drooping beauty; it made him wish to hear it speak, made him desire to touch it, and see whether or not it would alter under that touch—whether it had feeling—whether it could sadden into harshness, brighten into broad laughs, as other faces do—or whether it was always plaintively sweet, droopingly beautiful, and nothing more.

He tried, lying there, prone and helpless—for his had been a fever, and he could not move—to recall what he had known last, before this blest oblivion had been his. He forgot the walk he had taken, he forgot the prostration of spirit he had known during it, he forgot the dog who had stood by him to the last—he only remembered that he still had work to do!

That uncompleted novel, that unfinished plot, those waiting devils! He lifted his head from the pillow as he thought of them, and his head was very weak. It fell back again, and the soothing influence of peace and prettiness that were around him kept it there.

There was a charm—he knew it was a charm, because he had heard, or had he read? of such things—in the atmosphere. But suddenly it occurred to him that he might as well break it, as it could not last for ever—break it, and get back to that—whatever it might be that was waiting for him. So he moved and spoke. Moved with a jerk, and spoke out in a spasm—spoke words that had voice, and desperate uncertainty, and desolation in them—nothing else.

Poor fellow! I declare, that for this semblance of the truth whom I have conjured up, I have such a deep pity, such a sad sympathy! That horrible dread of wasting the time that was his rock, his anchor, his all, was upon him. He dared not be at peace, even for his own good.

So he broke the spell by means of which he enjoyed this charmed rest, and spoke. His words rang in their irrelevance deep into the quiet of the room, and the peace fled, and that reflection in the glass broke from its stillness, threw aside its drooping beauty, and was, in the one instant he saw it after its alteration, the young woman of this world once more.

He would not be at peace, even for his own good. He would test the tangibility of this vision that was fleeing. Even in his present state of semi-unconsciousness, he remembered that illusions might be his at any moment: this was a seeming fact—he would dare to stay it.

It was all very dreamy; the first stage of a recovery from a bad fever is apt to be so. That unfinished work of his, that thing still to be done within a given time, was running in his head, as he half turned on the pillow and asked vaguely "what it was."

The vision in the glass had started when he had first moved restlessly, and now he turned his head, half hoping that it might be she on whom his eyes would rest in the flesh. Such hopes were not realised; and yet I can scarcely say that he was disappointed, as his looks lighted on a clean old woman with a kind face, who did not look as if a legion of small bills were behind her, which was what his later experience of old women rather led him to expect.

There was no fear of losing oneself in shadowy depths in her face. It was a healthy, rosy, round, kind, old face, commonplace, and addicted to smiling without due cause, but not at all to be evaded by one on a bed of pain or weakness. Immediately at sight of her, Stanley Villars had pleasant thoughts of nice thick arrowroot and complete rest—of downy idleness, and egg and sherry at eleven; thoughts, happy thoughts of a period of being ill or convalescent, as the case might be, comfortably, with the consciousness of its not behoving him to do anything, save take his restoratives regularly.

He lay there looking at her in perfect peace for a while, wondering, with a gentle wonder, whether she would change into anything else presently; for he associated that vision in the glass with her, and looked beneath the border of her cap with his weak eyes, marvelling curiously whither that red glory had vanished. But she remained an old woman sufficiently long to reassure him—an old woman in a dark dress and a mob cap, who might have pursued Mr. Banting's system with advantage for a period—an everyday old woman, whose kindly, commonplace, stupid, round, rosy face banished the fairy faces from the bursting rosebuds that were blooming round the room.

"You feel yourself to be yourself, as one may say, again, sir; and heartily glad my missus and I are to see it," she said, when he had stared at her for a short time.

He smiled as graciously as his wanness would admit of his doing in response, and his smile was echoed, as it were, by a relieved sigh from a corner, which he could not command from his position on the pillow.

"I'm not certain about feeling myself, for I'm not clear who I am," he said, presently, on which the everyday old woman laughed, as if this uncertainty of his were a great joke, and deftly prepared him a draught the while, with which she presently dosed him.

"It not being for sleeping, speech is not forbid," she said, solemnly, when he had taken it; on which encouragement he combated his desire to sleep again and know nothing, and asked her "where he was? and, if she could tell him, how he came there?"

She became terse, not to say uncommunicative, at this point. He was "where the Lord Mayor, to say nothing of the Prince of Wales, might be, and no shame to them," she replied; "more than this she would leave for her mistress to tell, if so it pleased her."

"Then your mistress is——" He looked towards the glass, and left his question incomplete.

"She *was* sitting there—bless her!" the old woman answered. "She has been sitting there more days and nights than I would count to you till you're strong enough to add them up of yourself, sir. But this is not the talk she'd have me hold to you now, nor the talk I'd hold of myself, if I were not that stupid when I think of her." The tears came into the old woman's eyes at this juncture, and she drifted into vague and rambling statements respecting her own weakness on this point, which, in Stanley's current state, were neither amusing nor instructive.

He made a great effort to recall himself. "How did I come here?—tell me that first," he said; and then there was a faint whisper of "Rayner, not yet—not *yet* I tell you!" from that same portion of the room from which the sigh had proceeded but just now. Altogether, between his great effort to get at the truth, and that faintly whispered entreaty to retain it, poor Rayner was much bewildered, and not a trifle aggrieved.

By-and-by, after a short interval of waiting, and wondering what it all meant, he remembered Rock.

"Hadn't I a dog!" he asked—"a big dog—a setter?" He was endeavouring to recall Rock to his own mind by this full description, as much as essaying to paint him to Rayner. He was not sure whether he had not dreamt the dog, and the dog having been very pleasant to him he hoped it was no dream.

"There *is* a dog; but, bless his heart! he would be like a mad thing if I was to let him up!" the old woman replied.

There was a dog—ah! and that dog had been given him by Bella Vane—the girl he was going to marry—the woman who had jilted him for his old school-friend, Claude Walsingham! He remembered everything now—the woe, and the work, and the walk, and the way those two latter things had grown out of the former. He remembered everything now. "God! what a life to take up again!" he thought bitterly, remembering these things.

Presently a sound smote upon his ears—an impatient scraping afar, then a bounding, scratching footstep—a rough scramble up on to the bed, and Rock's great, loving, yellow-brown eyes were looking into his, and Rock's big, feathery tail was wagging its delight at the meeting. It was only a dog that was so joyed to welcome him back to saneness; it was only a dog that seemed to smile upon the prospect of returning strength; it was only a dog that seemed to say to him, "You would have been missed!" But the dog's sympathy was very sweet to the lonely man, whose soul but a minute before had sunk at the thought of taking up his burden of life again.

He laid hold, with his weak, thin hands, of the long, silky ears of the setter; he looked into the honest, loving, yellowish-brown eyes; and as he thought of how she had often patted and caressed the dog thus, the anguish of his life came back with all its force, and freshly as at first he mourned for the woman, and cursed the perfidy that had wrecked him! Better to have died, down on the road-side, like a dog, than to have come back to life—to the knowledge of the heart's disgrace—to the remembrance of how faithless had been his friend, how false his love, how frail his faith in all things—how utterly they had each and all failed him!

The remembrance aroused him—stirred him out of his peacefulness, and made him uneasily conscious that his portion was not to lie still when stillness was essential to his well-being, but that he must be up and doing whether he were fit for it or no. There was some poor task to be done—some mean goal to be won—and, living or dying, he must do and strive to win. This was incumbent upon him—he had no appeal against it. Fate was a pitiless monster to him, and she decreed that he should know no rest.

He would obey, since he could not resist. In pursuance of his plan of obedience, he raised his head from the pillow once more, to Rock's great delight—muttering some words to himself, which were intended as stimulants, but which, by some curious process, though dictated by his own mind, failed when uttered to reach the same again, but drifted off upon the empty air, and mocked him, as it were. Then his head flattened upon his shoulders, and his eyes appeared to be loose in his head, and his whole form went down many yards, with a thump in the bed, and the flesh came off conqueror in that never-ceasing combat between itself and the spirit. He was entirely broken down.

It was at this moment that she whose drooping beauty—whose babyish, innocent beauty—

had seemed so sweet and touching a thing to him, when he looked upon it in the glass, came before him bodily. She crept up to the side of the bed, by which the old woman still stood, and paused there, a mere girl, with a woman's pity for him beaming from her eyes, and the great tawny dog leaping up at her as at a tried friend.

She was wonderfully pretty—exquisitely pretty and innocent-looking—touchingly simple, and youthful in appearance. No child's mouth could be more perfectly pure in colour, outline, and expression than hers. No angel's brow could be more stainless. No woman's eyes more loving than the sweet, full, blue ones that looked down through a tender dew upon him.

Her tones were very mortal though. Impressionable as he was, through his great weakness, he could but be aware of this fact, as the childlike mouth opened, and through the parted lips came the words—

"I'm so glad you're better, sir! Is there any one I can send for?"

"No one," he replied. He had not spoken so softly to any one for months as he now spoke to her. Then he put his hand out to her over Rock's head, and added, "Have you been my little nurse?"

"The odd hours, when I was in, and Rayner asleep, I have taken," she replied in a matter-of-fact tone.

"Then it is to the odd hours I must owe my recovery," he said softly, and a little ungratefully to Rayner, it must also be confessed.

"It was Rayner made you everything and gave you your draughts," the girl answered, in her quaint, matter-of-fact way; "but I fed the dog, and looked in your pockets to try and find out who you were," she went on candidly.

A return of that uncertainty as to his own identity pervaded his mind dimly for an instant, as he asked—

"And did you find out?"

She shook her head in the negative and blushed, as she remembered that in the course of the search she had opened his purse, and found therein the sum of one shilling and sixpence.

"So we could not let your friends know how ill you were, or where you were," she continued, pursuing her own thought.

"I have none!—no matter!" he answered suddenly. Then observing that the old woman looked curious, and the young one pained, he added, "None with whom you could have communicated—none in London—none" (this with a great access of feeling) "who would have been kind to me, as you have been."

The girl looked pleased. "I have done what I could, and so has Rayner."

Stanley glanced gratitude at Rayner on the spot, but his eyes quickly went back to the baby face that was so very fair, with its look of innocent pleasure upon it.

"God will bless you for your kindness and your goodness."

"You are not to agitate yourself," she interrupted hastily; "the doctor says you're not to agitate yourself."

"But you must tell me——" he began.

"No, sir, not now. Rayner, his cooling draught—quick! I must go out now; when I come in I'll tell you all about yourself."

"And all about *yourself* too," he said, with a smile. "Well, meanwhile I shall obey you, and not agitate myself."

"Not yet—no questions yet," the girl said with a touch of childish imperiousness that was as pleasing to look upon as the rosebuds on the walls and curtains. "Don't leave him, Rayner, I shall take the key and let myself in. Good-bye!" and with that the vision was gone.

He looked after her lazily as she flitted from the room—looked after the slight girlish figure with a languid wonder in his eyes. Then when the door had closed behind her, he drank the cooling draught; then he looked at the woman those dewy lips had addressed as "Rayner," and observed that Rayner had pursed her own aught but dewy lips up with decision, as one who was resolved that no speech should filter through.

"Is that your mistress?" he asked.

Rayner nodded, and then shook her head at him monotonously, under the impression that such motion on her part would conduce to his quiet, and so to his restoration.

"And you are Rayner?" he went on.

Again she nodded assent.

"Who is that young lady?"

"My mistress, sir."

The conversation ceased here for awhile, and Stanley was conscious that he had made small—not to say no—progress. Presently he resumed:

"How long have I been here?"

"My mistress's memory is better than mine, and she'll tell you all you want to know when she comes in," Rayner replied, with a dogged nervousness that defeated her own amiable intention, and caused him to feel that he must, indeed, have been there a long time, since she dared not affix a date to his advent.

"Do tell me, my good woman," he said imploringly.

"Now don't you ask till the doctor comes in; he will tell you."

"When will he come?—the doctor for *me!*"

"He will come to-morrow."

"But you must tell me this before to-morrow," he said quietly. "I must know it—at once!"

"Six weeks; and Miss Marian will never forgive me for telling you yet," Rayner answered in a melancholy tone.

"Six weeks! My God, six weeks!" he groaned feebly. It was overwhelming to him. Six weeks! Evil as his case had been before, it was nothing compared to what it would be now. Six hours inactivity at that period, when he left off his life as it were, would have been detrimental to such miserable prospects as had been his. But six weeks! It was destruction!

Wearily he made one more effort when the stunning effect of this blow had worn off a trifle.

"Tell me all you can—all that you think want to know," he said hoarsely.

Gently, with her toil-hardened hands, sh smoothed the pillow, with a coaxing, tender touch, that soothed him in spite of himself.

"Not yet, sir," she said, with tears in her voice; "not yet, dearie!" she repeated with a downright assumption of affectionate authority that was very good for him, desolate as he felt himself to be.

He tried to smile at her. Failing in that, he moved his wasted hand against hers, and seemed to himself to be holding her in a firm grasp. Ah! how she sorrowed for his weakness as the thin fingers went round and held her strong old hand in their feeble clasp.

"Do tell me in kindness? don't make me ask."

The piteous appeal for information respecting himself, from the handsome young gentleman over whom she had watched night and day, with unremitting care and attention, for six weeks, overcame her scruples. So after a few more soothing touches had been administered to the pillow and to the coverlid, and after she had wiped her eyes on her apron, and apostrophised her "goodness," after she had driven him to the brink of insanity, in fact, by her preliminaries, she started fairly on the story he wanted to hear.

She told him that Miss Marian coming home one blustering March evening, "between the lights, as one might say," had been drawn to the spot where he was lying by the howls of the big dog. That Miss Marian had then run into her own house (this abode in which he was at present), screaming out, "Rayner, there's a man dead outside!" That she (Rayner) had forthwith made the "poor, frightened lamb," the aforesaid Miss Marian, lie down while she went out to investigate. That she found he was neither dead, as Miss Marian had feared, nor drunk, as she herself had first fancied, but faint only; that she half dragged, half carried him in, and placed him on a sofa. And that when he came out of his faint he had gone into a fever, through which Miss Marian and herself had nursed him. That was all.

That was the extent of her voluntary information; and he was too weak, too weary to ask for more, though he longed to hear it. He lay there after she had brought her brief narrative to a close, conscious only of two things. The one was that he must be up and at that tale of bricks that were over-due ere long—at that odious work over which he had broken down; and the other was a faint desire to know more about "Miss Marian," his baby-faced saviour.

The consciousness of these two things finally overpowered him, and he fell asleep. When he woke it was night, the curtains were drawn across the window, and by the light of the candle that stood on the toilet-table, he saw in the glass the reflection of her face precisely as he had seen it on his first awakening. Saw it, and saw that it was unconscious of his observation—marked its expression of purity, and its youth, and (being more himself than he had been before) felt sorrowfully that it was a hard thing that he should have broken down at the feet of this girl—a hard, a bad, a bitter thing for some one—perhaps for the lonely, baby-faced beauty.

—o—

CHAPTER XXX.

"NOT A JOT! NOT A JOT!"

THE fall from his horse, and the period he had passed down among the tadpoles at the bottom of the brook, were insufficient to affect Claude Walsingham unpleasantly after a day or two. But though the effect they had upon his constitution was so small, their influence upon the relations between himself and his wife was mighty, and bid fair to be lasting.

Her alarm about him had taught her how very dear he was to her; and the ravages that alarm had made upon her, brief as was the time for which she had endured it, appealed to him, and awoke all his slumbering tenderness into a fuller life than it had known before. They were drawn closer together by this danger which he had escaped, and Bella no longer found it dull at the Court.

All the old joy which she had felt in the old Denham days, when to feel it was treachery to Stanley Villars, came over her soul once more. She marvelled how she could ever have felt anything else in Claude's presence. She strove to put away the remembrance that she had been feeling quite the reverse rather fervently of late, as she would have put away an ugly dream.

In her re-awakened tenderness for and trust in her husband, she took the whole neighbourhood nearer to her heart, and forgave Lady Lexley's existence—a thing that was the more easy to do as Lady Lexley left the Harpers about this time, and crossed her path no more. Still she told herself that she would have been equally magnanimous had Lady Lexley remained, which proves that she meant well.

A something called for a celebration at the Court at this epoch. Some one had a birthday, or there was a long list of festivities to be requited, or some equally cogent reason for giving a ball arose, and stared Mrs. Walsingham senior in the face.

It was to be a tremendous affair. I may say that it was to be a serious affair—giving the word serious in its two meanings of solemn and important. People were coming to it from either end of the county—from the extreme ends, even; and the inns of the two nearest country towns promised themselves that they "would be crowded to excess, and full to overflowing," in the columns of their respective journals, for a fortnight previous to the ball.

Mrs. Claude showed in her brightest colours from the moment it was first mooted up to the night of its realisation. She threw herself heart and soul into the scheme, and made Mrs. Walsingham feel that after all a daughter-in-law who liked gaiety was no bad thing to have near at hand when the promotion of gaiety was the object in view. Bella was ubiquitous and incessant—Bella rode and drove about, and gave all the orders for the hundred and one things that were forgotten day by day as the scheme progressed—Bella wrote all the notes of invitation, checked off all the acceptances, organised the order of reception, vigorously restrained unhallowed hands from interfering with the flowers in the conservatory, by which means she secured a full and plentiful supply of the same; and, in the intervals of this serious business, taught Jack to waltz without putting his feet through his partner's dress while she was "doing the back steps"—a triumph of management Jack had been powerless to attain heretofore—in each and all of which good works she was applauded and encouraged, not to say goaded on to greater efforts, by Claude, and jealously watched by Claude's sister.

She never thought of Stanley Villars. This relapse into being "in love" with her husband, together with the projected ball, entirely obscured her first lover's claims upon her memory. She forgot that semi-plaintive, semi-imprudent appeal she had made to him, by writing to him without obvious end or aim. She forgot the assertion she had made respecting their speedy return to town—a return she had blithely assented to deferring for no particular reason; she forgot the desire she had expressed to see him. In fact, she forgot everything save her present happiness and her husband, which was right from one point of view, and wrong from another. It was her "nature to" forget the past when the present was agreeable at all points. It was constitutional; she may no more be blamed for it with justice than one may be blamed for any other physical defect, or applauded for any physical perfection. She was neither heartless nor undeserving. When she remembered, she could be as considerate, as tender, as remorseful for her venial errors, as any one—only she was very apt to entirely forget.

So, while the weary weeks dragged on during which Stanley Villars was wasting under that fever of body and soul of which she was the remote cause, she was making preparations, with that earnestness which comes from intense interest alone, for the greater success of the ball at the Court.

Grace Harper came into her confidence greatly, by a series of almost imperceptible gradations, in these days. At first Mrs. Markham marvelled, in her own hard, honest soul, at this intimacy between her spotless friend and her brother's wife. But presently Grace explained, and made all things clear in a way that enhanced her own merits in Mrs. Markham's stern eyes, and depreciated Bella's with the most consummate tact.

"If I stand aloof from her I may have cause to reproach myself by-and-by," Grace said, with that sort of stolid satisfaction in the performance of a meritorious though unpleasant act which it is hard to stand by and see sometimes. "She's not congenial to me, but, at any rate, *I* can do *her* no harm," she went on, in a tone that implied that Mrs. Claude might do much harm to one who was not encased in such well-tried moral armour as she (Gracie) wore. Mrs. Markham received this sentiment, and endorsed it with a bony kiss on the brow of the "fair brave." Mrs. Markham was one of those women with their mouths full of long teeth whose kisses have the effects of bites on the unprepared recipient. But Grace was never unprepared for any little outburst of the kind, therefore she stood it—"like a man," I was about to write, but far more tolerantly than any man would have done Grace was accustomed to having Mrs. Markham's fangs gnashed upon her. In the days gone by, she had endured it gallantly because Mrs. Markham was Claude Walsingham's sister; and a girl on promotion will put up with much from the sister of the probable or possible promoter. Now she endured it for custom's sake, and because it was easier to go on enduring chronic unpleasantnesses from a neighbour than to rebel against them. It may be an unamiable thing on the part of the portrayer of her character to lay bare the causes which conduced to this outwardly amiable quiescence on the part of Miss Harper; but, when painting from the life, it is so hard to be pleasant—one can but see the reason of many bony kisses being patiently taken, if one will but look.

Gradually, it came about that Miss Harper spent long hours alone with Mrs. Claude Walsingham, "seeking to improve her, and give her tone and stability." Mrs. Markham opined, when conversing with her mamma on the subject, "Grace's society could but do Claude's wife good," they both averred, and as Bella took to that society very kindly, they began to think better things of her.

Gradually, too, it dawned upon Bella that she had, all unconsciously, led on by heaven alone knew what unfortunate combination of circumstances, laid bare her whole soul, the complete plan of her life, to this plump, placid young lady, who had told her so little in return. The giddinesses of her gushing girlhood, the flightinesses before and during her first engagement, her meeting with Claude in that old country inn alone at night, her young conjugal distrust of him when they first came to the Court, her relapse for a few hours into the ancient kindly feeling towards Stanley, her repentance concerning that relapse when Claude was in danger, their restoration to perfect bliss, and love, and trust in one another, which was contemporaneous with Claude's restoration to health—all these and many other things Bella told in full confidence to the admirable young lady who was so ready to see, and deplore, and amend all that was amiss in the young wife of the man whose wife she herself had fully intended to be for more years than she now cared to count.

These friendly confidences—rather this friendly confidence, for it was one-sided—had gone on uninterruptedly for ten days or a fortnight, when one day, and that the very day before the ball, it received a slight shock. The pale devil of jealous hate would not be quieted any longer; it rose up and forced Grace to say——

"Thank goodness! when I marry I shall not live in dread of any such old memories being brought to light! Poor girl! I can understand your being a little nervous sometimes."

"I'm never a little nervous—and when I am, it's not that I'm afraid of any of these 'old memories,' as you call them? Why in the world should I be afraid of them? What nonsense!" The first portion of Bella's disclaimer was slightly contradictory. Grace made Bella feel that she marked its being so, by shaking her head and smiling in melancholy toleration.

"Old memories! Why, my husband knows about the worst—I mean the most important things I have been telling you of," Bella went on pettishly, feeling excessively annoyed with herself for having told Miss Harper anything at all.

"Oh! *does* he?" Grace asked, elevating her faintly marked eyebrows.

"Does he? Of course he does!"

"Then, at any rate, you have the satisfaction of feeling that you have concealed nothing from him. Take my advice, though—I have known Claude from a boy—don't *you* be the one to renew the acquaintance with Mr. Villars!"

Miss Harper spoke in apparently absolute forgetfulness of Mrs. Claude having written to Stanley Villars—a fact Mrs. Claude had cursorily alluded to three days before.

"For what reason?"

"Well! for many; your quick wit will supply you with more in a minute, if you think about it, than my slower tongue."

"But Claude wishes to meet him again," Bella said energetically.

"*Does* he?" Miss Harper asked with a dubious air.

"Does he? Of course he does! Claude has a generous nature, and he couldn't help feeling—though he would never allow——" Bella stammered and stopped.

"That's the very reason. I quite feel with you that you could never be the one to bring them together again," Grace said, with a great air of frank sympathy with and appreciation of Bella's motives.

"But Claude told him the day we were married that he hoped he would soon be with us again."

"Poor Claude! I can understand how you will always shrink from putting him to the test," Grace said admiringly. Bella felt provoked at being so entirely misconstrued; but, at the same time, she had grave doubts as to whether it would really be well to make her real feelings on the subject patent to Miss Grace. She had no thought of how patent they were already to the unsophisticated Miss Harper. At the same time the influence of this apparently guileless cross-examination was to make her wish that she had never indited that letter, all harmless as it was, to Stanley Villars, or that she had told her husband that she had done so at the time. It was too late now. It was all trifling. A thing that was of no account one way or the other. Still, for all that, a thing that she almost wished she had not done.

The two ladies had been sitting alone during this conversation; but soon after it had reached the point of Grace telling Bella that she could "well understand her shrinking from putting her husband to the test of a meeting with Mr. Villars, brought about through her agency," and, while Bella was giving in her adhesion to this noble sentiment, by her silence, Claude himself sauntered in and sat down by his wife.

"The conversation has foundered, apparently, can't I start it again?" he asked.

"Well, no; I don't think you can," Bella said, half laughing, and leaning her head on his shoulder as she spoke; "we had talked the subject out. You can give us a fresh one, if you please."

"I had rather take up the one you have exhausted, and say something new about it," he said, merely for the sake of saying something.

"There is nothing new to be said about it, Claude," Bella exclaimed quickly.

"Let me try; what was your theme, Grace?" he continued, turning to the gentle blonde, who was not greatly softened by the sight of Bella's head burying itself on his shoulder. "What was your theme, Gracie? Gloves?"

Grace Harper shook her head.

"What then? Crosbie's chances of getting quit of Lady Alexandrina and going back to Lily Dale? Bella takes a great interest in Crosbie; I suppose you do also?"

"No, I don't," Grace replied, almost sharply. She was very much afraid the conversation was about to drift into space, just as she had thought it making straight for a rock on which Bella might get broken up.

"I thought all the women liked Crosbie," Claude went on carelessly; "they are not quite clear why they like him; but there is a vein of heartlessness in him that they find pleasant in a book."

"I certainly am not clear about the heartlessness," Bella put in. She felt annoyed with Grace for not being interested in the popular current hero, added to which she had a mingled feeling of tenderness and sympathy for Crosbie as a fellow-sinner, that rendered her sensitive to the smallest slur being cast upon him.

"He is worse than heartless; he's unprincipled," Miss Harper said quietly.

"I can only say I don't see it," Bella replied.

"Oh! Mrs. Claude, I'm sure you do," Grace said earnestly; "you, holding such sentiments as you expressed to me just now, cannot think a man anything but unprincipled who jilts one girl and marries another, and then wrongs his wife by thinking tenderly of the first."

"Of course, when you put it in bald hard words it sounds very bad," Bella answered warmly.

"Have you been giving way to noble sentiments, old lady?" her husband asked, laughingly.

"I didn't know that I had," Bella replied, "at any rate we'll have no more of them," she continued, hoping to change the conversation.

"They come so naturally to her, you see," Grace said; and, if it had not been the plump, placid, good-natured Grace who spoke, Claude could have fancied it was said with a sneer.

"I hope they do! but what were the special ones, pet?" he asked, smoothing the hair away from Bella's forehead. As Grace looked upon them, she could have cut her tongue out, quiet as she seemed, for that it had not already uttered words that should have caused him to take that hand away.

"The special ones," she said slowly, "were a very natural and profound contempt for and distrust of any woman who could have a thought of or communication with a former lover, which was not held in common with her husband. I should have thought the same onus of honour was upon a man." The last sentence robbed her speech of all intentional bitter personal meaning. Nevertheless Bella, loyal as she was, blanched in her soul as she listened.

"I should think so! I should rather think so!" Claude said sternly.

"What, Claude?" Bella asked hurriedly.

"Why, that it behoves a woman to be ten times more careful than a man in such a case," he replied.

"*That* was scarcely the meaning of Miss Harper's remark," Bella said scornfully.

"Wasn't it, by Jove? it was, though."

"Oh! you mistake me, Major Walsingham, if I seemed to you to judge more rigorously of a woman in such a case than of a man," Grace said softly.

"You would surely not be more lenient to her?" Claude asked hastily.

"More lenient? well, I hardly know. It would be so terrible to judge, you know—to decide *against* a woman, you know, however faulty she might be." Grace spoke with such a frankly uplifted face, such a very ingenuous voice, that these seemed sweet, sober sentiments, not spiteful snaps.

Bella began to feel indignant. A suspicion of there being something in the air that would be antagonistic to her happiness, and to her husband, had come over her. But she was not quite clear where or what it was. An unwary woman is, perforce, at a fearful disadvantage in such a warfare as this. The nobler the animal, the more liable it is to be injured by attacks from curs which it has overlooked. If one would scent out mean foes in time to render them innocuous, one must needs grovel in their level.

"You take a great interest in faithlessness, and conjugal faultinesses, Miss Harper," Mrs. Claude said, trying to speak in a sweet, unaffected voice, and failing, even in her own ears.

"Theoretically, yes; practically, I have had no experience, you know, having no brothers or sisters," Grace replied, with a great air of maiden innocence and virgin purity. Bella felt strongly tempted to throw courtesy to the winds, and the gauntlet down, by saying, "No, and you're not likely to gain it either, in your proper person;" but she restrained herself. Instinct sometimes teaches us that that suspicion which is the result of hate and theory is a far subtler foe than the offspring of experience and practice.

This instinct was strengthened within her the following night, when she was dressing for the ball. Claude came to her then; and when he had sent her maid away to get him a cup of coffee, he put his arms round her and drew her close to him, and said—

"I'm glad you get on so well with Gracie, Bella dear; she's an uncommonly prudent, sensible girl."

"Do I need the companionship of such? Really, Claude! you're going the wrong way to recommend your friend to me."

"That's right! be off into a rage about the Lord knows what, for I don't!"

"But I do, Claude. I got over her being hurled at me as your mother's pet; but as your paragon!—no, never!"

There was a slight infusion of jealousy in the tone in which she said this—just enough to be pleasing to Claude, who was not entirely averse to his pretty wife being a little jealous of him.

"My paragon! my darling; as if you believed she was that! However, she's a sensible, staid, kind-hearted girl; and she likes you, and she represents the mass of public opinion down here."

"Does she?" Bella made a face at herself in the glass, but her husband saw it over her shoulder.

"You doubt it?" he asked.

"No, I don't; I simply don't care for it," she replied.

"That's your mistake," he said; and he said it in measured tones that portended wrath to come.

"Now, Claude, don't be cross, and I will care," she said, turning round hurriedly. "How do I look? Nice!"

"As you do always," he replied, kissing her.

"That's a good boy. Now, in return for that charming speech (oh! Claude, *what* charming speeches you *used* to make to me!), 'I will defer to public opinion,' if you'll tell me what she says."

"What 'it' says; speak correctly, Bella."

"I was speaking correctly, for I mean Miss Grace Harper. How have I transgressed?"

"You have not transgressed."

"And a word from you will save me from doing so; say the word, Claude." Then she laughed, and added, "Make yourself the mouthpiece of public opinion."

He flushed up to his brow when she said this, and she tried to cool down the flush with her kisses.

"Dear Claude, I was flippant."

"Well, don't be so again, for I can't stand it," he replied.

She put a diamond star in her hair, and another on her breast, and hummed a waltz air.

"Ain't I as 'beautiful as a butterfly?'" she asked, flashing round upon him.

"Yes, and——" He stopped abruptly.

"Finish your sentence—'and as frivolous,' you meant to say," she cried, with her eyes sparkling. Then she remembered what pangs of doubt she had suffered through him—and how he had been in danger—and how dearly she loved him, and she held her face and her arms up to him.

"Claude! what a booby I am to try and make you believe that I wouldn't give up anything, or do anything in the world for you," she said, tenderly.

"Then give up a very little thing to-night, and don't make yourself ill by tearing about in any of their waltzes and gallops?"

He asked this very affectionately of her, and she desired to please him. But these round dances! She was very fond of them. Fond of them as she was of peaches, and of rides on Devilskin, and of Anthony Trollope's novels! Why should he ask her to give up what was so harmless and so sweet?

"They don't hurt me," she said soberly.

"They do hurt me," he replied.

"Then don't dance them, dear."

"*I* dance! if I do, it will be with certain people"—("So shall I," she laughed)—"with whom I have to do it, just as certain other marks of esteem and honour have to be accorded them in this house. *I* dance! Gad, I should be devilish glad never to see any more of it!" His tone was almost surly now, and her sweet, smiling visage fell as she listened to him.

"Very well, Claude; you shall see no more of it from me," she said softly. But she felt that she could have made the concession ten thousand times more blithely, small as it was, had not the firm conviction been hers, that it was required of her at Miss Grace Harper's instigation. While as for Claude, he was not jealous of her, "not a jot, not a jot;" still he was well satisfied that it should be patent to the most discriminating beholder that he had no cause to be. Within the last few days he had felt this remembrance growing upon him—that she had deceived another man—had lapped a cleverer man than himself into security for awhile. Still remembering this, even he would not be jealous of her, "not a jot, not a jot!"

CHAPTER XXXI.

MISTAKES.

"He will return, I know him well,
He will not leave me here to die."

WHEN Stanley Villars had looked, till his eyes ached, at the reflection of the girl who had enacted the part of good Samaritan towards him, he had a strangely earnest little debate with himself as to whether or not he should get up, and away out of her vicinity at once, before she could discern and arrest his intention. While he was faintly arguing that it would be better that she should go about all her life with a black sense of man's ingratitude weighing on her mind, than that she should ever know him as he really was, or rather as he believed himself to be, she saw that he was awake, and came up and defeated him.

The baby face looked down upon him from a background of Rayner, with a very hopeful smile upon it. He was much pleasanter to look upon than he had been during fever and insensibility. Besides she had a sort of vested right in him as her own patient, and now he began to do her credit.

"I have waited till you woke to say good-night. Rayner will sit up with you till you have had your sleeping draught," she explained, taking up his hand, and giving it a gentle friendly shake of extreme satisfaction. It was a very muscular hand which took his in that friendly clasp, but it was warm and womanly notwithstanding.

"Have I been unfortunate enough to have been the cause of your staying up sometimes?" he asked.

She nodded. "I have sat up half the night several times. Don't speak; it was nothing. Why, I'd have done it for any one."

"How good you are," he murmured, faintly; he did not feel flattered by the statement of these broadly charitable views, for some reason or other.

"Good! I'm afraid I'm no better than other people," she replied; but she laughed a little, low, childlike laugh as she spoke, and her dancing eyes and dewy lips looked far better and more innocent than any that had come under his ken since he had parted with Florence.

"I can tell you what you are, and that's tired," Rayner interposed. "Do go, my dearie! do now, Miss Marian."

"Do," Stanley urged, warmly seconding the old woman's suggestion, and warmly hating her the while for having made it. "Pray do, you need rest."

"Well, I will; but it won't be to rest for three or four hours yet. Good night."

Once more she lifted up his hand, and gave it that muscular clasp which corresponded so ill with her soft baby face. Once more the cloudless child's eyes looked out at him confidingly from under the clear brow, over which the rich masses of that glorious ruddy hair clustered. Once more he found himself being sorry for her, and irresistibly impelled to curse the hour and the fate which had cast him athwart her path.

"Where is she going, that she won't have any rest for hours?" he asked of Rayner, as soon as the girl whom Rayner called "Miss Marian" had closed the door behind her.

"Is it Miss Marian, sir?" his nurse interrogated, in a way that made him feel that he was reproved, he scarcely knew how or for what.

"Yes; where is Miss Marian——"

"You'd far better not talk to-night, sir; take my advice, and lie quiet," Rayner replied, earnestly, and in simple faith. She was desirous of nothing more than to keep her patient calm. He believed that she was evading his question, and so worried himself fearfully in seeking in his own mind for a reason why she should do so.

"If you would rather not tell," he began; and then she interrupted him, in her deep anxiety that he should remain entirely undisturbed, in order that the opiate he had taken might have the due effect, and said that she "certainly would rather not tell to-night." Which decision gave birth to a dread in his mind that grew to be almost a tangible monster oppressing and maddening him, as the soporific worked, and sight and sense were gradually artificially dimmed.

It seemed to him that the monster dread, whatever it might have been, was being charmed away after a time by a strain that welled up to him faint and low from some other sphere. When the notes first fell upon his ears, he started with a throb; but presently he settled the question of "whence came they?" satisfactorily; it was fairy music from the rose-bud faces on the walls. When he had assured himself of this he left off trying "to be" any more, and went away into nothingness without further effort. He was a feather floating in an atmosphere of sweet sounds; he was a rose-leaf, with a nightingale for his private property; he was Joachim's own favourite violin; he was a south breeze sweeping o'er a bank of violets; he was a song without words; he was the soul of music at large in Tara's halls. In short, he was under the influence of a powerful opiate, and some one was playing the piano in a room at no very great distance from the one he occupied.

Late into the night that indefatigable player went on, practising the same piece—a tender, plaintive melody it was, with a wealth of sad meaning in its every chord—over and over again, till the piano seemed to be speaking the sad story in the mother tongue of each one who heard it. And while the strain went on, and for hours after, indeed, till the morning light streamed in through the cloudy muslin curtains, Stanley Villars continued to be all those incongruous things mentioned above.

He woke a better man. Not morally better, but physically better, and found himself alone. Then he thought he would get up and dress himself, and begin to think about going away. But when he set about carrying out this idea, by getting out of bed, the floor made an angry rush at him, and when he grew calmer, he crept humbly into bed again, acknowledging that he must needs wait.

The monster doubt which had been put to flight by the combined effects of the opiate and the music was about to resume its sway, and make him unhappy, when Rayner came in with his breakfast, and banished it again. He drank his tea and ate his toast with the feeling one is apt to have after a long illness, that this life, namely, is well worth retaining—if it be only for the sake of the tea and toast which may be denied to us in the next. It was a very material reflection; but it was born of returning health. The rose-leaf and soul-of-music notions came of sickness of spirit and drunkenness from opium. The gracious acceptance of the goods that were going was a very good sign.

He did not question the old servant further about her young mistress. He spoke of himself now, telling her that it was essential that he should be up and doing as soon as possible, and that he should relieve them of the burden of his presence before the day was many hours older; which insane idea Rayner was far too deeply versed in the weaknesses of the invalid mind to attempt to combat, but encouraged, rather as a thing that might be if he would only make a good breakfast, and not exert himself to say too much.

But though she gave such a cordial assent to his plans, they were not carried into execution on that day, nor the next, nor for many a succeeding one. Not only did he feel that it would be well, when he came to see himself in the glass, that he should look less like an attenuated and broken reed before he ventured into the haunts of men, but the floor continued to rush madly up at him whenever he essayed to stand upon it. Therefore, for awhile he gave up the contest, and ceased from his efforts to stand upon it at all.

When he was able to get out of his room he found that it was a mere doll's-house of a place which had been his haven of refuge. A neat, trim, tiny, fanciful bit of a place, that gave itself up to having one "good" bed-room, which he had occupied, cheaply furnished, but pretty and graceful notwithstanding—strangely like the girl, its mistress, in fact.

He had learnt all that there was to be learnt of the divinity before seeing the rest of the shrine. The "all" was prosaic enough. She was "first-hand" at a second-rate milliner's establishment, and she made enough by her labours to keep this diminutive roof over the head of the woman who had nursed her mother in her dying illness, and her own. Her ideas on the subject of her paternity were undefined, but exalted. Her mother had kept an inn. There was no romance to be extracted from her surroundings. But Marian had heard that her father was a gentleman, and that she resembled him strongly in beauty of person. That was all she knew about him, and all she knew she believed.

The pretty little milliner, the baby-faced beauty, was a thing to study. She had her ambitions, her hopes, her aspirations, and she confided them all to him. She had a deep genuine love of music, and lately she had saved enough from her salary to buy an old piano, and take lessons of a lady who had fired her with the idea of being "professional" in time. "She was no more than me at one time," she said, simply, "and now she's quite the lady, and goes out to play at grand houses, and goes down to supper with the best."

Her lovely blue eyes dilated at this glorious prospect in such a bewitching way, and the mouth that uttered these words looked so opposed in its refinement to the vulgarity of the sentiment enunciated, that he could but study her with interest, and suffer her to perceive that he did so. The race was low, the breed was bad; the manners and customs by which she had ever been surrounded probably were against her, and still the true artist feeling was there. It was mixed with lower and more paltry ones, unfortunately; but it was there, nevertheless, a vein of fine gold in a coarse soil.

He was warmly and earnestly interested in her. Who would not have been in such an anomaly as she was? Who would not have been interested in that fragile, tender, childish loveliness, marred as it was by the manner of a self-sufficient little show-girl? Who would not have been interested in that rich vein of artist feeling which was choked and buried beneath so much that was paltry and little? To hear her one moment playing some piece that was far beyond her executive powers as yet, with a depth and intensity of feeling that blinded one to all mechanical errors; while in the next she would be raising her voice exultantly at the thought of being fitted in time, through her fingers, for admission into the drawing-rooms of these whose dressing-rooms alone were open to her now! He was warmly interested in the baby-faced beauty; but though there was much tenderness, much pity in that interest, there was not a grain of passion. The glorious beauty of her hair, the childlike, delicate loveliness of her face and form, might have won upon his man's heart had she never spoken. But the sweet lips were their own antidote as soon as they parted. What that genuine artist feeling might do for her in time he could not tell. At present, the little beauty was more than a little vulgar.

His clearness of vision on this point could have been a safeguard to him, even had he not been possessed of another, in his vivid remembrance of Bella. But the baby-faced beauty had no such safeguard, and, in his gratitude, he was very kind.

The generous little creature had been ready, ay, eager, to take care of him—to tend, and succour, and perhaps restore him, when he was nothing to her but a fellow-creature in distress.

She had denied herself necessaries, and impoverished herself cheerfully, never thinking for an instant that there was aught out of the way in her doing so during his illness. It would have been just the same to her—she would have done as much, with a willing hand and heart—had it been an infant or an old woman whom she had found by the roadside that night. Her generous charity was pure enough, only, unfortunately, the object of it chanced to be a young, handsome man.

He was not a selfish man, but his early training had not prepared him for giving much thought to small sordid things. He had no idea of how many sacrifices she had been compelled to make for him, and of how surely she was coming to love, through having thus sacrificed and suffered for him. In his own mind he was quite resolved that the dear little thing, with the honesty of purpose, and the artist feeling, and the unfortunate inability to be a lady, should be well repaid for all she had done for him some day or other. He little knew how impossible it would be for him ever to repay her, save in a way that would be odious to himself. She was as pleasant and as dear to him as a kitten, but he felt no repugnance to the plan when she told him that an artist had begged her to sit to him as a model for "Hetty" in her first meeting with "Arth‸r Donnithorne."

By-and-by the day came when he could leave her—leave the sanctuary where she had held him secure—without fear of the floor playing wild antics. He was much better, he was nearly well, and he found that strength was given him to go back, and take up the burden of life again, at the spot where he had laid it down before going out for that fatal walk.

So Rock and he removed themselves from the tiny, fanciful, pretty doll's-house, and the doll went to her work with swollen eyes and a heavy heart that day. At night, she came home and sat down, at once playing her saddest strains, till the faithful old woman, who was half-friend, half-servant, and whole blind devotee of hers, took heart of grace to whisper that "he would come again."

Thus the thin veil of secresy which had been long between them was swept away, and the girl told to the woman, who knew it already—told to her own heart, which trembled at hearing the truth spoken—that she loved the stranger whom she had saved.

The gloomy room in the grim house, that was so conveniently situated, seemed duller and drearier than ever when he went back to it, and his landlady, kind and cordial as she essayed to be, according to her lights, was as harsh and unbending as his fate, when contrasted with those two women who had been his nurses for more than seven weeks. He had no time to waste in drawing comparisons, however. There was much work over due, and he put his feeble shoulder to the wheel manfully, and tried to do it.

The necessity of working hard while the faintest power of work is left in one, is apt to make many a well-meaning man appear neglectful and careless of his best friends. The impossibility of concentrating one's whole faculties on a wearisome thing that must be done, and at the same time of attending to various little conventionalities, to which it behoves civilized man to attend, is an impossibility, that those who neither toil nor spin find it hard to realise. It is a hard thing to be affable when straining every nerve for existence—next to impossible to be polite while purchasing future popularity, prosperity, or the power of living on at all, at the price of all current peace of mind and body.

Still there are some things which have such a holy claim upon humanity, that we blush for the latter when those claims are overlooked. It was the force of circumstances; it was the result of that sad war he had been so unwisely wrought upon by disappointment to wage; it was, for all this, *inexcusable* on the part of Stanley Villars to grind on wearily, unremittingly, for a fortnight, at his loathsome task, without giving a thought to the brave little beauty whose good Samaritanism was likely to cost her very dear.

I have said how she went to her work when he was gone, with swollen eyes and a heavy heart, and how, when she came home at night, she played the saddest strains her skill could draw from the keys. She might have indulged plenteously in this last pastime with impunity. Artistically speaking, it did her good indeed, for it ("it" being that sensation about him which was the offspring of her care for him) taught her to play with feeling and expression! Who cares for the cause when the effect is admirable?

But though her artist-life was enriched by this experience of the loving and riding away habits of mankind, her working-life was impoverished, not to say endangered. Swollen eyes and a heavy heart were matters of small moment when she was sitting, with Rayner for an audience, making the shrill piano discourse most eloquent music; but swollen eyes and a heavy step in the show-room of the west-central Mantalini for whom she worked, were grave offences.

She had other qualities essential to a success in "the millinery," as she called it, in addition to her ingenious fingers and nice taste in the disposition of ribbons, and laces, and flowers. She had a gracefully poised head, and a lissom form, and these two things disposed of many a mantle, wreath, and scarf. There was a limber ease about her manner of putting on and off these things, for their better inspection by possible purchasers, that induced the credulous to believe that the grace was in the garment. But in these days of which I am writing the limber ease deserted her, and the sale grew stagnant in the show-room, and a briny tear had been seen to fall from her clear blue eyes down on to a fragile idea she was carrying out in tulle for a querulous customer.

The poor baby-faced beauty! She had nothing in her home life to distract her thoughts from dwelling all too fondly, all unwisely, on the one who had broken up the calm current of that life, and caused it to seem so miserably wanting without him. She had taken an innocent child's innocent pleasure before in playing at keeping a house of her own, and in believing that she was doing it all by herself—a belief which Rayner fostered, keeping things straight the while in an earnest matter-of-fact way, that came from her romantic devotion to the loving beauty of the girl who was as dear to her "as her own flesh and blood could have been," she said. Now, alas! that innocent pleasure was a pale memory only—a flat, insipid thing, that had been—that was all!

The home life was insufficient, and the freshness of the beauty was fleeing under the influence of alternate hope and despair. Brightly every morning did she hope that she would see him again before nightfall; bitterly each night did she bewail the falsity of that hope. There was nothing mean in the hope—nothing ungenerous in the regretful despair. She never gave one single thought to aught that she had done for him. She never reproached him in her innermost heart with ingratitude or thoughtlessness towards one who had thought well for him. She only sighed to see him again, because she loved him.

When a fortnight or so had passed, the current of those thoughts of hers, which were undoubtedly dwelling far too exclusively on him for her own good, was disturbed. A whisper had reached her employer that there was "a cause" for that change in her which was so detrimental to the business. A perverted statement—in which truth was so entangled with falsehood, that she, in her confusion, hardly knew which was which—was abroad respecting her; and as she had been the brightest star in that little firmament, there were many who gloried in her fall.

It was a rigorously respectable establishment. Its mistress had not always been a milliner, but she had seen the error of her ways when a good, remunerative opportunity of amending them offered, and so now was unequalled in the promptitude with which she saw the error of other people's. Had the dark whisper respecting Marian not been contemporaneous with the swollen eyes, the heavy step, and the loss of limber ease, the estimable woman would not have hearkened thereunto. As it was she felt that it behoved her to hear and to act "like a Christian," she said. Accordingly, after rating Marian Wallis till the poor girl's cheeks tingled with anger, and her soul with a sense of bitter injustice, she dismissed her without a character, on the strength of sundry whispered words.

Poor baby-faced beauty! She went back to the little house which she had played at keeping, with her cheeks hot with such shame and fury as must bring down God's curse upon the sister woman who can cause it. She went home feeling herself stained by the foul suspicion that had fallen upon her, by the foul words in which that cruel suspicion had been given voice—went home and hid herself, as though she had been the thing they said, and would not hear the voice of comfort that her faithful, fond old friend elevated, and would not seek solace in the strains she loved—went home and piteously bewailed herself, like the child she was; but never once, even in her childish wrath, had other than a softly tender thought for the man through whom this sorrow had come upon her—by whom she was forgotten.

For she told herself, now that she was forgotten by him—and as she deemed him as beautiful and as high above her as a star, she simply thought it in the order of things that she should be so,—it was no fault of his that he, being a gentleman, should regard her as lightly as the majority of the great, according to her experience, appeared to regard the very small. So she excused him to herself, crouching down under her sorrow, with no thought of that rich gift of loveliness, which was hers, and which a queen might have envied.

She turned a little, burning ear of unbelief to Rayner's tales of startling reappearances after long absences, and longer apparent forgetfulness than this which their late patient was displaying. Rayner's stories were all of the King Cophetua and Lord of Burleigh order. She was always bringing Stanley Villars back to her young mistress's feet under circumstances more or less gorgeous. Coaches and four—to say nothing of an army of servants, in and out of livery—played a prominent part in the programme of procession she constantly insisted upon arranging outside the doll's-house door—a procession that was to be formed in honour of Miss Marian, when the man she had nursed should return in the state of splendour that was natural to him to bear that mistress away. But these pictures had no effect upon Marian; she would not look upon them. Sadly poor old Rayner felt that they were painted in vain.

One soft May evening, coming home after a weary day passed in seeking employment, and finding none, the big, tawny setter bounded forth from the door to meet her. Going in with a rush, and a cry of such delight as might not be subdued, she found him—the bright stranger—in their little room, and Rayner standing talking to him, and crying, as was customary with Rayner when she was agitated.

"My poor little Marian! my dear little nurse! what you have suffered through me!" he said, in a deep, thrilling tone, as, together with Rock, she nearly fell through the doorway into his arms. Suffered! There was no trace of suffering in her face now. "He had returned—he had not left her there to die!" Oh, glorious sun of youth, and love, and hope! Such intense bliss as the girl felt in that moment repays one for years of sorrow and despair!

—o—

CHAPTER XXXII.

WHO WROUGHT THE WRONG?

A few months have passed since that soft May evening which restored happiness and Stanley Villars to poor little Marian Wallis. It is August, and the Claude Walsinghams are thinking of going out of town.

The sweet peace that was their portion just after Claude's accident—that was hanging over them, in fact, like a mantle when we saw them last—had been disturbed when we met them again. Mrs. Markham had accompanied them when they left the Court—accompanied them sorely against Bella's will—and during the whole of her visit she had justified Bella's repugnance to having her at all, by being very observant and disagreeable.

Stanley Villars had called on them once. It was on the occasion of his visit that peace took the opportunity of fleeing. His visit had been paid shortly after their return to town, as had been originally intended. It was August before he saw them.

Claude was not with his wife when her old lover was admitted to his presence, but Claude's sister was sitting with Bella, irritating her nerves by cutting the leaves of a new book slowly and methodically, and with a grating sound that was simply intolerable.

All those confidences which had leaked from Bella during those hours of idleness she had known with Miss Harper had been zealously passed on by that sweet girl to Mrs. Markham. From the moment she had heard them, Mrs. Markham had been on the alert to catch Bella tripping even so slightly, "for love of Claude." Therefore, now when Stanley Villars came into the room, she mounted guard at once in a palpable way, that would have caused Bella to evince confusion at the entrance of a saint with whom she had never had love passages, or indeed met at all.

Fondly and fervently did Mrs. Claude hope that oblivion or discretion would keep Stanley from making any mention of that innocent letter which she so bitterly repented having written. But poor Stanley, feeling miserably conscious now that he was in her presence again, that the wound she had made was as fresh as the day it was given—feeling moreover that he had taken a step of which she was still ignorant, and so was there in a measure under false pretences—mooted the subject of that miserable letter, as a drowning man clutches at a straw.

"I had a bad fever just after I heard from you: it laid me up for six or seven weeks," he said, striving hard to speak to her as he would speak to any other woman, and failing.

Mrs. Claude was not one to grow nervous and excited before the enemy, and she felt that her husband's sister was her enemy now.

"That was bad—Claude will be so sorry when he comes in," she said quickly.

"Claude will doubtless have wondered why his letter was not answered," Mrs. Markham remarked grimly.

Mr. Villars looked at the last speaker quietly for a moment or two, and then glanced quickly at Bella's blushing face. He saw that he had made some mistake, but he did not know what his mistake had been.

Bella's old reverence for his perfect truthfulness uprose at once as he looked at her, and banished temporarily her dread of Mrs. Markham and mischief.

"It was of *my* letter, not Claude's, that Mr. Villars spoke, Ellen," she explained, in such a cool, firm voice that Mrs. Markham was more than half inclined to think well of her. Then Mrs. Markham remembered the relations that had existed between the man who was before her and her brother's wife, and conquered the half-inclination—like a woman.

"Oh, indeed! *your* letter!" she said, in such a tone that Bella felt she was on her trial.

"And what have you been doing since your illness?" Mrs. Claude asked, with a slight fall in her voice—a sympathetic inflexion that she could not restrain, as her eyes fell on the altered worn face and habiliments of the man whom she had once been going to marry.

"Since then! God knows, I can hardly tell," he replied drearily. "My life would hardly interest you—I mean any of my old friends, I fancy."

"Is it so changed, Stanley?"

The deep, true woman's pity that would well up, as she marked pitifully how changed it was, would make itself heard in her tone.

She could but remember how different he had been; she could but remember who had changed him thus.

He dared not risk a repetition of that pitying tone. He dared not, for his own sake, and for hers, and for the sake of one other whose heart would break to know him moved by it. So he answered carelessly—recklessly almost—

"It's a life made up of excitements, of which you fashionable people can have no conception."

"You were one of us not so long ago," Mrs. Claude exclaimed unguardedly. She could not bear to hear him abjure his class in this way.

"But I'm not one of you now; therefore I have no time to be idle," he said hurriedly. Then he rose up and said, "Morning calls were not much in his way, therefore he should like to see Claude, as he might not be able to come again."

Bella went to look for her husband in order that she might be free from observation for a few moments. He was so horribly altered! so sadly, so painfully altered! She would have given much not to have seen him at all, since she saw him thus. She would have given much to have been able to drug the conviction to rest that *she* had caused that change.

"Stanley Villars is here, Claude," she said abruptly, opening the door of the room where her husband sat writing; but not putting her face in, or suffering him to see it. "Come and speak to him, will you?"

He got up instantly. "Stanley Villars!—I'm coming."

"You'll hardly know him," she said, turning away and walking along the hall before Claude when he came out. Then they went in together to the room where Stanley was awaiting them, and attempted to be cordial and unconstrained, and failed—failed miserably!

Soon Stanley went away. It was the best thing he could do, considering all things. Claude stood looking out of the window and whistling for a minute or two after his departure. Bella sat with her elbows on the table and her hands supporting her chin, gazing intently at vacancy, and not finding the view agreeable.

"*What* a change!" she said impatiently at last. "Claude, ain't you sorry?" She asked it eagerly. Stanley Villars seemed so far removed from her now, changed as he was, that she dared to speak of him eagerly and freely to her husband.

"He's a complete wreck," Claude replied, rather mournfully. He was feeling more than he cared to make manifest, for this man whose plan of life *he* had spoilt.

"He looks as if he drank," Mrs. Markham put in quietly. "Your plan of a renewal of intercourse with him won't do, I fear, Bella."

"Why not? had Bella any plan?" Claude asked vaguely.

"I thought at one time it would be pleasant to see and be friendly with him again," Bella replied. "I have given up that idea now."

"So she wrote to him, as he mentioned just now, when he was telling us about his fever," Mrs. Markham went on, with much simplicity, but keeping a keen watch on her sister-in-law the while.

"You wrote to him?" Claude interrogated, turning round and frowning a little; "when?"

"Oh! long ago," Bella replied, crimsoning up to her very brow with anger at his tone and his sister's interference.

"What did you write to him for?"

"To tell him that we should be glad to see him."

"I'm not glad to see him as he is now," Claude said, harshly. "Why didn't you tell me that you had written?"

Mrs. Markham nodded her head at nothing, as though she were saying, "Why not? Why not, indeed?" The gesture annoyed Bella.

"It did not occur to me to tell you, Claude," she replied coldly. Had they been alone she would have made free confession—have told him why, and how that letter was written, and how penitent, not to say remorseful, she had been about it often since. But not now; not with Mrs. Markham's stony eyes watching, and Mrs. Markham's stony heart judging her.

"I should have been better pleased then if it had never occurred to you to launch out in condemnation of the very thing you have done—writing to a man without your husband's knowledge," he said gloomily. "It was a piece of deceit I should never have believed you would have been guilty of, Bella."

"Don't believe it now——" she began eagerly; but he would not listen to her; but went away, leaving Bella alone with his sister, who proceeded to improve the occasion, till Bella felt that a brace of murders and a successful attempt at arson would have lain more lightly on her soul than did this letter which had cropped up against her thus unexpectedly. This innocent letter—indited without guile, but all-sufficient to wreck her nevertheless.

She would not stoop to defend herself to Mrs. Markham. She would not attempt to offer any explanation as to the creative cause of that epistle. Mrs. Markham was striving earnestly, according to her light, to arrest the progress of this disease with which she firmly believed her sister-in-law's mind to be infected, and she had not the art to keep her instruments from the eyes of her patient. She believed that it behoved her to cut deep to cure, and so she had no false delicacy about letting the one to be cut see the knife; that was all!

"If every tiny thing of this sort that comes up is to create a coldness between Claude and me, well! the sooner things come to a climax, and I'm 'frozen out' altogether, the better," Bella exclaimed at last, taking up arms abruptly, and breaking off patient endurance with a snap.

"It *being* an error on your part, and your being far too sensible not to be fully conscious that it *is* an error, it would be more becoming, to say the least of it, Bella, if you regarded the consequences in a more patient spirit."

Mrs. Markham cut through the sides and top of a sheet, as she spoke, with a sliding, sure motion, and a grating relentless sound that made Bella's blood run cold. For about the first time in her life, Bella felt that she must not give way to impulse. For about the first time in her life she calculated the effect the speech she was going to make would have on her hearer. While Mrs. Markham continued cool and self-possessed, the power was hers, palpably, of stinging Bella into making the most unwary speeches. To shatter that self-possession by fair means, if possible—by foul, if fair failed her—was the first task Bella set herself to achieve.

"'It being an error on my part!' Do you really think me in error when I feel hurt at my husband being cold to me?" she asked, with a simple earnestness, which Mrs. Markham hated her for, feeling sure that it was assumed for her discomfiture.

"You are wilfully misunderstanding me, Bella," she began angrily. "I did not mean that it was an error——"

"I thought you didn't mean it, though you said you did," Bella interrupted. "I'm glad you acknowledge that, Ellen. I have no liking for misunderstandings."

"If you will *allow* me to speak," Mrs. Markham resumed nippingly.

Bella expressed interrogatory astonishment with her eyes and shoulders.

"Why not?" she asked.

"I was saying when you stopped me," Mrs. Markham said, severely, in a tone that would have been very telling had Bella not seen her fingers nervously working between the leaves of the volume she held on her lap—"I was saying, when you stopped me, that it *being* an error——"

"Excuse me, you'd said that before," Bella said, shaking her head and looking intensely interested; "that was where you started. I know how annoying it is to lose one's thread—I often do; but you'll remember what you want to say presently."

Mrs. Claude Walsingham spoke with provoking calmness. She hardly knew herself why she parried the blow her sister-in-law was evidently bent upon dealing. In the end she could gain nothing by a brief delay—a temporary warding off of that blame from which she shrank. But then women love to fence with fate, and Bella Walsingham was a thorough woman.

"Pardon me—I know perfectly well what I am going to say—if you will be polite enough to listen to me," Mrs. Markham said, with such severity that Bella rose up saying, "Excuse me, I will listen another time. Claude will be going out almost directly, and I must see him before he goes." Her intention of seeking her husband, however, failed her when she got out into the hall and found the door of his room closed. It seemed to be closed more especially against her, she thought, so she went away moodily to her own chamber to be miserable; and Mrs. Markham, marching after her unseen, marked the failure of that intention, and put down the swerving from the declared purpose as another proof of Bella's "confirmed duplicity."

Claude Walsingham, when he found himself alone, had first asked, in a hot mutter, "Why the devil Bella shouldn't write to Stanley if she liked? It was like Ellen's malicious spite to think it fishy—and to try and make him think it so too. He had perfect confidence ——" Then he paused. Truth to tell, he had not perfect confidence in Bella. It had been his misfortune—it would be his misery—not to have perfect confidence in any woman. Then he asked himself, "Why the devil she *should* write to Stanley Villars—and be confoundedly sly and confused about it? It was fishy and no mistake, and he had been an ass to marry."

The angry young husband had no pity now for the old friend, the more than brother, who had gone to the dogs before that prowess of his (Claude's), which had never failed him with women. He had no pity for him. On the contrary, he had a certain feeling of disgust for the man who looked "like a cad," and was at the same time the recipient of a letter from Bella, the contents of which were a sealed book to him, her rightful lord. He had no pity for the changed man; no kindly desire to learn the cause of the change—the immediate, commonplace cause—and ameliorate it if possible. He told himself that Stanley Villars was "turning out very badly (precisely as those fellows who commence by being pious prigs invariably do turn out), and that Bella was as deceitful as was usual with her sex." But, for all these unpleasant convictions respecting both of them, "By God, I'll have none of Ellen's interference!" he added morosely. "I can guard my own honour better than a dozen old women can do it for me!" Mrs. Markham would have been sorely grieved had she known that her brother included her in the list of those whose assistance he despised, and whose youthful intelligence and efficacy he doubted. Claude was not wont even to "think" unseemly things of the sex—unseemly things relating to their age and appearance, that is. But to-day he was very much aggrieved. He had "shown jealous" before his sister, and he could not forgive his sister for having witnessed the sight.

He determined to put down anything like an approach to former intimacy with Stanley Villars, with the strong hand of common sense and marital authority. On the occasion of his marriage he had been "a romantic ass," he called himself now. It had been an unwise—an extraordinarily generous, but desperately unwise thing on his part to press upon Stanley the office which made Stanley appear so noble and self-sacrificing, so loftily resigned, in Bella's eyes. A sensible woman would have thought Stanley an idiot, under the circumstances, for accepting that office. But he began to fear that Bella, with all her charm, was *not* a sensible woman—not sensible enough, at least, to think Stanley Villars an idiot.

He was not jealous—he assured himself that he was not jealous; but it behoved him to take care of Bella, and not subject her to the temptation of seeing Stanley Villars look woe-begone and blighted on her account. He remembered that women were very weak, very liable to be affected by the sight of certain things that were utterly repulsive to a man. In masculine eyes, Stanley's abnegation of all things, his dolour and despair, were simply imbecile. In Bella's dazzled orbs they would probably appear interesting.

Besides, he had another reason for not caring to see much of Stanley. He had amused himself to his heart's content with Florence for several months; and there was a look in Stanley's face very often—he had remarked it vividly to-day—that reminded him of Florence in a way he did not care to be reminded of her. A rumour had reached him that Florence had never been so sweetly, softly glowing and bright, since that time at Denham. His heart told him the reason why; and he wished to banish the remembrance of what she had been, and the reflection of what she might be. She would marry in time, there was no doubt of that; but till she did marry and exhibit a surface happiness, he would rather not see a face that brought hers, in its saddest aspect, to his mind. He was not more subject to remorse than are the majority of men, but he did feel its throes sometimes about Florry Villars.

In recalling past passages with numberless fair daughters of the land, reprobation, happily for him, mingled largely with his remorse. They had been as ready to take as he to give. They had surrendered without discretion. They had been reliant and kind; and when he left them, he left no blank—his place had been filled precipitately. But with Florence it had been different. The welcome she had blushed for him had been blushed for none other. The light that love for him had lit in her eyes had not been rekindled yet. She had been very fond! so had many another woman. She had been very faithful! and in that he believed her singular.

He did not see his wife again till they sat down to dinner at seven; and then the soup was far from clear, and he was not far from cross. Bella had forgotten her fears of mischief ensuing from Mrs. Markham's active endeavours to keep her straight, and had recovered her animation in a way that was not pleasing to him, since he had not recovered his. She wanted to talk. There was nothing very reprehensible in this. Her subject, however, was ill chosen: out of no bravado, but rather out of a very gentle feeling of good will towards the man who had loved her so much better than she deserved, she selected Stanley Villars as her theme.

"Have you been riding, Claude?" she began.

He shook his head, "No."

"Where then? the club?"

"I went in there," he replied, in a constrained tone, as if her asking the question were an infringement of the liberty of the subject which he scorned to resent, and still could but mark.

"I didn't go out at all," she said, looking up with a blithe expectation of his being interested, that he would respond to by word or glance. "I didn't go out at all," she repeated.

"Then I think you were wrong,' Mrs. Markham put in quickly.

"Ah! you often think me wrong," Bella replied laughing. "But, Claude! don't you wonder what kept me in such a bright day?"

"Really I had not marvelled very much about it," he said, without looking at her. She could but remember how he had looked at her once—with what eager love—with what passionate pleading! Well! she was his wife now. It was her duty to put up with his altered looks; to win them back to their original softness, if she might. After all, this reserve on his part might only be the effect of fatigue. He was weak still, perhaps; may be he had not quite recovered the accident which had threatened to rend him from her. At the thought all her tenderness arose, and she went on making her subtly sweet efforts to win him to a gentler bearing.

"Well, I didn't go out to-day, because——"

"You've told us that twice, dear," he interrupted.

"Because I sent out for that magazine—the *Metropolitan.* You know, Claude, that Stanley Villars writes for it."

"I should hope that imbecility that's 'to be continued' isn't Stanley's?" Claude asked languidly.

"The story that's running in it is his," Bella replied, trying not to show that the contemptuous condemnation of it in anywise affected her, and failing.

"I'm really astonished at Stanley's condescending to write such maudlin rubbish; the fellow has talent of a certain kind, but he is wasting it and throwing himself away entirely," Claude remarked with an air of superiority, that Bella, remembering certain things, girded at in her soul.

"Why does he do such things, since it is evidently not his vocation?" said Mrs. Markham.

"A little because he does it well, and a little because there was nothing else for him to do, I suppose," Bella replied shortly.

Claude smiled superciliously. "My dear Bella, Stanley Villars ought to thank the Lord that all men who could 'do it well' don't set about doing it at once; if they did, he and his compeers would be in a sorry plight, I'm thinking."

"And wasn't there anything else for him to do?" Mrs. Markham asked suspiciously.

"How should there be when he didn't stay in the Church?" Bella answered, with a lack of relevancy that was reasonable under the circumstances.

"The whole thing lies in a nutshell, and is not by any means so gloriously uncommon as you seem to think it," Claude explained. "He got tired of slow promotion—dozens of men do that—and he fancied that he was a genius, and would make himself famous by his pen if he cast himself upon literature entirely. The delusion is common enough."

"Foolish young man! How very unpleasant for his family!" Mrs. Markham remarked.

"Then why don't his family do something better for him?" Bella said it with warmth, and was instantly made to feel, by the depression of her husband's eyebrows, that she had been unwise to do so.

"It is unpleasant for his family. However, he'll get tired of the Bohemian brotherhood by-and-by, and then Gerald's interest will set him on his legs again. He's a nice fellow; but there is an atmosphere of gin and water about the band he belongs to at present that it may be as well to avoid."

Claude strove to speak in a monotone expressive of absolute unconcern. He slightly overdid it, unfortunately. His wife saw through the effort he made, and was so sorry for him and for herself that he should think it necessary to make one at all in this matter. "He might trust me, and feel a little as a man *should* feel for Stanley," she thought, and her heart swelled painfully. Now that she had come in contact with Stanley again, now that this contact brought her to her mind once more, she did so fervently desire that Claude should go with her in making what atonement might be made to the man they had both wronged and wrecked.

"An atmosphere of gin-and-water! that's a hard thing to say of Stanley Villars, Claude," she said softly.

"And I'm sorry to say it; but it's one of the conditions of the life he is leading—those fellows all use themselves up, and the more brains they have the faster they go."

"Then you think he'll 'go,' as you call it?" she asked, anxiously.

"His appearance this morning rather favours that supposition," he replied. The conversation was eminently distasteful to him. There were servants in the room, and he felt that they were listening with understanding; still he could not turn it, or stop Bella, or refrain from saying severe things.

"His appearance this morning rather favours that supposition." Bella repeated those words to herself, and she felt that they were very cold words—that they were words, indeed, which it ill became Claude to use with reference to Stanley Villars. However low the latter might have fallen, it ill became the man who had, in a measure, caused that fall, to condemn or be caustic. She gave a quick sigh, that was half pain and half anger, and asked—

"Do you remember what he was at Denham?"

"An intense bore about matters parochial," Claude replied.

"I don't know that," Bella rejoined—not quite truthfully, it must be admitted, since, as has been seen, the discussion of matters parochial had occasionally bored her in those Denham days—"I don't know that; but he was very earnest."

"As earnest as he is now in running the orthodox career of a press-man of to-day."

"As earnest as he was in love," she said, quietly. "Shall we go into the drawing-room, Ellen?" Then she marched off in her sister-in-law's wake, with a heart that was very heavy, and very repentant as to that parting shot. But she could not keep the peace when Claude disparaged Stanley—when the victor was ungenerous to the victim.

All through that evening she perused and reperused, with an interest that was intensely aggravating to her husband, those pages of the *Metropolitan* which Stanley had penned. She tried to trace him through his work, as the weak and the wise alike persist in doing whenever they chance to know a luckless writer in the flesh.

Constantly as she read her brow flushed and her lips quivered. The light regard for women, the disbelief in truth, the doubt of honour, the damning dread of being deceived at every turn, —good God! of what had all this been born? Her conscience answered that question; and still she read and re-read, and asked it again.

——o——

CHAPTER XXXIII.

DOMESTIC BLISS.

WHILE Bella—his lost love, the sweet rock on which he had split, the wife of his friend, the one woman in the world to him—was wrangling with her sister-in-law and wrestling with her own spirit, Stanley Villars was walking slowly home through the dry, dusty streets, with his eye-balls burning and his temples feeling painfully compressed, and a general sensation over him of having been up all the previous night, and of having to be up all through the night to come.

He was very glad when he got away from the precincts of the Walsinghams' house, which was situated in a region where he might at any moment come upon any member of his old set —at Princes Gate, namely. The walk across the park was pleasant enough in itself, but there were too many people still in town for him to walk there freely now. He sneered at himself for giving a thought to such things; but he was conscious of whiter seams than were well in his coat, and of a certain limpness about his hat that was aught but seemly in that place. He despised himself for doing it; but still he did avert his eyes, or abstractedly study the ground, whenever a carriage approached whose occupants might possibly know him.

When he reached the Marble Arch, he heaved a sigh of relief for that he was nearing home; not that home was a pleasant place to him, or, indeed, one from which he would not have abstained for ever could he have done so in honour, but simply because he was physically worn out, and he could not afford a cab. Besides, there was a shady side to the streets through which his way lay, and he could keep on that side, and so be more likely to evade observation.

There had been no slight courage in that determination which carried him over Claude Walsingham's threshold. He was a worn, haggard, shabby man now, and he clearly saw himself to be what he was. It was no light thing to show himself in such a plight to those two. But he did it because he yearned so to see them again; and because he hoped that he should see that there was no longer semblance of a cause for that appeal which he had fancied he detected in Bella's letter.

He had not found the meeting pleasant. He had never anticipated its being that, indeed; but it had been wanting in so much that should have been there. Bella had been what she always must be; her nature would not admit of her being other than warm and womanly. But Claude's manner had said plainly, "My dear fellow, you've put yourself out of the pale. Can I do anything for you? If so, mention it; if not, the sooner we part the pleasanter for both parties."

He thought over this manner of Claude's; he looked at it in every light as he shambled along Oxford street. I use the word shamble advisedly; the gait indicated by it is not uncommon in men who have been utterly worsted, and who still have to keep going, loathing the onus humanity lays upon them of struggling for life, envying the desolate dogs who lie down in the gutter and die at their ease.

"Perhaps after all Claude was right." He tried to think him right, for their ways of life were so different; they were so utterly separated in reality that occasional communion in seeming could only prove painful to both. But after all that had come and gone, by the memory of their boyhood, by the pleasure and the pain they had been to one another, by the love they both had felt for one object, by the doubt and agony, by the thousand nameless things which had been and were not, Claude's manner of showing him this should have had more manliness in it.

Presently he turned out of Oxford Street to the right, and shortly came to a street near the Strand that had a living pattern of infant Arabs in its centre, and a border of broken windows, in the majority of which there were attractive announcements respecting accommodation for single men. It was a disheartening street! How vividly, with what frightful force, it contrasted with the surroundings of the house at which he had been calling!

The day, bright as it had been beyond, seemed gloomy in this street. The sun did not find it worth his while to smile upon so dolefu a corner of the earth. There were a vast num ber of women moving hither and thither in it in that marvellous manner peculiar to the se: in these shades—of appearing to be going fo. something which they are not likely to get. There was a man with a flute and a wry neck walking its length to his own sorrowful strains. There were several dispirited cats, whose case was too sad for them to care to keep their paws clean. Beyond these there were no signs of life in the street down which Stanley Villars walked to his own door.

When he reached it he gave an impatient knock; he was eager to get in, and no wonder. The position he occupied while waiting for admission was not an agreeable one for a moderately sensitive man. Sundry heads came out of the windows of the houses immediately adjoining his own on either side, and a woman came on to the door-step of the opposite dwelling, affording her infant sustenance in the most Arcadian manner, the while she called to him that his "good lady had gone out and left the latch-key with her, and would he excuse her crossing with it, her feet being that swelled with the heat that she could scarce stand, far less walk."

He crossed over and got his key, and returned with it, cursing his degradation with deep and bitter oaths. His hand trembled to such a degree that he had difficulty in getting the key into the door, and a street boy marked his bungling efforts and chaffed him freely on the subject in the street-boy style.

He opened it at last and got into his own house, to the place that was his sole sanctuary

—his home. A narrow, little, stifling passage led to a low, stifling, little room, in which there was dust and disarray and stuffiness; and yet despite all these, some trifling evidences of a woman's presence. A long table in the corner covered with papers, books, and slips, with stubby pens and grimy ink-bottles, with uncorrected proofs, with recent novels to review, with suspicious-looking letters, over which there was that unwholesome shade of blue which bespeaks the bill, with dust and dead flies, with the pitiable litter, in fact, which distinguishes the careless, uncared-for "literary man's" writing-table. A little piano in a recess by the fireplace, a workstand near it, and a low lounge chair and footstool in close proximity to the stand, indicating a woman's presence habitually in that room—a round centre-table, with a soiled green cloth very much awry upon it—a few despondent chairs that seemed to say, "Sit upon me, do; but I'm very uncomfortable"—pale green chintz curtains to the windows, that looked as though they had been put to that test which Shetland shawls proudly assert they can stand, namely, being passed through a ring—a small effort at colour and cleanliness, in the shape of a pink paper cut into a honeycomb pattern and draped round a chimney-glass, that gave the rash one who gazed in it one swollen cheek and one oblique eye—an abrupt cessation from all such effort immediately the precincts of that paper were passed,—this was all Stanley Villars found when he got home that hot August day.

Heavily he drew a chair along to the side of that table in the corner, and sat down, trying to fall to his work without further thought. He was a machine for turning out copy now. Every moment of his time—every effort of his brain—was brought up, and pretty well paid for on the whole. He had a hard day's work before him on the next month's instalment of that novel, the earlier chapters of which Bella was contemporaneously perusing. By the time that was done he would be due at the office of the daily paper for which he wrote; but the season was dull just then, and there was every chance of his soon being released, instead of the latest telegrams bringing such news as would compel him to sit up half the night writing a leader that should be utterly passed over by many, and superciliously criticised by more, at the breakfast tables of the great majority, on the following morning.

But he could not work. The horror that crept over him as he felt that the time was stealing away, weighting every minute to come with a ghastly weight of work that he shrank from contemplating—the horror he felt at this was really one of those things that must be endured to be appreciated. But it was nothing; it was a weak, poor, puerile horror to that which seized his soul and stultified his brain, as the reflection arose that in his rash wrath at the downfall of his first idol he himself had marred his plan of life—had gone wilfully into the groove from which there was no escaping.

It was a soul-deadening thought. This wrong—this bitter wrong which had been done him—had been wrought by his own hand. He had given way, just as the veriest fool might have done, to that feeblest passion which induces a man to revenge some injury, real or fancied, upon himself, if none other be by to bear the blow. He had cast off those ropes and anchors which at the time he had deemed to be fetters, but which now he knew to have been merely saving responsibilities. He had gone to perdition at a slinging trot. He had taken the road from which there was no turning back—bound, as he was, hand and foot—clogged, as he was, through his own folly; so the faster he followed it the better.

As his bitter, distorted thoughts reached this point, he laid his head down upon his arms, and groaned in that bitterness of spirit—that weariness of body—that fainting of the soul—that doubting of its God—which parents had better strangle their children in the cradle than let them live to feel,—laid his head down and groaned over the folly of that despair which led him to believe that all was lost when a woman jilted him—that all was gone when his first scheme for life was proved faulty.

This knocking under—this breaking down and giving way—was owing much more to his pitiful surroundings than to the sight of *her*—the lovely rock who had wrecked him. Had he gone back to plenty and peace—to nothing to do and iced wine—to an earnest groom's doubt of a blood mare's dam—to a coachman's groaning over the way the carriage "was kept out at night"—to any of the multifarious discomforts (!) of wealth, in fact, he might have held a gloomy debate in his soul on the Bella question, but he would not have groaned, and found the cup too bitter for him even to pray that it might pass away from him.

Time fleeted on—the shadows lengthened on the floor, and did not decrease in his heart; and at last he raised his head to the sound of a knock at the door, and knew that it was evening. He rose wearily to answer that knock, and struggled to throw off so much of the blackness he was steeped in as was in his eyes and on his brow. Then he went out into the narrow passage, and opened the door, and tried—and cursed his own weakness as he felt that he failed—to give something like a welcoming smile to the childish beauty wistfully glancing at him from the step, and to the solemn-faced dog, whose loving wisdom had taught him to keep close to his master's wife.

You will have guessed the secret—you will have decided what that step was which he had taken—remembering which, he felt himself to be in Bella's presence under false pretences. You will have pierced through the tiny mystery I have made—you will have comprehended that the baby-faced beauty and Stanley Villars had cast in their lots together "for better, for worse."

Even so! He had gone there, to her quiet little house—to the doll's-house, where the doll had tended him so unweariedly—on that soft May evening, meaning to repay her with such measure as he had for that which she had done for him. He had found her absent, and all things altered. The peace and the quiet had fled, and in their place had come a doleful dread of what was to follow—a bitter sense of things being about to close over and swamp the butterfly-bark that had put out to sea so blithely, disregarding the idea of possible squalls.

He did not come in procession, as she had prognosticated; nevertheless, he was very eligible in Rayner's eyes. Accordingly, that well-meaning woman made the most of Miss Marian's forlorn state. For a while he had no very clear idea of what he ought to do in the case; but eventually it dawned upon him that he was called upon to refund, not only the actual filthy lucre which Marian had expended upon him, but something else that he had cost her.

He told himself, sitting there, and listening to Rayner's wails about Marian's woes, that he had nothing more to lose, let him do what he would. He was cut off utterly; truly, it was by his own hand, but still he was utterly cut off from his class and his kindred. If this poor little girl loved him—if she had indeed already lost something she could never regain through him—why should he not do all he could to repay and make her happy?

Why not?

He asked the question idly, and never stayed to hear his instincts answer, as they would have done had he not rushed along recklessly, bidding him beware of this worst, last folly of linking himself for the rest of his life with that for which his previous life had entirely unfitted him. He was a man, and he thought of her beauty, and told himself that he could not blight it, and that it behoved him, since he could do so, to lift the load that had come upon her through him. So when she came home he made her poor little heart happy, and let her perceive that she might love him without fear and without reproach. This was enough for her. She gave no thought to the strangeness of that wooing which accepted merely, and offered nothing in return. He let her love him, but he neither loved her, nor lied to her about it. Still, she was satisfied, with a loving wealth of satisfaction that almost refined her for the time, and married him without a doubt as to the glory and grandeur of that fate which had commenced for her when she found him by the wayside, with his dog howling over him.

Not that he had deceived her as to his position. At one fell blow he had demolished the lordly mansions with which Rayner had endowed him, and had exploded the King Cophetua and Co. theories. He tried to make her understand that he was only a working man—a hard-working, ill-paid man. But she looked at his white hands, and her ears—so open to soft, sweet sounds—drank in the tones of his voice, and she disregarded everything that he said to her in a cautionary strain.

They were soon married, and he removed her from the doll's-house to a lodging in the heart of London that was more conveniently situated, in relation to his daily haunts. Rayner accompanied them, nominally as a servant, in reality as Marian's own familiar friend; and though Stanley Villars' sense told him that this was a natural consequence of former conditions, it was a loathsome arrangement to him.

It must be admitted that Rayner was a trial. She would take no wages; she wept when he hinted that such being the case, she had better, in justice to herself, leave them, and left the room in a prominent manner whenever Mr. Villars came into it, in a way that made him feel himself to be a brute, he knew not why. Marian, too, had a habit of slinking out meekly after Rayner, evidently with the design of appeasing her aggrieved spirit, and causing her to feel that they were not *both* ungrateful. When he remonstrated with Marian for doing this—he having wanted her on one occasion—Mrs. Stanley Villars proved her inability to cope with circumstances, and adopt a medium manner, by becoming imperious to her self-sacrificing old friend, after the fashion of a "haughty lady," by whom she had been profoundly impressed, one blissful and never-to-be-forgotten night long ago on the boards of the Victoria Theatre. Then Rayner was resigned, and remorseful, and reproachful all at once, in a bewildering way, till Stanley Villars would have entreated her to take the seat of honour at his board and the upper chamber in his mansion, had he had either, rather than be subjected any longer to poor Marian's laments over the impossibility of her "keeping Rayner in her proper place." At last things came to such a pass that he made another move, and told Rayner he could not afford such a luxury as she was any longer. At which dire decision, Rayner—whose love for the girl, to whom she had been as a mother, was strong and true—lifted up her voice and wept, and pressed the savings of a lifetime upon him earnestly.

Stanley Villars had realised his mistake even while in the act of making it. He had not stood at the altar, and called God to witness that there "was no just cause or impediment" to his marriage, as many better men do when something whispers them to the contrary. He had not forsworn himself before God. In his own heart there existed the impediment which, while it did exist, should have prevented his calling any other woman but Bella wife. He knew this, so he made their union binding and respectable by wedding Marian Wallis at a registrar office. But though there were no words to stay him on the occasion, he fully realised his mistake the whole time he was making it.

Perhaps you will understand more fully why he did so when you have seen a little more of Marian. A mere dry catalogue of his reasons for doing so from my pen would be worse than wasted.

"Where have you been, Marian?" he asked, as he opened the door. He did not ask it sternly or anxiously, as most husbands would of a beautiful young wife. He merely asked it because he felt that she expected him to speak to her, that he ought to speak to her, and he never knew what to say.

"I've been shopping. I hope you haven't been waiting for me long, Stanley," she replied, walking in before him, and pulling her bonnet off as she preceded him into the sitting-room.

"Not very long," he answered, returning to his writing, and taking up the pen, in which, truth to tell, the ink had been dry for more than two hours.

"I left the key with Mrs. Watts, over the way, and——"

"Why the devil did you?" he interrupted; "when I found you were not at home, I could have gone on somewhere; besides, if you were going out, you should have left the girl in."

"It was her half-holiday," Marian explained,

with a tremble in her voice. Though she was always jarring upon his finer feelings, and making him writhe, and feeling, poor thing! that she was doing these things, this man was as a god to her—a thing to love and tremble at, to adore and kneel before.

"Her half-holidays come devilish quick!" he muttered; and then he made another effort to send the pen over the paper, and found he could not do it.

"Can I have something to eat, Marian?" he asked, throwing himself back in his chair, and looking at her, as she stood smoothing her ruddy, glorious hair before the glass.

She stopped her evolutions suddenly, and glanced round at him.

"I'll go and get you something, Stanley. Haven't you had any dinner?"

He shook his head. "And I don't like you to get it for me in that nice dress," he said; "but I'm quite knocked up."

She brightened wonderfully; all the soul of the little milliner sparkled up into her soft blue eyes, and irradiated the lovely childish face, at his observation and praise of her dress.

"I won't hurt it, Stanley; I'll light this fire and cook you a rasher," she said, with animation; but he had no appetite for a rasher, and she saw that he had not, in his face.

"Never mind, Marian; I'll get something to eat as I go down to the office." Then he took out his watch, and said he "must go presently, and she had better not sit up for him, as he might be late, and would have to write again when he came home."

She looked disappointed for a minute or two; it might be at the downfall of the rasher plan; it might be at the hearing that she would not have more of her husband's society that night. Whatever it was, it clouded her brow only for a minute or two. Then she brightened up again, and resumed her occupation before the glass, taking a delicate violet ribbon from her pocket, and passing it through her richly tinted hair with excellent effect.

She looked so very young, so innocently pretty, standing there, that he could but think of her tenderly and pityingly; could but think of her as she was individually, and not as a clog in relation to himself. In this uncongenial union of theirs, *he* only was unhappy, but *she* was equally alone. Dangerously, pitiably alone!

"Where did you say you had been, dear?" he asked, trying to speak as though he cared to know.

"Shopping," she replied, blushing a little; "and if you can wait, I'll tell you where, Stanley?"

He had risen and was looking for his hat; but he ceased his search when she said that, and went up and kissed her, telling her "that, of course, he could wait." He pitied her so profoundly for being so utterly, hopelessly powerless as she was to efface the past from his memory—to make the present endurable—to shed one ray of warmth into the heart Bella Vane had chilled.

"I went to the place where I used to work," she began, hesitatingly, feeling her way, as it were.

"Ah, indeed! what for, dear?"

"Well, I want a bonnet, you know, so I thought I'd go there and order it; and while I was there——" She stopped again, uneasily twisting her wedding-ring upon her finger, and growing full and flushed in the face, as a confused child does. She was quite conscious that she had gone to the old place in order to display herself as a married woman and a gentleman's wife to her old companions, and she half feared that he would fathom the motive and despise her, or be angry.

"And is this the new bonnet?" he asked, laughing, and taking up the one she had pulled off but just now.

"Oh, *dear*, no! the new one isn't home yet; but, Stanley, I saw some one there."

"Whom did you see?"

"Your sister, Flor—— Miss Villars," she answered, hastily correcting herself. He had only mentioned his sister Florence once, when she had asked him if he had any sisters. But this brief mention had been all-sufficient to show her that Florence was a very sacred thing in his estimation, one that might not even be looked upon lightly.

His brow darkened a little. "How did you know that it was my sister—Florence?" he asked.

"I'll tell you; you won't be angry?"

"Angry with you, child! God forgive me for having ever made you fear it!"

"I was in the show-room, and one of the young ladies who was great friends with me while I was there, asked me to show off some mantles to some good customers who were coming up."

"You didn't do it!" he exclaimed.

"Ye—es, I did."

"And it was Florence," he almost groaned. "Oh, Marian! Well, don't mind me, dear; but don't do it again! How did you know her?"

"Miss Simpson (that's my friend, and I have asked her here) whispered to me that the young lady, the youngest lady, for they were both young, was Miss Villars, 'the same name as the gentleman you've married,' she said; for I'd told her all about you, and she *does* wish to see you so much, Stanley."

"God!" Stanley ejaculated.

"And then I heard the other lady call her 'Florence,' so I knew. Wasn't it funny? I wonder what she would have thought, if she'd known."

It was very funny, very funny indeed! So funny, that Stanley Villars almost staggered under the superb humour of it. His darling sister unconsciously accepting humiliating service from his wife, and the shop-girls speculating as to the similarity of name! Very funny!

"Marian," he said gravely, "you must not do that again; I'm not angry with you, dear, but I wish you not to do that again; you won't, will you?"

In dealing with this girl, whom he did not love, he never made use of the old authoritative tone and manner which had so chafed Bella, whom he had adored.

"No, I won't," she said, promptly. "I've asked Miss Simpson—and—and—one or two of the others to come here to tea with me, Stanley; you won't mind that?"

What could he say? This society for which she sighed, was the society for which she was fitted; and he saw with unlucky clearness of vision that she would never be fitted for any other. "Not that it mattered, for what other could she have, poor little thing!" he thought. His own acquaintances—the men with whom he was thrown in daily contact—the men who shared and understood these later interests of his—scarcely noticed her at all, or, if they did, plainly regarded her as a pretty toy, which Stanley had been "weak, rather," to tie to himself so securely. She was nice to look at, but a bore when they had anything to do; for they often congregated about Stanley, he having a "local habitation and a name," they were good enough to remark; wrote their articles at his house, and gave themselves the freedom of it generally, in the frankness of that good fellowship which would have redeemed more faults than any of which these reckless, harmless, clever young Bohemians were guilty. Sad as Stanley's worldly plight was, when compared with that of his past and his class, it was far better than that in which some of his brethren of the craft were plunged. The days were very dark for some of them; but they were struggling on through the darkness with the light-hearted, plucky determination to win their laurels, which is so frequent a characteristic of the bright brotherhood to which they belonged.

Stanley Villars felt that Miss Simpson's presence would not impart the flavour that was already wanting to make his wife acceptable to his guests. She was very much alone—more alone, perhaps, when he was with her, than at any other time. He had no plan for her improvement. He had no hopes of amending anything connected with himself. As she was, so he would leave her. He had put such a clog round his neck, that no amount of gilding on the padlock that secured it could dazzle the world to the extent of making it oblivious of the crushing weight it was to him. It would crush him down in time—the sooner the better; meanwhile it was useless to try and alter anything that was. So he swallowed his repugnance to the plan, and promised Marian the exquisite bliss of seeing her friend whenever it seemed good to her.

Having made her happy so far, he whistled his dog and went away to dinner, if he could eat—to work, if work was to be done. It was a very rare thing for him to get anything to eat in his own house. The "girl" was always alarming her mistress into granting her half-holidays, and Marian always grew down-hearted when the subject of meals at home was mooted. Her share in the organisation of the doll's-house arrangements had obviously been very small, he learnt after Rayner's departure.

———o———

CHAPTER XXXIV.

RATHER HARD.

It may have occurred to the reader while following this little history through the last few chapters, that Florence, whom I described as being singularly fond of and faithful to her brother, has but scantily proved the justice of her claim to these qualities. Naturally, I who know "what she means" do not so misjudge her. Equally naturally the majority will feel that "another of the characters has utterly broken down."

The fact is, after that one visit to her brother's lodgings—that one stolen indulgence in the literary sweets he was preparing for the delicate palate of that many-headed monster, the reading public—Florence found herself a sort of prisoner on parole. She was living under her brother Gerald's roof at this time, and her brother Gerald's wife was, of course, her guardian and supervisor. Now Lady Villars had a habit of ill health—scarcely that, but of most extortionate delicacy. She was always in a state of verbal dread of being upset. She went a "little low" on the smallest provocation. She unselfishly bewailed these things on account of the effect they might have on her only child, the little heir. Sir Gerald was but a man and a baronet. He shrank from Carrie's being "upset," for many reasons that will be readily appreciated by husbands whose wives are addicted to disorganisations of the sort, and utterly unintelligible to the untried men who have had no such experience. He shrank from this as a man and a husband. As a baronet and father he was more sensitive still, therefore he cautioned Florence never to "put Carrie out," and Florence promised "not to do so," and forthwith became a white slave.

"I must *entreat* you never to go to Stanley's lodgings again, without telling me of your intention beforehand, Florence," Lady Villars said to her sister-in-law, shortly after Florry's first raid upon Stanley's premises.

Florence allowed herself to be entreated with effect; but still, while acquiescing in the demand made on her obedience, ventured to ask "why?"

"I have my reasons, and you must attend to them, believing them to be good, even though I can't explain, dear." Carrie's reply was accompanied by a kiss; so the affectionate Florry tried to look her faith, but failed, poor child, in feeling it.

As time went on, and no answer came to the little imploring note she had left for Stanley on the top of his pile of MS., Florence began to feel cut to the heart, and doubtful of his love for her. At last she wrote to him again—she had given Gerald and Carrie no promise as to not writing—telling him unconsciously, for she was not given to complaint, how weary she was of this life she was leading; how willing to change it for one anywhere, anyhow, with him.

She had given no promise as to not writing, still she said nothing about this letter; not out of any desire for secresy, but out of a dread of discussing Stanley and Stanley's doings with Carrie. Young Lady Villars was very hard upon her brother-in-law. It is difficult to determine what feeling it was that biased her judgment so sternly against him. Whatever it was the feeling was genuine. She did feel him to be a very faulty man—a man whose sufferings were surpassed by his sins—a man who deserved all he got, however bad it might be. She believed that he must have been well inclined for evil, to have seized so sharply upon the first excuse for going into it, as he had done. "He made being jilted a mean excuse," she said; "there had been but little good in him ever, or it would not have fled at the first wrong note that was struck in the melody of his life. Happily the family honour and family name were not *entirely* in his keeping." Then she would look at her little son, and feel more rigorous still towards Stanley if that little son looked pale or flushed, or anything unbecoming to an infant.

These things that were said of her favourite brother—of that brother who had been all that a man should be till Claude had played him false—were very hard for Florence to hear. She was a patient girl, and she gave but few signs of the sorrow that she felt. But her soft, tawny eyes—the eyes that were like a setter's in their tender, loving beauty—would swim in tears that she would not suffer to fall lest "Carrie should be upset," and her heart ached to be with Stanley again.

She said nothing about the letter; but she laid it down with the family epistles on the hall table when she was going into luncheon one day. Lady Villars, following her, stopped her, and read the superscription. Florence had been desirous only of evading conversation on the subject. She was careless as to whether Carrie saw the letter or not.

Lady Villars did not touch that letter—the purloining of other people's correspondence is not an attribute of the English ladies—but she went hastily back into the drawing-room, where she had left her husband sitting by the fire. It was a cold April day—one of the days poor Stanley was passing in dreamy doubt in the doll's-house; it might, therefore, be the cold which imparted an extra glitter to Lady Villars' eyes, and a heightened flush to her round, fair cheek.

"Gerald," she began, hurriedly, "here's Florence writing again to Stanley! You must speak!"

"What shall I say? Oh, let her!" he replied, in a vexed tone.

"Say! *you* must know what to say. It's for Florence's good I'm anxious. You might give me credit for that." She sat herself down as she spoke, and looked as though she were going to be upset.

"So I do, dear," he replied, getting up and standing before the fire, and making a feeble effort to twist his moustache unconcernedly. "It's a difficult matter to interfere in. Dear old Stanley! I wish to God he'd come back and be with us again!"

"So do I, if he did but see the error of his ways. But to throw up his profession in that wicked way, and go off and lead a godless life as he is doing; I cannot think of him affectionately."

"A godless life! Come, Carrie, that's rather strong, you know."

"At all events, the life he leads is not the life you, as her guardian, ought to suffer that child Florence to know anything about."

Gerald made a faint protest: "Writing to her brother can't harm her."

"Writing! yes, as if it would end there. Florence has a tinge of romance about her; and if it gets inflamed, where are her prospects? Being spoken about with Claude Walsingham (another of Stanley's precious friends) did her no good. You *must* be careful of Florence, Gerald."

"So I will."

"Ay, but very careful. Florence is a little unhappy about that Claude still; and more than a little inclined to believe Stanley a noble martyr. Really the responsibility will be too much for me, if you *won't* assist me."

"What shall I do, Carrie? Play the tyrant, and forbid her writing to her brother and mine, because he's gone to the devil for a time about a woman? No, no!"

Lady Villars rose and went nearer to him, sinking her voice to a whisper nearly, but speaking energetically. "I tell you, Gerald, you *must*. He has formed a low connection."

"Whew! How do *you* know?" he asked, quickly.

"Pollock" (mentioning her maid) "heard of it in the show-room at Mrs. Mitchell's the other day. It's one of her girls. Now fancy, Gerald!"

Carrie clasped her hands, and stretched them down before her as she spoke. She was one of those pinky-faced women, with short noses, who always look simple and well-meaning, whether they be so or not. The attitude matched the face; it was innocent and appealing.

"I can't fancy it," he replied. He could have believed any amount of downright depravity of Stanley just then, because he felt certain that Stanley's frame of mind was very sore and reckless. But a *liaison* with a milliner's girl! He did his brother the justice of disbelieving it. He could not accredit Stanley with being guilty of such a fatal folly.

"But I know it, Gerald." How convincing Lady Villars' tones were when she wanted to convince. "I know it. Pollock will talk, you know———"

"Why the devil about my brother?" Gerald interrogated hastily. But Carrie went on—

"She will talk; and when I found that she had something to say I listened—something concerning Stanley, I mean."

"Deuced insolent of her!"

"Well, I confess I asked her, Gerald. She's very right-thinking, and knows her place, and is thoroughly attached to the family; therefore when I found she knew something about Stanley, I *did* ask her. The girl is to be dismissed."

"Were there any truth in it she'd have dismissed herself. But let us go in to luncheon; Florry will be wondering, as well she may, why we stay."

Accordingly they went in to luncheon, and after it Gerald took occasion to tell Florry that "Carrie was very anxious about her—very much feared she was not happy, and—and—all that sort of thing."

"Not exactly unhappy, Gerald."

"Well, a good imitation of it, dear—pining after Stanley, we're afraid."

"And isn't that natural?"

She went up close to him as she asked it. She put both her hands on his shoulders, and bent her head down on his chest, then lifted it again suddenly, and looked into his face with her soft, loving eyes.

"And isn't that natural??"

It nearly upset his resolution. The fraternal element is very strong amongst us English, try to hide it as we may. But he remembered his wife, and his heir. Carrie had told him that did he not assist her, "her responsibilities in this matter of Florence would be too much for her."

"Well, it is natural, my darling sister. Poor little Florence, don't cry; it will all be well in time, dear. Meanwhile it's better both for Stanley and for you that you shouldn't try to mix yourself up with him—indeed it is."

"I don't—believe—it," Florence sobbed.

"My dear Florry, it is—believe me." Then he began to feel weak of purpose before the strength of her love for that absent brother of whom they had hoped such bright things in his youth, and he struck an unfair blow.

"Doesn't Stanley tell you so himself by his silence?"

"No-o."

"Now, you're blind, Florry," he said gravely. "Had he thought it wise or well for you to see him, wouldn't he have acknowledged your visit and your note?"

Florence lifted her hands and her head away from him; but she was only stung, not conquered yet.

"Perhaps not. I know Stanley so well, Gerald: he'd never be the one to come halfway to meet any one who didn't seem to want him very much."

"You have seemed to want him very much, and he hasn't come."

"*Don't*— don't make me doubt Stanley!" she cried, bursting out into a passion of tears that made Sir Gerald pity her, and himself, profoundly.

"I don't want to make you doubt him, dear! There, there, say no more about it! By Jove! what *is* a fellow to do? Florry, do be reasonable!"

She heaved and sighed in answer to this adjuration, but did not sob any more.

"It's so awkward to explain," he muttered. "The long and the short of it is, Florry, that you'd better not send that letter you've written to Stanley. Don't look at me as if I were your jailer. I'd better out with it, I suppose!" he continued, confusedly. "Stanley's not leading the sort of life you ought to countenance. There, I've done it now." He almost groaned as Florence turned away and sat down, looking very pale and terribly shocked, but speaking not a word.

"I'll send Carrie to you, dear," he said hastily, kissing her brow. "Don't think about it: we'll have him back all right by-and-by. Meantime *don't* upset Carrie—there's a darling girl!"

"No, Gerald, no; I won't."

"Shall I send her to you—and the boy?" he asked cheerily, walking to the door. "The boy," in his opinion, was an infallible panacea for every ailment, mental or bodily, that could assail humanity. He himself had found much comfort in perusing those infant lineaments at divers times. He offered him to Florence now as a perfect cure, and was rather astonished she didn't bound in spirit towards the acceptance of it.

He was very glad to get himself away out of his sister's presence. He felt that he had defiled it by aspersing Stanley to her—Stanley, with whom she had ever been so much more intimate—Stanley, who had always been so much "better a fellow" than himself. Sir Gerald had never made Florence his friend and confidante in his boyish scrapes, and in the dilemmas of his riper years. To touch upon this topic for the first time with her in relation to Stanley made him feel very unhappy, and ashamed of himself.

Shortly Lady Villars came to her, offering her restoratives, and counselling warmth as though the chill she had received had been bodily. And Lady Villars enlarged upon the theme which her husband had merely broached, till Florence of the yielding spirit felt that Stanley was a being bad and dangerous to know—a thing to dearly love, and shrink from.

She gave up the letter, and saw it deftly rent into narrow strips, and then curled into matches between her sister-in-law's plump fingers, and she had to subdue her own sentiments at the sight, for Carrie was quite ready to be agitated and upset. In fact, she put herself under Lady Villars' plump little white thumb that day, and remained there while Lady Villars saturated her with wise saws and modern instances.

In the nursery in the evening Lady Villars had it all her own way with Florence more completely still. They sat by the fire, and passed little Gerald backwards and forwards from lap to lap till that unconscious little innocent had set the ball of good feeling and conversation rolling smoothly between them. Then Lady Villars mooted the matter again, and imparted additional poignancy to it by introducing Claude Walsingham's name, till Florence, between her agony of dread lest the nursemaids should hear, and her agony of shame of what she had deemed the secret of her heart being known at all, was ready to promise anything.

"It is kinder in reality to keep entirely apart from Stanley now, Florry: indeed it is. He's more likely to stop on his road to ruin than if we countenanced him as though he were doing something very fine."

"I hope it may prove kindness, but it's harsh kindness."

"I little thought that I should ever have been accused of unjust cruelty by one member of Gerald's family in relation to another!" Lady Villars said, with touching resignation.

"I don't mean to accuse you, Carrie; indeed I don't!" Florence answered in an agony of dread. Lady Villars had an alarming power of going pale and contracting her nostrils, and these were usually held to be preliminaries to her being upset.

"It's uncommonly like accusing me, and it does hurt me when it is only *your* interest that I have at heart. Gerald and I are in such a position that we might venture to do anything of the sort; but for you to appear to be vindicating Stanley *now*, when he's——"

Florence made a deprecating gesture with her hands; but Lady Villars only paused for an instant, and then resumed—

"Well, it would be simply wrong on our part to see you doing it and not to warn you; unjust to you and unkind to Stanley. He's far more likely to leave off evil doing if he finds that it cuts him off from us, than if we took no notice; to seek him would be to encourage him, and, if your love for Stanley is genuine, you won't do it."

If her love for Stanley were genuine! Florence made no answer in words, but she glanced, with a piteous reproach in her eyes, at her sister-in-law—a reproach that was so eloquent that even Lady Villars was touched by it. "Even Lady Villars," do I say; this implies a doubt of Lady Villars' integrity of purpose in this business, which I am far from feeling. The motives which influenced her were honest enough, only she was rather hard.

"There, Florry, I didn't mean to say that quite. I know *how* genuine your love for Stanley is—therefore I feel sure that you will not refuse to put a little temporary restraint on your feelings, for his ultimate good."

"Ultimate good!" The phrase was a nice, magnanimous, well-sounding one. Florence was rather impressed by it on the whole. Of course she was quite ready to do anything that might conduce to Stanley's ultimate good.

So she was induced, through her love for him, to give up seeking for a renewal of intercourse with the brother who was under a cloud. So she was influenced to fall away from him outwardly for his ultimate good.

Some few days after this, Lady Villars told her, with a very well conceived casual air, that "the Walsinghams were in town! didn't she think it would be well to call?"

"No; I don't," Florence replied, nervously.

"Why not? it would look better."

"I couldn't go!" Florence said, imploringly.

"My dear child, surely you are not going to bear malice against Bella all your life because she discovered, happily before it was too late (Lady Villars said this with virtuous fervour), that she did not love your brother?"

Florence made no answer. She was very truthful, and she knew that Bella's making this discovery had not been the worst offence towards herself. Lady Villars had some notion of this kind also; but she judged it better to ignore what would not be altered by mention.

"Oh! I'm sure you would not do that, Florry; I'm not Stanley's own sister, but I believe I know him well enough to be sure that he would not wish such a display of petty feeling. Of course you will go with me to call on her?"

"Why must I go, Carrie?"

"It would look pointed if you didn't; besides," Lady Villars went on, looking straight between Florence's eyes as she spoke, "people might make mistakes, and attribute your remaining away to a cause that you wouldn't care to have it attributed to. From every point of view"—(Lady Villars, in common with the rest of the world, merely meant her own, when she said this)—"from every point of view such a course would be unwise—unwise to the last degree."

Once more Florence permitted herself to be convinced; but she felt it to be rather hard that she should be put to the test in this way without an end or aim, as it seemed. Meek and gentle, timid and soft as she was, she had that in her which would have carried her over hot ploughshares without shrinking, had the doing so been essential to the well-being of the one she loved. But her heart fainted within her at being thus called upon to perform a painful task, in order that people to whom she was indifferent might not attribute her letting said task alone to some bygone cause, in which, at least, there was no shame.

However, Lady Villars had set her heart on Florence going to call on Mrs. Claude Walsingham. Need it be said, after this statement, that Florence went.

On the whole, Mrs. Claude would far rather that they had not extended the olive branch in person just yet. She was much disturbed at the sight of them, and desperately uncertain as to what it would be well to talk about. With Lady Villars alone she would have been at her ease, for Lady Villars was great at forgiving other people's injuries. But with Florence she could not be at ease for several reasons. Florence had been down at Denham during the days of doubt and of struggling. Florence had at one time held her own Claude's fickle fancy—had dearly loved him, and been wofully deceived by them both. With her usual pleasant power of putting away unpleasant thoughts, Mrs. Claude had thrown these facts off her mind while Florence was neither seen by nor mentioned to her. But now, that Florence was before her in the flesh—and, alas! in less of it than of yore—Bella remembered vividly, and felt penitent and uncomfortable.

It was difficult to know what to speak about. Everything of which she could think had some relation—even if remote—to *the* subject which, she was morally certain, was occupying the thoughts of all. She wronged Lady Villars there, though! Carrie was thinking only of a pair of Venetian glasses, in antique silver frames, and wondering where Claude had got them.

The same difficulty was oppressing Florence with tenfold force. Say what she would, it was safe to refer to Claude, it seemed to her. In addition, too, the dread was upon her of Claude's coming in suddenly and finding them there. She began to wonder how he would look if he did come in, and what he would say, and what he would think? These conjectures caused her to miss the thread of a poor little conversation that had been gallantly started—a conversation about dogs—not living dogs—but dogs of Dresden.

"Have you got Rock still?" she asked, thinking that by thus asking she was proving that she had taken an interest in and followed the subject.

Bella blushed a little, and one hand that was lying upon a table gave a convulsive twitch.

"No; I gave him to your brother, Stanley," she said, in a low tone, "when I married."

"How is Major Walsingham?" Lady Villars asked, quite cheerfully. And then Bella told them of the accident which had befallen him in the hunting field, and tried not to seem to see the tears that gathered in Florence's eyes as she listened. Mrs. Claude addressed herself to Lady Villars, as she told the story; but when she had finished it, there was a touch of true womanly feeling in the way she turned to Florence, and said, as one sure of sympathy, "I thought I should have lost my husband then!"

And that the sympathy she had sought was given, no one could doubt who saw Florence's face.

"Ah!" Lady Villars broke in adroitly, coming to the rescue with a bit of practicality that was invaluable at the moment. "Ah! I remember, Gerald was pitched into a ditch half full of water once, and we agreed then that in every field there ought to be a surgeon and a stomach-pump."

"They should be attached to the kennel, in fact," Bella said, laughing; and then the visit came to an end.

——o——

CHAPTER XXXV.

A STAB IN THE DARK.

Mrs. Markham brought her visit to a close almost immediately after that call Stanley Villars had designed so well, and executed so badly. She went back to a home that wanted her—to a husband that welcomed her—to duties that she performed with a flawless exactitude that may not be excelled; and when she was gone, Bella raised her arms over her head, and clasped her hands together, with a child's action of relief when its period of behaving with circumspection is over for a term.

Mrs. Claude breathed more freely when her sister-in-law left. She had never taken things easily—never gone her own way, and suffered her guest to do the like—as she would have done with any other relation or intimate friend. From first to last she had treated Mrs. Markham with marked consideration; and the doing so had only been one degree more laborious to her than to Mrs. Markham.

Mrs. Markham had quickly detected this resolve of Bella's to be on guard against anything like careless intimacy with her, and to treat her with such grave, unremitting attention as should be shown by a well-bred hostess to a distinguished but not specially dear denizen of her house. There was nothing absolutely suspicious on the face of it in this. Nevertheless Mrs. Markham, failing to account for it in the right way, namely, by comprehending the simple truth, which was that Bella didn't like her, imagined that Bella feared her—consequently had cause for it.

But it was in vain she watched for a cause which should appear sufficiently strong, even to her prejudiced mind, to account for such fear. She watched and waited with a patient assiduity that almost ennobled her task, being truly zealous in the good work of detecting something that might make her brother miserable for life.

However, she watched and waited in vain. It might be a folly, but it could hardly be termed a crime, that Bella should have written to Stanley Villars without her husband's knowledge. It was a misdirected literary taste which led her to peruse that same gentleman's works of fiction; but not a convincing proof of unholy affection for said gentleman. Even Mrs. Markham was obliged to admit these things, and that she had watched and waited in vain.

Friendship also made her warmly welcome on her return to her own sphere. Grace Harper was unfeignedly rejoiced to see her, and really made her feel that her stony society was a thing to be sought; and Grace was an attentive listener to all that had transpired in Major Walsingham's house, and to all that had *not* transpired about Major Walsingham's wife.

"I am only sure of one thing, and that is, that it would have been a happy thing for my brother if he had never seen her," Mrs. Markham said, with a sort of solemn satisfaction in being able to fall back upon a strong sentiment that shall not be shaken, that is frequently adopted when facts fail.

Grace Harper looked up stolidly. In reality she was more excited on this subject than on any other that had ever been brought under her notice; for Claude Walsingham was hale and handsome, powerful and passionate again now. She looked up stolidly, and said—

"Even now, if anything were found out, they might be separated, mightn't they?"

Eager as Mrs. Markham had been to find Bella unworthy in ever so small degree—patiently as she had watched and waited for something wrong—the result of such finding and waiting had never shaped itself clearly in her mind before. The blood came up into her face, and she looked less hard than usual, as she asked—

"Do you mean divorced?"

"They would be, I suppose, if anything——" Grace was commencing phlegmatically, when Mrs. Markham burst in with—

"Pray God there may never be found a cause for it! Pray God such disgrace may be averted from my brother and our name! How could you, Grace? how could you say it?"

Miss Grace offering no explanation, Mrs. Markham went on—

"What right have you to judge her in that way—to suspect her, and think, because she has been a flighty girl, that there is anything——" She stopped, choked by her anger and pride; and then Grace spoke.

"I only drew deductions from what you said yourself, and from those reports one can't take hold of and examine, about her way of going on when she was Miss Vane. I should be as shocked as you could be, Ellen, at anything befalling Claude."

In spite of this assertion of hers, Miss Harper's mind dwelt much on the subject of a separation between Major Walsingham and his wife. She found herself planning out a future for him, did such a thing occur, as she drove home after that visit to Mrs. Markham. In time his father would die. Her father had said but yesterday that "Walsingham, who appeared so well preserved, would probably break down suddenly, and go off, very much to the surprise of those who regarded him as looking so wonderfully well for his years." And when he died, Claude, his son, would reign in his stead.

Why, it might be very soon; and he might—would probably—settle at the Court, and take his place in the county. The Court would be a good place to come to in order to get over the loss of his wife.

"The loss of his wife!" She started, stolid as she was, as the words formed themselves, and she thought them out. Then she comforted herself, telling herself that she was not wishing evil to Bella: separation, a divorce, might ensue from other causes than Bella being proved guilty.

Her brain was very busy during the rest of the journey. She saw herself mutely consoling a man who had been wronged by others, and in time rewarded by that man. Her brain was very busy, even when she reached home, and retailed to her father and mother during dinner the light, idle gossip of the uneventful day.

About a week after Mrs. Markham's departure, Claude and Bella had arranged to go out for a ride together, an unusual thing in those days, and one, therefore, for which Bella prepared herself in good time, in order that Claude might not be put to the trying test of waiting for her. The consequence of this precaution was that she was ready long before it had come to him to think about preparing to go out with her. Therefore, being in her habit, she had nothing for it but to hang about between the rooms, and while away the time, while he kept her waiting.

She walked well and freely in her habit. The clinging cloth makes no manner of difference to the gait of the woman accustomed to it. She takes longer steps than are hers ordinarily, that is all. So it came about that she beguiled the tiresome time by moving about and altering the position of a few of her favourite ornaments, with whose place in the world she was never *quite* satisfied, as was natural. What woman is ever quite satisfied that the situation of the thing dear to her is not to be improved upon? She walked about the drawing-room, therefore, happily enough for a while—as happily, that is, as any woman can walk about and waste the time, when she knows that her horse is awaiting her outside the door, and that the flies are teasing him, and making him impatient to be off.

At last she had moved all she could move in the room with effect. She had put the Venus de' Medici on a broad crimson-backed bracket, and the life-size Clytie on a pedestal, and the Venus of Milo on a stand, where the glorious figure looked "not out of place"—she never can look that; but sorry for the world that had no better place to offer her; grandly compassionate to its bad taste; loyally resigned to a false position.

When she had achieved these ends Bella grew petulant. "Claude *might* have remembered!" she muttered to herself. "Poor Devilskin! a sweet temper he'll be in when we do start, after waiting so long!"

She passed before a glass in order to tip her hat a bit more forward over her brow, and see if the stand-up collar set well. Then she picked up her gloves and whip, and walked with that long, gliding step so suitable to a habit, out of the room, and down into the hall, to be ready there "when Claude came."

The twelve o'clock postman knocked as she set her foot on the last stair, and she watched proceedings lazily, as the man who was waiting to let Claude and herself out took the letters in, and placed them on a salver on the hall table. It was a practice of hers never to open a letter in the middle of the day. The morning and evening were all-sufficient for such toil. Experience had taught her that a letter lost nothing by waiting, and that answers to effusions which came in haste at mid-day might always be deferred with safety.

However, she had nothing better—*i.e.*, pleasanter—to do now than to see what that post had brought her. So she walked idly up to the table, and commenced burrowing with her doe-skin covered hand (she always rode in doe-skin gloves, the reins did not slip through them) amongst the packet of letters that had just arrived. There were a lot for her husband. These she passed over, merely looking at his name without a second glance. She was a very faulty woman, this Bella; apt to forget what she ought to have remembered, and to remember what she ought to have forgotten. But she had no low curiosity. It was one of the articles in her erring creed of faith, that if her husband desired her to see a thing he would show it to her. If not, she would not seek for it. So now she tossed these letters of his over with a careless hand, and searched for any stray ones that might have arrived for herself, just to beguile the time.

Suddenly she came upon one in a long, narrow, cream-laid envelope, which she turned over leisurely, thinking that the seal or stamped monogram would tell from whom it came, and so save her the trouble of reading it. There was no stamped monogram, however, and the seal was one of those puerile conceits which belong to nobody in particular. With one little, impatient glance at the stairs, down which Claude came not, she broke that seal away and read.

Such a letter! No civil invitation; no false form of inquiry; no friendly platitudes; no tradesman's puff! Any or all of these she would have counted tedious ten minutes before. Any or all of these would have been wildly welcomed by her in place of this miserable epistle which she held in her hand.

It commenced, "My dear Mrs. Walsingham;" and seeing this friendly commencement Bella was led on into the weakness of reading it before looking at the signature. Reading a portion of it—that is, an all-sufficient portion, since it made her brain reel, and her foot trip in her habit as she hurried upstairs again, and into the drawing-room she had been lounging about so pleasantly just now.

The letter told her of things that her brow burnt to read about; of things that her heart sank to hear; of deeds which make a woman shrink from their perpetrator when that perpetrator is the woman's husband. All Claude's wild oats were brought in a sheaf and placed before her in this letter; and the jealousy of Lady Lexley, which she taught herself to consider unjust and unmeaning, was cruelly justified.

She was told of so many things, poor girl, that Claude would rather have blown his brains out than that she should have learnt. And she sat almost paralysed till she came to the end of the letter and found that it was anonymous.

So! she could not return it to the writer, as she had hazily resolved to do, without a word of acknowledgment. She could not meet her (Bella intuitively felt that it was penned by a woman), and cut her and scorn her as such a she-devil deserved to be cut and scorned. Agonized as she had been by that reading, paralysed as her faculties were for the moment, it had not occurred to her to take any other notice of this stab. But now she found that it was a stab in the back, and she must forego the taking such notice as that even.

For a few moments—they were only moments, but they were so long—the young wife sat uncertain how to act. Then her colour and her heart rose, and she tore it into a hundred fragments, saying to herself, "Thank God, Claude need never know it!" This was her first active impulse. The doubt what to do had been merely born of passive pain—of bewilderment and surprise.

No! he should never know it! She took it all in now. The pain he would feel at her pain. The sore agony that would be his at her doubting him, or thinking that she had cause to doubt him. She shook off the devil of distrust, and, lighting a taper, burnt every scrap of the paper that had told the shameful tale to tinder, and was all herself again, bright, unclouded, sunny, and loving, when he came down at last to ride with her.

She felt so sorry for having read such things about him! It seemed to her that she had been so far baser than Claude, the exalted in appearance, would have been under the same circumstances. She had read on to the end. Claude would never have gone beyond the first line that aspersed her. The feeling of being so immeasurably beneath him in point of honour and generosity made her bear on the snaffle with a heavier hand than was her wont, and adapt herself less readily to the curvature of the spine with which Devilskin marked his resentment of the change in her.

"Now, do be careful, Bella, and don't wobble," Claude said, somewhat testily. He was dearly fond of his wife, but they were going into the park now, and he desired that she should have a good seat in the eyes of all men. This spirit of exaction was only another form of the same deep love she was showing for him by her toleration in regard to this matter which had been thrust before her to-day.

Bella came down to her saddle tighter than before, as he spoke. She was conscious of an uncertainty of seat and hand this morning, that must, she felt, be equally trying to her husband and her horse. She wished so much to please him now—to please him entirely, and without reservation, and to make him feel that she was a good thing for a man to have, even though he had hankered after other things before her. She would no more now have suffered his heart to be made sore by a knowledge of that vile letter than she would have stabbed him with her own hand. It almost seemed to her, as she rode along by his side, that she had been in error; that she had been the faulty one, to have received such a letter.

Who had dared to write it? Her heart swelled, and her small, well-bred hand grasped the reins with such convulsive energy, that the additional intensity of purpose in the rider communicated itself to the fine nerves of Devilskin's mouth, and caused him to concentrate himself, and break into a canter that was grand, as far as the appearances went, but of little value where progress was concerned: his feet, that is to say, went up very high, and came down almost precisely in the same spot; and he arched his neck, and put at least ten pounds on himself by the way he carried his tail; and, altogether, made a very pretty little performance.

"I say, Bella! that won't do, you know!" Claude exclaimed, holding his own horse in with difficulty, and looking with annoyance at the very questionable effect his wife was producing on the minds of some bystanders. "Stop that Astley business, do!"

"Then I must give him his head, and then he'll bolt," she replied, getting Devilskin well in hand as she spoke, and evidently not regarding the possibility of his bolting in a very serious light.

"No, he won't!—steady, boy, steady!—wo-ho, old fellow!" Claude answered, under the mistaken impression that his voice would show Devilskin the folly of it, whatever the "it" might be that Devilskin was contemplating.

"Come on, Claude, then," she said, brightly, "don't stop at the top, but wheel, and give them a breather all the length of the Row." They were nearing the end of the row by Apsley House as she spoke, and, when her husband had agreed, they drew nearer to the left hand rails; she lowered her hands, and the two horses went off at a fleet gallop, that seemed to bring their riders closer to the earth, and slackened the girths, and made the air whizz as they cut through it.

They reached the end, and wheeled cleverly, the two horses keeping stride for stride, and neither showing signs of taking trouble about it. Suddenly, both horses swerved; a woman was crossing, in the idiotic, temper-trying way women will cross the Row, regardless alike of the knees of the horses who are sweeping along, of the necks of the riders, who get many an evil jerk through their means, and of their own stupidly-risked lives. As Tom Hood says, it must be "a horrible thing to be groomed by a horse." Nevertheless, innumerable women, all of the readily-confounded, easily-overpowered, and perpetually-surprised order, do apparently endeavour to test the horror of it daily throughout the season.

With an impatient exclamation, Claude touched his horse with the spur directly the swerve was recovered, and the horse responded freely, and went along even as he had been going before. As a slight relief to the feelings which that swerve had ruffled, he commenced cursing the cause of it aloud to Bella, as he thought; but he pulled up on finding Bella did not answer him, and riding back a few yards, espied her at the spot where she had paused, apparently for no better purpose than to look after the ill-timed human interruption to that deliciously soul-and-body-freshening breather they had been having.

"What is it?" Claude asked affably, riding back.

"I'm sure it's Rock!" she replied.

"Where?" he asked, less affably. He remembered that she had given Rock to Stanley Villars, and he did not care to see her betray the smallest further interest in him. It was ungenerous, considering all things; but, on the other hand, he must be forgiven for not considering "all things," since he was ignorant of many of them.

"There! following that girl—see!"

"That ass, do you mean, who rushed right across us just now?"

"Yes," she replied, agreeing, in her haste, to the uncomplimentary epithet he bestowed upon her sister-woman, without the expostulation that might have ensued under ordinary circumstances. Then she rode hastily up to the rails, Claude keeping by her side, until she was on a line with the woman who had crossed the Row and had now gained the greensward; and close by that woman a red setter was flaunting along.

"I'm sure it's Rock," Bella said aloud, leaning forward over the near pommel as she spoke. At the sound of the name, a pretty, fair young face was turned towards her inquiringly, and the dog came forward in a series of airy curves, and leapt up on to her habit, showing that he liked to meet her once more, by the shimmer of his tawny eyes, and the waving of his well-fringed tail.

"Rock, old dog! Poor boy! see how glad he is, Claude!"

"Yes, wonderfully! Will you come on now?" Claude replied, coolly. It did not appear to be upon the cards that Rock should come into his own possession, and he had no morbid feeling in favour of another man's dog, more especially since that dog had become that other man's under circumstances that were interesting to himself, but not agreeable to look back upon.

"Yes; wait a minute, though. I wonder how he came here!" she continued, in a lower voice, to her husband. "You know that I gave him to Stanley—do you think he is stolen?"

Claude felt uncomfortable. Instinctively he perceived that the young woman with the pretty, fair face was not a thief. Let her be what she would, there was not that amount of diabolical iniquity in her which is essential to the professed dog-stealer.

"No, come along—nonsense!" Major Walsingham replied, riding on slowly, and wishing that his wife would not make a "spectacle of herself in this way."

"But, Claude!" she expostulated, riding after him, and still encouraging Rock to follow with her hand—"But, Claude! do stop! He's such a dog, to be about with anybody. I'm sure Stanley would have taken better care of him, because he's valuable, you see. I will ask her how she came by him."

The owner of the pretty, fair face was sauntering along just inside the railings all this time, watching Claude and his wife attentively. The baby-faced beauty had taken very kindly to the big, tawny, loving dog; but she had done so in unconsciousness. Stanley had never told her how Rock became his, nor indeed had she ever cared to enquire as to Rock's antecedents. But now that a beautiful woman caressed the dog as an old familiar friend, and alluded to Stanley as though he had been even as the dog (an old familiar friend, namely), Rock's antecedents became of interest to her instantaneously, and her memory went back jealously to every glance, every word, every touch of affection he had ever bestowed in her sight and hearing on the red setter, Rock.

"Ask her nothing of the kind. Come along, Bella!" Claude exclaimed, impatiently. "What the devil's the difference to you whether the dog is stolen or not?"

But, in such matters, Bella could still be wilful when an opportunity for being so arose. It might be a little thing to Claude that there should be doubt and uncertainty as to whom Rock belonged to now; but it was not a little thing to her. She had been very fond of the dog, and the dog had been very fond of her, while their union lasted. She had been welcomed boisterously by him a thousand times in a way that showed her that she had been missed. He had been her own—he had been very much admired—he seemed so unfeignedly rejoiced to meet her again to-day, though there was no bone in the case. Besides, it was not a little thing to her that Stanley should have so lightly regarded her present as either to have lost or given it away. Accordingly she was wilful, and would not attend to Claude's rather decided suggestion that she should "come along."

Still leaning forward to pat the dog, who kept jumping up at her horse's side every minute, Mrs. Claude Walsingham turned sharply to the railings, and drew up at about three yards from the woman who was sauntering along over the sunny sward.

The owner of the lovely, simple face paused and looked straight in the bright, brilliant, beautiful one of her rival—looked into it with a child's admiration for what is beautiful, with a child's transient feeling of jealousy, dread, and distrust. Bella glanced at the girl a trifle superciliously. "Stanley's landlady's daughter, I should say," she thought. "Impertinence! to take Rock out." "I beg your pardon," she said, aloud, "but I used to know this dog. Can you tell me to whom he belongs now?" And the answer was—"The dog belongs to my husband, Mr. Stanley Villars."

Then Bella was silent, and rode on.

CHAPTER XXXVI.

DOUBT.

It is not in the heart of man to triumph outwardly over a fallen, or say tottering, foe, in the "I told you so" strain. That form of consolation is one specially affected by the gentler sex, who lilt these little lays of love lachrymosely whenever occasion serves. But though it is not in the heart of man to triumph outwardly, he has still a certain feeling of sore satisfaction when an evil, which attention to his counsel would have obviated, comes, through disregard of that counsel, to pass.

Major Walsingham had counselled his wife to "come along;" had asked her not to mix herself up with possible dog-stealing and other matters in which she had no concern, merely out of a manly dislike to betraying active interest in anything that was out of his own orbit. He had no intense desire to be fully acquainted with Rock's present—no loosely-packed, but still valuable to the owner, bundle of memories connected with Rock's past. The girl so idly sauntering along, through the noon-tide heat of an August day, was too pretty, too marked, tawdry, and observation-compelling altogether, for intercourse between her and his well-known Bella to be desirable in that place. Therefore, he had not alone wished, but had told his wife to pass on and be silent. And his wife had developed her old infirmity, wilfulness, and had pulled up effusively to speak to a girl whom she didn't know, about a dog for whom she ought no longer to have cared.

The punishment came quickly after the offence. Delicacy of feeling restrained him from looking direct at her, to see how deep the lash, contained in that single sentence the baby-faced beauty had spoken, cut. But that it had cut, and cut deeply too, he knew, through the agency of that animal magnetism which makes us writhe, and wince, and shiver, when the one we love is doing these things in our immediate atmosphere. For two minutes and a half he felt sympathetically tender towards Bella; she had "got it," he knew, from a quarter whence she had so little anticipated it. Then he reflected that Bella had no right to care about Stanley Villars having allied himself to what he (Claude) denominated "a queer lot;" and when he thus reflected, the delicacy which had caused him to refrain from looking at the slightly wounded, deserted him, and he glanced askance at his wife, and grew red and resentful.

Bella's feelings, meanwhile, were mixed; but the worst ingredients in that mixture were of a nobler sort than Claude imagined them to be. Whenever she had thought about Stanley at all (and she had, woman-like, thought about him several times since she had learnt, through the medium of his writings, that he had it in him to rise and distinguish himself), she had been conscious of a half-hope that the wound she had made would be healed in time. She had thought, in a sketchy, undefined way, that Stanley would get over her defalcation and be happy, after an exalted pattern, with an exalted wife—a superior woman, with a lofty forehead and a bone in her nose. A woman whom she (Bella) could respect and like, and never feel an atom jealous of, as being one able to supplant her. A woman with money and good connections, and a power altogether of making Stanley thoroughly comfortable. A woman of whom she could never, for one instant, entertain the idea that Stanley had loved her, with a duplicate of that passion he had felt for herself. A woman, sensible, good, and discreet, who would keep Stanley straight, and redeem him from the poverty-stricken bondage and slavery he was now in; and who would be wise enough to accept the fact that she was powerless to efface from his memory his love's young dream.

Her feelings were very mixed. This girl, with the face that was lovely as an angel's—ay, lovelier than any pictured angel's can be, for there was human warmth and womanly love in it!—this girl was wanting, on the surface, in all those attributes with which she, Bella, had accredited the one whom it might be well for Stanley to marry. She was young, lovely, love-inspiring! but she was not a lady. Stanley's marriage with her had been the result of her effect on his heart; therefore it was not the offspring of judgment only, as Bella would have liked to think of any alliance he formed. Her heart swelled and her colour rose. To have been cast out from Stanley's heart—from the heart of *any one* who had once loved her—by such an one as this.

They had kept the silence so long after that sentence the baby-faced beauty had uttered, that there was something awkward in breaking it. At length, when Bella did so, she was the first to speak naturally. Claude was conscious of feeling suspicious—she was unconscious of anything of the kind.

"Do you think she told the truth, Claude?" she asked abruptly, as their horses went up that slight elevation in the Row at a steady gallop, that admitted of no excuse for further silence, as the stirring trot of a few minutes before had done. "Do you think she told the truth, Claude?"

"Probably!"

"I don't think it probable," Mrs. Walsingham exclaimed determinately. She thought it quite the reverse of probable, in fact; and it seemed to her a mean estimate for Claude to have formed of Stanley Villars.

"It's not worth arguing about. Slacken your curb, Bella; if you go on pulling at him in that way, he'll serve you a trick some fine day, and be off when you don't expect it."

"But it is worth arguing about, Claude. I'm interested in Stanley's well-being still, whatever you may be; and I do think, after all, that you might feel a little for him."

"My feeling for him wouldn't do any good; he has chosen his own path; for God's sake let him follow it in peace."

"How can I—how can you *expect* me to be so indifferent about an old friend?" she asked, almost piteously.

"I thought the old flame of friendship had died out. If it hasn't, and its ashes are liable to burst out into a blaze at any moment, I can only say that it will be unpleasant for me."

She shook her head vehemently, and drew Devilskin nearer to his side.

"Not for you, Claude—don't say that; whatever you may be, you're not ungenerous."

He made no reply. To him it seemed that she was begging the question. He did not recognise the truth, which was, that the qualities she most adored, she strove to deck her husband in.

"You're not that," she repeated; "besides, if I may not speak to you about a thing, to whom may I speak?"

"Couldn't you hold your tongue about it?" he suggested, quietly. In his heart he was sorry that things should be going so utterly wrong as they appeared to be going with Stanley Villars. But he remembered the past, and it went against his taste—to the dictates of which he paid more attention than to those of his heart—that his wife should mix herself up, identify herself in any way, with Stanley's dearer interests. Added to this feeling, which he would have experienced under any circumstances, there was the natural shrinking a man would be sure to feel against aught dubious coming in contact with one dear and precious to him. Now Bella was very dear and precious to him, for all his occasional lack of judgment in his treatment of her. She was very dear and precious to him, and there was a very dubious air about the baby-faced beauty who was sauntering through the sunbeams.

Major Walsingham asked, "Couldn't you hold your tongue about it?" in a quiet, amiably superior, tolerant-to-your-weakness way, that it is hard to listen to and maintain repose. He intended his remark to be taken as a definite and satisfactory conclusion to the subject by Bella. He meant it to stop further discussion, to wind up the matter gracefully, leaving her in the position of one whose erring judgment had been set straight, and who was silently grateful, as became one conscious of inferiority in experience and mind. But this was Bella's misfortune. She did not think about Claude's larger experience, and had she thought about it at all, she would have been in doubt as to his having the larger mind of the two. Had she felt that he did possess it, sorely as she might have disliked his snubbing her, she would have known through it all that he *was* to be obeyed, and so would have stood it better. As it was, she fretted under his assumption of power and superiority, even as her horse fretted under the curb, of which she was giving him more than a touch.

"No, I can't hold my tongue about it, Claude; and why should I? Her 'husband, Mr. Stanley Villars,' indeed! Couldn't we find out about him? It will be shocking if he has married in such a way! Shocking for Florry!"

He laughed. They were walking their horses now, and on across the grass their eyes would travel after the forms of the woman and the dog who had given rise to the discussion.

"You were not always so careful of Florry's feelings," he said.

"It was love for you made me careless then; come, sir!"

She turned her face to him as she said it, and the softened light in her eyes, the heightened colour on her cheeks, and, above all, that marvellous inflection of the voice which cannot be affected, did its rightful work.

"My dear girl, I know that," he replied; "show your love for me, dear, by not disturbing yourself and bothering me about what is done and can't be helped. Stanley has chosen his own path—it mayn't be a pleasant one, but it's one from which you can't turn him; and it isn't pleasant for me to hear you always going into rhapsodies about him; the day's gone by for your being his guardian angel."

She looked at him keenly, in the attempt to discover whether jealousy had a share in the feeling which prompted him to utter these words, or not. He ought not to have been jealous of her—of her who had put the paltry feeling so entirely out of court about him. Her love for him was to the full as deep and true as his for her; and still, poison-fraught as was that letter she had received this morning, it had caused her no pang save the one grand one that any person could have deemed her weak and base enough to be influenced against her husband for one instant without sufficient cause. Whereas he was jealous now of her openly betraying that she still felt an interest in whether Stanley Villars sank or swam. He sat his horse like a centaur, and she had run the gauntlet of opposition for his dear sake; yet for all these things (and they were mighty links) she wished that he possessed more magnanimity.

CHAPTER XXXVII.

A HARD CASE.

We have probably all heard that the merry, merry sunshine makes the heart so gay. It is an axiom that has been set to music, and harmony always imparts an appearance of truth to a statement. When the sentiment is trilled out by a songstress in satin under a glaring gaselier, it naturally strikes us as veracious. The heat of the sun in the open—anything, anywhere!—is sure to be regarded as enviable, even as gaiety-provoking, when our heads are throbbing from artificial heat, strongly impregnated with patchouli.

But there are certain conditions of mind when the merry, merry sunshine stabs rather than soothes. When we are unappreciated, unsuccessful, uncared for. When the light of love has gleamed over us, and for some reason gleams over us no longer. When the present is very dark and dull, and there seems to be nothing better in store. When all the hopes we ever had, lowly as they may have been, are fading fast. When the sense of our own inability is upon us crushingly, and we perceive the wounding truth that we are powerless of ourselves to help ourselves. When we feel left behind—not alone that, but trampled down by Fate, against whom we sulkily acknowledge that it is useless to struggle. When any or all of these things are, how terrible is the sunshine!

I suppose that we have all felt the terror of it—all of us, at least, who have temporal hopes, fears, and aspirations beyond the day. The brightness of it mocks, and the warmth of it burns us, and the glory of it irradiates each one but ourselves. We lose sight of the fact, that all these sensations are born of our own sense of defeat, perhaps—or of dyspepsia, or disappointment—therefore we do not look further back for causes, and discern that each one of these things is probably the offspring of incompetence, unworthiness, or—more likely still—of a weakness of will, a faltering of purpose, which prevented our grasping and retaining firmly that which we desired to have. All things come to him who knows how to wait. All things are to be had by him who knows how to take.

> "He either fears his fate too much,
> Or his deserts are small,
> Who dares not put it to the touch,
> And win or lose it all."

That which has been done before may be done again; but there are certain phases of feeling when one loses sight of this fact, be one's determination to win eventually what it may. It is while in the state of bodily and mental languor that these phases produce, that the merry, merry sunshine becomes a trifle overpowering, and altogether a thing from which to shrink, as one that places your misery in a stronger light.

Now, poor Marian Villars had no particular will, and no design of life worth carrying out, even had the will to do so been hers. Had things been bright and well with her, had her home been happy, and her husband loving, and her wardrobe well furnished, she would have been as blithe as a bird even when a fog was hovering over the land. But none of these things were, nor were they likely to be, as far as she could see, and her lights led her tolerably correctly. Therefore depression reigned in her soul, and the sunshine could not remove it. There was no gaiety in the heart of the poor pretty little saunterer through the sunbeams; the latter merely made the fact of her cloak being rusty and her dress shabby more patent to her.

She had come out this day for a walk, because the monotony of sitting at home, surrounded by ugliness, and stifled by the heat, had become almost unbearable. Stanley had asked her to "go out and get a little air," too, partly because he fancied that, like a bird, she was pining for the sunshine, and partly because she had a restless way of moving about in the room, causing his brain to reel.

His brain often reeled now, poor fellow! He told himself that it was the heat, and that when the winter came he should be all right again—more especially if he could take that "little rest" which amiable outsiders were always recommending to him in the fervent way people do recommend things which, if accepted, will cost them nothing. But in the meantime that reeling of the brain was a hard thing to bear.

Day by day the dread grew and strengthened within him that he was missing his chance—doing himself an injustice which he could never recall—burning his candle at both ends—wasting material which, if properly managed, might have made such a blaze as should have commanded observation. Day by day this dread grew and strengthened within him, until it attained such power, that to think of it was to paralyse his hand and numb his faculties, and drive him to seek oblivion in anything that came to hand—so hastening the end he feared.

He was getting irritably alive to sounds; not only to those which render day hideous in the streets, but to such as were partly the conjurations of his own brain. Noise and pressure, that was all he suffered from, he said, when any one had time to ask him, "What was the matter?" or "Whether he wasn't quite right?" Noise and pressure!—that was all.

Heads—editorial heads—had been shaken once or twice over the results of several hours of his hardest and most earnest labour, and he had been entreated sharply to write more carefully—more coherently—more as if he had something to say and were capable of saying it. At last, the day before Bella and Rock met in the park, he was given to understand by the ruling power of a journal to whose staff he was attached, that he might go his ways without let or hindrance from them. "His writings had been ravings merely lately," he was told, "and the public wouldn't stand them."

Dreamily he accepted his dismissal—hazily he held that there was justice in the fiat which, pronounced, left him a more completely ruined man than he had been before. A little sooner or a little later, it was of small consequence. The end that was inevitable—that he had felt for some time to be inevitable—would come. He would fall and be forgotten, and the place where he fell would be unmarked! He went home with his head aching, as the head whose brain is overtasked will ache, and lay down, caring little whether or not he should ever rise up again.

There had been a little balm brought even to him in the evening. One of his own fraternity—a man who was living a from-hand-to-mouth existence by his pen, and living it in a light-hearted way, as yet—came and stirred him up, sacrificing his own leisure to the by no means easy task, and not alone offering to do him good service, but doing it.

"It will be all right, old boy," he said to Stanley, in reference to that dismissal from the journal, which had left him in a worse plight than before. "It will be all right, old boy; they've put me on in your place for a few days."

Stanley looked at him vaguely. It mattered very little to him by whom he was superseded, since he held himself dismissed. He believed the man meant it kindly; but it was a queer form for kindness to take, the promotion being on the occasion of his (Stanley's) downfall.

"Only for a few days—only to keep it open for you," his colleague went on quickly. "I tell you what; it's all settled. I've arranged up there" ("up there" meant the office of the newspaper) "that I'll do your work till you're all right again, on the understanding that you'll do mine by-and-by when I knock up; do you see?"

Stanley felt very wooden about the head, but he contrived to nod, and say "Yes." Dimly he felt that "that young fellow Bligh" was being kind and generous to him—but only dimly.

"So that's all arranged then, and don't bother yourself about it any more," Bligh went on, as cheerily as he could, with the conviction oppressing him that "poor Villars would never do any fellow's work, or his own either." He had seen this thing creeping over other men before, but he had never been touched as now, for the men had been older than Stanley Villars, and their breaking down more gradual.

Very quietly, for a few hours, did Stanley resign himself to the repose which was thrust upon him. But the next day he grew restless, and declared that while he lived he must write. Then the stabbing and the reeling assailed him afresh, and he became agonizingly alive to the lightest sound in the room. Then it was that he begged Marian to go out for a walk. "Do go and leave me to myself, dear, till I have done this," he said, letting his pen stray down and then ramble over a slip; "and take that dog." Rock's regular breathing fell upon something in the top of his head as the incessant droppings of water might have done. When he was left, he drank brandy with laudanum in it till the present passed from him, and he found himself once more in a broad old rose-embowered window, at the feet of Bella Vane.

He was haggard, wild-eyed, terrible to look upon, when his wife came home. "You have been working till your head aches again, Stanley," she said complainingly; "and so does mine—the sun's so hot to-day."

"Is it?" he asked absently.

"Is it! How can you say that? Aud oh! how *can* you bear to sit with it pouring down on your head in that way?" Then she turned to the table on which their dinner was already placed, and asked him, "Would he not come and have some!"

"No," he replied peevishly. "And I wish, Marian, you would teach that girl not to come in to this room; her elbows are enough to drive a man mad."

The girl's—the luckless maid-of-all-work's—elbows had always been a sore point with Stanley, as obviously they were sore points with their unhappily raw-boned possessor. They protruded themselves into everything—they courted observation, it appeared to him. Those elbows, and the way their owner had of charging at the stairs, and then stumbling up or down them, as the case might be, had been colossal tributary streams to the ocean of his woe. He had been ready to beseech the girl, more than once, to pull her sleeves down and pick up her feet—to cultivate a higher action, in fact. But he had never done it, and now the sight and the hearing of her had become unendurable.

"She shall not come near you again, Stanley," the poor little wife half sobbed. "I'd send her away, dear, for I hate her, and her elbows, too—but I have no money left."

Instinctively he put his hand in his pocket and pulled out his purse. "Then pay her—get rid of her at once," he said, handing it to his wife. When she opened it her face fell a little, and a few tears came into her eyes.

"What is it?" he asked carelessly.

"It's empty, Stanley," she said, showing it to him.

"Then I have no money left either, and—and—" and then he burst into tears. As he wept on a change came over her; those tears of his touched that "right chord" in her which is, I believe, in every human being; and the thrill it caused strung her up to do the work that was needed of her.

Her little idle dreams, her little venial vanities, her little childish discontents and repinings, vanished into thin air before this woe which she felt to be coming upon him—upon them both. She got up, fraught with that feeling of concealment, that beautiful deceit which God gives to women in such hours as these—got up and went over to him, seeming not to see his grief, not to be affected by it, smiling and being at once brighter and softer than she had ever been before.

For a time, a brief time, she soothed him strangely. He forgot his rapidly-increasing incapacity, he forgot that he had no money in his purse—no prospect in his profession—no friends in the world, as she sat on a low stool by the side of the couch on which he had stretched himself, and talked him into the dreamy state he had been in when first he opened his eyes upon her away in the little house by the Regent's Park.

"Marian, pet!" he said to her at last, "if it were not for what is before *you*, poor child, I couldn't be thankful enough for having married you."

Then the change that had come upon her when he shed those hot tears deepened, and she almost coo'd forth a low, murmuring answer that was like a song of gratitude and love.

But their case was very hard!

—o—

CHAPTER XXXVIII.

ENGAGED.

THERE was much sober satisfaction in Sir Gerald Villars' house. Florence had repaid all Lady Villars' care and anxiety. Florence had approved herself sweet and amenable to good advice, as Lady Villars had always trusted that she would do some day or other. Florence, in a word, was going to be married!

The bridegroom elect—a Mr. Chester—was as different as light from darkness, milk from brandy, from her first love, Claude Walsingham. He was a handsome young man, tall, with beautiful eyes, and a booby.

He had been a playmate of Lady Villars' in her childish days, a "great friend" of the immaculate Carrie's in her girlish unmarried ones. Since her marriage with Sir Gerald, Fred Chester had been given the freedom of her house. He came in and out like a tame dog; he was so very inoffensive.

In addition to being inoffensive he was very kind-hearted. Florence had melted towards him because he looked depressed whenever Stanley was spoken of. She thought that it was warm feeling and tender interest for Stanley which caused this depression. In reality, it arose from a shadowy notion he had that he ought to say something, and an utter inability to think of anything to say on the subject. However, his looks touched Florence. *He* would never, she felt sure of that, keep a sister from a dearly-loved brother merely because that brother was under a cloud. *He* would help her to seek, and redeem (if redemption were necessary, which she doubted), and make Stanley happy and comfortable again! This conviction, and a certain feeling of being an incubus upon Carrie, of which she could not dispossess herself, swayed her. So when Fred Chester proposed to her she accepted him; Lady Villars having paved the way well for him, by telling her sister-in-law many times during the week previous to said proposal, that "her own sisters wanted to come and stay with her; but of course, though she wished it very much, she couldn't have them *yet*." And when Florence asked "Why not?" she had gone on to say, "When you are married I shall be able to, but Gerald wouldn't like the house be-sistered in that way."

Florence's heart went out more tenderly than ever to Stanley after it thus being made manifest that she was not too highly prized by the brother who was left. She began to feel in the way; she began to yearn for a stand-point of her own, from whence she should dare to stretch out her hand to Stanley. Here she was hampered by a dozen of those heavy chains which, though invisible to the casual visitor, too often eat into the flesh of the denizen on sufferance in a house. Gerald himself was kind and loving to her, but he did not "notice things," and he had a pious horror of Carrie being upset. Florence was a very soft and gentle woman. Had she been other, she could easily have brought her sister-in-law to understand that she gave fair payment by her presence for all favours received. But she was meek, and with the meek Lady Villars was apt to be merciless.

In reality, Lady Villars meant very kindly by her husband's sister. It seemed to her a sad and a sorrowful thing that Florence should be suffered to pursue her path in solitude any longer; therefore any gentle spurrings that might urge her to quit said path, Lady Villars deemed herself perfectly justified in administering. It was for Florence's good she desired to see her with an active, living, present interest once more. When Florence had this she would leave off mutely raking over those ashes of the past — her shattered girlish devotion to her brother and to her brother's friend.

Moreover, Lady Villars was a woman on whom the claims of her own kindred pressed strongly. She had three sisters—three fair unwedded young beings, all with short noses and plump faces, and a marked disinclination to remain longer than was absolutely necessary in maiden meditation.

"It does seem unkind never to have the girls to stay with me," she would say to Florence; "I am sure they would be very much admired." On which poor Florence would feel guiltily that her unmarried presence in her own brother's house was held by her brother's wife to be detrimental to that lady's sisters.

There was kindness to a certain degree, and vast magnanimity, in Lady Villars ordaining that Fred Chester should marry Florence. He was very tractable, and would have bowed himself at the feet of one of the short-faced beauties had the word of command been given. But it was not given, for Lady Villars had ideas on the subject of justice; and it appeared to her only fair that Florence, being the sister of the head of the house, should be given the first chance.

So Florence was given it, and Florence took it—not very gladly it must be admitted, but gratefully nevertheless. She had no ecstatic notions of beatitude resulting to herself from this marriage—such notions faded away from her for ever the day she heard Bella was to marry Claude—but she did hope great things from it for Stanley. For Fred Chester was wealthy and tractable, and he always, as I have said before, looked depressed when Stanley was spoken about.

It was now August, and they were to be married in the first week in September, then to go off and be happy on the Continent for a month, and then return in October to Fred Chester's place in Suffolk for the partridge shooting. It was a long time to be out of town. They would not be back till January. Florence grew brave as she thought of it, and determined that she would ask Fred to take her to see Stanley. It would be best to obey him in future; the onus was off her of attending longer to Lady Villars' ideas.

But Lady Villars had been beforehand with her. "If Florence—dear girl! she has some sentimental notions—wants you to countenance her intercourse with Stanley, don't do it, Fred," she had said to her favourite vassal.

"No, I think she'd better not, because there's something wrong, by Jove! or he'd have turned up before now," Mr. Chester replied. On which Lady Villars nodded her fair little head and threw up her short nose, and said—

"Yes—low connection I believe; *misfortune* he has been to his family; I never did like him." Hearing which Fred Chester became depressed as usual when he had nothing further to say on a topic.

There were those extant who said that in days gone-by Lady Villars had not disliked the younger brother. But she had always been a prudent girl; so, when he passed her by heedlessly, and the elder brother proposed, she took to seeing Stanley's faults, and cured herself, as was wise and well.

So when Florence asked her betrothed "if she mightn't go and see her brother now?" he cast her down into the depths by replying—

"Well, I think not yet, Flo; it will be bette to wait—to wait a little, you know."

"But waiting only widens the distance between us. Just fancy what he'll feel if he hear from any one else that I am going to be married!" Florence said, pleadingly.

"It will be all right by-and-by," Fred said, in a down-hearted way, that belied his words. He could not bear the Stanley Villars question, for the simple reason that it was made a vexed one between his paragon Lady Villars, and his future bride. Had Carrie not put her veto upon it, he would have drifted away amiably into the most distasteful purlieus of our great metropolis in search of Stanley, had Florence ordered him to do so. As it was, straight sailing appeared impossible, and he was not gifted with the tacking mind.

"That's what Gerald and Carrie always say," Florence replied, mournfully. "All right by-and by! They have tried to comfort me with that assurance for months!"

"They know best, you see," Fred Chester said, persuasively, looking at her with the clear, large, well-shaped, blue eyes, that were so perfect in form and deficient in expression—in the expression of that sympathy which she craved.

"I had so set my heart on seeing him now, and introducing you to him!" Florence said, trying to feel that warmth of interest in Fred which the latter part of his sentence implied.

"Oh, you'll see him by-and-by, Flo; but at present they must be careful, you know, and try to guard you from the least thing—that isn't quite —you know——"

"That's one of Carrie's sentiments," Florence cried, with a sudden flash of spirit. Patiently had she suffered herself to be dictated to by Carrie the dictatorial; but she could not suffer it patiently from the man who was to be her husband. "That's one of Carrie's sentiments," she said, almost fiercely. I believe that there is nothing sweeter, softer, more gentle, lovable, and harmonious in humanity, than one of these richly-coloured women, with golden brown hair, and luscious, melting, tawny eyes, like a setter's. But they can develop determination and spirit—ay, and even angry resentment, when tried too far.

It was trying her too far now. Florence felt that it was, as she reflected on how her husband was to be made the instrument of her more complete separation from her brother. She could not be patient any longer. This was such a low form for rightful authority to take.

"Carrie is generally right," the lover said, somewhat abjectly. He cared very much for Florence, but he could not forget that Lady Villars had had a habit of ordering him about, and regulating his opinions for many years.

"But you can judge for yourself, Fred. Say now—do *you* think it right that I should fall off from my own darling brother because other friends fell off from him when his fortunes failed!" She asked it earnestly of him, laying her white hand on his arm as she spoke, and Fred Chester began to think that there was something in that view of the case, by Jove!—but for all that conviction, to wish that Lady Villars would come in and help him out of this difficulty!

"Yes; I can judge for myself," he said, with a small, self-satisfied air, that was too little for his person, and too big for his mind. "I can judge for myself, Flo—any man can do that!"

"Any man should do it," she said, quickly. "Come now—a bargain, Fred! In every other matter I will be guided entirely by you; but let my heart guide you in this; let me see my brother—not once or twice, but always—freely as a sister should see her brother—if you love me?"

The handsome young man with the beautiful eyes was embarrassed. Willingly, with all his heart and soul, would he have made this compact with "Flo" had not Carrie loomed before him—an avenging spirit, prone to be down upon any weakness committed by other than herself. He felt like a booby, and he looked like a booby, as he sat silent in his embarrassment. I think Florence would have done more wisely had she resolved upon steering her own bark.

"We'll talk about it another time, Flo," he pleaded presently. "You don't know, you see, and I can't tell you, you see; but Carrie seems to think that you had better let things rest for a time."

"And if I let them 'rest' now, will you do what I ask by-and-by?" she cried.

"Yes—oh, of course, dear!" and then he kissed Florence, and she shrank and shuddered as his lips touched her brow, and tried to make herself believe that she only did so because these kisses were such very new things.

Lady Villars got hold of him before he quitted the house after that interview with Florence. The gentle Carrie sent for him to her own little sitting-room, with the friendly design of making him feel what a delightful woman she was herself to have for a confidante, and of strengthening the purpose Florence might have undermined.

"You can sit there, Fred," she said, pointing to a low stool, a seat on which brought the occupier to a level with her feet; "you can sit there, Fred; and you shall have some tea with me, won't you?"

"No; I don't want the tea," he said, taking the seat she indicated, and bringing his beautiful eyes to bear upon her without the slightest meaning in them; "but I want to talk to you—you're such a sensible woman, and can tell a fellow what he ought to do. There's Flo got it into her head that she ought to run after her brother Stanley, you know; and I don't care, you know, only——"

"Only, of course, you wouldn't—you *couldn't* allow her to do it. Oh, no! I quite see your objections," Lady Villars interrupted, sweetly.

"No: you—see—the fact is, I was thinking that *you* could put it to her, you know, if it had better not be, you see—at least, not now."

"Certainly not now, Fred; *your* wife compromise herself by mixing herself up with that young profligate's low intrigue!" Lady Villars' voice almost fizzed as she said "profligate;" it was so nice to apply this term to the man who had passed her over.

"That would be rather out of the way, by Jove! But I don't think she quite wanted that," Fred Chester remarked, meditatively.

"Oh, she doesn't know *what* she wants—dear girl!" Carrie said, with a plain snap, the epithet coming in as an ornamental after-thought. "Florence is very young, you know, and *we* must guard her, since she is incapable; in fact, it isn't to be desired that she should be alive to all the danger; but then, *we* know."

"To be sure *we* know!" Fred Chester replied, with a sapient air, that was refreshing to behold, if you were not going to be allied to him.

"If you took my advice," Lady Villars went on, in a sweet, small voice, "it may not be worth much—but it's well meant——"

She paused, and Fred took the opportunity of observing that he knew its value as well as any fellow; that he really would take it (and so would Florence) gladly.

"Then, if you really care for my poor opinion," Lady Villars resumed, sweetly, "I should say, keep our dear Florence away from Stanley's influence. It would be ridiculous to affect before you anything but a full knowledge of the brilliant—yes, *brilliant* future that awaits our darling." (Lady Villars grew as tenderly tearful at this point as regard for the hue of her short nose, which was apt to become inflamed, would permit.) "It would also be *unfair* to you not to tell you that Florence's tendency to generosity amounts to weakness—positive weakness!—and to warn you that it may be played upon to your cost by those who have influence over her."

Fred Chester felt himself to be a mark for foul designs, all of a mercenary order, on the spot. Of course he was much too sharp to be taken in—he had that satisfactory self-assurance! But he would show Florence that he was the master, and that he was not disposed to lavish his red, red gold on unworthy objects!

He made this intention clear to Lady Villars, sitting at that sensible matron's feet, in the solitude of her little room, and looking at her with his beautiful eyes, in which was no dangerous meaning. When he had done that, Lady Villars sent him away; he was apt to become tedious after ten minutes, for all his good looks, if the truth be told.

If the truth be told about all things, too, it must be admitted that Florence had made a mistake—a second mistake—and a far larger one than that she had made about Claude Walsingham. It was only her heart that had been deceived in her intercourse with the man who had been in action and come out scatheless dozens of times, only to fall at last before Bella Vane! It was only her heart that had led her astray then. But now her head, her judgment, her knowledge of a by no means profound character, were all at fault. The wish—the hope that he would go hand in hand with her about Stanley was father to the thought and belief that he would do so; and now that she had gone too far to recede—now that she had pledged herself, and made herself believe that she loved him—now that her sister-in-law had lavished sums at Marshall and Snelgrove's, and held countless consultations with Elise, and told everybody "what a delightful match it was—quite a marriage of affection"—now she discovered that, as Mrs. Chester, she would be as far from Stanley as she was at present! There would be a double guard over her to save her from the imaginary harm.

CHAPTER XXXIX.

"THOSE ROSES!"

WE left Stanley Villars, and the poor, pretty, helpless little girl whom he had married, to his own immediate cost and her ultimate sorrow, in a very evil case. Things had come to a very terrible pass with him on that August day when last we looked upon him. Now, a little later in the month, there was a ray of hope lighting up even his dim, dull, dark path.

It did not radiate from Florence. Had that once cherished sister realised how sadly he sickened for her whenever he did think of aught beyond the murky, miserable present, she would surely have burst the rotten chains they loaded her with for safety's sake, and have gone to him, and essayed to offer him such comfort as could still be shed upon that wasted, misused mind of his. Had she known him as he was, lying there, day after day, in poverty, peevishness, and almost solitude, she would—she must have got herself together, for the leap that should carry her free of all the prejudices that held her from him.

Late on the night of that day when we looked upon them last, Stanley Villars made a solemn request of his wife. "Promise me one thing, pet," he said—he had grown strangely fond of and tender to her since he had begun to fear what was coming upon her in her youth through him—"Promise me one thing, pet."

"Anything you ask me, Stanley," she said, with a little tremble.

"You'll never, let what will come, make any appeal to my family. God! I couldn't stand that!" He asked it almost fiercely, and she shook as she answered—

"Never!"

"They—I don't blame them, mind—but they don't want to have more to do with me; and I won't have them refuse *you* anything, poor child," he went on bitterly.

"Your sister Florence was very fond of you, wasn't she?" Marian asked, with a little, feverish feminine desire to hear something about the mighty family into which she had married—the family who utterly scouted her.

"*She* was fond of me, poor Florence! but that's past evidently."

"How?—why do you say so?"

"I have written to her, and had no answer," he said with a sob. "There, let's have done with the subject. It's the hardest thing of all that they should have turned that loving child from me utterly. Swear to me by your soul, Marian, that you'll make no appeal—take nothing from one of them—come what may!"

He was almost choked by the emotion with which he asked it. She hastened eagerly to give him the assurance he sought.

This conversation had taken place on the night of that day when Marian had sauntered out with Rock and seen Bella. When we see them again, a week or ten days later, things looked a little brighter.

Stanley's novel—the one he had been running through the magazine—had come out, and reviewers had been generous, as it decidedly is the wont of the majority to be when aught like merit can be discerned. He was very weakly, and worn, and weary, in these days; but Bligh, the kindly, hard-working young fellow, who was stopping the gap, and keeping his place on the paper open for him, used to "look in" daily, if only for a minute or two, and bring him the notices, and tell him how things were going.

He was very weakly, and worn, and weary, in these days; so weak that the exertion of reading a favourable review, and the flash of hope the same would cause him, would be almost too much for him; so weak that he put a power of faith in the prospect others seemed to think was in store for him, for the non-committal assertion that his "work was full of great promise" was liberally indulged in. There was plenty in store for the future, he began to tell himself, and not absolute want in the present; for his salary came to him as usual from the daily journal for which he did *not* write, and Marian was always going out brightly to make purchases, and coming in brighter than she went out.

She was such a loving wife to him, such a patient, tender little nurse, that he might well feel it to be a cause for thankfulness that he had married her. So the days drew on to the close of August, and that reeling of the brain went on more wildly than before.

One morning when she had got him up, and helped him down-stairs (the once strong erect man stooped now, and leant heavily on the slight arm and rounded shoulder of the lithe young girl whose slender form had shown off mantles and shawls so well), she knelt down by the side of his couch, and told him she had made a friend—such a nice one, and her friend was coming to see him to-day.

She told him this with dancing eyes and other signs of animation, and he tried so feebly now to respond, because of the deep pity he had for this girl who had none now for herself. Still, with a hazy recollection floating about in his mind of Miss Simpson, the model milliner, who was looming over him, he could not succeed in responding to Marian's communication with anything like the degree of warmth with which it was made.

"Your friend mustn't mind my keeping my face to the back of the sofa, Marian?—I can't be bored—I can't manage any talking till Bligh comes at night to tell me how things are going, and hear whether I can get into harness again to-morrow."

Bligh never omitted this formula, though no one knew better than he that Stanley Villars would never get into harness again—that he was one more added to the long list of those who have broken down.

"Perhaps you'll care to talk when you see her," Marian said, softly. And when she said that, a gnawing desire to ask "Was it Florence?" seized the failing man.

But he would not ask it—partly because he would not put the idea of its being possible that she should come in Marian's head, and partly because he shrank from hearing an answer in the negative. He knew that he should wince and shrink did such answer smite him. He was so weak, so uncertain of himself, that he dared not risk a blow, though more than half prepared for it.

So he curbed the gnawing desire, and remained quiet with his face to the wall, with a cold dew of expectation on his brow, and a panting eagerness in his heart. Sternly as he had forbidden Florence to be sought, he was more than rejoiced that at last, though late, she was seeking him.

Marian busied herself about the room, trying to give it an air of brightness and cheerfulness, and failing by reason of there being nothing bright and cheerful in it. Dusting his books and papers, and fidgeting him wofully by the rustle she made, and the disarray she would be safe to introduce amongst his slips. Endeavouring to give the scanty curtains a graceful sweep and fall, which they could not achieve. Polishing up the surface of her little work-table till all the reels of cotton danced aloud within it, making Stanley's head stab, and causing him to curse this suddenly-developed domesticity. Flashing hither and thither in the room, and being very energetic and busy altogether.

By-and-by she went out of the room, and presently returned with a tall vase of roses—red and white roses—not overblown, and most delicately scented; autumnal roses, that had been born of the late summer sun, and had the fervour of it upon them.

Weak as he was, languid as he was, heart-sick as, heaven knows, he had good cause to be, he quickened at the sight and scent of them, and his old love for the beautiful sparkled up in the dull eyes that so seldom saw cause for sparkling now. It was the first time Marian had ever brought him flowers; and from him, needing essentials as he so often did, a request for such frail luxuries would have come strangely.

But now that he had them—now, that she of her own free will had brought them to him—he let her see how he loved them, and she revelled in the sight. They were such dainty flowers!—deep crimson and creamy white. He would have them on her work-stand, close by his side, where his hand could rest caressingly on the vase that held them; where their perfume could reach him, bathing him in an atmosphere that brought back the vision of that rose-embowered window which had been Bella's shrine in the halcyon days of his adoration for her. There's something so graceful, refined, and elevating about those roses, that he felt more like a gentleman—more like his old self—than he had done for many months.

"I feel better already for the flowers," he said, calling her over to him, when she had done all she could do to the room, and was pausing to look at the effect of her labours; and finding the "all" very insufficient—"I feel better already for the flowers. What good taste it was to get all roses, dear."

She blushed, and smiled, and looked pleased.

"Ain't they lovely and expensive?" she asked, simply.

"Expensive! are they?" with a sigh of disappointment. "Ah! I never thought of that; poor child, you shouldn't have got them for me!"

"They were given," she explained, opening her eyes like stars. "Here, Rock! get up," she called to the dog. "He shall have one in his collar, Stanley," she continued.

"Given, were they? by whom? No, I won't have one wasted on the dog! they must last me for so long."

He spoke peevishly, petulantly, as a sick child might have done. He did not like to hear that the rare flowers had been given to his wife. And yet he could not part with them—they were too sweet and dear.

"When they're dead you shall have some more. Do let me put one in Rock's collar!"

He took hold of her hand in his own almost transparent one.

"You must not accept presents, Marian, from ——" He stopped, and she asked, "Why not?"

"Don't bother about the dog. Who gave them to you?"

She put the rose she had taken out back into the vase, and replied—

"That's a secret! You'll know by-and-by, but it's a secret now!"

Then he looked at her small, pure face, and never doubted but that it was a "secret" which she might indulge herself in with perfect safety to them both. Perchance, even, the flowers that were so sweet to him were from Florence.

As the hours passed, Marian grew very watchful and uneasy, and he saw that she was getting anxious about her expected visitor. She kept on going to the window and looking out eagerly; and she made Rock stand up, with his large white paws on the sill, in order that he might sight the arrival at once, and give notice by one of his deep, rolling barks.

Presently the notice was given. There was a sound of wheels; then an angry bark from Rock, which was quickly changed into a joyous one, as he caught sight of some one coming up the steps. The red setter rushed round the room in intense excitement, his white feathered tail flaunting like a pennon; and some of the dog's excitement communicated itself to the master. Poor Stanley Villars was too weak to rise, and too nervous to remain quiescent. He could only flutter, as an old woman or a young girl might have done.

Marian had rushed out to meet her guest; and he heard them speaking in the passage, but they spoke in whispers, and he could not, therefore, recognise the stranger's tone. "I shall die the happier for having seen Florry," he thought. Then a sob, that he could not check, sent the burning tears, that he would have given all he had not to shed, rushing from his eyes. Involuntarily, as the door opened, he clasped his hands over his face, in order that his sister should not see the change that he knew too well was upon him. There was a quick movement, as of rustling skirts, through the room, and a light hand was laid on his. He uncovered his eyes then, and looking up, saw a beautiful face, burning with emotion, and trembling with passionate helpless pity, bending over him, and a slight hand trying to repulse the rough caresses of the dog. And the face was not that of his sister Florence, but of her who had been Bella Vane.

——o——

CHAPTER XL.

MAKING A BOOK.

LEAVING Bella to gaze undisturbed with no very enviable feelings on the form of the man whose downfall had dated from the day he learnt that she was false as she was fair; leaving that man in a maze of bewilderment as to how she came near him now—how this miracle came to pass, that she, his old love, should be his wife's new friend; leaving that poor little wife panting, partly with hope and partly with fear, for the result of this combination which she had effected—I will go back a few steps, and strive to make clear to my readers the maze through which Mrs. Claude had come to the meeting.

A day or two after that encounter with Marian and Rock in the park, Major Walsingham had been summoned to "the Court." His father was very ill, and he, the heir, was needed. Before he went he said to his wife—

"By the way, Lady Lexley has been ill, Bella: I wish you would call and enquire for her."

"I will, if I am going that way," Bella replied coldly. She could not conquer her dislike to Lady Lexley, and she felt annoyed with Claude for thrusting her into communion with that lady, to say nothing of feeling annoyed with herself for entertaining the dislike.

"Certainly, don't go out of your way to do it," he replied carelessly; "that wouldn't be well, in fact; but there's no harm in being civil to her, since every one else is." With which rather sketchy rule for her safe conduct, he left his wife and went down to "the Court."

Two days after his departure she received a letter from Claude, containing a request to which she had no inclination to accede, and which she had no reason for refusing. "My mother tells me that Grace Harper wants to go to town for a week or two; the aunt with whom she usually stays (old Lady Lexley) is in Wales; you had better invite her to be your guest. By doing so you'll oblige an old friend of my family's, and please my mother." Having written thus much, he went off into another subject—his father's ill-health namely. But later in the epistle the Grace Harper topic came upon the board again. "I shall tell Ellen to arrange for you with Miss Grace, and one of them will drop you a line to-morrow, telling you what time you may expect her." Then he wound up with expressions of his unalterable affection for her; and Bella, in the pleasure of perusing these, forgot her slight annoyance at Miss Harper's expected advent.

"Besides, I rather like the girl, and of course Claude's free to ask whomsoever he pleases to the house. Only I had *such* a time of it with Mrs. Markham, that I would have preferred a longer respite from lady visitors. However, there's no help for it."

There was no help for it. The day after a kindly-worded letter from Grace arrived, thanking Bella for *her* "kind consideration in wishing to have her (Grace)," and utterly ignoring Claude's share in the arrangement. "Dear Claude! he has made it seem to be entirely my own idea. I suppose he really does want the people down there to like me very much," she said to herself, as she laid the letter down; "but why didn't she go to Lady Lexley's, I wonder?"

Miss Harper, and her maid and her man, arrived in the course of the following day. She was far too precious a thing to have been entrusted to the tender mercies of the railway company without these adjuncts. She arrived, and her young hostess made her frankly welcome, and even asked after "her friend Mrs. Markham" with something like interest.

"For, though she's Claude's sister, I always feel that you're much more intimate with her than I am," Bella explained, on Grace making large eyes at the question.

"Don't you write to each other?" Grace asked.

"No, never."

"How odd! At least I suppose it's antipathy. Do you know," she said, with a well-affected effort, "I have the same feeling against my cousin's wife."

Bella blushed: so had she the same feeling, only she was half-ashamed of it.

"It all comes, in the case of Lady Lexley," Miss Harper went on, "of her having been professional. There are sure to be rumours, you know; but it's unchristian to regard them."

"Do you know anything against Lady Lexley?" Bella asked eagerly.

"Oh, *no!* and don't let *us* be the ones, dear

Mrs. Walsingham, to give rise to scandal," Miss Harper said with emphasis.

"Give rise to it!"—all Bella's generous impulses were stirred within her—"now do you think I could be so base?"

"No, I do not," Miss Harper rejoined; "but still, dear, you must promise never to hint a word that I have said. I *don't* believe it (though I'm not fond of her); it would be cruel to believe it, to act as if we believed it."

"Believed what?" Bella was getting bewildered.

"Why, that she is not all that a woman ought to be. Oh, dear, it's so hard to do right! God knows what is in my heart!" Miss Harper went on, piously lowering her yellow eyelashes over her cheeks as she spoke.

"I don't wish not to think her that," Bella said remorsefully. She felt so sorry now that she had not been to inquire for Lady Lexley.

"I shall never forgive myself if you ever hint that I have spoken on the subject," Miss Grace exclaimed; "it was so wrong of me to speak. I believe her to be as pure as I am myself. Promise me that you will never, by either word or manner, to any one, let a hint of this escape you."

Bella promised nervously and hurriedly. Why should *she* be supposed to be anxious to run down an innocent woman? She promised that she would not do so, rather more fervently than was perhaps necessary. There was nothing mean in the girl's nature; had there been, she would have distrusted this hedging on the part of Miss Harper—this late circumspection—this pious prudence.

Almost immediately Mrs. Claude Walsingham called to inquire for Lady Lexley. Lady Lexley was not at home. With almost royal celerity Lady Lexley returned the visit, and Bella began to feel that there was something pleasant about the woman—something pleasant in the dramatic character of her beauty—something pleasant in her openly-expressed admiration for Bella herself.

Grace was more than friendly in her demeanour to her cousin's wife. She was loving and affectionate to a degree that made Bella feel herself to be but a cold sinner in comparison. She called Lady Lexley "dear," and sat on a little stool at her feet. She offered to do all sorts of things for Lady Lexley, and then disappointed Lady Lexley when the time for fulfilment came, in the most engaging manner.

Lady Lexley knew something—as did the majority of people in their world—of Mrs. Claude's former engagement. She had heard it spoken of in a hundred ways, as broken engagements, to the cost of those who break them, are ever spoken about. In her own often-erring heart she did full justice to all that was good, all that was true, all that was undesigning, in Mrs. Claude Walsingham. She knew Bella to be thoughtless, careless, too quick to feel and to act. She also knew Bella to be honest in her impulses, no matter into what evil those impulses led her; and she believed Mrs. Claude to be endowed with that sort of generosity which risks its possessor very often, and revolts at all meanness. "If she knew what that man was suffering she wouldn't go on her way smiling," Lady Lexley said to herself one day, when she had heard from the indefatigable Simpson the story of "her (Simpson's) friend Mrs. Stanley Villars' sorrows." "The man has cut his own throat, of course; but that child will feel that she put the knife in his way, and will bless any one who'll help her to heal the wound."

Fraught with this idea, she speedily made an opportunity of telling Mrs. Claude all she knew; and then Mrs. Claude confided to her in turn how she had "heard Stanley Villars had a wife, and how she had disbelieved it."

"But it's true for all that," Lady Lexley replied; "the girl he has married isn't a lady, but she's honest and pure; help to keep her so, Mrs. Walsingham, for they're in horrible distress."

"I will tell Claude the instant he comes home," Bella replied; "how he'll feel it, poor boy!" In the midst of her own grief for the evil that had come upon Stanley Villars, her greatest sorrow was for the grief of the man she loved. "How he'll feel it, poor boy!" she half sobbed.

"Yes, it's very hard to see one who has been swimming with us go to the bottom," Lady Lexley replied; "but you may as well see his wife, as you and Major Walsingham were such old friends of her husband's. Nearly every one gets spoken about in this world; but there's not a breath against that poor child Mr. Villars married. It's pitiable," Lady Lexley continued, waxing warm, "to see her sauntering about in the park by herself, because she's weary of the streets, and needs air. See her, Mrs. Walsingham, and see her soon."

"When Claude comes home," Bella said.

"When will he come? The man is dying, I tell you. Write to your husband about it."

But from this Bella most unwisely shrank. "I can tell him everything in two minutes—how I heard of it and all; but to write, it is different. Claude is so fastidious; I should like to see *her* soon, though; and to help them, if I could."

"I tell you how you can manage, then," Lady Lexley replied, eagerly; "come to luncheon with me. Ah! there's Grace. Well, bring her, and come to luncheon with me to-morrow; then we'll go to the shop where she used to be, and Miss Simpson can tell you her address; something must be done, and done quickly—the man is dying."

Bella blenched.

"But what can *I* do?"

"See them for yourself, and then let his family know. Had *I* the right of old friendship which *you* have, wouldn't I do it, think you! It's hideous to think about, even to me, who only knew Mr. Villars by name and repute." She stopped, breathless with genuine horror at that fate which had befallen Stanley—a fate she, better than Bella, could realise.

"Then it shall be so. How could I ever have hesitated?" Bella said, with tears in her eyes. "It's all I can do to go and see him—them, I mean—and show him that my friendship is unaltered."

"Of course it's all you can do—till your husband comes back; but do it without delay, for heaven's sake!" Lady Lexley cried, energetically. "Come to me to-morrow, and I'll put you in the way of doing it."

On the morrow, shortly after Mrs. Claude had mooted the subject of going out to Lady Lexley's to her companion, Miss Harper was seized with a violent headache. "*Would* dear Mrs. Claude go without her, and give her best love and a thousand apologies for her non-appearance, to Adèle?" Mrs. Claude would, but still regretted very much that Grace should fail her.

"I don't like to leave you, as you are so ill, Grace," she said.

"Oh, my dear, for you not to go would be a dreadful slight to Lady Lexley. Poor thing! why should you wish to hurt her? Do go, and be kind to her; you see she lost her old friends by her marriage, and hasn't made many new ones since."

"Kind to her; it's no question of kindness or unkindness," Bella exclaimed. She began to fear that she must have a most uncharitable disposition, and that Miss Harper had detected the same, and was trying to guard her from its ill effects, and to re-mould it as became a Christian.

"Then, do be careful. Pray, be very careful," Miss Harper replied. And Bella, not feeling at all sure as to what she was to be careful of, went off with a confusion in her brain.

Went off, and partook of the aforesaid luncheon with Lady Lexley, and then ordered her carriage round, and asked for the address of the shop at which Mrs. Stanley Villars was to be "heard about."

"But I'll go with you, if you will allow me; we shall see *her* there," Lady Lexley said, fixing her eyes on Mrs. Claude's. On which Mrs. Claude felt confused as to something, she knew not what, and replied, "Oh, certainly; most happy."

But she was not happy, and she taxed her mind to the utmost to supply herself with a valid reason for being otherwise. She had given her jealousy of Lady Lexley to the winds, and Lady Lexley had lately been showing a very womanly and generous desire to put her (Bella) in the way of doing good to one whom she had formerly injured. Lady Lexley had done this, too, in a way at which no one could have taken offence. She had put it on the score of their old friendship for Stanley, not of Bella's old fondness for and falseness to him. Lady Lexley had approved herself a generous-natured, kind-hearted, quick-feeling woman in the business. Yet, for all that, Bella felt that she would rather be elsewhere, when she found herself driving along the "ladies' mile," in an open carriage, with Lady Lexley.

"Why can't we go straight across the park, and out at the Marble Arch?" Mrs. Claude asked. She had not heard the order that had been given to her own footman to pass on to the coachman. She had taken it for granted that Lady Lexley would have given the address of the shop, and that they should have driven there at once.

Lady Lexley blushed. She was not a malicious woman. She did not desire to harm any other woman. But she had no intimate female acquaintances, and in the course of transacting the amiable business which was to result in good for the Villarses, it occurred to her that she might as well achieve good for herself, and be "seen" a good deal with young Mrs. Walsingham. She had no desire to be the cause of a breath of ill-odour passing over Mrs. Claude's bright head; but she could not refrain from risking giving rise to this breath, in the hope that it might temper the breeze that was abroad about herself—a breeze that was bitingly sharp sometimes, and not to be lulled even by her present, prudent, open course. Lady Lexley would have been very sorry to overshade Mrs. Claude Walsingham; she would not do so wittingly. But she was far from certain that she should overshade her, and she was very certain that being seen with Mrs. Claude could not be other than a reassuring thing in the eyes of all men who beheld the sight, about herself. In fact, she did not wish to work evil to her neighbour; she only wished, and wished strongly too, that her neighbour might work good for her. It was very natural. None can blame the womanly yearning for good, pure, womanly society. It is a thing to be desired—a thing to be striven for—a thing to be attained at any price, Lady Lexley felt, especially in the open.

So now, when Mrs. Claude Walsingham asked rather confusedly why they could not drive straight across the park, and out by the Marble Arch, Lady Lexley answered that "it was too soon to go to the shop yet awhile." "That Miss Simpson told me," she added, "that Mrs. Stanley Villars was coming this afternoon, but it would be too soon to think of seeing her yet. If you want to go anywhere else, we can go, of course; but it's pleasant here, isn't i '

"Very pleasant," Bella replied, and there came a blush upon her cheek as she spoke. The air was very soft and balmy; but men gave not "impertinent," but long looks into the carriage as they passed, and Bella began to wish that Lady Lexley had elected to use her own carriage for her morning's drive.

"Very pleasant! By-the bye, I must go into Regent Street. Stay! I'll put you down at the corner, and you can sit there and talk to people till I come back."

Lady Lexley made no reply for a moment or two. She was well inclined towards Mrs. Claude Walsingham; at the cost of pain to herself, she would have shrunk from doing Mrs. Claude Walsingham harm. But here was no tangible harm to be done, she thought; on the contrary, here was a very tangible good to herself. She did not wish to injure Bella; but sho did desire that Bella should serve her.

"I don't see any people to whom I care to talk. No, I'll go with you to Regent Street, if you'll allow me," she said at last, looking Bella straight in the face as she spoke. Then Bella blushed again under her gaze, and said—

"Oh, certainly! I only thought—" and then broke down in her explanation, and condemned herself in her own heart for having suffered Miss Harper's undefined shadowings to cloud over Lady Lexley in her (Bella's) eyes.

The park had been bad enough, but Regent Street was worse. It was full for the time of year; full of people who knew her and her companion. There were two or three blocks. Everybody was shopping this day; and their progress along the street, till they came to the repository for carved oak, at which Mrs. Walsingham was going to alight, was slow, mercilessly slow. Mrs. Claude Walsingham grew more and more flushed, and her manner more and more constrained, as they moved along at a foot-pace. And she was conscious of these things, and sorry for them, believing as she did, in her innermost heart, that there was uncharitableness and narrow-mindedness in her being even inwardly influenced by an idle word, idly spoken.

For Grace's manner of speaking had been idle, when looked upon in cold blood. True, she had seemed to strive to render it impressive at the time, by calling upon God to witness that she meant well, and was earnestly set upon doing right. But then Bella reflected that some people are very apt to do this on slight grounds, and she argued that had Miss Harper believed that at which she had guardedly hinted in apparent agony of spirit, that she would either have said less or more; and that she would have refrained from being effusively affectionate as she had been since to Lady Lexley.

"At any rate, if it gives her any pleasure to be with me, I don't see that I need grudge her that pleasure," Mrs. Claude Walsingham thought, heaving a sigh, and trying to get rid of a portion of the weight that was upon her. "How wicked I am to think evil on the strength of the actual *nothing*—the mere whisper—Grace said." Then she spoke out quite freely and joyously to Lady Lexley, spoke in a more intimate tone than she usually assumed towards more intimate friends, out of the fulness of that foolish generosity on which Miss Harper had counted when she played the card of the impalpable suspicion.

She was so foolish, this poor Bella. She had always been so addicted to going from one extreme to the other without due consideration; so apt to forget what was not immediately before her; so awfully ready to please herself and others at the moment, without counting the cost. Granted that she was all this, still she had such rare redeeming qualities. She was so ready always to repent and make amends; so incapable of seeing the bad side of things at the first; so very sorry to see them ever, in fact.

I do not mean to imply that she was slow to wrath, or meekly resigned when she fancied she had been injured or deceived. On the contrary, she was very quick to feel slight or injury, and to flame up about either. But till she did so feel, she did not invest her time in looking about for weak places in people's characters, motives, or assertions. She had a habit of just letting them go on. It might have been amiability on her part, or it might have been mere idleness; at all events, whatever it was, it saved her from being a mischief-maker or a busy-body. It also saved her from the misery many more loudly professing Christians declare that they endure—the misery, namely, of too clearly discerning other people's faults and follies.

My heroine was far from perfect, though, it must be confessed; this day, for example, she had come out fraught with the determination of doing all that might be done for poor Stanley Villars and his wife, without an instant's unnecessary delay. Yet now, not a couple of hours after that determination had been in full bloom, it faded away, leaving her blithely regardless of the old friend's sad strait, as soon as she found herself in the midst of the carved oak. Her face flushed with a widely different glow to that which had been upon it as she drove along Regent Street, and her eyes sparkled with a natural, but, perhaps, less praiseworthy excitement, than the one which had blazed in them when she had first listened to the tale of the trials of the baby-faced beauty who had been with Rock in the park.

Mrs. Claude Walsingham had come out with her purse well filled; and the contents had all been devoted, in her mind, to the holy purpose of making things pleasanter for Stanley and his wife. She knew well that he would rather die than suffer her to relieve his need. But from his wife—from the girl who was beautiful, but who was not a lady—no such delicacy of feeling was to be expected; at any rate, Bella did not expect it. Mrs. Stanley Villars should be drilled into silence for her own good, as to favours received—that, of course; equally of course would it be that she should receive them.

Now, however, that she found herself amongst things that were very dear to her taste, the latter came to the fore, and would be obeyed. Its government over Bella was an absolute monarchy: it always would give the law. So now she forgot what was not immediately before her, as was her wont, and the purse began to empty itself with fatal rapidity.

"I'm going to fit up a study for myself," she explained to Lady Lexley, when Lady Lexley commenced a series of impatient movements, all tending towards the door. "Oh dear! *how* I wish I could get a Robinson Crusoe writing-table, like that lovely sideboard that was in the '62 Exhibition! Do you remember it?"

Lady Lexley nodded. She did not remember anything about it; but it was easier to nod than to listen to a description of it.

"If you furnish your own design—any design—madam, we could carry it out for you *as* cheaply as any house in the trade," the man who was waiting on her here ventured to suggest.

"Ah! but I like to get what I see, you see," Mrs. Claude replied; "it might be all very well in my imagination, and a dead failure when carved; but a writing-table, like that Robinson Crusoe sideboard," she went on lingeringly, "would be charming."

The shopman, with the fell rapidity of his tribe, had his order-book out at once. "You will allow us to make a memorandum of it for you, madam?"

Bella shook her head despondingly. Their house was very fully and completely furnished, she knew. The writing-table that had been appropriated to her own special use was of oak, well carved; *but* it was not a "Robinson Crusoe" writing-table and for this she pined.

"I think we had better be going on, or we shall miss her to-day?" Lady Lexley whispered; "that is, if you are ready?"

"Oh! I'm ready—to be sure I'm ready! Just wait one moment, though—*those* candlesticks; did you ever see anything so exquisite!"

Lady Lexley affirmed that she never had seen "anything so exquisite; but would Mrs. Claude come now?"

"In one moment. I'll have those candlesticks. No I won't—I'll have the taller ones with the gnomes' heads peeping out through the flowers. And just let me see that inkstand. Oh, *charming!* Of course I must have that; wood sprites, and such wonderful leaves; it might be Gibbons' carving, mightn't it?"

Again Lady Lexley nodded. She had never heard of the individual referred to; but it occured to her that, if his carving was so superior, Mrs. Claude might as well have gone to him direct, instead of purchasing what, after all, was to his work as "cowslip unto oxslip is."

"I have a piece of furniture that will please madam," the man here remarked, with that subtle air of seeming to detect an artistically appreciative power in the purchaser, which sellers acquire by sharp practice. "A table, a square table, carved by Gibbons himself; it is very old."

"Wouldn't you rather have Gibbons do you a new one?" Lady Lexley asked aloud.

"We mean the eighteenth century Gibbons," Bella replied quietly. "There is such a lot of his charming works in Holland House. I wonder whether that is owed to the Countess of Warwick's taste or to Addison's?"

"This table I was speaking of belonged to Addison," the man struck in gravely. He had been casting about in his own mind for a fitting person on whom to fix the former ownership of this excellent article. Addison was as good for the purpose as any other man; therefore without hesitation he asserted that it had belonged to Addison, and so made Mrs. Claude Walsingham happy.

Her happiness was so patent to him, however, that he could but charge her a few pounds extra for it—a proceeding which made no manner of difference to her, since she was unconscious of it. He smiled in gentle pity for her inexperience when he was bowing her into her carriage. But I, for one, think that pity misplaced. It is so nice to think that you have in your possession a table on which some of those wonderful *Tatler* and *Spectator* papers might have been written.

"Perhaps he did some of his 'Sir Roger de Coverley' at it!" Bella cried in a burst of enthusiasm when they were driving off.

"Who? Gibbons?" Lady Lexley replied absently. "I do *hope* we shan't miss her."

Which remark brought Bella's mind back from thoughts of that golden age—that time when Addison had lived and loved, and drank and written—to these degenerate modern days, when one gifted even as she believed Stanley Villars to be, could not live by his pen. She thought about these things sadly till they came to the shop where they were to see the girl who was asserted to be Stanley Villars' wife. My judgment may be faulty on the subject, but I confess to a feeling of preference for Bella, the woman who never doubted that assertion, though appearances might be said to be against its truth, over the always-correct-in-conduct Lady Villars, whose Christian horror of evil-doing led her to detect it frequently before it was.

The poor little milliner, who had deemed it such a golden thing that she should marry a gentleman, was, as has been seen, in the habit of drifting back here to the society that was most congenial to her. She was rather at a premium in the show-room. She served as a subject for conversation amongst the "young ladies" in their hours of idleness. She could be let off as a successful fact—a genuine case of "risen from the ranks"—at the heads of languid lady customers, who were willing to linger over garments of divers shapes in wearying uncertainty. When expatiating on the "elegance" and "perfect style" of an opera cloak, for example, the adroit Miss Simpson would tell in touching tones how sure said opera cloak would have been to win the hearts of all beholders, had it but been seen over the shoulders of the late Miss Wallis, promoted. "This grew," till half the habitual customers of the place knew that, in some way or other, "the man that Bella Vane had jilted had made a mess of it."

—o—

CHAPTER XLI.

A PRACTICAL CHRISTIAN.

It need not be told how, even at this their first meeting, the kindly lady who was "the cause," she felt, in a measure, of the sorrow that had come upon the girl, and the gentle, unpretending girl on whom the sorrow had fallen, understood one another, and came together as it were. There was something inexpressibly winning to Marian, who had never met with it before, in the rich, fearless warmth of Mrs. Walsingham's manner towards her. Bella turned to her at once when she came into the room, and found her there already installed, and, it must be confessed, gratingly familiar with her not too refined former companions. Turned to her at once—with no crushing condescension—with no mock "I am as thou art" demeanour—with no false superiority—no degrading to one as to the other patronage—but with a great big hearty kindness, that proved she took the girl at once for what she stated herself to be, and looked. Turned to her as Bella would have turned to a duchess in distress—in a way that made Lady Lexley's eyes dilate with womanly sympathy, as belladonna had never caused them to do.

Their interview was not very long. When a few facts had been stated by the young wife, and listened to by Bella, they both found that they had little left to say. "I should like to come and see you, and him; we are such old friends," Mrs. Walsingham said with a little gasp, when Marian said "she must go now, or Stanley would be cross." On the statement of which desire Marian shook her head dubiously, and replied that she "was sure Stanley wouldn't bear to see any of his old friends," and let her lip quiver as she said it, and suffered a round, quickly-dried tear to fall.

"But I must see you both," Bella urged, "now we have met again, and he is ill."

"He has made me promise never to go near any of his family, or let them come near him," Marian said sorrowfully. And at that even kind-hearted Lady Lexley shook her head, and said to herself, "That looks bad."

But Bella was above suspicion as regarded Stanley Villars. It was all very well, or rather it was perhaps natural, that others should distrust him, and think that, because his first guard had been broken down, that evil should have entered in to the once well-defenced citadel, and have its own way entirely. It was perhaps natural that others should think this. But it would have been unnatural for her to think it, knowing the man as she did. The wrong he had wrought, whatever it might be, that had made him desire to cut himself off from his family, had not been a wrong to this innocent, fond, trusting girl.

"At any rate let me come and see him," Mrs. Walsingham urged. "As to his own family, between him and them I can't interfere, of course; but my husband was like his brother; why should he wish to cut us?"

"I never heard him name *you*," Marian said wonderingly.

Bella blushed. "How wrong of him," she said quickly; "he should have brought us together, and made us friends. Are you fond of Rock?"

The brief pang that had been Marian's portion that day in the park, when Rock had leapt with a dog's enthusiasm about his old mistress, assailed her (Marian) again now.

"Did *you* give him to Stanley?" she asked in a low tone.

"Yes, I gave him Rock; and now Rock has rewarded me by first making you known to me," Bella replied heartily. She understood perfectly well the nature of that pang which caused the baby-faced beauty to speak in a lower voice.

The interview ended satisfactorily. Marian was persuaded to give up her address. She was also induced to "try and think" whether there was anything Stanley might possibly like. But she shook her head in resolute refusal to "think" even that he might possibly care for anything save some flowers. On being put to the test, she showed herself in fact to be far from deficient in that special phase of delicacy which Mrs. Walsingham had felt sure would not be a conspicuous attribute in one "of her class."

So the roses were procured from the sacred recesses of a damp drawer in a shop in Covent Garden market. Lovely roses—not cut off, and wired-up, and gummed, and otherwise manufactured—but fresh, fair, natural flowers, with long stalks and lots of leaves, and fragrance unimpaired. Lovely roses! that brought back the memory of bygone summer-days to Bella, even as they brought them back the following morning to poor, sick, suffering Stanley.

Before they parted, Marian acceded to Mrs. Walsingham's proposition of calling to see Stanley on the following day; and, as is the habit of women, she had no sooner acceded to it, than she began to entertain it enthusiastically, pressing Bella to "make it early," with a half-shy familiarity, that Bella would have watched with a feeling of semi-amusement in any woman save Stanley's wife.

When they were driving back to Eaton Square, in order that Lady Lexley might be deposited before Mrs. Walsingham proceeded home, the evil spirit of over-caution seized the usually unguarded Circe.

"If I were you, as those poor people want to keep close for reasons best known to themselves, my dear, I wouldn't say a word of the matter to Grace Harper; she has a way of telling things that makes them change colour."

Bella winced. It is always unpleasant when two people take it into their well-meaning heads to put you—the luckless third—on guard against each other.

"Well, I won't, till Claude thinks I may."

"Oh, of course, you'll do as you please in the matter; I have no motive for concealment," Lady Lexley replied, carelessly; "but I have seen a good deal of Miss Grace, you know, and, as I said before, she has a way of telling things that makes them change colour."

"Do you mean that she tells stories?" Bella asked quickly.

"That's such an angular way of putting it. No; you'll never catch her out in a story, if you lie in wait for her till the day of judgment; she really does stick to the letter—excuse the idiom."

"Then how does she change the colour of things?" Bella inquired.

"Mother of God! how should I know?" Lady Lexley cried, almost passionately. "She does it, she does it—but how? What does it matter, though?" she continued, with a sudden change of manner.

"Only that some time or other harm may come of her peculiar—talent," Bella said, hesitatingly.

"Harm come of it!" Lady Lexley replied, laughing. Then the slumbering southern fire in her blood blazed up, and she added, "If harm came through it to *me*, I would tear her thick white skin off her face in strips, and have her hissed at the church door; that would sting her more than anything!" she continued, with a bright laugh, that made Bella's blood curdle, coming as it did immediately after the enunciation of such sanguinary sentiments.

Miss Harper's head was quite well when Mrs. Walsingham got home. Grace looked so cool, so good, and unemotional, as she raised her head to greet her hostess, that Bella felt her to be almost a relief, after turbulent Lady Lexley.

"I am sorry you could not go——" "with me," Bella was going to say, but she paused on the brink of the polite perfidy, and substituted "out for a drive."

"Oh, thank you; but I have been very well amused, dear Mrs. Walsingham," Grace replied, indicating, as she spoke, the book she held in her hand as the source of her amusement.

"What is it?" Mrs. Walsingham asked. Then she looked again, and added, "Oh! Stanley Villars' novel!"

Miss Harper nodded. "Perhaps the worst thing about such works," she said in a sort of humble and contrite tone, "is that they absorb you against your convictions."

"You mean they amuse you, I suppose, whether you want to go on reading just at the time or not; that's my idea of what a novel should do," Bella replied, hardily.

Grace shook her head. "The novelist has so much in his power, if he only uses his gifts aright," she said, in the same tone as before.

"If he gets good prices, he has as much and no more in his power than other men with money," Bella replied, wilfully misunderstanding the fair critic, and trusting fondly that by so doing, she should avert the bolt of censure which she perceived was in readiness to be let fly at her.

"I can only say that I am glad the man who wrote *that* book is no friend of mine," Grace went on, with the faintest tinge of colour coming upon her cheeks. That is one of the great advantages fair women have over duskier ones; they can get into a terrible passion without at the same time getting red in the face.

"I dare say you wouldn't care for literary society." Bella spoke coolly; but her heart was hot within her. It was hard to hear the man who had nearly burst his brain over the work that was daily bread to him—who had broken down as Stanley Villars had!—it was hard to hear him thus lightly judged by a mediocre woman with yellow eyelashes.

But she would not have put in this plea—that he had striven while strength was his to strive, and failed in agony—for all the goods the gods had ever given her. She would not have done it. She could not have done it. There are some people whom even their friends dare not attempt to excuse.

The battle is not always to the strong, nor is the race invariably to the swift. Miss Harper was mentally a far weaker woman than the one with whom she was combating. That she was "slow," no man could be found to deny. But for all these things she was likely to come in winner in this contest upon which she had entered. For her blood ran coldly in her veins about all things that did not immediately concern herself, and when the circulation is thus well-regulated, success in all matters of feeling is inevitable.

"I can only say," Miss Harper repeated, dogmatically, "that I am very glad that the man who wrote that book is no friend of mine."

Mrs. Claude Walsingham heaved, but held her peace.

"It must be very painful to you, dear Mrs. Claude, to peruse such sentiments as I find here," Grace persisted, tapping the book with her soft, white finger as she spoke. It was a peculiarity of those fingers of hers, that, soft, white, and well rounded as they were, they yet had a lazy, cruel look. Mrs. Claude Walsingham was fascinated into glancing wistfully at them, as though they were things that must be watched and warded off, as she answered—

"The author being a friend of mine, maybe I have lost judgment about his work."

"Then the book is likely to be more pernicious to you than to me," Grace replied, calmly; "you ought not to read it."

"I am greatly obliged to you for the caution; but on such a point you must allow me to judge for myself," Bella answered, speaking with that fatal coolness which is the sure precursor of a storm.

Grace Harper smiled inwardly. Inwardly, too, she told herself that she was really only doing her duty in striving to irritate Bella, and depreciate the work of the man whose views differed from her own. What those views were is very immaterial to my story. They are simply alluded to in order that Bella's motive for acting as she is going to act may be made manifest.

"I should be false to myself, and to everything that I have ever been taught," Miss Harper said in her stolid way, "if I did not tell you what I think about Mr. Stanley Villars' ideas."

"You have told me." (Then the servant came in, and announced dinner.) "Very well, Hill. Now, Grace, we must escort ourselves in to the dining-room. "Oh dear!" she continued, as they were coming down stairs, "how I wish my husband were back!"

Miss Harper did not echo the wish. She only smiled, and thought "I hope he won't be back yet. What a nuisance that 'dinner' should have come in the way just then! She was ready to say anything."

Later in the evening the subject was renewed in this way. Mrs. Claude rang the bell, and ordered Hill, when he came, to "take back the two volumes that are lying on that table to Mudie's, to-morrow morning, and ask for the third."

"Is it 'Never a Chance,' that you're sending back?" Miss Harper asked, mentioning the title of that work of poor Stanley's which was indeed but a reflex of his life.

"Yes," Bella replied, briefly.

"Oh, I'm sorry!—I haven't done with it."

"Put it down, Hill—don't take it!" his mistress exclaimed, sharply, to the hesitating servant. As soon as he was out of the room, she continued, "I beg your pardon—but I could not imagine, after what you said, that you were going on with the book; otherwise, of course, I should not have thought of sending it away."

"Oh, yes! I confess to being interested in it; and that's just where I feel the book will work evil—the trail of the serpent is there, covered with flowers."

Grace came forward as she spoke, and seated herself on a low stool near the feet of her hostess, with her own back to the light, and her yellow lashes lowered. Bella was facing what light there was left in the sky, and her eyes were open—wide open—and filled with an honest anger.

"Once more I must remind you, Grace, that Stanley Villars is my husband's friend and mine; I cannot hear him spoken of in this way."

"I should be untrue to the principles—the holy principles in which I have been reared—if I did not tell you what I think about it—if I did not lift up my voice in warning," Miss Harper said, humbly, just glancing through the pale lashes at the flushed, excited enemy.

"Having told me, let there be an end of it. I am not responsible for a line that may be in that book. I neither care to uphold nor to defend it. I simply want not to talk to you about it."

A sudden fear seized Bella that this girl, whom she had liked and trusted as a nice, soft, womanly creature, would be too many for her were warfare declared. Miss Harper was forcing the subject into a serious light; she was being solemn in her severity, and seeming to threaten darkly. Bella grew very nervous.

Was there anything so bad in the book that first holy principles—principles Bella revered to the full as much as did the fair Pharisee at her side—were assailed by it? Bella grew very nervous; but nervous as she was, it was farther than before from her mind to desert Stanley Villars.

"We should not shrink from a subject simply because it's unpleasant to us," Miss Harper rejoined.

"Now, Grace, that is all very well; but we all *do* shrink from an unpleasant subject. You'd shrink from it if it were unpleasant to you."

"Can it be pleasant to me to run the risk of offending you, dear?" Miss Harper asked, more effusively than was her wont.

"I don't know; but it's certainly pleasant to you to censure Stanley Villars."

"I want to spare you pain in the future. God knows what is in my heart!"

"Well, I don't!" Bella cried, almost writhing away from Grace's side. There was something terrible—something horrible—in this mixture of worldly animus with piety.

"Don't use a tone of levity about such things, dear!" Grace pleaded, with an earnestness that would have been very effective, had not Bella caught the quick glance that was levelled simultaneously through the yellow lashes.

"I am not going to use a tone of levity, or any other tone, about it any more!" Mrs. Claude replied, firmly. "You will please to recall two things to your mind that you appear to have forgotten: I am neither a child to be reprimanded, nor a heathen to be converted!"

"A word spoken in season——" Miss Grace was commencing, when Bella interrupted her.

"This is really too much, Miss Harper!" she cried indignantly. "Once for all—I will not hear another word, in season or out of season, on the subject!"

"*Only* this—oh, do, for your own sake!" Grace said, with a mild persistence, that was hard—very hard—to endure. "I know the Walsinghams so well—perhaps even better than you do—though you've married into the family. Forgive me—it's all interest for you, and desire to see you keep straight with them. They'd one and all think there was *pollution* in coming in contact with one who could sympathise with the man who wrote that book!"

With that, she rose from her little stool at Bella's side, and Bella—her heart swelling with a dozen conflicting feelings—registered a vow on the spot to seek that man and his poor little wife on the morrow, and give them such comfort as it was in her poor power to bestow.

"It has been a thankless office, but I shall have my reward," Grace said modestly to herself, after saying her prayers that night; and deceitful as she was, she really meant it. In fact, her deceit was of so fine a kind, that it imposed upon herself. She really believed that she had been actuated by some higher motive than a desire to irritate Bella into too warm a partisanship for Stanley Villars. She really fancied at some moments that there had been more sincerity than spite in her endeavours. She really imagined that she had been a practical as well as a professing Christian this night! And so she told herself, with a sort of humble unction, "that she would have her reward"—which I sincerely hope she will.

——o——

CHAPTER XLII.

"THAT WAS RATHER STRANGE."

ALL this time, while I have been tracing out, link by link, the chain of events which led her there, Bella has been waiting by the side of Stanley Villars' couch. She had come to the meeting this morning with a sort of defiant secresy. Openly at breakfast had she ordered her carriage. Openly had she declared to Miss Harper that she was bent on a mission on which it did not suit her to be accompanied, to which declaration Miss Harper had listened calmly, with an unsuspicious air. It did not seem well to Grace to make Mrs. Claude confide. The withholding of confidence did not look so well; and, somehow or other, Miss Harper was not averse to seeing things that did not look well about Bella.

Bella had received a letter from her husband again this morning. "Ellen has been reading 'Never a Chance,'" he told her; "and she has done nothing but shudder ever since. I suppose he has run his head against a stone wall; but it's of no use saying a syllable about him here that can be considered justificatory. As we have drifted apart now, it's just as well that you never mention him, as you're apt to do, in your warm, honest way."

So her husband even, Claude the magnificent, on whose generosity she would far sooner have relied than on her own, thought that as the man was down—as he had fallen in the struggle—it would be quite as well to leave him there! Her blood curdled as she thought of what Stanley had been in those Denham days, and all his life before them. Her blood curdled; for when she remembered things at all, she remembered them with a terrible vividness that makes each recalled moment one of vital agony. "What *they* do, the cold-blooded wretches" (by "they" she meant her husband's family, and their own familiar friend, Miss Grace), "is nothing; but Claude should be different—Claude should remember my part in the business, and be merciful, or at least just.

She could not answer her husband's letter at once. She thought she would go and see Stanley first, and then, with the sight of him fresh in her mind, would come back and write such a letter to Claude as should at once bring him over triumphantly to her side. She had no design, when she started, of keeping aught she had done or was going to do from her husband. She meant to tell him all, the hour he returned. She had done no wrong; she was neither doing nor contemplating wrong. She was merely obeying the dictates of humanity; yet she took the first step into danger when she went off to see Stanley Villars without first writing to tell her husband that she was going to do so.

All hard feeling, all anger and indignation, against those who trampled on his name, and passed him by, vanished from her heart when she stood by the side of the man she had once loved, and marked as the stranger who sees him not daily is quick to mark, that he was dying. It might be a little sooner or a little later. He might linger here and there, could any stage be made easy and pleasant for him; but the last journey was entered upon—he was dying!

He opened his eyes, expecting, as I have said, to see his sister Florence; but he gave no start when he saw Bella, only his heart thumped audibly, as he asked—

"Ah! how did you find us out?"

He said "us," holding out a hand towards the wife, who stood in the background. There was something very touching to Bella in that gesture, which identified the poor girl he had married at once and entirely with himself. He was such a thorough gentleman, you see! Bella proudly and promptly recognised the old trait—a thorough gentleman! quick to spare the feelings of any one who was weaker than himself.

His old love, his former friend's wife, gave her hand into his with the willing warmth a sister might have shown.

"I found you out through your wife, Stanley," she said simply. "God forgive us all," she added passionately, "for not having found you out before!"

Her thought showed itself clearly to him. *She* saw that it was too late, that he was a dying man. He had felt this sorrowful truth strongly within himself once or twice of late; but it oppressed him with a new horror, now that it was illustrated, as it were, by the manner of another.

Wearily he turned his head round on the sofa pillow till only his profile was seen by the two women who stood over him, the one weeping with a wounding pain, the other wondering why this meeting, towards which she had decked the room, should be turning out so dismally. "I thought you would cheer him," she whispered presently to Bella; "he only wants rousing. He gets so dull when none of the men he knows are with him."

"They come often, I hope?" Bella asked, half hoping that "they" might be some of his old friends.

"Oh, yes! often; but then they smoke, and that makes him cough. When he gets rid of that cough, and needn't work so hard, he'll be all right, won't he? Won't you, Stanley?"

Marian asked this as we sometimes ask that which, in our own hearts, we dare not hope to have truly answered. For the first time it had struck her this day—this very hour, indeed—that there was a huge sorrow in store for her. For the first time she had come to the knowledge of the wounding truth that her husband's was no mere ordinary illness.

He managed to bring his head round to face them again, as his wife's words died away.

"Marian, my pet!" he said; and Bella loved him so dearly then, in her own pure, honest heart, for thus addressing the woman who had superseded her—"Marian, my pet, you must tell Mrs. Walsingham how we met first. You must tell her what an angel you have been to me; and then, dear, she will love you, and understand how I love you too! Come, cheer up, pet!"

He smiled his old, sweet, protecting smile upon Marian; but the poor "pet" could not "cheer up." The dread that had seized her was so heavy and so strange; she could not cheer up under it.

"You shall tell me yourself, Stanley," Bella said, softly, drawing the lovely young face, down which the scalding tears were now pouring, on to her own shoulders. "You shall tell me, yourself; and first tell me were you married when you came to see Claude and me?"

"Yes," he said.

"And you did not tell us. Oh! Stanley, that was not fair to me!"

"And he's been so ill since, and not one of his old friends has been near him; and I know that it's all because he married me-e-e," Marian sobbed out, miserably.

"Not a bit; his old friends will come, now they know where to find him, you silly child! Oh! I *wish* Claude were here," Bella said impetuously; "he's away now with his father, who's ill, you know; but as soon as he comes back I shall bring him."

Stanley's face fell.

"I shall not ask you many more favours, Mrs. Walsingham," he began, in a low voice. "Will you grant me one?"

"One, Stanley! a thousand if you will!" He looked at her very kindly.

"Rash, as of old, I see. Well,"—with a slight movement of his head, as though he would have thrown off the very memory of it—"that's past. This is my favour—I can't ask you not to come near us, now I see you, and find you——" He gulped, and could not finish his sentence, and Bella did what women are sure to do when they feel perplexed—wept copiously.

"Marian, go and get me a glass of lemonade, dear," he said, suddenly; and when Marian was gone on his mission, he went on, hurriedly—

"I couldn't say it before *her*, poor darling; but I'm dying, Bella, *you* know that."

"Don't, don't!" she implored; "don't say it, Stanley!"

"It's true—I know it—and as I have little enough to live for, it's as well. Don't let me think, though, that you press Claude to see me against his will, or that he refuses to grant your request, as I shall think, whether he comes or does not come, if you go away intending to ask him. Don't let me think that."

"He will come; you don't know Claude."

"I *do* know him," he cried, starting up on his elbow. "Bella! by the old love that was between us once, don't subject me to such a cursed humiliation. It's nearly all over with me; don't you be the one to stab me at the last."

Her voice went up almost with a wail as she replied—

"It is *too* hard, *too* hard!"

"It is too hard—don't you make it harder."

"Stanley, I *can't* argue, but how you wrong my husband!"

He sank back again, flushed and breathless.

"Do you see what I am now?" he asked. "Do you see that it must be over soon? Bella! it's the last thing I ask of you. You have found me out—God knows, through no will of mine—respect the secret you have surprised; let no one hear, through you, of me, and of my misery!"

He spoke bitterly and sternly, and Bella's heart throbbed to each accent of his, in fear, as it had never done in love.

"You are mistaken," she was beginning to plead; but he checked her, and repeated his charge, that through her no one should know of him and of his misery. "Unless you will promise me this, I will cut off the only pleasure left to me from the past. I will never see *you* again, and thus my poor little wife may lose a friend."

"But, unless I let it be known that she *is* your wife, how can I be her friend? as I will be, heaven help me, if I am permitted!"

But, with a man's perverseness, he would not see the force of this.

"You may be a friend to her when I am gone, but, while I live, I will live out of sight of the sneers that are given about me."

"Oh, Stanley! what a distorted view to take," she said; and then Marian came back with the lemonade, and the subject was dropped.

Mrs. Claude Walsingham sat there for an hour, after Marian came back with the lemonade, listening to the story of "how she (Marian) had met with Stanley." It was not such a very long story in itself, as the reader already knows; but it took a long time to tell, nevertheless, for Marian had not the art of telling things concisely. She interlarded her account with discursive passages—bringing in, without sufficient cause, the suggestions and suppositions Rayner, Miss Simpson, and others of that ilk, had indulged in. She told very artlessly how different her wedding had been to what she had always felt sure it would be if she married a gentleman. She did not say how different her after-married life had been! Poor girl! there was not the faintest shadow of complaint in the story that she told. It might have been bravery, or it might have been love, which kept her silent on this point. But whatever it was, Bella respected her for it.

I am not by any means sure that Mrs. Claude Walsingham listened attentively throughout the recital. Anxious, as she was, to know all about it—to hear how he had come down to the depths he was in now—she could not avoid letting her mind wander. Her attention would lapse perpetually, and she would find herself thinking of the life of love and comparative leisure and literary ease he had led down at the little village when her first engagement had been made. She could but think of this, and compare it with this dismal room, which even the rich roses could not brighten—this room, rife with evidences of his penury—this room, in which his life seemed doomed to ebb away. The contrast would have been saddening to any woman; to one of Bella's temperament, it was nearly maddening.

When the story of how he had met with and married Marian had been told, they spoke of his book—of that "Never a Chance" which she had read with a sickening interest, feeling it to be partly a reflection of its author's life. He mentioned it in a tone that strove to be slighting at first; but, with a woman's quickness, she discovered that he had a little pleasure in it still, and she fanned that pleasure as only a woman can.

"Everybody is speaking of it," she said, with the polite and surely pardonable deception that loving-kindness is apt to attempt to practise upon tyros in the craft sometimes—"everybody is speaking about it, and I see it so well mentioned by the reviews."

"Yes, it's gone into a third edition; but that means nothing; and several of the dailies have gone into raptures over it, which means less," he replied, with assumed indifference. "I shall do better than 'Never a Chance' by-and-by."

An eager look came over his pallid face as he said it, and his eyes kindled with such a terribly bright fire that the blinding tears came into Bella's eyes. It was hard for her to hear him say that, and to see him wasting away so surely and so fast. Whatever her sins towards him, grant that she was sufficiently punished for them now.

"And directly he makes a great deal of money by his books, we are going away to live in the country—ain't we, Stanley?" Marian asked.

"Somewhere near us, I hope," Bella suggested. And then the idleness of her hope, the bitter mockery of it, the futility of it, struck her with a hard, stunning force: it is so bad when pain ceases to be sharp and stinging, and becomes crushingly weighty and dull! Bella could not sit under hers any longer, so she rose abruptly, saying—

"May I come again to-morrow with more roses?"

They both said "Yes," in a tone that told her what a gleam of sunshine in the darkness of their lives her presence was to them. Then she bade them adieu, and drove home, bitterly lamenting that she had been surprised into giving a promise of keeping Claude in the dark as to Stanley's state and Stanley's straits.

Perhaps it would place poor Stanley Villars in a more noble and exalted light before the reader if I said, on Bella's departure he disburdened himself to his wife of the secret of that engagement the rupture of which had ruined him. But I cannot say that he did, since, in fact, he did nothing of the kind; and I hold him to be right in thus maintaining reserve on a point which it could do no manner of good to make public.

There is probably a closed closet in every man's heart—a little cell that may not be dark as the suspicious are apt to think it, but that is simply closed reverently in order to keep out prying eyes. Why should that closet be unlocked and ransacked for the benefit of one who is occupying or about to occupy the rest of the heart of which this cell is now but an unimportant corner? Whether the one who filled it once be dead or "only" gone away, she should at least be nameless to the new love, who will be wise if she never search for the little key that may open the door of the closet a man seems disposed to keep closed.

At any rate, Stanley Villars was not the style of man who opens his closet needlessly. Had the girl he married been of his own rank in life, she would probably have heard about the Bella Vane episode—heard of it as one hears of such things every day, carelessly. But since she had known nothing of it before, his tenderness for her—a tenderness that was less than love, perhaps, but more than friendship—determined him on keeping it from her still, on keeping silence and the closet closed.

I said that Bella went home bitterly lamenting having been surprised into giving a promise to Stanley of keeping Claude in the dark. She bitterly lamented something else also, which was the loss of that belief in the good that is in all men, which Stanley had once possessed. It was gone from him now. It was patent to her in everything he wrote, and said, and looked, that a mighty distrust had come in its place—a distrust that was so hard, bitter, and deep, that it poisoned all it dwelt upon. Remorsefully she thought about it, for his eyes had silently questioned her when she was reproaching him with it once, during her visit.

> "How could it different be?
> Since thou hast been pouring poison
> O'er the bloom of life for me!"

Grace had had a pleasant morning's shopping, and was very satisfied with the result of her labours, when Bella met her, before dinner. Miss Harper appeared to have quite got over the little difference of the day before. She had that great art of being able to seem as if she had not only entirely forgiven, but entirely forgotten—a thing which renders lymphatic women dangerous to deal with. Bella, on the contrary, was one of those unfortunates who cannot forget being intentionally offended immediately, however it may be about forgiving. So now she met Miss Harper a little more coldly than a wary woman would have done, and suffered Miss Harper to perceive that silence would be agreeable to her. She only addressed one question to Grace during dinner, in fact, which was—

"You went out with Lady Lexley this morning, I suppose?" To which Grace replied—"No, dear Mrs. Walsingham; by myself—I preferred it."

"That was rather strange, I think," Bella rejoined. Then she forgot the subject, and began wondering how she could at the same time be true to Stanley and to Claude.

——o——

CHAPTER XLIII.

VERY SORROWFUL.

Either the new novel, "Never a Chance," was having a tremendous run, or Mr. Mudie had taken a very insufficient number of copies. Whatever the cause, the result was that the subscriber who was, perhaps, most interested in the work, could not get the third volume the day she wanted it.

"It's really very annoying," Bella said, when they were back in the drawing-room after dinner; "*too* annoying! You're sure you've been more than once for it, Hill?"

Hill, standing at ease in the doorway, was very sure he had been more than once.

"Very annoying indeed," his mistress repeated in a thoroughly vexed tone; "a perfect nuisance! I wanted it particularly to-night. However!"

This "however" was intended, as the word at the end of a touchy sentence is usually intended, to terminate discussion, namely, and to be taken as a declaration of the speaker's feeling the futility of saying more about it.

But Hill had been in the disappointed lady's service many years, and he took an old servant's interest in whatever interested her. He never, by any chance, omitted to look for that special paragraph in the advertisement-sheet of the *Times*—"Notice. The new novel, 'Never a Chance,' at all the libraries"—in these days. He almost took a personal pride in it, pointing it out to the select in the servants' hall, and dwelling upon it as upon a work in which, some way or other, he had a share. Many had been the surreptitious glances he had given to the contents of the two first volumes at odd moments, while his mistress had kept them near her favourite couch, to be at hand the instant she was seated. And the fact of the third volume being unattainable just now was to the full as distressing to him as it was to her. For a very tender heart beat beneath that plush, and the plight in which the heroine was left at the end of the second volume was sorely harassing to his feelings. So now, when his mistress said "however," in a very dejected, disappointed tone, he conceived an idea, and delivered himself of it with surprising rapidity—

"There's the large library at Knightsbridge, Ma'am. No doubt it might be got there."

"You can't get it from Westerton's any more than from Mudie's, at night."

"It might be tried. Shall I go, ma'am?"

"Yes; I'm very anxious for it. Manage it if you can, Hill," Bella replied, looking steadfastly at Miss Harper, who was trying to look grieved at such a perverted taste, and failing. On which Hill departed, leaving his mistress hopeful about getting the book, but rather inclined to think she had been rash in bringing it to the front as she had done before this calm enemy.

As soon as the man was gone the calm enemy arrayed herself for battle; in other words, took up some netting, which she always had on hand, and placed herself with her back to the light.

"You seem tired, dear," she commenced.

"I am tired," Bella replied, briefly; then she felt aggrieved at her fatigue, which was purely mental, being noticed, and added, "What makes you think me so?"

"You look so pale and harassed; besides, your craving for the book is a sign that you're not up to doing anything better than reading it."

Bella gave a little gasping sigh. She was beginning to hate Miss Harper.

"Do let the book alone!" she said, almost angrily.

"Don't be afraid that I am going to reiterate what I said about it last night, dear!" she said gently. "I have made my protest. I have spoken once."

"Well, well, I know; don't, don't say any more about it, please."

"Not about the book, certainly," Grace replied, blithely, "since you can't listen to a dispassionate critique on anything that's written by any one you have known, but about the author—or, rather, about his sister."

In spite of herself, Bella made a small movement indicative of curiosity. She turned her head round slightly towards Miss Harper, and evidently listened. Miss Harper marked that she did this, and, therefore, kept silence and bided her time.

"Well?" Bella said, interrogatively, after a minute.

"Two, three—that's right," Grace said, counting her stitches aloud. "I thought I had got into a mess. What did you say?"

"I didn't say anything—I mean, I asked you what you said," Bella replied, giving a glance of deadly hatred at the netting.

"I! I didn't speak, dear."

"I beg your pardon; you did just now," Bella said, with difficulty restraining her inclination to tell Miss Harper not to call her "dear" any more, but to come into an open field and fight it out.

"What did I say?" Grace asked, artlessly. How odious a frank manner is when we see behind it, and discern the treachery it seeks to mask. Bella saw behind the artlessness now; but the clearness of vision would do her small service, she began to fear.

"What did you say? as if you had forgotten already. Why, something about Mr. Stanley Villars' sister that you want to tell me, and I want to hear."

"Oh-o! Oh-o!" Grace said, with a prolonged sound on the "o" that was meant to express how very unimportant the whole thing was to her. "Oh-o! yes, to be sure; she's going to be married."

"Florence?" She asked it with a blending of relief and amazement. There was balm in this at least, that the sister should be able to bury her dead and be happy, though the brother had been unable to so. Memories of Denham days—of the days when Florence had loved Claude, and let her love be seen—came back to Claude's wife now, as she uttered the single word "Florence."

"Yes, Florence is her name; a very pretty girl, but not too clever, I understand. That's rather well though, as the man she's going to marry is not too clever either."

"Her brother doesn't know it!" Bella said hastily, and then Grace glanced sharply at her, and she felt that she had made a mistake, and faltered.

"I mean, *does* her brother know of it?" she said, blushing, and trying to keep the colour down by speaking very distinctly; as if anything would keep the colour down in a woman's face when she has made a false step, and is liable to be found out. "I mean, *does* her brother know of it?"

"Of course you meant that, for how should you know that he didn't know of it, not having seen him," Miss Grace replied, letting each word fall steadily on her listener's ear. "No, I don't suppose Mr. Chester has thought it necessary to have an official communication made to Mr. Stanley Villars."

"Who's Mr. Chester?" Bella asked. She felt that there was animus against Stanley in these speeches which Grace Harper let fall. She felt that there was animus; but after all she was moving in the dark, being utterly at a loss to account for it in any way.

"Mr. Chester is the man Miss Villars is going to marry."

"Do you know him?"

"I have met him two or three times. Lord Lexley knows him very well. He's such a booby."

"Poor Florence!" Bella cried, warmly. "You don't mean that, do you, Grace?"

"Well, I do mean it. Funny, isn't it, my giving you news of the Villarses? Oh! and I'll tell you something else, too. Don't picture your pet author pining in solitude. He's doing nothing of the kind."

She laughed as she said it. Laughed with a wicked meaning, that shot like a bolt of ice through Bella's frame. Yet Mrs. Claude fancied that the promise he had extorted from her bound her to keep his secret and sit silent when he was aspersed. A sentence or two of the truth would have stopped the persecution she was enduring from innuendo, and left her nothing to fear. But, like a woman, she was over honourable in the wrong place, and so harm came of it.

As Grace's wicked laugh died away, Hill came in, radiant with success, and with the book, the coveted third volume, in his hand. Then Bella took it, and with a faint hope that she might stop the conversation, and put an end to what would have sounded to her like insulting hints, had she been able to fix a motive for them on Grace, said—

"You must excuse my talking any more, now I have got my book. I am tired, and I want to read. After tea I'll play."

"Certainly, I'll excuse you, dear. Just wait one moment though. Of course I couldn't tell you before Hill, but Mr. Stanley Villars has gone down indeed! He's leading an *awful* life, awful! Isn't it shocking?"

"I don't believe it," Bella said, with a sick qualm at her heart. "Who's your informant?"

"Lady Villars herself," Grace said, quietly, "I forgot to tell you I met her this morning."

"I thought you didn't know her."

"No more I did before to-day, but Fred Chester was with her, and he introduced me. You see he hunts down about us, so he introduced me to Lady Villars and his fair betrothed. It's always pleasant, if people are likely to meet in the country, to have met first in town, isn't it?"

Grace was relapsing into the old stolid simplicity, but Bella's belief in this quality was shaken now.

"It's strange you shouldn't have mentioned all this to me before, as you are staying with me," Mrs. Claude said, with a slight air of the injured hostess about her.

"Yes, it always does seem so mean not to say where one has been, and whom one has seen, doesn't it?" Grace asked, innocently.

"It also sounds strangely that Lady Villars should have reposed a confidence in you immediately. What did Florence say when Lady Villars told that—that *falsehood* about Stanley?"

"Miss Villars and Mr. Chester had moved to another counter—they didn't hear it; after all," Grace continued, in an explanatory tone, "it wasn't a confidence. I said I was staying with you, and then we spoke of other things."

"Suppose we speak of other things now,"

Bella rejoined, with a lightness she was far from feeling. She scented danger, or, if not danger, at least difficulty, of some sort or other, but she did not know from which quarter to expect it; she was far from sure as to whether she feared it for herself entirely, even.

"I *wish* I had written to dear Claude before I went there yesterday," she thought; "I should have told him, and then there would have been an end of it; now I don't know what to do."

After this she was suffered to peruse her hardly-gained volume in peace, but there was no pleasure in the perusal. She was haunted the whole time by an uneasy feeling of having been indiscreet, and of therefore being on the high road to mischief—a feeling that very fortunately pervades the breast of every conscientious woman whenever she is guilty of that which, if less than a crime, is unquestionably more than a folly—concealment and secresy.

Mrs. Claude Walsingham had a burning desire the following morning to ask Miss Harper when she was going, and to hint that she need not stand upon the order of her departure, but take it at once. However, hospitality is a sacred thing. This well-reputed young woman, with the colossal power of making herself unpleasant faultlessly, had been entrusted to her charge; therefore she must keep the precious deposit until time, or chance, or something equally kind, relieved her of it.

"When Claude comes back, I'll confess to him that I *hate her*, and her thick white skin," Bella thought to herself. "Oh! good gracious! the Markham was bad enough, but she was better than this!"

Miss Harper really was like a huge white elephant upon her hands. Grace was just one of those "fine" creatures that when hated at all, are hated with a tall, fat hatred that corresponds with their bulk, and is a wearisome burden to the feeler of it. Miss Harper was ponderous, mentally and bodily, when once you regarded her as other than a vast expanse of harmless, well-meaning white flesh.

For two hours and a half after breakfast, Mrs. Claude Walsingham sat and loathed her guest and her guest's netting. The round, well-covered white fingers caught her eyes and chained them, turn which way she would. Had the girl been awkward with these fingers, or quick with them—had they been other than the subtly slow, unvarying-in-purpose things they were, Bella could have borne them better. As it was, they acted on her nerves as organ-grinding or street ballad-singing does on mine and yours, fellow-sufferer from metropolitan harmony. They made her feel that she couldn't sit still, and that there was no relief to be gained by motion, and that anything on earth would be preferable to that combination of white cotton and whiter hands. They made her wish that Miss Harper ended at her throat like a cherub. They wrought her up into a highly nervous frame of mind, in fact, in which she went forth once more to see Stanley Villars.

She found Mrs. Stanley in tears in the passage when she arrived, and she took the poor little baby-faced beauty, who was learning this world's sharp lesson of sorrow so early, to her warm, womanly heart, literally as well as figuratively. She put her arms round the girl and held her within them closely, never thinking of Marian as other than of one to whom Stanley was dear, and who, she trusted, was dear to Stanley.

"I'm so glad you're come!" Marian sobbed. "Oh!" I'm so glad you're come!"

"What is it—tell me?" Bella asked soothingly. "How is your husband? See! I have brought him grapes with the roses to-day!"

Marian looked at the basket—the basket Bella had arranged with her own hands—of grapes, and mosses, and roses. It was very pretty—very pretty, indeed; but the sight of it evidently brought no comfort to Marian to-day.

"Shall we go in to him?" Bella suggested, trying to edge her way out of the passage, which, by reason of being partially blocked up with all the rubbish that had accumulated during the whole term of their residence, was not a pleasant place to stand in.

"It's no use," Marian said, rocking her head backwards and forwards on her shoulders, dolefully.

"Why no use?" Bella asked, in a whisper.

"He's gone o—out!" Marian said, getting on her feet, and relapsing into the manner of her sex and time of life, by trying to smoothe her hair and adjust her belt and collar simultaneously.

"Gone out!" Bella repeated after her. Then Mrs. Walsingham walked in and sat down on the couch where Stanley had been lying the day before. "Gone out—in the state he is in!"

"He's ever so much worse to-day!" Marian said, piteously; "he was ever so much worse after you left yesterday. He *would* sit up, all I coudl say; and then it was nothing but drink and write, drink and write, all day, and all night, till he's half mad, I think!"

"Do you know where he is gone?" Bella asked—not, in truth, with any real desire for information respecting his destination, but simply because she felt that it would be better for them both that there should be speech, than that silence should reign.

"I don't know—perhaps down to the office, or up to Mr. Bligh's; shall we go and see?" Marian said eagerly. It seemed to her quite in the order of things that the pair of them should forthwith form an expedition, and start in search of Stanley, and bring him back bodily when found; but it did not seem in the order of things to Mrs. Claude Walsingham.

"We can send my man with a note, that you shall write, to either of those places you speak of," Bella said, "and I will wait here with you till he comes back. What's the office?"

"His newspaper place. He would be sure to go there, if he could get as far; but he lost so much blood last night!"

"Lost so much *what?*" Bella asked, with a tremble in her tone that told of the pain she felt. "Lost so much *what?*"

"Blood! Oh, I didn't tell you that he broke a blood-vessel! It is all *so* miserable, Mrs. Walsingham; there is such a lot of it to tell," Marian said, putting up her hands, and hiding the light of day from her pale-worn young face.

——o——

CHAPTER XLIV.

A TRIO OF MATRONS.

POOR BELLA! She wanted so much to be "good," very, very good now, and to make everything pleasant for all in whom she was interested. But the time seemed past for doing this. It was "too late" to make amends.

Her heart ached with a gnawing anguish that is only known to those who feel they have been guilty, as she sat there in that dingy room, and thought of Stanley Villars, and, shudderingly, of the broken blood-vessel. She knew so well—for she was a quick-feeling, sympathetic woman—how this last evil had been caused. Mental exertion and mental pain had strained some delicate fibre; and the tide of life had rushed out, and would be liable to rush out at any moment.

To say that she was very sorry, very miserable, for all this, would not express to you a tithe of what such a woman as Bella suffers under such circumstances. The wages of her fault were not paid to herself; they were paid, seemingly, to the one against whom the fault had been committed. She, the sinner, was in purple and fine linen, while he, the sinned against, was in sackcloth and ashes.

The sense of her own helplessness in the matter depressed her, and made her appear so far less bright a woman than Marian had hitherto deemed her new friend to be. There had been previously an amount of warmth, earnestness, force, and brilliancy, about Mrs. Claude Walsingham: and these things are calculated to give the casual observer the idea of carrying all things before them. Marian had imagined all manner of good resulting from the dawning of Bella. But now Bella looked overcast—overcast as any common mortal, who wasn't full of beauty and vigour, might have looked. Marian stood looking at her with a vague sense of disappointment, as she sat on the couch, doing no more, and making things no better, than any other woman.

At last the wife spoke, and her words were wise, with the wonderful wisdom of love.

"Mrs. Walsingham, could you help me to find out his sister? Never mind what they say of me, or think of me. I ought, as he won't do it, to find out his sister, and tell how ill he is."

"I can take you to her," Bella replied, starting up; "I will take you at once."

"Is it very far? should we be long away?"

"We could go there and tell Florence all she need know, and be back in an hour," Mrs. Walsingham replied. "It *is* Stanley's doing, you know. He has cut himself off from his family. They would never have left him in the lurch."

"He had some good reason for it, I think," Marian answered, putting on a shawl that was lying on the table as she spoke. "He has not turned to what he is now for any little thing, I'm sure. Sometimes, when he is quite himself, I seem to see what he must have been before he had his grief. *You've* known him a long time; do *you* know what changed him?"

The question was asked in perfect simplicity and good faith, but the questioned shrank within herself as she heard it. She *did* know, God help her! The knowledge of it was the cross she had to bear. She did know; and, as she hoped and prayed to serve, she dared not tell his wife.

"He has not got on well; I suppose that's it." She tried to say it steadily, but her voice shook.

"And his marriage has kept him back more, hasn't it?" Marian asked mournfully. "But he did tell me once that he was glad he married me. I wish he hadn't, if it has harmed him; I wouldn't have harmed him for the world."

The girl was weeping wearily before her sentence closed; and wearily the lady, who knew the truth so well, answered—

"*You* are not the one who has harmed him; the harm was done before he knew you."

"How do you know?"

The sudden cessation of Marian Villars' tears, the quick glance she flashed out through her wet eyelashes, put Claude Walsingham's wife on her guard at once. She remembered that she was Claude Walsingham's wife, and that to reproach or point to herself as unworthy would be to reproach and ask for condemnation for him. She gulped down the desire to make a clean breast of it, which had almost overcome her when Marian so piteously bewailed her own supposed share in Stanley's downfall; and replied quietly—

"Didn't you tell me yourself how you found him first? His grief and his restlessness had come before then, evidently."

"I suppose they had," Marian said softly. "I'm ready now. Do you think I shall do good?"

"You can do no harm," Bella replied; but though she said this, she was rather nervous as to the result of their mission. That her nervousness was fully shared she was well aware; for more than once on their way to Sir Gerald Villars', Marian broke the silence with a gasping sigh, and the words—

"I won't care what they say, or look, or think of *me*, if they'll only remember that he is their brother." The unaccredited ambassador was unmistakably quailing.

As for Bella, the only way in which she supported her courage was by reminding herself constantly that she "was in for it now." She had undertaken it, and must perforce go through with it; but she felt morally sure that, both by Claude and Stanley, she would be made to pay for having mixed herself up in the business.

Yet she had done no more than humanity had a right to expect from her. She had found a man in dark despair, in penury, in ill health; and the certain conviction was hers that she had been the cause of his fall into these things. However weak and erring he had been—however blindly perverse, and wickedly wasteful of the good gifts God had given him, which no woman could destroy—she could but feel herself to have been the first cause of the weakness and error, of the blind perversity and reckless wastfulness. What amends she could it was her bounden duty to make. This she knew. She also knew that she had set about making it in the wrong way. "*Why* didn't I write and tell Claude about it yesterday, before it grew?" she thought, as she found herself walking alone into Lady Villars' room, having thought it well that Marian should wait in the carriage till the ice was broken.

There were three of Lady Villars' sisters in the room when Bella entered. She saw at once that they were sisters, and shrewdly guessed that they had come up for the wedding.

"I think Florence is taking off her habit," Lady Villars said, "or else she's trying on some dresses; would you hear?" addressing one of her sisters; "she'd so like to see Mrs. Walsingham."

"And I want to see her very much," Bella commenced in an agitated tone. "The fact is —I hope you won't think——" She broke down, and Lady Villars began to smile, and continued the same till her little short nose was almost lost in the plumpness of her cheeks.

"Think you late in your congratulations? Oh, dear, no! It's a very recently arranged affair—a brilliant match for the dear girl—if she were my own sister I couldn't have desired a better."

"I suppose not," Bella replied, looking at the aforesaid sisters. She did not mean to look sarcastic or anything else antagonistic to the "Carrie" interest just now; but she could not help feeling and showing that she felt that Lady Villars' fraternal toleration would not have been very severely taxed. The marriage that was pronounced fitting for Miss Villars, might surely have been held suitable for one who owed all of social consideration that she enjoyed to the Villars alliance.

"I suppose not. No, it was not congratulations I came to offer." Then she rose from the seat she had taken on first entering the room, and said hurriedly, "I had better not go round the subject. Stanley is dying—and his wife has come here with me (she's in my carriage) to tell you so."

Lady Villars shook her well-arranged little head resolutely.

"I'm sorry you've permitted yourself to be made a tool of," she said. Then she turned her head slightly over her shoulder, fixed an obedient sister with her cool blue eyes, and whispered in a tone that was not intended to reach, and that did not reach Bella's ear—"Stop Florry from coming."

"A tool of!" Bella repeated the words warmly. She had anticipated its all being such easy work, as far as the Villarses were concerned. The sole difficulties she had foreseen had been with Stanley and her husband.

"A tool of! you don't understand——"

Lady Villars stopped her with an ejaculation.

"Good gracious! how cruelly you have been imposed on!" she cried. "*We* know all about it—the whole story."

"And you're leaving him to live if he can, and die if he must?" Bella asked it with a biting scorn, that made Lady Villars tingle. "You can't know the whole story: your brother has struggled till he can struggle no longer; don't stay to think whether he has been to blame or not, but help him up again."

"I am sure you mean well," Lady Villars replied, in the tone evil-disposed people use to little children when wrath is in possession of the latter; "but you are so *dreadfully* mistaken. It's shameful of Stanley—it's the worst thing I have heard of him yet—to have let you mix yourself up with the matter!"

"Won't you see his wife?"

"His wife, Mrs. Walsingham!"

"Won't you send his brother to him?—there's his address;" she forced a card, on which she had written down the name and number of the street in which Stanley lived, into Lady Villars' unwilling hand.

"Sir Gerald will please himself about going," Lady Villars replied, adjusting her fair plump face and insignificant features as severely as she could; "but as a married man, I should *hope* he'd have the good taste to keep clear of a den of profligacy!"

"You do not believe what you are saying, Lady Villars! You are trying to harden your own heart with phrases."

"I am striving to save myself from being influenced by unhealthy sham emotions," Lady Villars replied, spitefully.

"Let me see Florence!" Bella urged, not heeding the insinuation.

The third sister, who had remained quiescent during the interview, now rose, and said she would "go and look for Florry." Presently she came back. "Florence is not come home," she said.

Bella gave vent to an impatient exclamation.

"She is out, you tell me, now; but will you tell her what I came about when she comes home?"

Lady Villars paused for an instant or two before she answered; then she said—

"You can hardly be serious, Mrs. Walsingham, in wishing to bring Miss Villars into communication with her brother's mistress; if you choose to risk your own reputation so recklessly, I must ask you to consider Miss Villars'."

"No woman's reputation will be endangered by intercourse with the poor young girl Stanley has married, to their mutual cost——"

"Married!" Lady Villars struck in scoffingly. "Really, Mrs. Walsingham, if you persist in showing yourself all over London with her, I must beg that you will not again subject me to the insult of having that creature seen at my door. I wonder Major Walsingham permits it —if he knows anything about it!"

She added this last clause suddenly, on seeing Bella wince when surprise at her husband's "permitting it" was expressed. It was a very telling volley. It routed the already nearly exhausted enemy.

"My husband will judge for himself, Lady Villars."

"And I will judge for *myself* in this matter," Lady Villars replied. She was very much afraid that Florence might perchance escape from her guileless detainers, and come down and find Bella, when the whole thing would explode in an explanation.

Mrs. Claude Walsingham felt that she was vanquished, and it was very hard for her to feel this, with her love of ordering things according to her own inclination. It was very hard to go out of that room, and that little, plump, short-nosed woman's presence, with a sense of defeat upon her. It was harder still to feel that the defeat must be made known at once to that anxious young watcher in the carriage.

She made no pretence of offering her hand to Lady Villars. There was hostility in her heart against that admirable matron, whose course of conduct was so correct that all men's tongues wagged in praise of "it," but never of "her." Bella felt that, on the surface, right was with Lady Villars. The latter was cold-blooded, cold-hearted, calculating, cruel, but she was very correct. The diabolical ingenuity with which she brought her virtuous scruples to the aid of her old spite against Stanley, staggered the woman in whose breast resentment and malice never obtained.

As Mrs. Claude Walsingham walked away through the hall, after bidding her hostess farewell with a cold bow, Lady Villars asked her sister—

"How did you keep Florence away?"

"I told her there was a bore calling—that was enough." Then the truthful, honest, young creature got behind the curtain, and peeped out at Mrs. Walsingham's carriage and contents.

"Don't look! What's she like?" Lady Villars asked in a breath.

"An impudent-looking thing."

"Don't let them see you on any account! Golden hair, hasn't she?"

"Yellow!" the sister answered, scornfully.

"Ah! Piesse and Lubin are universal benefactors in these days. I hope Mrs. Walsingham will get it from her husband," Lady Villars continued, letting her words out in a series of snaps.

"So wrong of her," the sisters chimed in. The sisters had a habit of chiming in with any sentiment, and of chorussing any remark the wealthy married one of their band elected to make. They too, young innocents, saw visions and dreamt dreams; and the dreams were all of days of delight at Gerald's shooting-box, in the autumn; and the visions were more glorious still, of a season in town, next year, under Carrie's wing.

"Wrong! it's idiotic!" Lady Villars said, sharply.

"Yes; what has she to do with it?" the obliging sister went on. "How violent she was, Carrie; I expected to see ever so much prettier a woman. There was such a fuss about her."

"There was only a fuss about her because there was no one else to make a fuss about. Florence is much better looking."

Lady Villars knew that Florence's beauty was not precisely the theme which would be most pleasant to her present auditors. But she was thoroughly sisterly in her treatment of the three young beings whose hopes for the future she held in her own plump hand. She kept them under by allusions to Florence's manifold superiorities over them, just as she kept Florence under by allusions to the many losses they sustained through her.

"Well, I don't so over-much admire Florence either; she has but one expression."

"Ah! but that's such a sweet one," Lady Villars replied, laughing. "She never troubles herself to be envious and jealous, and so her face keeps fair and smooth."

Mr. Chester was coming to Sir Gerald's to dinner this day, and whenever he was asked to dinner he had a habit of coming an hour-and-a-half too soon in order, as he expressed, that he "might have a little talk with them." As the whole family were generally engaged in their dressing-rooms at these times, he ordinarily spent this hour-and-a-half in standing about desolately, and wishing he "hadn't come so soon." This day, however, Lady Villars left word that when he came he should be shown into the library, and she herself told at once that he had arrived.

She was down upon him before he had had time to offer up one regret on the shrine of his self-importance, for that he had come to solitude. She was cool and crisp, and entirely herself again, now; indeed it was an attribute of hers to be neither readily nor long ruffled by anything.

Extending both hands to him as she entered (how he wished that Florence would learn that "little way" of Carrie's!), she commenced—

"My dear Fred, I have something very important to say to you; how *good* of you to have come in such nice time."

He thought that it was very good of himself, considering how often he had done it before, and how invariably melancholy had claimed him for her own in consequence.

"I haven't even told my husband yet. I feel that it's so essential that *you* should know it at once."

"Nothing gone amiss, eh?" he asked, nervously. He knew very little of Florence's character. It occurred to him as just within the bounds of possibility, that she might have gone away through a back window, with a little bundle, to the arms of some young Lochinvar of whom he had never heard.

"No; nothing gone wrong *yet*," Lady Villars replied, with an emphasis that made him feel that something had intervened to stop the flight—say a nail, on which Florence's dress had caught, or an accident on the railway along which she was speeding.

"No; nothing gone wrong *yet*, and I do hope that your sound sense will step in and save us from anything going wrong at all. You know about Stanley?"

She asked it with a very well done look of pity for the sinner, and detestation for the sin. Fred Chester nodded assent.

"I positively shudder," Lady Villars continued, with a little shake that was not nearly as well done as the look—"I positively shudder to think of it!"

"So would any one," Fred Chester said, nobly forgetting, in the pleasure of being the chosen witness of the shudderings of such a "charming woman" as Lady Villars, even to attempt the smallest bit of "business" on his own account.

"The woman! the creature! forced her way here to-day." Lady Villars spoke in a low tone, as though she were afraid of polluting the silky ears of a King Charles spaniel, who was lying on the rug, with the infamous tidings.

"By Jove! you don't mean to say so?"

"I do. Oh! it's shocking! Mrs. Claude Walsingham came with her."

"Hulloa! if Mrs. Claude Walsingham came with her, that looks rather—eh?—doesn't it?—eh?"

"Doesn't it look what?" she replied sharply.

"Why, rather as if there were some truth in what Flo thinks—that he's married!"

"Flo thinks!" she repeated, sarcastically. "You *must* know so *much* better."

"But Mrs. Walsingham is——"

"A very foolish, rash, impetuous person," she interrupted, "and I fear, I very much fear, not at all too strait-laced herself. We shall hear more of Mrs. Claude Walsingham one day, I'm afraid. That's not the point, however. What do *you* wish about Florry?"

She asked him "what he wished?" as a matter of form, in order that she might tell her husband afterwards "what Fred Chester said."

"I hardly know."

"Of course one hardly does know," she said, encouragingly. "I suppose you'll never suffer Florence to see her."

"Oh! never!" he answered with as much decision as an imperfect comprehension of what she had said could supply him with.

"And till Stanley gives up the connection you'll never suffer Florry to see him either?"

To this he replied, "Certainly not!" and then Lady Villars, having got all she wanted out of him, left him to his own devices and desolation, and went up to her husband's dressing-room, and told him of the raid that had been made upon her respectability that day, and of Fred Chester's firm, and "certainly proper," determination "never to let one of the lot come in contact with Flo while Stanley had that creature with him."

"What I have gone through to-day no one can tell!" Carrie said, as she saw her husband look black.

"It's an astonishing thing that you women will always be deuced hard just where you should be lenient," he said angrily. "I have known you so uncommonly gentle in your judgment of other men, and so wonderfully ready with the argument that if you examine the private characters of all your male acquaintances, with a view to purging your list, you'd soon not have a name left upon it, that I can't quite understand your animosity against Stanley."

"Then I must be content to do my duty and be misjudged, Gerald," she said, meekly. "I will only say that dear Florry has been a great anxiety—thank God, I shall soon be relieved of it!"

"Thank God that you will—since you're always hurling it at my head," he replied without looking at her.

Mrs. Claude Walsingham had gone back to her carriage with a sense of her defeat upon her strongly. How should she tell the hard truth—that they had no pity for and no faith in her—to the poor, worn-out young wife, who was waiting? How should she do it? How could she have the heart to do it? She asked herself this question, sadly, and she could give herself no answer.

She was saved the trouble of telling it in words. Marian lent forward eagerly as Bella came through the doorway and down the steps, and saw that in the face of her beautiful friend there was sorrow and rage, and little else.

"They don't care for him any more," the girl said, in a low harsh voice, as Bella seated herself in the carriage. "I can see they don't care—they'll let him die, and I'm the one——"

She stopped and burst into tears, and Bella said—

"I did not see his own brother or sister—I only saw his sister-in-law. She's cold and heartless; but the others are different—don't despair."

But the girl only shrank more closely into the corner of the carriage, sobbing.

"Oh, Mrs. Walsingham! if I could only be unmarried from him, I'd leave him at once, and—then—they'd come to him; and I'd—do—it—though I love him so."

The words came out from the bursting heart with such a mighty power of truth, that they forced from Bella the inward prayer—

"God forgive those who are trying to fix the stigma on her of *not* being his wife—I can't."

Stanley had not returned when they went back.

"I shall come again to-morrow," Bella said, and then she kissed Marian, and tried to force something into the girl's hand. But Marian started, and shook her head, and put the proffered gift back.

"No, Mrs. Walsingham; not that," she said, shaking her head. "It may come, but not yet."

"Oh, Marian! and I have so much," Bella pleaded.

"And I have *nothing*, but the hope that Stanley will never be brought so low as to live on charity through *me*. Don't be angry, Mrs. Walsingham, it's all I have."

—o—

CHAPTER XLV.

A THUNDERSTORM.

THE servant who opened the door to Mrs. Claude Walsingham on her return home from her mission of mercy, looked so pleasurably excited that Bella naturally felt convinced that something horrible had happened. "Master's home, m'm," he said, as his mistress stepped into the hall.

"Home is he? where?" she asked hastily.

"And master's father is dead, m'm," the man replied, with the proud resolve to be the one to break the bad news, which is a strong passion in the breasts of the lower ten thousand. The man had no ill or any other feeling connected with Mr. Walsingham deceased, but he told of that gentleman's death with an unctuous satisfaction, slightly—and but slightly—dashed with sorrow, that was refreshing to behold.

Mrs. Walsingham started. So the kindly, polite old gentleman, her father-in-law, was dead! Well, she would have felt it very much had she been down at the Court at the time. She had been away from his atmosphere for some months now, however; so, though she started, it was neither with great sorrow nor great horror. It was merely with surprise.

"Dead is he! Where's your master?"

"Gone out, m'm. Mrs. Markham came back with master."

"Oh, did she!" Bella said, walking on. She did not ask "where Mrs. Markham was?" It occurred to her that she would know that soon enough. "I wish Claude had waited in till I came home," she thought, as she went into her dressing-room, "then I could have told him about poor Stanley at once."

It came upon her strongly now, as she reflected how much she had to tell "about Stanley," that she had been unwise in that she had not written some of it to her husband. It was rather a long story. Not so much a long story, perhaps, as a difficult story to tell with the conviction upon her that a portion of it should have been told before.

It lengthened and grew more intricate as she sat there thinking about it. Lady Villars' remarks would have to be repeated; and Lady Villars' remarks and Lady Villars' manner had not been pleasant to Bella, even in the midst of the fervour and heat of her philanthropic mission. But now, when that fervour had toned down a bit, and that heat had cooled by reason of her having come out of the presence of the creators of it, Lady Villars' manners and remarks seemed more unpleasant still, and she felt that Claude would be righteously angry at his wife having subjected herself to them.

There was an element in Claude's nature which his wife had always been conscious of, without ever having called upon herself to define. It was an element which he kept under greatly, but still it was *there*. It was that which brought the red spots to his eyes when anger seized his soul. It was a strong, hot, furious fierceness, in fact, which could be very cruel. He had given vent to a little of it on the occasion of that fall she had had from Devilskin under Jack's auspices. "Ah! it doesn't do to sit and think when one's nervous," she said, abruptly starting to her feet, after dwelling for a minute or two on that incident. "I'll go and see the Markham, and apologise for not having been in to receive her, when I didn't know she was coming."

Accordingly, Bella having heard from her own maid that Mrs. Markham had installed herself in a suite of rooms that seemed good to her, went off to welcome and condole with her guest. Went prepared to fulfil all the rites of hospitality, and avert with kindly words any wrath, the seeds of which might have been sown during her inopportune absence.

Her tap at the door was answered by a lachrymose "come in" from Grace Harper, and entering, she found that young lady installed on the little couch at the foot of the bed, with a brace of pearly tears on her nose, and a list of mourning habiliments to be procured in her hand—all for the deceased Mr. Walsingham. Mrs. Markham was seated opposite to her friend, recruiting herself after her journey with sherry and biscuits, and enlivening the repast by giving details connected with the "late mournful event."

"I am so grieved to hear," Bella was commencing as she hastily advanced towards her sister-in-law; and, to do her justice, she *was* grieved the instant she saw Mrs. Markham, for Mrs. Markham's face was care-worn and pain-lined. "I am so grieved, Ellen; and that I should have been out too!"

She had given out her hand frankly towards Claude's sister, and now she bent her face forward to greet Mrs. Markham with a kiss. It was such a sweet, glowing, lovely face that was extended, that no man or woman on earth could have resisted giving it the salute it asked for. Mrs. Markham bent her stiff neck with a jerk, and brought her mouth down with a bony kiss—a kiss in which Bella felt nothing so much as the teeth—on Mrs. Claude's bright cheek.

"We must submit to the Lord's decrees," she said, as she brought her kiss to a conclusion, snapping it off suddenly in a way that seemed to show that she inwardly protested against the weakness of which she had been guilty. The remark not being one that was exactly calculated to set the ball of conversation rolling, Bella held her peace for an instant or two, and then said—

"Yes; I'm so sorry I was not at home. I wish Claude had waited for me."

Mrs. Markham reseated herself, and then assumed that most terrific of all feminine expressions—the mysterious. When a woman puts on this, a home in the howling wilderness would be preferable to a boudoir, all silk taboret and Sèvres china, in her vicinity.

"It certainly would have been better had you been at home on Claude's arrival," Mrs. Markham said presently, and her tones were a degree and a half more mysterious than her looks. The stranger on whose ear they might have fallen might have been forgiven for imagining that murder, arson, and general unpleasantness had been the result caused by Bella's absence. "It would have been better—much better," she repeated, emphatically.

"I hope you've been made quite comfortable?" Bella asked, trying to ignore all the disagreeable meaning in her sister-in-law's voice.

"Thank you, I have," Mrs. Markham replied, icily.

"The woman won't let me like her, however well inclined I am," Bella thought. Then she asked aloud—

"Mind you command me absolutely, Ellen. Let me save you all trouble about the—about the mourning, I mean," she added in a lower key, touched to solemnity by her subject.

"You are very kind." Mrs. Markham spoke in a rigid tone. Intuitively Bella felt that something had gone wrong.

"Did Claude say where he was going? and what have you been about while I have been out, Grace?" Bella asked in a breath.

Miss Harper's lips parted, but before she could utter a word Mrs. Markham said—

"Claude did *not* say where he was going. He was met on his return home, in grief for the loss of a parent, by news which upset him considerably."

"What was that news? and who gave it to him?" Mrs. Claude asked quickly.

Mrs. Markham sipped her wine and crumbled her biscuit, not "nervously"—she was not the sort of woman to relapse into nervousness on slight provocation—but tremulously. Her tremulousness usually arose from anger, Bella knew; and, knowing this, Bella watched it somewhat anxiously.

"What was that news? and who gave it to him?" Mrs. Claude repeated her question with that slight additional emphasis which betokens the birth of an intention not to be trifled with in the speaker. It was very slight in her case, but she, not being a gusty or showy-mannered woman, marked all these fluctuations of feeling very delicately, though clearly.

"What the news was you will hear soon enough. I cannot tell you who told it to him."

Mrs. Markham spoke in a monotone. She had told herself that it behoved her to betray neither anger nor excitement; therefore she adopted that tone which is of all others most calculated to drive the one who hears it into angry despair. Turbulent violence may be endured and baffled; but calm virulence is simply maddening in its effects.

"Don't torture me by speaking in that way," Bella said quickly. "Do *you* know anything of this, Grace?" she continued, looking Miss Harper fixedly in the face.

'Nothing more than you've heard from dear Mrs. Markham," Grace replied, meekly.

Bella's heart swelled. It seemed to her that her husband had been wanting in certain attributes with which she had loved to endow him, in having left her to the mercy of these discreet women, who knew, and looked, and thought all manner of things which they were too guarded to say. Her heart swelled, and the angry tears started into her eyes. She had no intention of suffering them to fall in such company, however, so she walked to the door, saying—

"Since I can be of no assistance to you now, I'll leave you till Claude comes home."

"You dine at the old hour, I suppose?" Mrs. Markham asked, coldly.

"Yes, the same. I shall go and rest now." Then she went off to her own dressing-room again, and coiled herself up on a couch, and tried to care for the last pages of "Never a Chance," and forget the shadowy doubts that had been created in her mind. But she could do nothing but move about restlessly, and wish that Claude would come and say out the news that he had heard when he came home.

He came at last. She, starting up and throwing down her book at the sound of his foot in the passage which led down to her dressing-room, went forward to the door to meet him. Even as she went forward hastily, her quick ear detected in the sound of his step that there was something wrong.

His gaze met hers the instant the door was opened, and the red spots that came into his eyes when he was angry were in them now, as they met his wife's. He kept his hand on the door-handle still, too, instead of putting it round Bella, as he was wont to put it when she had her arms round his neck and her face on his breast, as she had them now.

She had seen in the momentary glance she had given that his face looked pale and hard. Perhaps he was grief-stricken only, for he had loved his father well, though with none of the warm affection his father had lavished upon him. "Dear Claude!" she said, and her voice was very soothing and sympathetic, "I am so sorry, dear! and that I shouldn't have been in to hear it from you first when you came."

He just brushed her brow with his lips in reply, and then he moved her away from him and said—

"Here! let me get into the room!"

She stood back then, feeling rebuffed and discomfited, and let him get into the room. When he was in, he flung himself on the couch, first flinging the volume that she had been reading into the corner of the room.

His doing that reminded her of the Stanley Villarses, and of all she had to tell him. "He is worn out with his journey and his loss, poor boy," she thought. "It will take his mind from his own sorrows a little if I tell him about poor Stanley."

"Claude, dear, I have something to say to you," she began, sitting down by his side, and laying her hand on his shoulder. She gave a wistful, pleading look into his face as she spoke, and somehow the expression recalled the one she had worn the first night of their meeting in that old cathedral town, when she had implored him to remain at the inn, "in order that she might feel that she had a friend in the house."

"And I've something to say to *you*," he replied, banishing the remembrance of that expression, with all its softening influences, as he spoke. At the same time he took a letter from his pocket, and half opened it, glancing down at its contents in a way that seemed to imply that it had some connection with that matter on which he was going to speak to her.

"What is it, Claude?" she asked; and her breath failed her as she asked it, for she, too, had glanced at the half-opened letter, and recognised the characters in which it was written as being identical with that anonymous letter of which mention has been already made.

"Is it true that you have been—by Jove! I won't give you an opportunity of deceiving me further," he interrupted himself, savagely—"it *is* true that you have been flaunting about town with a couple of—of women with whom it's not too creditable to be seen, and picking up with nice associates!"

"Claude, stop——"

"When I have done," he went on, ruthlessly. "It's true—I see it in your face. Why the devil didn't you attend to what Miss Harper said?"

"Attend to what Miss Harper said?" she repeated wonderingly.

"Yes. When I read this letter—*there's* a pleasant epistle to greet a fellow the first thing after such an absence from home as mine has been." He picked the letter from his pocket again as he spoke, and flung it into her lap.

"What is it?" she asked. "Who's it from?"

"It's anonymous———"

Before the word was well out of his mouth, she had flung the letter from her with a gesture of loathing and contempt that was so genuine and so strong that he paused to look at her. Presently he resumed—

"If you'll read it you'll see———"

"If I'll read it?" she repeated, sorrowfully. "Claude! Can you ask me to do it—can you believe I would do it?"

"Then I must speak to you about its contents," he said, sternly; "which may be more unpleasant to you still. It was to save you the pain of hearing the truth in so many hard words that I gave you the option of reading the letter which made me acquainted with it."

"With what?"

"The truth."

She bowed her head. "I will hear it from you, Claude," she said, quietly. She was remembering very vividly now how remorse had oppressed her for having read an anonymous slander of him.

"You will not deny, I suppose, that you have been exhibiting yourself about with Lady Lexley in the park, and in Regent Street, and God knows where else?"

"Of course I have!" she replied, wonderingly.

"Why on earth did you do it? Why select her from every other woman under heaven to help you in carrying out your sentimental, half-philanthropic, imbecile intrigue?"

"I do not understand you," she said, firmly; but, though she spoke firmly, her heart was very low. She saw herself entangled in the web that had been partially woven by her own absurd reticence.

He rose up and began to pace about the room, by way of keeping his anger active.

"Not understand me!—you do. If it's true that you have been day after day in some low purlieu to see Stanley Villars, and the girl he has picked up—and you'll scarcely deny *that*—you must understand me."

"Claude, don't be hard and hasty. I will tell you all—everything," she cried, starting up and clinging to his arm.

"By Jove! I have heard enough already to turn a fellow sick," he said, hotly. "Here this letter meets me on my return———"

"And *you* regard it for an instant? Oh, Claude!" She thought again of the one she had received; but she was not made of the stuff that strives to make others display generosity by vaunting its own.

"Regard it! Well, it annoyed me preciously, I confess, to learn that you should be spoken about at all; and then to hear what I have heard since."

"Will you tell me all you have heard? then I will defend myself," she said; "but before you tell *me* anything, I want to say that I *have* been to Stanley Villars and his wife; and you must go too, for, Claude, he's dying."

Her voice broke down as she said that; it seemed so unnatural a thing that Claude should be hard on the subject of Stanley now.

"Dying! what nonsense you women talk!" Major Walsingham said, angrily. Then he looked at her, and softened a little—"Poor girl!" he said, kissing her, "I really think you believe it."

"Believe it! Oh, Claude!" and then she poured out a portion of her story.

"The broken blood-vessel is bosh! simply a fabrication of the ingenious young lady who induced you to compromise yourself by taking her to Lady Villars'. I was coming through the Strand just now, and I saw Mr. Stanley reel out of some tavern. It's disgusting—actually disgusting!"

"He must have reeled from some other cause than intoxication," she said, sorrowfully.

"He's gone to the bad entirely, I tell you, Bella. It's absurd of you to affect to disbelieve what every one knows; he's lost to every decent feeling," he continued, angrily, "or he would never have made the parade he has of being driven to despair by your—your throwing him over"

She blenched. "Don't speak of it in that way, Claude," she said, quickly. "God knows I am telling you what I firmly believe to be the truth, when I tell you that Stanley Villars is dying now. His poor wife was broken-hearted to-day—that's why I took her to Lady Villars; I wanted to see Florence."

"His wife! Well, I'll say nothing of that part of it; only I won't have you mixing yourself up with her. How on earth did you ferret her out?"

She told him "how kind Lady Lexley had been."

"Very imprudent of you," he said, with a scowl—"very imprudent, indeed!—you couldn't have made a more injudicious selection of a companion into a romantic scrape if you had tried."

"You told me yourself to call on her, Claude."

"To call on her, but not to career about all over town with her. Grace Harper says she told you to be careful—didn't she?"

"Sketchily."

"In what other way could a girl tell you?" he asked.

"So *she* has been improving the aspect of things in your eyes, while I was absent and undefended, Claude?"

He hesitated.

"I was so annoyed that I let Ellen see that cursed letter, warning me of 'your imprudence!'" he said at last; "and then she told Grace."

"But—excuse me, Claude, for speaking in such a way of your friend—it seems to me that she had no right to discuss my conduct."

"She tried to make the best of it," he began. "She said she felt sure you hadn't done any of these things, as she had cautioned you against doing anything that might annoy my family. Now, Bella, you must feel conscious that this picking up with Stanley Villars and that girl is not at all the sort of thing which my wife may do with credit."

"Claude, I didn't believe that Stanley has forfeited his claim to our friendship when Lady Villars said it, and I don't believe it now. He has been unhappy, and in his unhappiness he has been reckless, to the injury of his health."

"He's a dissipated drunkard," Claude said sternly.

"Claude! those are cruel words! Oh! my dear husband, don't use them about Stanley; he's failing so fast!"

"And no wonder, when he drinks at the rate he must to have been in the state I saw him in, in the Strand, to-day. 'Failing fast' is a shallow euphemism; he's softening his brain with gin and water."

Major Walsingham believed that what he was saying was true, otherwise he wouldn't have said it. But there was little sorrow in his heart for this truth. He forgot his old friendship for Stanley now. He could only remember that Stanley, through what Claude termed "his cursed maudlin sentimentality," had kept the fact of having been jilted by Bella fresher in the minds of men than was desirable.

Bella shuddered. "How you have changed to him!" she said presently. "He knew you better than I did!"

"What did he say about me?" he asked.

"He asked me not to humiliate him by begging you to go and see him, as he felt sure you wouldn't."

"I wish he had had the decent feeling not to try and link your name with his again. He's had the good taste to keep clear of his own family; I wish to God he had extended his consideration to mine!"

So they talked the subject over, neither convincing the other, nor being shaken for an instant in their respective beliefs and opinions. But Bella was a woman; and it is the woman's part to give up, whether convinced or not. She played her part very gracefully.

"I grieve for everything connected with the business, dearest Claude; but I hope you'll believe me when I say that I grieve for nothing so much as for having acted in a way you don't approve of. Will you forgive me?" She looked at him very lovingly as she spoke; so lovingly that he bitterly repented him of his harshness. She was not the type of woman to need it.

"Forgive you! I should think so! but you mustn't perform romantic exploits again, dear."

"I won't," she said; "but I wish——"

"There! not another word!" he interrupted. "I wish, too, all sorts of things. If Stanley doesn't drink himself to death, the time will come when he'll shake himself clear of all this mire, and be ashamed of it. Then I'll hold out my hand to him, not before; and mind you, Bella, I'll not have you do it either!"

He was all the lord and master, the man to be obeyed, without question or demur, as he said this.

"So be it, Claude," she said quite meekly; love had thoroughly tamed her.

They separated to dress then; but when she was ready, she went and knocked at his door, and asked him, "might she come in?" On his giving her permission, she went in and talked to him of his father's death, and of their own altered condition.

"Shall you live much at the Court?" she asked.

"Oh, yes! a good deal. We'll go to the Highlands for a few weeks after the funeral? And I tell you what, Bella—you may as well ask your mother to meet us at the Court on our return, and stay a short time with us."

"Thank you, dear; that will be very nice," she replied absently.

"And when Mrs. Vane goes, it may be as well to give my mother to understand—very delicately, you know, but clearly—that it perhaps will be well for all parties that there shouldn't be two mistresses at the Court, and that it would be better for her to live in the village; *you* must do that, dear."

"Very well; as you please, Claude," she said slowly.

"Is there anything the matter?" he asked, advancing towards her as he was tying his cravat. "Don't think any more of our difference, dear. I have told you what I think and what I feel, and now it's over. Be a sensible little woman, and don't dwell gloomily upon it."

She got up and utterly spoilt the symmetry of the bow of the carefully tied cravat.

"Oh! Claude!" she moaned sorrowfully, clinging to him, "I feel as if a boat were going down before my eyes! I wish so to do right! I wish so to do right! and it *is* right to obey you; but my heart is torn!"

"I should rather think it was right to obey me!" he said good-humouredly. "You silly girl! to go into heroics for nothing!"

"Well, I won't again, Claude; but grant me one favour."

"What is it?"

"Don't let either Mrs. Markham or Miss Harper"—and her eyes flashed as she named them—"feel that I am in the pitiable position of a distrusted or an indiscreet wife."

"What an absurd girl you are!"

"Not so absurd! Your sister is your sister, and means well by you, I'm sure. Remembering this, I can forgive, and but just forgive, the insultingly suspicious guard she has attempted to mount over me from the moment of my first meeting with her. But that white-faced hypocrite has no such claim on me; and when she leaves my house this time, she shall never darken my doors again."

"This is absurd prejudice, dear," he said carelessly; "you'll think better of it by-and-by." Then they went down to dinner, and rather puzzled their guests by their demeanour to one another.

——o——

CHAPTER XLVI.

DEAL GENTLY WITH THE ERRING.

THE majority of us have seen a boat go down. I do not mean that we have, most of us, stood on a shingly beach, and looked over the leaping waves at the terrible sight of a slight thing of planks and spars battling with the awful, angry element! Some of us have witnessed that spectacle, and sickened at it, and prayed earnestly enough to the great God of Mercy to save us from a repetition of it. But there is another and a sadder wrecking—the wrecking of a human bark on the ocean of life, and that, the most of us who have looked at life with open eyes must have seen!

It is almost invariably the most gallant barks that fall to pieces in this way. They go out so bravely! with such a gay disregard of danger, and the first rock they strike upon bruises them just sufficiently to admit of the waters of bitterness welling in, and then they fill with fell rapidity, and go to the bottom.

The barks that rigour, and routine, and respectability—all these such good things in their way—have wrecked! How many "hopes of the family" have been court-martialed out of all care for the future for some ward-room joke or mess-table excess that rigour would not, or routine dared not overlook. The boyish escapade may be no very dark thing in itself: just a vinous defiance of a superior officer; just a bacchanalian boast; just a few idle words said out of the lavishness of high spirits; nothing very desperate, nothing very dark, but sufficient, very often, God knows, to cause a man to be given over to all manner of devilries and despair, by reason of the crushing punishment it calls forth.

Take from a man all hope in his career, or, as is frequently done, dismiss him from it with disgrace, and he is in the position of a woman whose fair fame has been dimmed. All is over for him in this world, however it may be in the next. We should deal very gently with the erring, they deal so hardly with themselves.

Those, and those alone who have known a man who is under a cloud in the flesh, as well as in books; who have seen the one who went from his home a star, return to it a fallen one; who have marked a father grow stern to a favourite son, because that son and a profession that was as dear to him as a son had parted ignominiously; who have witnessed the agony of late repentance in the severely punished man; the shrinking from former friends; the withdrawal of former friends from him; the gloomy turning away from those who show affection for him still, and who wound him by showing it pityingly; the morose doubts as to that justice and mercy which have not been extended to himself, existing at all; those who have sorrowed for the blackness that is his sole portion now, for whom all had been brightness formerly; those and those alone will understand this chapter and the feelings which dictate it.

Stanley Villars had not been wrecked by rigour, or routine, or respectability. On the contrary, his ruin had been wrought by his own hand entirely. He owed his destruction to no stingingly sharp, horribly public reprimand; to no over severity; to no official animus. He had "gone to the bad," as Claude Walsingham called it, simply because he had not been able to brook disappointment, and the downfall of all those mere tender hopes which made up, despite his outward sternness, a larger portion of his than most men's lives. Love was to him more than it is to most men; he was chary of it, he gave it with hesitation. When it got rudely treated, and thrown back to him as a thing of no worth, there seemed to be nothing left to him. So he suffered himself to drift into unseemly paths, and took no heed as to what he did with himself.

He did all things that he was compelled to do, or was led into doing, without the smallest particle of heart, the smallest atom of interest, the smallest semblance of feeling. He wrote carelessly, not with the carelessness of joyousness and thoughtlessness, but with the carelessness of black, dogged indifference; and that he did so was marked, and marked to his detriment. He married lovelessly, and quickly came to feel that his wife's lot was as black and hard and arid as his own—a sorrowful conclusion for a sensitive man to arrive at. He ceased to take an interest in all that he had hitherto been interested in; and when he had done so, and found that all ceased to take an interest in him, as was natural, the stultifying sense of utter stagnation came down and utterly crushed him. Worst of all, he felt himself to be an erring man, and also felt that the time for retracing his steps, for redeeming his error, was gone by. There was no opportunity for amending, for death was staring him in the face. For it was quite true, that statement which Claude Walsingham had declared to be but "an ingenious fabrication of that girl's." Stanley Villars had broken a blood-vessel, and there was now upon his brow the pallor of fast-approaching dissolution. He looked such a haggard, pallid man, that the stranger turned to look upon him as he passed along the street, and the casual acquaintance passed by on the other side, because life is too short and too brisk in London to admit of any dallying on the road.

Two or three men whom he knew well, who had been employed with him on the same journal, who had thought rather good things of him when he came among them first, met him this day, and looked upon him with the eyes of men whose judgment he had disappointed, and whose verdict he had made faulty. They told him "distinctly," as they afterwards said, that "if he didn't put a stop to this sort of thing, and go away somewhere for a rest, he'd be sorry for it." He thanked them for their advice, and said, "he'd think about it," as he did, truth to tell, somewhat bitterly.

You see he had no very intimate associates among these men. The majority, though running a career of work equally hard, and of dissipation far harder than his own, were running it unencumbered. They had had the wit not to hamper themselves with wives without money. If they lived in dingy lodgings, they dined at good clubs, and it was at their clubs that other men saw them. Moreover, it was very few of them who did live in dingy lodgings, and these only the youngest and most unassuming of the band. The older men had neat little sets of chambers, and some of them possessed a fine taste in books and pictures, and engraved glass, which they gratified. The most of them, too, dressed well, and in consequence fought shy of a man whose new clothes were worse than his old threadbare ones, in that they were so execrably cut.

Had he been "alone in his hole," as they said, there were many who would have sought him out and striven to urge him forward, with hand and voice, ay, and pen too. But it was not congenial to them to go and sit in a dull room, with a downcast man and a little girl who had nothing in common with them—who was "left behind" invariably, when they did try to talk to her. Bad as such a position was, a lady would have been better placed in it; that is to say, she would have made it better to his friends, and through them to her husband. It was not the fault of his fellow-labourers that he slipped away from them entirely, save just when they chanced to meet him at the office. The man whose home will not stand inspection must do this eventually, no matter how warm the original feeling towards him. He was care-worn, downcast, and badly dressed! With the best intentions in the world, other men could not invite him to make these facts more public still, by "joining them anywhere."

Bligh, the man who had taken his work for him, held on to him with the rèsolute staunchness of youth and strength; also with the tenacity which comes of having a certain amount of spare time in which to display such tenaciousness. Bligh went to him daily, writing what he couldn't write, and revising what he wrote, and bidding him cheer up, with an earnest hopefulness of better things being in store for Stanley, which proved that he was looking upon the spectacle of a boat going down for the first time. Went to him daily, feeling the whole time that Stanley's wife was not quite sure of what her manner should have been to him, she being palpably in doubt as to whether he was really a friend or only a portion of the printing machine with which Stanley had to do, in a way that was likewise not clear to her.

This day, however, on which he had gone out, leaving Marian crying in the passage, he had not met with Bligh. He had only fallen in with those men who tendered him advice which was admirable, but difficult to act upon under existing circumstances; it was not upon the cards that he should "cut work for a time and go to the sea-side," which was what his advisers recommended, in the liberal manner in which people are wont to recommend pleasant extravagances to their impoverished friends.

He had come to the stage of pitying himself profoundly before this juncture, of pitying himself almost as if he were another man; he could stand aside, as it were, in his cooler moments, and watch the creature he had become, and feel sure of what the end would be, almost as clearly as the most circumspect among his acquaintances could have done. He knew that his bark was stove in and rapidly filling; and he felt a pity for that it was so. But he never thought of attempting to bale out the water that was swamping him. He was wrecked, and it seemed to him too late to avoid going down.

I do not think, after all, that the sight of Bella the day before, in all the bravery of her beauty, and with her beauty set off by all those little toilet elegancies which money alone can deck a woman in, no matter how good her taste may be,—I do not think that the sight of Bella had been good for him. It was like the spirit of the past he had known, coming to mock him in his present dark poverty. There was about her such refinement, brightness, beauty, and wealth; and all these things were gone from his life.

The meagreness of the room, the meanness of his own and his wife's habiliments, the miserable lack of all that was graceful and refined in their surroundings, the poverty and barrenness, the arid nature of the soil on which he was stranded for ever, had never struck him so vividly before. He thought bitterly of the contrast between now and then—very, very bitterly of it!

He had drifted away into this dismal swamp, this slough of despond, and no man had put out a hand to hold him back. They had, one and all, let him drift. Had he been wealthy, or at any rate independent, his gloomy despair would have rendered him interesting perhaps, and society might have set itself the pleasing task of comforting him—taking him to its bosom as it has taken other "stricken deer," however mad, bad, and dangerous to know, they have been. But he was not wealthy, or even independent, and gloomy despair in a poor man is a bore in a drawing-room. He had no club of his own, and he was not convivial enough to be carried away perforce by other men to expensive little club dinners which he could never return. He was a literary man, out at elbows, in a barefaced, pinched, despicable way, and, as such, was no credit to the fraternity. Consequently, without meaning it exactly—wishing him well, but being unable to serve him—the fraternity felt that the whirl of London life was separating him from them, carrying him out of their orbit, and didn't precisely see why, and how, and where!

It was no one's fault, but he was a very friendless man. The knowledge that he had a poor, patient little wife at home, had kept him at first from accepting invitations to enter into that masculine society which all men need, and which would have braced him up. This knowledge kept him from accepting their invitations at first; and by-and-by the same knowledge kept the men from inviting him. It was no one's fault, but he was a very friendless man. The full knowledge that he was so, the full horror of being so, had seized upon him after Bella had left that day. He had endeavoured to dispel it by that course of drinking and writing and smoking which Marian had recounted to Mrs Claude Walsingham. He had failed in his endeavour, and broken a blood-vessel into the bargain, and then he had risen up, swearing that he "would not lie there and die like a dog!"

The yearning to see his family again—his brother and sisters, especially Florence—came upon him as he went along the streets alone. It was hard, very hard, that the gulf which he had created between them and himself, in his first rash wrath, should be between them till the end. The end! yes, it was coming. Men in his state did not live long, he knew, when the strain that reduced them to such a state was kept up. He was told off for death surely enough. It was hard, very hard, to think that those who had been little children with him but the other day as it seemed, he was still so young, should go on their way rejoicing, indifferent to or unconscious of the fiat that had gone forth.

They were his brother and his sister still. Such a little thing would bring them together again for the short time that was left to him—such a little thing would do it, if only the opportunity were given. The days were not so very long past in which Gerald had looked up to him, and his sisters had relied upon him beyond all others, and even Carrie herself had given in to his decree.

Those days were not so long past in reality, but they were a long way off in seeming, as he turned round the corner of the square and came in sight of Gerald's house. He had wandered on and on, never intending to go so far, never owning to himself that it was towards Gerald's house that his steps were tending. When he found himself close upon it he started, and stopped! and his heart began to thump ominously, and the dew to gather on his brow. They were "so near, and yet so far." It would have been such a little thing to have gone forward and lifted the knocker that he had lifted a thousand times before, in the days when he was a son of that house, and as free to pass its threshold as Gerald himself. It would have been such a little thing! But he did not do it. He thought of the stare the man who opened the door would give; he thought of the signs of decay that were about him; he thought of how they all—even Florence—had let him go; and as he thought of these things, he told himself that the time "was gone by." And yet he was dying! and the desire in his heart to see them once more was such a big one!

While he was standing there, too weak to go on, too weak to go back, too weak to conquer his desire or give way to it, a carriage drew up at the door of the house at which he stood gazing, and with a dreamy wonder he recognised in the occupants of it Bella Vane and the baby-faced beauty. Then he remembered that Bella Vane was Mrs. Claude Walsingham, and that the baby-faced beauty was his wife. And then he saw it all! His wife had been brought there to seek for him, or to sue for him! He leant against the corner shuddering. It was too late to interfere. That which he had shrunk from doing was being done for him, and he was conscious of a sick wild hope that it might end well—that his wife would win admission for herself and re-admission for him, and that they would see and forgive and love him at the last. You see his pride was pretty well broken, poor fellow! He was, in truth, humbled and softened in a way that it is very sad to see.

It has already been told how that visit ended. By-and-by he saw Bella come out again and enter her carriage; and as he saw the expression of the women's faces as they drove past him (for he never thought of attempting to hide himself), he saw that it was all over—that his sick, wild hope had been born to perish. Then he turned himself away resolutely, thinking, as we are apt to think when we only see one side of the shield, that "his own" had been more bitter and harder to him than was the case in reality. As he so thought, he swore a solemn oath never to hold communion with one of them again. They "had cast him off utterly, evidently; repudiated his wife, perhaps; made him a by-word, a thing of scorn, in the eyes and mouths of their blackguard flunkies! Come what would now, he would never nurse a soft thought of one of them again." Those of whom he thought and muttered had been little children with him, and had at the same mother's knees lisped their little prayers!

There can be no worse hell than was in this man's heart as he walked away. Whatever his faults had been, whatever his sin had been, he was being punished for it in the flesh in a way that must have purified his spirit; he was having it here in a way that entitled him to the brightest hereafter. How horrible it is, that the actions of others, erring, weak, and faulty as himself, can make a human being so hopelessly wretched.

He did not go straight home. Miserable as he was himself, he shrank from seeing the misery and disappointment that he fancied would be upon the pretty face of the poor little log he had tied to him. She was not very deep, still he did not fathom her. He knew no more of what she was capable when put to the test, than a man can know of a woman he does not love. He went to a house in the Strand, and smoked and drank brandy till the pain within him was dulled a trifle. Then, as the shadows grew long, and the house began to fill with men, the majority of whom seemed unpleasantly happy and well-pleased with life, he got himself away out into the street once more, where he was seen by Claude, who shrank out of his way quickly, as a thing who staggered in the daylight, and was otherwise disreputable.

Stanley had marked little this day save that door which was barred to him, and the occupant of the carriage that had waited at it; but he marked his old friend now, and his old friend's avoidance of him. He had borne a good deal, but this was the last drop in the cup. He turned away down one of those little streets that lead to the river.

—o—

CHAPTER XLVII.

FOUND OUT.

Before Mrs. Markham went down to dinner on the day of her arrival at her brother's house, she made a progress into Mrs. Claude's dressing-room, expecting to find her sister-in-law there. But her sister-in-law was not there; accordingly Mrs. Markham looked round the room in order to see what additions had been made to its decorations since she last saw it.

She found out one or two new ornaments, and disapproved of them, as became a woman who had no taste for such things herself, and no indulgence for those who had, and gratified it. "Absurdly he indulges her, to be sure," she thought severely, as though every one of the frivolities she censured had been wrung from the sweat of Claude's brow. Then she saw something else—a letter lying in the corner—and pounced upon it in all honour, not intending for an instant to read it, but meaning to deliver it up to Bella with a reprimand for being "so careless."

She did not intend for an instant to read it; but as soon as she got it into her hand she saw that it was that letter which Claude had found awaiting him on his return—that special letter which he had given her to read. "I see how it is," she thought; "she's explained everything, and there's been a reconciliation. Thank God!"

She meant this thoroughly. Hard and stern as she was, she was also just, and her soul recoiled from the means that had been used to bring Bella to justice. She was very glad that those means had failed—very glad indeed—though she was still ready and willing to swoop down upon any of her sister-in-law's shortcomings in fair fight.

She put the letter away in her pocket, meaning to return it to Bella with a reprimand, as I said before, on the first fitting opportunity. Then she walked grimly down-stairs, revolving many things in her mind; amongst others, whether "Jay" or "Marshall and Snellgrove" should execute the large order she had to give on the morrow.

Mrs. Markham was, as I have said, a very just woman. When she came down and found that all was fair and smooth between the husband and wife, she felt that Bella must have explained very satisfactorily all that had not looked well, and that therefore it behoved her, Claude's sister, to say something apologetic about her manner previously. She felt that it would only be just to Bella to say this, and she would be just though she could not be gracious.

Now Mrs. Markham's justice was a harder thing to bear than most women's injustice would have been. It was so very hard, that even when it commended, you thought more of how it would be down upon you did it ever catch you tripping, than of its present commendation. There was a certain wintry brightness in her manner to Bella during dinner which was not pleasant, but which said plainly that Bella was not so bad as she (Mrs. Markham) had imagined, and that she was glad of it.

Mrs. Markham had resolved upon not saying her say, upon not speaking her words of justice, until they should all have re-assembled in the drawing-room after dinner. Her manner, however, made manifest to Bella that some such recantation of error was looming, and Bella forthwith tried to strengthen herself for the reception of one of the most unpleasant things in the world—a grim apology.

"I wish she'd drop it, but I see she won't," Bella thought, as she was walking up-stairs behind her sister-in-law after dinner. "I wish I'd made Claude come up with us; this eternal talkee talkee is tedious!" she mentally added, as she thought of what Mrs. Markham would say, and what she would have to say in return, and what Mrs. Markham would then reply, occurred to her.

She was spared the infliction yet awhile. "I shall go to my own room till Claude comes up, and you have tea, Bella," Mrs. Markham said, when they reached the top of the stairs. "I'm by no means sure that that list is complete, and as we've no time to lose, I'll just look over it again."

"Very well," Bella replied; "as you like, Ellen. I will help you to-morrow, of course; we shall only have the morning, remember. Claude means to take us off by the 3.40 train."

"Quite right too; we ought to get back to my poor mother as speedily as possible," Mrs. Markham replied, as grimly as if Bella were responsible for the desolation that had come upon Mrs. Walsingham. With that they separated, Mrs. Markham going on to her own room, and Bella and Grace Harper into the drawing-room.

Bella had been civil, scrupulously civil, to Miss Harper; but she had felt very savage with the fair Grace since that explanation with Claude. "What right has she—what right has any woman—to speak about me, to censure me, by word or implication to my husband?" Bella thought. "I can forgive Claude, dear Claude, for having listened; but I'll never forgive her for having spoken."

Accordingly, now when they found themselves alone, they found themselves uncomfortably placed, for Bella was not the sort of woman to conceive a deep antipathy, and conceal it. While Miss Harper was her guest, she would treat her as such; but there was that in her manner which assured Grace that she would never be Mrs. Claude Walsingham's guest again.

Miss Harper dried her eyes as soon as she found herself alone with Mrs. Claude. She had kept them damp during the whole day, and Mrs. Markham had been considerably touched thereby. The latter was not one of the weeping order of womankind herself, but the two tears which Grace had established as soon as she heard the tidings of Mr. Walsingham's death, had been accepted rather above their due worth as a just and proper tribute, by Mr. Walsingham's daughter. Miss Grace perceived this, and as her grief was not a disfiguring thing, she kept up the soft semblance, and gratified Mrs. Markham.

But now that she was alone with Bella, the tears were abolished at once. She felt that Bella saw through her. For this she cared little as matters were going; but she would not give Mrs. Claude Walsingham the satisfaction of seeing a transparent deception practised without an end or aim. So she dried her eyes, and subsided (it being after dinner, and she feeling a little sleepy) into tearless composure on a couch.

"She shall not infest 'the Court' when I'm the mistress of it," Bella thought, as she glanced towards her calm guest; "if my being cool to her huffs the Markham I can't help it. She must be huffed, for I won't have that girl about my house any more."

The evening was warm, quiet, conducive to thought, and Mrs. Claude Walsingham had much to think about, even though she would not permit her mind to dwell upon the Stanley Villarses. The whole plan of her life would be altered by Mr. Walsingham's death. Claude would, of course, have to go down and take up his part of big man in the county. Henceforth all her interests would centre in that neighbourhood which had seemed so dull to her when she was in it as a guest. She had no fears, however, of its seeming dull to her in future; the pleasure of possession was upon her already. She would be the queen of that little world; she would no longer be the jealously watched wife of the heir-apparent merely.

She would not permit her mind to dwell upon the Stanley Villarses any more, and this not out of heartless forgetfulness, but because she had promised her husband not to go near them again, and she felt that it was upon the cards that she might break her promise did she think about them. The hope that she might be permitted to alleviate, in a measure, in the present, the woe of which she had been the cause in the past, was dead. The only thing left to her was to bury it, and all appertaining to it, as speedily as possible,—to bury it entirely out of sight, and so fulfil, to the utmost, the compact she had made with her husband.

Love had thoroughly tamed her. She did not rebel, even in her innermost heart, against this decree of Claude's, to cease from all communion with the man they had both aided in blighting. Claude willed it, and that was enough for her. Like Tennyson's May Queen, she "had been wild and wayward; but she was not wayward now."

It was late in the evening before Claude and his sister came in to tea. When they did come, they came together—a fact that requires a brief explanation.

Mrs. Markham had gone back to her bedroom, to look over the list of articles required for the mourning, in which the whole establishment down at the Court had to be placed. After doing this, and jotting a few after-thoughts, in the way of handkerchiefs with broad hems, &c., she went over to the couch Grace had occupied during the greater portion of the day, and pensively placed herself upon it.

Then she, too, fell to thinking about the same subject that Bella was dwelling upon below—viz., the difference that her father's death would make in life at the Court. Mrs. Markham did not like Bella, therefore she adjudged her capable of actions that were iniquitous in her eyes. "I shouldn't wonder if she gets Claude to turn his mother out, and, after all, won't care to live there much herself," she thought, which, considering that she had warmly protested against the aged Mrs. Markham dwelling in the same tent with herself on the occasion of her own nuptials, was a little inconsistent. But then, people whose important actions are always marked by a perfect propriety, may be granted the liberty of being inconsistent about such trifling matters as their fellow-creatures, and the motives that rule the same.

"I wish they would have tea at a decent hour in this house," Mrs. Markham said to herself, petulantly, after about an hour had elapsed, and no summons had come to her from the region where the tea was to be consumed. "What must Grace Harper think of the management here? Everything so shockingly irregular!"

She turned round impatiently as she thought this. It had been very unpleasant to her that Grace Harper, than whom she firmly believed there was not a better regulated young woman in civilization—it had been very unpleasant to her that Grace Harper should have been cognisant of the fact of misunderstandings having arisen between Claude and his wife. The mischief was done, however, and nothing was left but to pray that Bella, the erring, might deport herself for the future with becoming solemnity, and so erase from Miss Harper's mind the impression former levity had made on it.

As the thought of the various irregularities of the house struck her, she turned round impatiently, and her eye lighted on an envelope that had fallen down between the cushion and the head of the couch. In a moment, her hand was upon it. It was addressed to Miss Harper, and it contained no letter, therefore she turned it round idly.

Turned it round idly, with the half design of looking at the monogram or seal, and then started up erect, with an exclamation of "Good heavens!" and commenced rapidly searching in her own pocket for the letter she had found in Bella's dressing-room, for the inside of the envelope, that evidently belonged to Miss Harper, was covered with duplicate words in duplicate handwriting to those which the anonymous epistle had contained.

She saw it all in an instant—saw the whole of the perfidy and the treachery that had been planned and partly carried out. She did not like her brother's wife, and she knew that her brother's wife did not like her. But for all that, the perfidy was very painful, and the treachery very terrible to her, of which it had been intended that Bella should be the victim.

She kept the two—the envelope that had been practised upon, and the letter, the result of that diabolical practice—in her hands for some few minutes, comparing them, and deciding "what she ought to do next." She was a very just woman, and she knew that obnoxious as anything like an open detection, and the bringing to justice of the offender, would be, that it behoved her to put her brother on guard against the real enemy, and to say to her brother's wife, "We have all wronged you."

But it would be hard, very hard to do this. They—her mother and herself—had a little to answer for in the matter, for they had both not only taught Grace in the old days to regard Claude as specially her own, but they had also suffered her to feel when Claude married that they regarded Bella as her special foe. They had been to blame in the matter; but then, "Who could have supposed her such a serpent?" Mrs. Markham said to herself, angrily.

I think Mrs. Markham hated her smooth-surfaced, well-ordered young friend in that hour of detection, debate, and uncertainty. "When she finds I know it, she ought to be ashamed to look one of the family in the face again," she thought. "How ever she'll dare to show herself in society, or take the sacrament, I can't think!" and Mrs. Markham shuddered.

But though she shuddered, and [illegible] that much shame would be upon her old friend and favourite, did she not hold her peace, Mrs. Markham never dreamt of holding it. She was a just woman, essentially a just woman, and though she would have no sensation scene, no idle conversation on the subject, there was something to be done, and something to be said, in justice to Claude's wife.

She went out of her room, and down the stairs, with the envelope and letter gathered together closely in one hand, looking as hard, firm, and cold as usual. But she was not hard and cold now, however firm she might be. She was thinking rather softly of the girl whom she didn't like, and who might have been wrecked by the girl she had liked till now.

She found her brother looking at the evening papers, and smoking a cigar. It had pleased him to remain longer by himself than was usual with him this night. He, too, had had much to think about. Despite of all those hard things he had said about Stanley Villars, the sight of his old friend staggering in the Strand had been a cruel one to him.

Mrs. Markham came in with no idle apologies for interrupting him. She had something to say; she had no scruples about the manner of saying it.

"I think you know that I don't like your wife, Claude," she began; to which Claude replied—

"I think you might select some one to impart that fact to who'd care a damn for it—*I* don't!"

"Hush!" she said, as though he had been a small boy still. "I was going to say that though I don't like her, I owe her some reparation—and so do you, for she has been very badly treated?"

He looked up from his paper, and asked, quickly, "By whom?"

"By all of us! Just look here!" and then she unfolded the letter and the envelope, and handed them to Claude, who said "Pooh!" and could make nothing fresh of the combination.

"But, Claude," she expostulated, "you must!"

"Oh, botheration! What's the good of it? —that's all done with now! Bella has told me the truth, and explained away the malice, and there's nothing more to be said."

"But there is much more to be said, Claude —the malice comes from a quarter where we least expect to find it."

"Answer for yourself! I expect to find malice in every quarter!"

Mrs. Markham moved her shoulders, and passed over the cynical remark. She was as cynical as her brother in her heart, but she put her cynicism on another score—as is the habit of professing Christians!

"There is this much more to be said about this, Claude—I am very much afraid that your wife has been very much wronged!"

"Why to God do you harp on that?" he asked. "She told me how it came about, and I'm quite satisfied. What more do you want?"

"I want to tell you that I'm very sorry for my share in the business."

"Your share in the business has been small enough, as far as I can see," Claude replied. He felt some of the younger brother sensations come over him as Mrs. Markham denounced herself.

"My share in the business has been, that I have made the writer of that letter my friend," she said—"that I've believed in her, and—come, I will out with it all now—allowed her to see that I thought less of Bella than I had any right to do. Bella has told you the truth, and you are satisfied; but that doesn't do away with the obligation that is on me to tell you that I have found out that it's Grace Harper who put the *truth* before you first in an unpleasant way—and—and—I'm disgusted with her!"

"Grace Harper!—the devil it is!" he said; and then he began to look at the letter and envelope. "What reason could *she* have for trying on that little game?" he asked, after a minute or two; and then he looked curiously at his sister, and his sister looked curiously at him.

"Never mind her motive—the way she has acted is plain enough. Claude, I'm sorry and ashamed that I should ever have thought her fit to hold a candle to Bella—she is not!"

"I always knew that," he replied, briefly.

"Whatever Bella's faults may be," Mrs. Markham went on—for even now she could not forget that Bella had faults—"whatever Bella's faults may be, she's neither cowardly, mean, nor sly. She doesn't like me, but I will say that for her."

"She likes you as well as you like her," Claude replied. "As for Miss Grace, and her small attempts to part us, you may as well give her to understand that my wife is dearer to me than ever. The devil might whisper to me now about her, and I should turn a deaf ear!"

He said this very warmly. He knew how the hearing of it would sting Grace Harper, and he desired nothing so much as that Grace Harper should be stung.

Mrs. Markham bowed her head. "After what I have told you, Claude, it will be better that Grace should go down with me alone, I think. Bella and you can follow—say the day after to-morrow. I shall say nothing till we get back to the Court, but I don't suppose your wife will care to keep Miss Harper's name on her visiting list."

"I suppose not," he replied—"that is, if you tell her."

With all his hot love for his wife, his sister was not only juster, but more generous, to Bella in that moment.

"She could not, after what has transpired," Mrs. Markham said—"she *could not*, Claude; there shall be no fuss, if you fear that. I can't forget that the families have been friendly for years before either of us was born—I can't forget," she continued, waxing a little warmer, "that I once hoped to see them united; but above all, I can't forget that Grace is not worthy to touch your wife's hand!"

"I don't think that she is myself," Claude replied. "It was devilish mean, and no mistake! but you women are queer animals when you get a jealous fit on!" By the light of which speech Mrs. Markham read that her brother was more lenient to Miss Grace's perfidy than she (Mrs. Markham) herself; more lenient also than he would have been had that perfidy not been the offspring of an unhealthy passion for himself. He detested and despised Miss Harper; but he remembered, through all that detestation and contempt, that Grace Harper loved him. A woman never forgives and never likes a man who acts, meanly and basely, even for love of her, to the man she loves; but a man placed in similar circumstances with relation to a brace of women, feels differently, and is more merciful. He forgets the base meanness, remembers the love alone, and is lenient. In fact, he is a little more selfish and a little nobler than a woman can possibly be.

"We won't talk about what her reason might have been for having acted as she has acted, Claude. All I say is, that she shall never be thrust upon your wife again through me," Mrs. Markham replied.

—o—

CHAPTER XLVIII.

A HUSBAND'S FIRST GIFT.

FLORENCE was married! She was Mrs. Chester now; and that proud destiny being achieved, far more toleration was shown to her weakness respecting Stanley than had been shown formerly. More toleration was shown to her weakness; but for all that Lady Villars took an early opportunity of suggesting to the happy bridegroom that he kept a tight hand on his pride in the matter, and made no rash promises under the influence of pardonable emotion.

The toleration that was shown to Florence was shown in this way. When Mrs. Chester went up to change her wedding dress for a travelling one, Carrie accompanied her out of the fulness of sisterly affection. Carrie was uncommonly well pleased with her own share in this business which had come to a climax to-day. There had been no forcing of a girl's inclination in the matter, she told herself and Gerald; she had only trained and pruned Florry's affections in a suitable direction, and taught Florry the tractable to feel that there was sin in suffering the thought of "what might have been" with Claude Walsingham to stand in the way of a very good thing.

Florry was loving, gentle, womanly, and good; she was also much given to seeing the things that were shown to her. Now, some women, equally well-endowed with her in other respects, are not blessed with that safest gift for their sex of seeing selected sights, and finding them good. But Florence having found brambles and stumbling-blocks in the path she had elected to follow of her own accord, when starting in life—having been sorely torn and bruised thereby—came back repentant, and ready to be guided by Carrie for the future.

It must be confessed that Carrie guided her well, all things considered. Lady Villars was well acquainted with the materials which Fate placed in her plump hands to mould according to her will. The path to the entrance of which she led Florry, and along which she gave Florry a gentle impetus when the ground seemed heavy, was an open, moderately pleasant, thoroughly safe one. It was the best, perhaps, that Florry could have travelled, after having "made tracks" in the wrong direction formerly. It was moderately pleasant and thoroughly safe, and the man who was to be her companion along it was as lovable, in his love for her and pride in her, as any man could have been coming after Claude.

"You have made me so happy, dear!" Lady Villars said, giving Florry a discreet little hug that expressed affection for the bride, and consideration for the bride's veil. "You have made me so happy, dear! and you look *so* nice!"

"I am glad of that, Carrie: you've been so kind to me."

In her natural emotion at the thought of the quickly coming parting, Florence remembered nothing but the kind, sweet little speeches Lady Villars had been in the habit of making at divers times to her. She forgot the hard meaning those speeches had sometimes hidden. So she said now, "you've been so kind to me," with a certain sudden swelling and reddening of the eyelids that betokened the approach of rain.

"And you've made Gerald very happy too, my darling," Lady Villars continued. "Oh! gracious! *how* tight that dress is round the waist! You've made Gerald so happy!"

"Dear Gerald!" Florence replied, hurriedly; "he's always so good! But then he has so much to make him happy! Now, there's dear Stanley—if—he—could—only——" She stopped, for the rain had come.

"Don't, *don't* cry, dear!" Lady Villars said, soothingly; "it's very natural for you to feel so, though, very natural indeed. Who could have believed that Stanley would ever have so heartlessly lost sight of us all?"

"Oh, Carrie! you don't know Stanley!"

"You must remember you are a married woman now, dear," Lady Villars resumed, patronisingly; "you must be very careful not to give way to any false sentimentality, not alone on your own account, but on Mr. Chester's. You will be more on your guard though, I'm sure, than Mrs. Claude Walsingham is."

"What is she doing?"

"I can't tell you now. What I was going to say is, don't try to work on Fred about Stanley, because that wouldn't be fair, and he would feel that it wasn't fair. I need not caution you though, dear; your own good heart will preserve you."

As Lady Villars did not state from what Florence's own good heart would preserve her, Florence went down with that sensation of elastic merit which is apt to come over the recipient of sketchy "honourable mentions."

Her good heart was touched to tears of grateful loving joy when she found herself alone in the carriage with her husband at last. He took up a black leather case that was lying by his side, and after handling it in apparent uncertainty for a few moments, he said—

"Flo, my darling, I thought this should be your first present from your husband."

As he spoke, he put a splendidly bound copy of Stanley's novel into her lap, and won his wife to himself entirely, and for ever.

It was no stroke of genius, it was no subtle plan, it was no pre-arranged sensational effect. It was simply a bit of pure good feeling for the girl he loved, designed to show her that he was not utterly regardless of her feelings at not having been suffered to ask her pet brother to her marriage. As such, it was accepted: as such, it was repaid.

It may easily be imagined how Florence leant upon his shoulder and cried then copiously, thanking him for what he had done, and, like a woman, asking him to do more. That entreaty of Carrie's that Fred might not be worked upon was utterly disregarded now; and Fred showed himself to be very ready to be worked upon, rather to like it, in fact.

"He shall be a great deal with us as soon as ever we come back—shan't he, Fred?"

"Rather! I should think so!" Mr. Chester replied. Then there came an interruption; they were compelled to get out at the terminus; but as soon as they were seated in the railway carriage, and the train was moving on, the conversation was resumed.

"I don't want you to think either Gerald or Carrie unkind to him *at all*, Fred, but Carrie has prejudices; she is very good herself, and she has no patience with other people who are not equally good."

Mr. Chester looked rather keenly for him at his wife.

"What prejudiced her against Stanley in the first place, Flo?"

"I don't know; she'll get over it. You dear boy" (taking up her books with effusion), "I'm so happy."

There was nothing more said about any person not present for a time; the brother was forgotten in the book, and the happiness the gift of the book had greatly enhanced. But at last Mr. Chester said, with an amount of decision he was almost surprised at himself for displaying—

"And, Flo, dear, give Lady Villars to understand clearly that you're mistress in your own house. I'll have no interference."

"She will never try to interfere, I think," Florence replied.

"That's right; but let her see from the first that you're mistress in your own house, Flo—it will save trouble."

We are seeing the last of Florence now. She has started on the journey of life fairly enough. Her life looked bright before her on that wedding morning—all the brighter that the prospect was hers of making Stanley's life happier on her return from the inevitable tour she was about to take. Her life looked bright before her; and bright it will probably be. She was not one to indulge in vain regrets for having declined on "a range of lower feelings and a narrower heart" than she had thought to rest upon once. The feelings were warm towards her, and the heart was broad enough to hold her well, and to honour her highly. She will be a happy woman, and when she looks upon her children, the very memory will be dead within her that she ever loved another than their father.

When Mrs. Markham had talked over the subject of that letter, and the cause of it, and the writer of it, with her brother, she came to the conclusion that it would be better to keep silence as to her discovery, both to Bella and Grace Harper, till the latter was back with her own people.

"She shall travel back with me," Mrs. Markham said to Claude; "you and Bella can follow."

"Very well," he replied.

"When I get down there I shall give her to understand that I have found her out, the mean, malicious monkey! and that she had better never attempt to show her face at the Court. I shall not say a word to Bella while Miss Harper is her guest; but it will only be fair to Bella to suffer Miss Harper to be her guest as short a time as possible."

"As you like, Ellen. There's no harm done, though, remember; so hold your punishing hand; don't make it too heavy." Claude could not be quite oblivious that the wrong had been wrought for love of him. He was scarcely the man to have sent Stanley Villars to destruction for, after all.

"It can't be made too heavy. The base wickedness of the girl we all thought so good frightens me."

"There's no harm done, as I said before," Claude replied. "Mine was the worst fault after all. I was a fool to pay the slightest attention to what any one said of a woman I know as well as I do Bella. She deserved better of me."

"She deserved better of us all," Mrs. Markham replied. She did not like her sister-in-law, nevertheless she would be just. Bella had deserved better of them all. Mrs. Markham would be the first to acknowledge it.

"She deserved better of us all, Claude," she said emphatically.

"Well, render her the 'better' now—it's not too late. As I said before, there is no harm done," Claude replied, rising up. "Come," he continued, "having settled that business, let us go in and see if Bella has a cup of tea for us."

So it came to pass that they walked into the drawing-room together, rather to Bella's amazement.

The evening passed rather heavily. Claude talked to his wife for a short time—talked to her in a lover-like, devotional way, that is very delightful to a woman; but he got tired of talking to her in this way, long, long before she got tired of listening to him; and then he went to sleep over a *Quarterly Review* in a fat armchair, and the evening commenced being very dreary.

How could the evening pass other than heavily indeed? Claude was asleep. Bella aggrieved. Mrs. Markham engaged in uprooting one of the traditions of her youth, which was, that a being whom she had elected to honour, and who belonged, moreover, to one of the county families, couldn't err. And Miss Grace Harper was uneasy in a semi-conscious manner, having a conviction that she had been found out, and not being sure by whom she had been so. The evening passed heavily, very heavily indeed. They were all glad when Claude roused himself from the depths of the fat chair and exclaimed, "By Jove! how late it is, Bella! Had you any idea of it?"

He drew his wife's hand down on to the arm of the fat chair as he spoke, and patted it, looking into her face the while, as he had been wont to look when he was "Major Walsingham" to her, and she only "Bella Vane." And Grace Harper saw that he did this, and felt that after all there were some things that might as well have been left undone, as this was the end of it.

The two ladies, Mrs. Markham and Mis Harper, journeyed down together to the Cour on the following day, leaving Claude and hi wife to follow. The widowed Mrs. Walsing ham met her old favourite with a warmth o. affection that it rather grated on Mrs. Markham's nerves to witness, and that contrasted harshly with the tone in which the mother said—

"So my son's wife has not thought fit to come to me in my trouble. Ah, well! I might have expected it."

"Claude and his wife will be here to-morrow, mamma."

"Claude *at least* might have escorted Grace and you, I think."

"And left his wife to follow by herself? No, indeed; Claude values Bella too highly to neglect her in such a way," Mrs. Markham replied, decisively.

"My dear child, *you* will stay with me to-night, will you not?" Mrs. Walsingham asked of Grace—"your dear mother will spare you to me to-night?"

"I have no doubt that her dear mother would do so," Mrs. Markham interposed; "but I believe it is arranged that Grace goes home to-night."

"That arrangement might be broken through," Mrs. Walsingham said; and then Mrs. Markham spoke rather sternly, and Grace Harper knew that her days of favour at the Court were over.

"That arrangement had better *not* be broken through, mother. Grace will agree with me that it will be well that she should not remain to meet my brother and his wife."

"Oh! I can go home, of course," Grace said, hurriedly. "I really never thought of staying—only dear Mrs. Walsingham seemed to wish me to stay."

Mrs. Walsingham looked from her daughter to her guest. "What is all this?" she asked.

"You had better not ask now, mamma."

"It means that Mrs. Markham—my—own—old friend, has been influenced by your daughter-in law into conceiving an unfounded dislike to me," Grace exclaimed, "I have known all along that Mrs. Claude Walsingham did not like me, but I never thought she would have been so mean——"

"Perhaps the less said about 'meanness' the better," Mrs. Markham said, in her most commonplace, resolute tones. "I certainly have no desire to make things worse by talking about them; but I think Grace will tell you, mamma," she continued, fixing her eyes steadily on Grace—"I think Grace will tell you, mamma, that she can never be Mrs. Claude Walsingham's guest again; and you must know," she added, quietly, "painful as the knowledge may be to you, that when Mrs. Claude arrives at the Court, it will be as the mistress of it."

Then old Mrs. Walsingham bewailed herself afresh, and in the sadder access of sorrow caused by this reminder which her intensely just daughter had given her, she suffered the vexed question of Grace's staying or leaving to be settled without further intervention on her part.

Miss Harper recovered her equanimity—her stolidity, rather—very soon. "If the carriage is ready to take me on, I'll go home now. It isn't nice arriving so very late at night, and it will be very late if I stay any longer," she said, after the expiration of a few minutes.

She kissed Mrs. Walsingham, who was still plunged in grief at the thought of her son's wife reigning in her stead, and then she held out a hand that was rather tremulous to Mrs. Markham in farewell.

"I'll see you out into the hall," the latter replied, stalking away to the door in a grim way that told Grace she was to hear the truth at length.

As soon as they reached the hall, Mrs. Markham put her hand on Grace's arm, and sank her voice to a whisper—

"I never was more shocked and sorry in my life than I was by the finding of that piece of paper," she said, handing the envelope to Grace. "Don't say a word either in deprecation or denial, for I shouldn't believe you. You will never come here again, of course?"

"I shall never care to come here again," Grace replied, in a very hard tone. "You needn't trouble yourself to put Mrs. Claude on her guard against me," she continued, crumpling up the envelope. "Let us leave each other off without a scene, please."

"It's the last favour I can ever do you—I will."

"You don't mean to be friendly with me, then, any more?"

"No!" Mrs. Markham replied, sharply; "I think you're the basest woman I know: but I'll not betray you to my mother; if you really care about her friendship, you shall not be deprived of it, if you'll promise not to attempt to poison her mind against Claude's wife."

"I don't care about keeping it—you needn't suppose I valued any of you on your own accounts—it was all for Claude!" the girl said, sullenly; then she passed on without another word to the carriage that was awaiting her. Thus ended her connection with the Walsingham family, and with my story.

CHAPTER XLIX.

THE END.

When Claude Walsingham and his wife arrived at the Court, Bella found herself very delicately situated. Everything that was to be said to Mrs. Walsingham, Claude told Bella to say. "It was her duty," he said to her, "and therefore she must fulfil it." She was most anxious to fulfil her duty and please her husband, but she did find it rather hard to be compelled to make "what was to be" manifest to Mrs. Walsingham, who would have learnt the lesson much more readily from her son.

After the funeral, Claude said to his wife, "I wish you would get my mother down to the village, Bella, to look over the house; she could point out to you what she would like to have done before she goes to it, better than she could to me."

"Very well, Claude," Bella rejoined; "will you ask her to go?"

"No; it will be much more gracious of you to ask her to go."

"She won't walk, of course?"

"It would do her good—an immense deal of good if she would walk," Claude replied; "dear old lady, she wants rousing!"

"I really think we had better wait till we come back from Scotland, Claude," Bella pleaded. "I'm sure your mother will hate me for hinting a word about the house yet."

"And have the business hanging over our heads the whole time we're away! That's just like a woman—avoid an unpleasantness, at any cost, as long as you can! No, it will be much better to get the thing over. I didn't think you were so weak, Bella, as to shrink from it. I don't."

"Ah! I feel so for her," Bella replied. When she commenced her speech she had intended saying, "Ah! but you don't do it yourself, you put it off upon me." But she waived that intention.

"So do I, dear old mother! but as the thing must be done (for she'd be wretched after a time in a house of which she wasn't both real and nominal mistress), it had better be done quickly. Find out how she'd like the place furnished, and show yourself interested, there's a dear girl."

Bella promised, and Bella tried to perform; but she merely won wrath to herself during the whole course of the transaction. "It is clearly not my own dear boy who wishes to get rid of me," the widowed mother observed to Mrs. Markham; "it's his wife. She is hurrying me away with the most indecent haste; she has just asked me to go to the village with her, and see if I can't suggest some alterations in the Vale House. I know what that means!"

Of course they knew what it meant. Mrs. Claude knew what it meant herself—namely, that her mother-in-law was to be made as comfortable as possible, and that she (Bella) was to bear the brunt of bringing those comforts into working order. It was horribly unpleasant to her to be regarded as one who was unduly impatient to reign, simply because she obeyed her husband, and strove to make things as pleasant as possible to the one who was dethroned. It was horribly unpleasant; but Bella was wiser in her generation than she had been in the days when we first made her acquaintance, and she bore the unpleasantness meekly, as being a portion of a young wife's lot—at least, the lot of all young wives whose lives are cast in the vicinity of their husbands' mothers.

Mrs. Walsingham, senior, hated the Vale House vehemently from the moment she looked upon it with the eyes of its future occupant. "I'm confident that I saw a black beetle in the kitchen," she said to Bella, as they were going up-stairs to look at the bed-rooms. "However, the place is good enough for *me!*" She said that the place was good enough for her in a tone that made Bella long to cry out, "And for me too, if I'm only permitted to inhabit it alone; you go back to the Court and be happy." But though she longed to say this with the longing that comes upon one after having been compelled to listen to the plaints of a discontented one for a time, she held her peace, remembering that the Court was not hers to give away magnanimously, and that she would only rule in it herself through the grace of Claude the great.

But she would be sorely harassed before she assumed the robes of queen-regnant, of that she felt very certain; the sovereign to be deposed was so very sensitive, not to say litigious, and the black beetles were so numerous, and the whole atmosphere of the Vale House so charged with quarrelling matter. "If Claude would only speak out to his mother, and have done with it," Bella thought wearily, when Mrs. Walsingham pointed out the tenth draught, and declared herself for the fortieth time ready and willing to submit to anything, no matter how unendurable—"If Claude would only speak out to his mother and have done with it, instead of making me 'imply,' and 'hint,' and do all sorts of things that she hates me for doing."

But Claude would not speak out. Things were going very well, according to his mind. His mother had been given to know that there could not be two queens at the Court, and that it would be well, therefore, that she should take up her abode at the Vale House. To the best of his belief, his mother had acquiesced very calmly and affably in this arrangement. He had heard nothing of the draughts and the black beetles. Bella to the best of her ability kept disagreeables, which he could not remedy, from his knowledge.

The day of their departure for the Highlands arrived, and they started, leaving all things in good order. It was clearly understood now that old Mrs. Walsingham should be found installed at the Vale House on their return. "I suppose your wife will not let you stay much at the Court, Claude, with *her* tastes and *her* habits," Mrs. Walsingham observed to her son. "However, though she may not be here much, I'm better out of the way, and I know it."

"That's nonsense, mother," Claude replied. "But what makes you think we shall not be here much? we mean to be here altogether."

"Oh, do you! then I'm very much mistaken, Claude. Those who live longest will see most!"

To which unanswerable argument Claude replied nothing. His mother was in the injured frame of mind, and his experience of women led him to avoid them at such times and in such conditions.

Mrs. Markham, too, had a few words with her brother before he left for Scotland.

"You know, Claude, that though I don't profess much love for Bella, I always do her justice?" she began.

He nodded. "I'm not going to interfere in any feminine squabbles," he said. "If you can't hit it off with Bella, you had better not come in her way, Ellen."

"But I can 'hit it off,' as you call it, with Bella; there is no reason existing why I should *not* hit it off with her—in other words, behave in a very friendly way towards her, as a sister should; but I want to warn you——"

"What the devil about now?"

"Don't let her mix herself up with that man she was engaged to—that Mr. Villars; I don't say that harm would come of it——"

"Well, I should rather hope you don't say so, indeed!"

"No, I don't, Claude; but harm may come of it. I don't like his ideas, and he might graft them upon Bella, eventually. His ideas strike me as being shocking."

"Why?"

Then Mrs. Markham said something about Stanley Villars being "evidently a free-thinker and an atheist," in the vilely inhuman way people are apt to denounce others whose faith they cannot gauge, and whose belief is broader, deeper, nobler than their own, in that it believes in the "good that is in all men," and in the mercy of God towards all his creatures. Mrs. Markham had gathered that Stanley Villars was not travelling along the road to eternity in the same class carriage as herself; therefore, she declared him to be a lost sheep, and settled the question as to his ultimate destination definitely in her own mind, after the manner of bitter Christians.

"That's all nonsense; but I don't fancy Bella will care to see any more of them. She believed him to be dying, or some stuff of the kind; it cured her when I told her I had seen him drunk in the Strand. Good God! how low the fellow's fallen!"

So Claude Walsingham spoke of his old friend, as he strapped one of the rugs that were going with him to Scotland a little tighter. And then he went to see if his wife was ready to start, and presently they were off.

But I must gather the scattered threads of my story together, before I tell you how the Claude Walsinghams enjoyed their trip into Scotland, and what they heard there.

When Stanley Villars turned down that narrow street that led from the Strand to the river, there was but one thought in his mind, and that one was, "how he should get out of it all most speedily." You see it was "all up" with him (how lightly we use and hear the phrase occasionally, never thinking of its deep, its terrible meaning)—it was "all up" with him. "Was it not pitiful, near a whole city-full, friends he had none!"

Morosely he went along down to a pier, where a river boat was waiting to discharge and take in passengers. There was a band on board the boat, pouring out blithe strains; and he stood and listened, only because he could not go down and drown himself before that gay company. The old habit of courtesy was upon the man still, even in this hour of blackest despair. He could not mar the festivity that appeared to be reigning amongst the crowd on board that boat, by a splash, and a sinking under, by causing that horrible sound, "Man overboard!" to arise.

So he waited there, leaning against the ticket-vendor's shed upon the pier. He was too weak to stand, almost; and as he leant there, fatigue, and the music, and the glare on the water (for the sun was on it still), made him sleepy, and caused him to shrink from the exertion of drowning himself at once.

"If I could only have a sleep first," he thought. "My God! when did I sleep last?—not for weeks!"

It was true, this, or partially true. He had not entirely forgotten himself and his misery for weeks. The power of sleep was gone from him. He was awfully open-eyed, shockingly conscious of a continual dull pain in the back of the head. Ah! that dull pain that comes on after many hours' continuous brain-labour! You who know what it is, "make no deep scrutiny into his mutiny," for he had suffered from it long

By-and-by that boat, with its band, telling how happy it could be in the Strand for evermore with Nancy, passed on, and another bumped against the pier in its stead, shaking him from his resting place as it bumped, and making him feel that he *must* take a little rest before he could get to the water's edge, and take the final plunge. So he sat down, making a pillow of his arm upon a stout post, that was used to fasten the boats' ropes to sometimes, and prepared to take the requisite rest.

He was very weak—entirely worn out by grief, despair, and hunger, for he had been fasting, from sheer forgetfulness, the whole day. Soon he slept, lying there, pillowing his head on a rude plank, like the outcast he felt himself to be—he who, but a year ago, had had so bright a fate before him!

The piermen, passing and re-passing him, looked down upon him with the sort of good-natured contempt that is shown to mangy dogs, beggars, and the like.

"He's a rum'un to choose this place of all others for his afternoon nap," one of them said to a comrade. And the comrade replied, "Ay, poor fellow! just heave that sack over him; we'll lay it across him; the river breeze is a sharp'un this evening."

So, there, with an old coal-sack over his shoulders, Stanley Villars lay sleeping, at about the same hour that Claude Walsingham was wringing the promise from Bella to "have no more to do with him."

For at least a couple of hours that sleep of his lasted. Then a man, in passing from one of the boats to the steps, paused to look at the recumbent form, and with a cry of—

"Good God, Villars! how came you here!" roused him.

"Ah, Bligh! is that you?" Stanley asked, rising up.

"Yes, I have been to Gravesend with a party; they're gone on now, and I must be after them."

"All right!" Stanley replied.

Suddenly, Bligh stopped. "What are you doing here?" he asked.

"Nothing."

"What are you going to do?"

"Nothing."

"Why don't you go home, then?" Bligh continued. His party had gone on now, but he did not care for that; he was determined not to lose sight of Stanley until Stanley had rejoined his wife.

"Why don't you go home then?" he said.

"Home! I have none," Stanley replied, thinking only of Gerald's house.

"Nonsense! come along." Then Bligh put his arm through Stanley's, and led him up the steps, and took him home in a cab, and never left him till poor, crying, frightened Marian was hanging over him, blessing him for having "come back to her."

The record of the days, of the weeks, that ensued would be mere weariness. A portion of his mind had given way on that day when he turned down the street that led to the river, and that portion was never restored. It was miserable for the only two who were with him—his wife and Bligh—to see what was left of that mind grow daily weaker and weaker; to hear him talking in a way that they knew he would have utterly scorned himself for talking in, had he been conscious of it; to know that reason had deserted her throne, and that he could never now be "himself again."

Sad, miserably sad, to see him writing, with a shaking hand, words that could never be printed; to see him making these up and counting the lines, and calculating the number of columns they would make.

It was very sad to see all this, and to feel themselves called upon to deceive him by pretending that his "copy" was sent, and inserted, and paid for, in order to give ever so small a gleam of satisfaction to his poor mind. But through all the sadness, all the sorrow, all the biting, horrible despair of that time, the baby-faced beauty nursed him with a loving, untiring devotion, that at last won him to know her.

She knew now that he had wrecked himself for another woman than herself. She knew that he had loved that other woman as he never could have loved her even had he lived—for he wandered much in his mind, and told the truth in his ravings. But this knowledge never embittered her—never rendered her one atom less tender in her devotion, less prompt in her service, less lovingly grateful to him for calling her to him constantly as he did with the words "Marian, pet."

They were often on the brink of bankruptcy,

but Marian kept the fact of their being so from Stanley. She had come to feel that she was a sort of protecting power over this man—that she was stronger in many ways than he, and that it behoved her to guard him. The sense of being needful to him—the sight of his absolute reliance upon her in all things—the sad knowledge that he had none other upon whom to rely, and the almost equally sad knowledge that he had lost his friends in gaining her—all these things strung her up to bear and to forbear such evils as none but those who have nursed the sick unto death in poverty can comprehend.

It was such a poor small bankruptcy, that upon the brink of which they were perpetually. They failed and fell short of such inglorious, such essential things. The great dread grew up in her heart that, brief as might be the time he had yet to live, he might be made to feel the want that was upon them in a physical way, that it was a terror to her to contemplate. But she kept up a bright air before him invariably, though generally he was not in a state to see anything with understanding—she kept up a bright air before him, and never suffered a tone of her voice to fall flat on his ear. It was only Bligh who saw the girlishness fading from her day by day—who heard the heart-wrung tones in which day after day she met him at the door, with the same weary tale of "Stanley being no better"—who knew that the baby-faced beauty was as true a heroine as any of the gallant women of ancient or modern times whose deeds have been sung melodiously.

Now that she knew that nothing could avert the doom that was upon her husband—the doom of early death—she grew very proud for him, and resolved to suffer anything, no matter how bad, herself, rather than make another appeal on his behalf to his family. She resolved upon something else too—resolved upon it with no flourish of trumpets—with no loudly-spoken oaths—with no callings of any one to regard with admiration the magnitude of the sacrifice she was determined upon making. She came to her decision with no outward sign, save an additional tightening of her lips, as she leant over him, bathing the poor head that had so little in it besides ache now. But she was very firmly set upon carrying out her decision, for all she made it so very, very quietly. The guard against possible communion with this girl which his brother's wife had wrought upon his family to erect was destined to be never tried.

Once and once only did Stanley Villars refer to the bright beautiful bane of his life after that visit of hers. "She never sent me those roses, you see?" he said, one morning, abruptly, to his wife. To which she replied, very sweetly, despite the sore feeling that would obtain at hearing another woman mentioned in a way that proved "she" alone had occupied his thoughts.

"But she will send them by-and-by, Stanley, dear. I'm sure she won't forget them, you see!"

In order that he might be made to see that she had not forgotten them, a journey was made to Covent Garden as soon as Stanley could be left with Mr. Bligh. A journey made in despair, almost by a heart-sick little wife—a weary little nurse; and though the roses were dear that day, Stanley's eyes were cheered shortly by a group of them as freshly white, as richly crimson, as the bunch "Mrs. Claude Walsingham had sent to him first," Marian said, simply. From that day forth Stanley had no reason to complain that "she never sent the roses." The roses were always there, though Mrs. Claude Walsingham was in the Highlands enjoying herself very much; and poor Marian was often on the brink of bankruptcy. He hungered and thirsted for the flowers, in a way that made Marian lie awake frequently, during the few short hours of the night in which he did not need her to attend upon him, when she was free to take repose—in a way that made her lie awake marvelling half fearfully as to how the supply should be kept up to the end—the woeful end that *would* come.

Claude Walsingham and his wife were having a very pleasant time of it in Scotland. The grouse were plentiful this year, and the dog Jack had lent Claude for the season was as good a pointer as had ever hooked his leg in the air, or done a field off into huge diamond squares with an equally intelligent fellow. The lodge Claude had taken was tolerably replete with creature comforts too. It was airily furnished, but there was no lack of soft seats in it, and now that Bella had Claude with her constantly, she did not care so much for books from Mudie's.

They were leading what Major Walsingham called a thoroughly "jolly" life. Bella did not knock up, and afflict him by a display of fine-ladyism, as to fatigue, on or without the smallest provocation. She approved herself capable of taking a great deal of pedestrian exercise without being a mere sleepy nuisance in the evening in consequence of the same. They got on so well alone in the wilds, up in their Highland shooting-box, in fact, that the receipt of letters and papers became a mere bore to them, and consequently they did not open the latter very often until they were three or four days old.

There were certain letters which they felt it to be their bounden duty to open and peruse, to read and inwardly digest, unpleasant as that duty was sometimes; and these were letters from the dowager Mrs. Walsingham. Claude's mother was desperately affectionate and discontented in her epistles.

"She calls me her 'dearest child,' and makes me feel like a criminal for being her child-in-law even," Bella said to her husband one morning, after reading a cross-barred letter in the palest ink, and with the deepest border of black that mortal eyes had ever beheld.

"Why?" Claude asked. "No, thank you" (as Bella made a feint of handing him the letter), "I never read plaid effusions."

"Oh! it's hard to say; the whole tone of the letter is calculated to depress the recipient; one has a vague sense of being guilty of some undiscovered crime while reading it."

"You may tell me the letter in brief bits—but mind, Bella, make them very brief!"

So cautioned, Bella commenced—

"Well, now, here she says, 'I went down to

the Vale House yesterday, to see about things; it is time that at least my bed-room and *own* sitting-room (humble as they are) should be ready. I know it to be Claude's wish that, though very *differently*, I shall be *comfortably* lodged, so I did venture to tell Thompson to mend the bell in the sitting-room.' Now, Claude, fancy! as if your mother didn't know that she was free to have a whole peal of bells in every room in her house, if she liked.

"And free to ring her servants out of their minds, into the bargain," Claude replied, with a laugh. "What a lark, to be sure!"

"Ah! but a lot of it isn't a lark. Just listen to this: 'I remembered, when Farmer Hopkins and his wife (good worthy people) lived there, they were always complaining of the damp, and I took the precaution of wrapping myself up in my sable cloak, and putting on goloshes, before I went into the house. Something must have struck a chill to me, however, for I have a tickling in my throat to-day, that warns me of the approach of bronchitis, and a stabbing pain in my left temple, that bids me beware of neuralgia.' There! I feel that these preliminary symptoms of your mother's will make my life miserable, Claude."

"You had better get to disregard them, my dear, that is all I can say."

"Do you really think the Vale House is damp?"

"Nonsense! damp—no!"

"Then why should Mrs. Walsingham go down to it 'in a sable cloak and goloshes?'"

Claude roared. "The damp is her pet grievance at present, my child; don't you want to deprive her of it until you're ready to give her another." Then he added more gravely, "You must know, Bell, that it is only to us that my mother will talk of the black beetles and the draught, and the damp, and the missing bells; to every one else the Vale House will be a little palace of delight."

"But hearing of all those disagreeables does exactly what she intends it to do—makes me feel guilty," Bella replied.

"Well, I hope to God you will never have greater reason to feel guilty about anything, my darling," her husband replied, opening the *Times* (that was several days old) as he spoke.

It is in the columns of this world-renowned institution that we come upon our greatest shocks in real life. There is nothing inartistic, therefore, in making the most severe shocks emanate from thence, in the mimic life with which it is the novelist's province to deal.

Claude Walsingham opened the *Times*, and after glancing over it for a couple of minutes or so, he let it fall with his hands on the table, and uttered an exclamation, a short one—"God!"

"What's the matter," Bella said. Then finding that he did not answer her, that he looked shocked into such pallor as she had never seen on Claude's face before, she jumped up and went over to him, and attempted to take the paper out of his hand.

"What is it, say? What is it, Claude?"

"Keep off for an instant!" he said; but he did not say it at all roughly. Her soul began to shake within her.

"Claude, Claude, tell me!"

"He's dead then!" Claude began in a loud voice, that ended in a big choking sob as his head fell upon his arms, and tears oozed from his eyes. Then Bella checked the utterence of the wail that was in her own heart, as she bent over and attempted to soothe her husband in his agony.

He remembered all things with such a dreadful distinctness now. His boyish days with Stanley, and the friendship that had been between them in their riper years. He remembered how love had battled with doubt in their hearts. How Stanley had believed their compact to be too sacred a thing to be foully soiled: and how he (Claude) had falsified that belief. He remembered all these things well; but better than them all, he remembered that he had loved this man who was dead, and that this man *was* dead.

It was a crushing conviction. Do what he would now, the late hardness, the worse than indifference that he had shown, could never be altered. He was utterly bowed—bowed and subdued, as entirely as any woman could have been, by the stunning weight of a most overpowering remorse. His superior scruples; his false fears as to future intercourse; his careful avoidance of contamination, were all shown to be uncalled for, unneeded, in such a solemn way, that the sight of that futility nearly burst his heart.

As for what Bella felt when she read the paragraph that had bent her husband's head. that may not be told too clearly. She had known, she had felt sure of "that" for some time which had come upon Claude as a shock. She was more than sorry, she was more than grieved! But there was just this unction which she could lay to her soul—she had parted from the dead man in kindness. Claude knew now that he had turned from Stanley in scorn, when, for his manhood, he should have gone to Stanley in humanity. Her husband's remorse took Bella away from too much thought of her lost lover's evil fate.

During the whole of that day Claude could do nothing but regret. He was as inefficient in his first sorrow as any woman could have been, as nervously uncertain "what to do at all" at first, and then "what to do for the best." The following day he vainly essayed to try and act as if this "had never been," to go out shooting as usual, to "shake off" the thought of that which had unmanned him. But he failed! He failed entirely. His better nature triumphed, and in the evening he said to his wife—

"Bella, dear! we'll go to London to-morrow. I'll go—to—his funeral, and you shall see after his poor little wife."

They talked freely of the miserable business after that. Claude was all the loving old friend again, instead of being the successful, but, notwithstanding that success, the needlessly embittered rival. They made plans to assuage so much of Marian's woe as might be assuaged, and in speaking of her Claude lapsed for a minute into injustice.

"Poor little thing! I pity her very much of course; but as she must have been utterly incapable of appreciating Stanley, I have not the least doubt that the consideration she'll receive as his widow will quite reconcile her to having been his wife for so short a time."

"I don't suppose she did appreciate him," Bella rejoined. She was conscious that she herself had not appreciated him, and she did not accredit Marian with higher powers than she had possessed in that respect.

The *Times* in which they had read of his death was five or six days old. Two more days were wasted in coming to a decision as to "what they should do." The result was that Stanley Villars had been dead nine days when they came at length to the door of his house to inquire for his widow.

The little house looked very gloomy and desolate when the door was opened by an old woman, and they stepped in.

"Is Mrs. Stanley Villars within?" Claude asked, while Bella began to cry.

"Are you any relatives of the late yonng gentleman's what's gone?" the woman asked, dubiously, by way of answer.

Claude felt like a brother towards Stanley now; in addition to which feeling, he thought that it would save trouble to say "Yes."

"Then I am to tell you," the woman replied, slowly, "that the young woman who lived here is gone away, and don't want to trouble you ever—no" (correcting herself) "I wasn't to say that—this is it, the young woman is gone away, and she wished it to be known to her gentleman's relatives, if they ever did chance to come nigh to inquire, while I was here, that the young gentleman never disgraced himself by marrying her—poor lamb!" the woman wound up with, heartily.

It was a staggering surprise to them both. They could only ask a few incoherent questions, and then go away discomfited. As they were leaving the door, Bella said—

"Claude, she's a noble little creature, mistaken as she is."

"How do you mean? Poor girl! God knows I would have judged her leniently enough, and done anything for her," he replied.

"You don't quite see what I do, yet," she answered. "I feel as sure as that I'm your wife, that she was Stanley Villars'; it's all of a piece with her wishing one day that she could have been unmarried to him. She has sacrificed her reputation in order that his family may not think he disgraced himself by a low marriage."

As she was saying this, Lady Villars' carriage drew up; and her ladyship, robed in the deepest mourning, leant out of it to speak to them.

"Have you heard of our grief?" she asked, with a little quiver in her voice, that told its own tale of the tears that had been shed, and Bella saw that Carrie's fair face was almost seamed by sorrow.

"We have just been there," Bella answered.

"Of that too;" but ours is a double grief, Mrs. Walsingham; my little boy is dead," the poor bereaved mother cried.

Then Bella told her how her visit was well-intentioned, but too late. "Stanley's widow was gone," she said; and then she gave the message Stanley's widow had left, as it had been given to her.

"Who could have foreseen *this?*" Lady Villars cried bitterly. "It will half kill Gerald to find that he can't make *any* amends."

"She meant well, I have no doubt; but it was a very imbecile precaution to take, to cut herself off from her husband's family just now, for Bella says there is no doubt about the marriage. A very imbecile precaution indeed," Claude said sorrowfully.

"Very!" Bella said emphatically, "as all the precautions have been that we have all taken about each other; even those dear Stanley took himself, from the very first. We have all been on guard against the wrong thing."

"He is dead now, and the acknowledgment of it can't help him," Lady Villars said; "but we have all been horribly hard to him."

"Let his memory make us softer to those who are left," Bella replied; and then they went their several ways.

But for all the toleration expressed in Mrs. Claude Walsingham's speech, she could not forbear saying to her husband, when they reached their own house, and found Rock awaiting them ("a dog that had been left for missus by a lady in black," the servant said)—

"Claude! she is the only one who has behaved unselfishly in the business—how much better she is than any of us!"

In addition, too, it must be said, that the black beetles and the draughts and the damp sometimes bore hard upon her.

THE END.

www.ingramcontent.com/pod-product-compliance
Lightning Source LLC
Chambersburg PA
CBHW020018030726
47500CB00002B/642

* 9 7 8 3 3 3 7 0 2 8 4 3 5 *